POKÉMON® GOLD & SILVER ADVENTURES

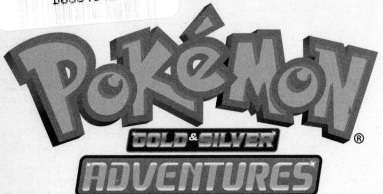

Pokémon ADVENTURES
Volume 8
Perfect Square Edition

Story by **HIDENORI KUSAKA**
Art by **MATO**

© 2010 Pokémon.
© 1995-2010 Nintendo/Creatures Inc./GAME FREAK inc.
TM, ®, and character names are trademarks of Nintendo.
POCKET MONSTERS SPECIAL Vol. 8
by Hidenori KUSAKA, MATO
© 1997 Hidenori KUSAKA, MATO
All rights reserved.
Original Japanese edition published by SHOGAKUKAN.
English translation rights in the United States of America, Canada, the
United Kingdom and Ireland arranged with SHOGAKUKAN.

English Adaptation/Gerard Jones
Translation/Kaori Inoue
Touch-up & Lettering/Annaliese Christman
Design/Sam Elzway
Editor, VIZ Kids Edition/Jann Jones

Printed in the U.S.A.

Published by VIZ Media, LLC
P.O. Box 77010
San Francisco, CA 94107

10 9 8 7 6 5
First printing, August 2010
Fifth printing, December 2013

PARENTAL ADVISORY
POKÉMON ADVENTURES
is rated A and is suitable
for readers of all ages.
ratings.viz.com

www.perfectsquare.com   www.viz.com

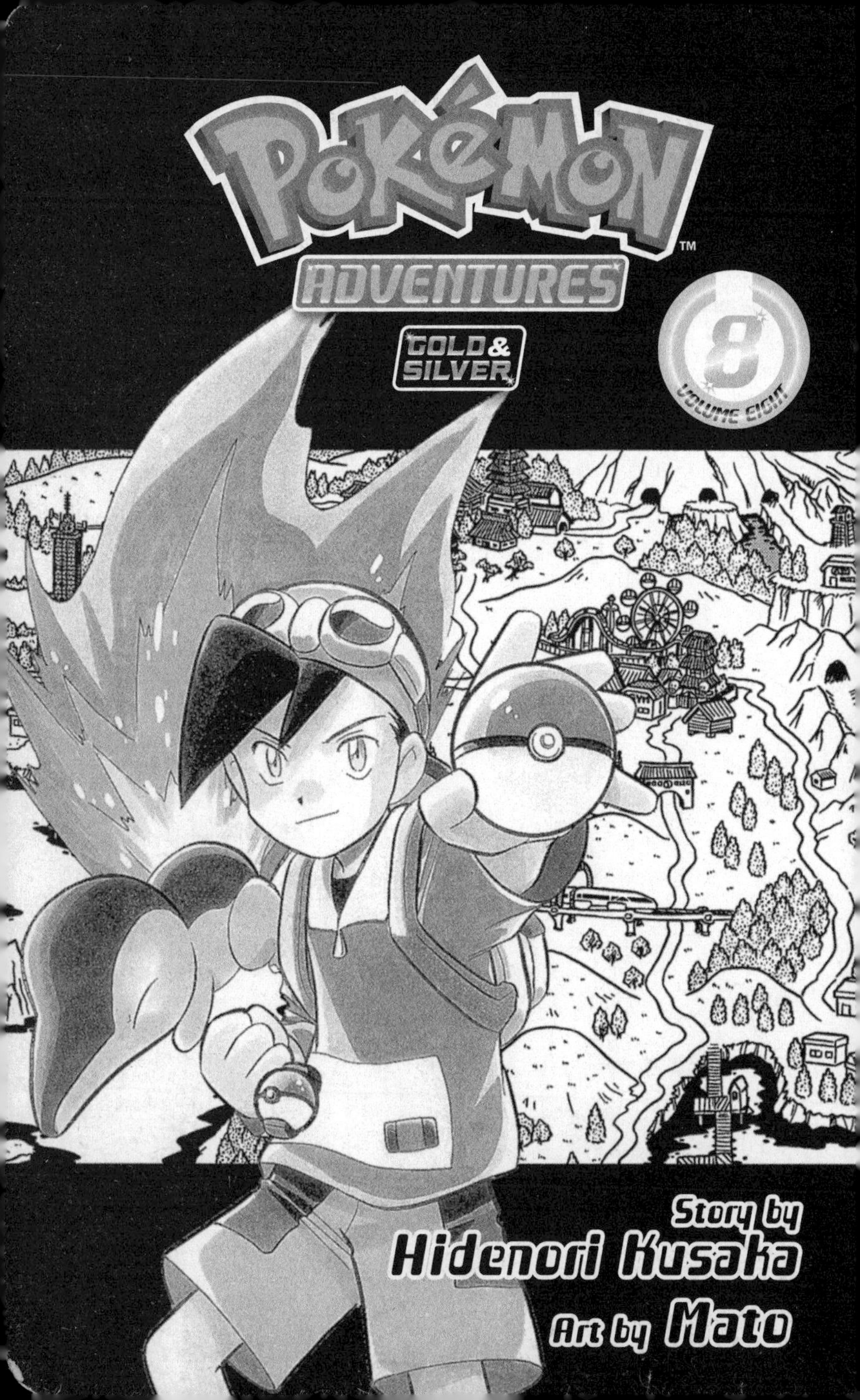

POKÉMON™
ADVENTURES
GOLD & SILVER
8
VOLUME EIGHT
Story by
Hidenori Kusaka
Art by
Mato

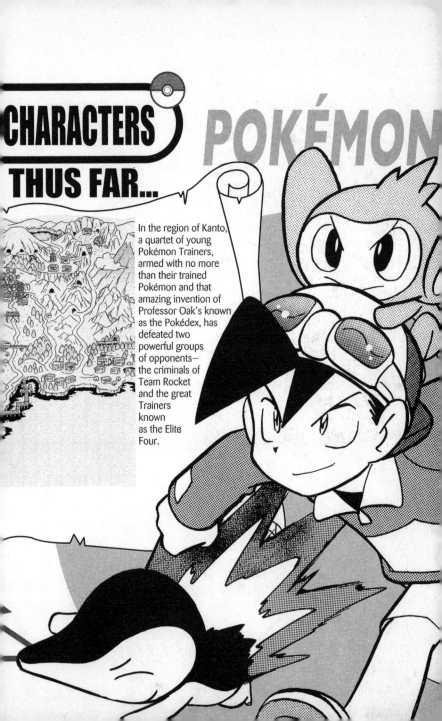

CHARACTERS THUS FAR...

POKÉMON

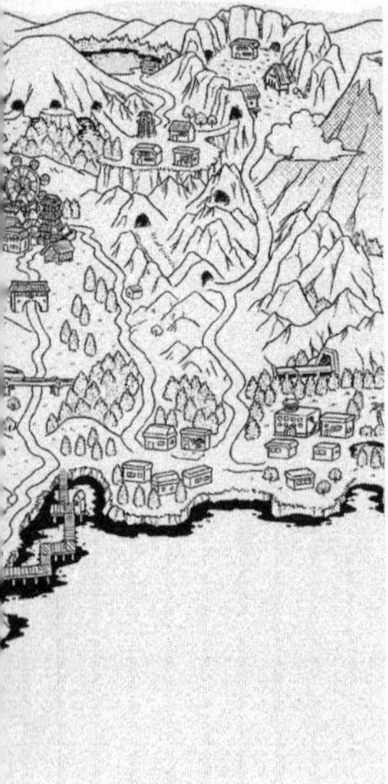

In the region of Kanto, a quartet of young Pokémon Trainers, armed with no more than their trained Pokémon and that amazing invention of Professor Oak's known as the Pokédex, has defeated two powerful groups of opponents—the criminals of Team Rocket and the great Trainers known as the Elite Four.

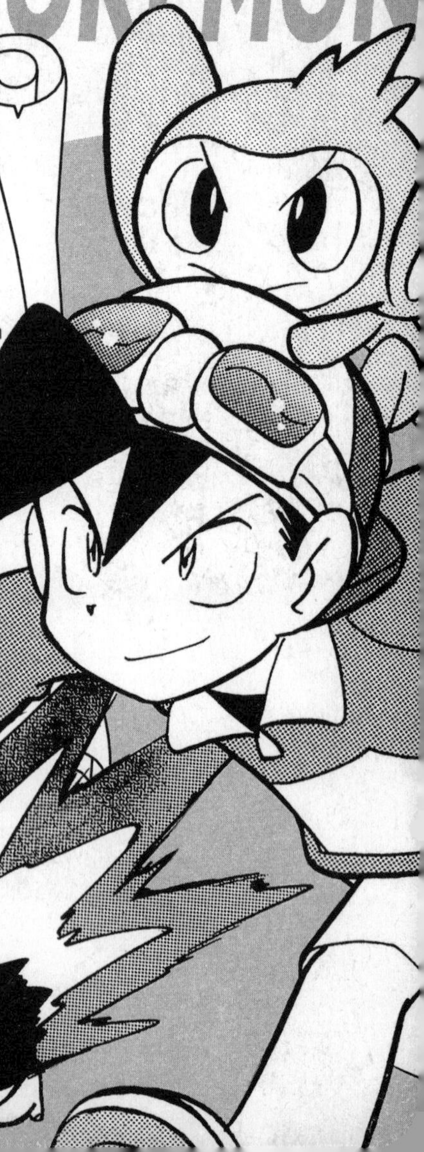

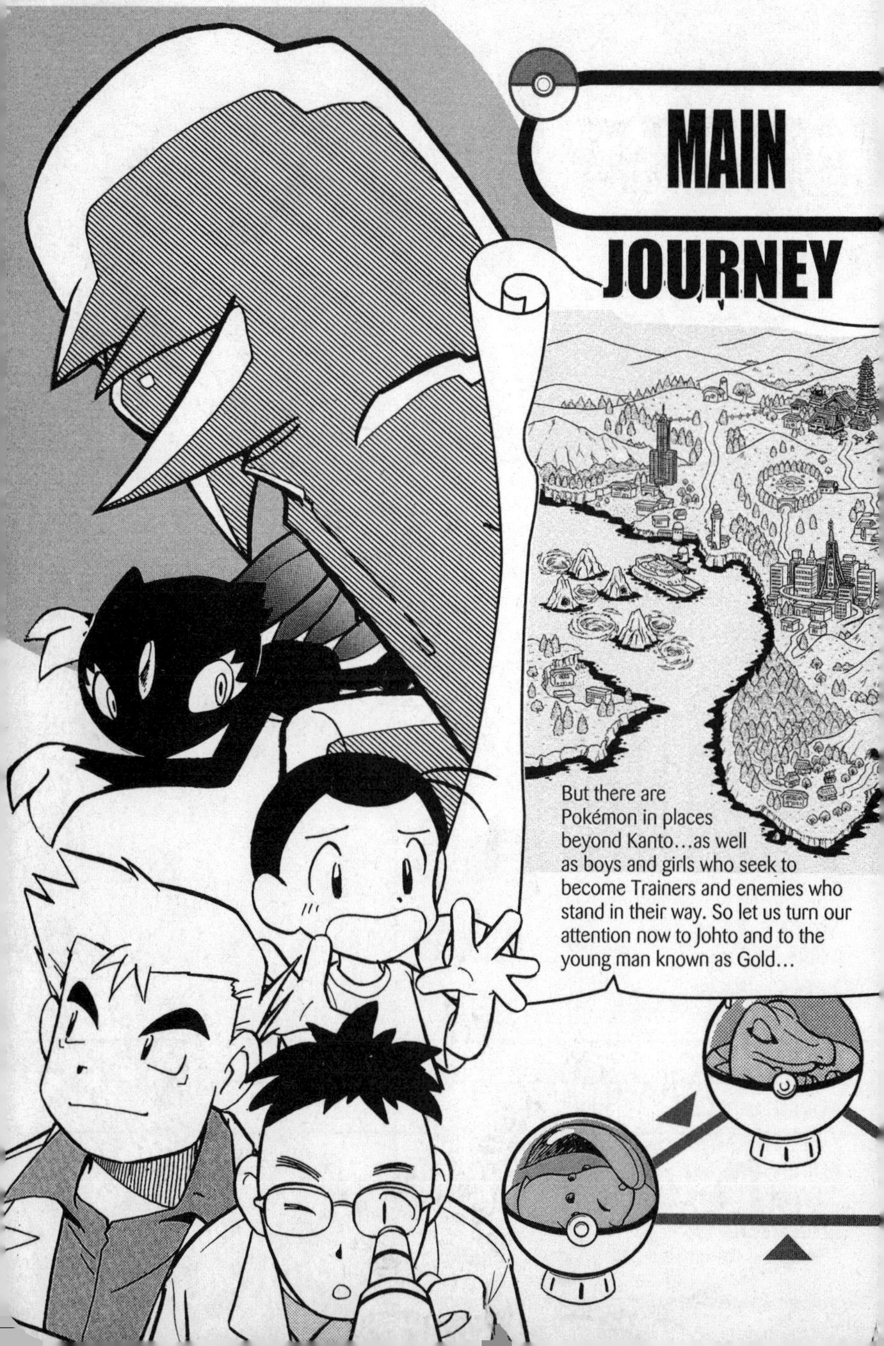
MAIN JOURNEY
But there are Pokémon in places beyond Kanto…as well as boys and girls who seek to become Trainers and enemies who stand in their way. So let us turn our attention now to Johto and to the young man known as Gold…

CONTENTS

GOLD

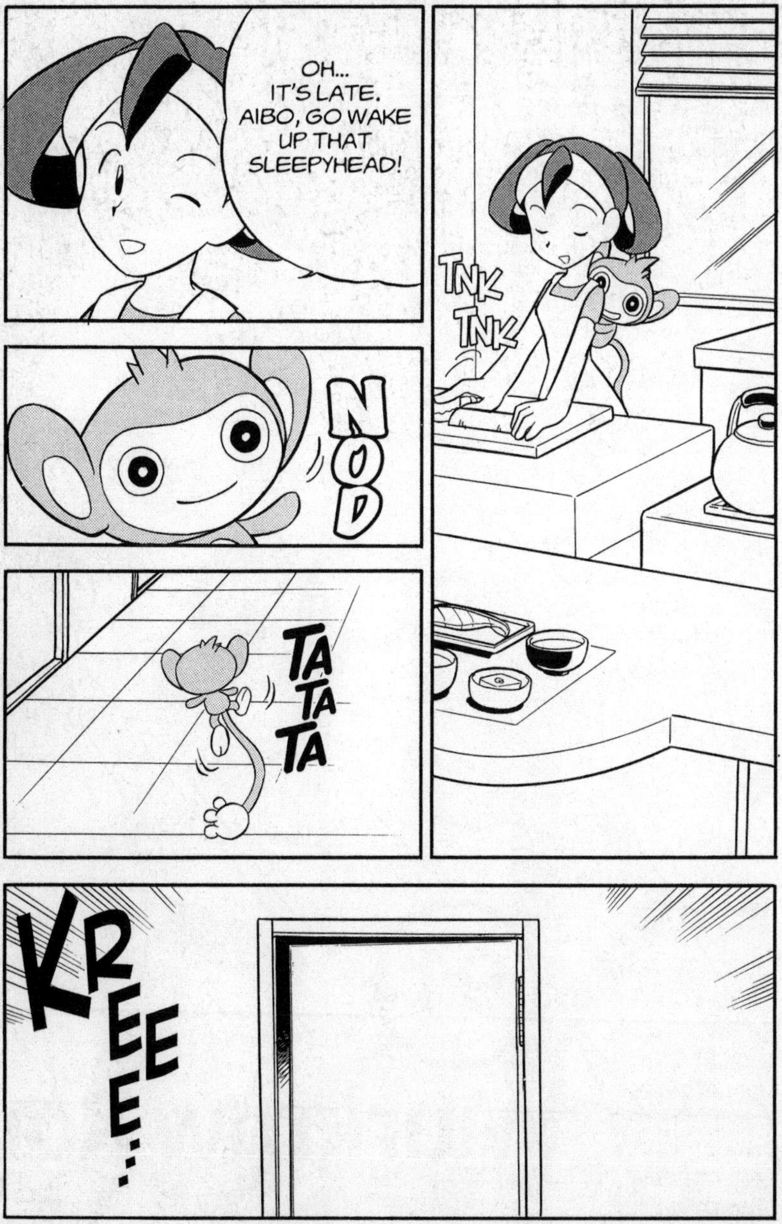
TNK
TNK
OH... IT'S LATE. AIBO, GO WAKE UP THAT SLEEPYHEAD!
NOD
TA TA TA TA
KREEE...

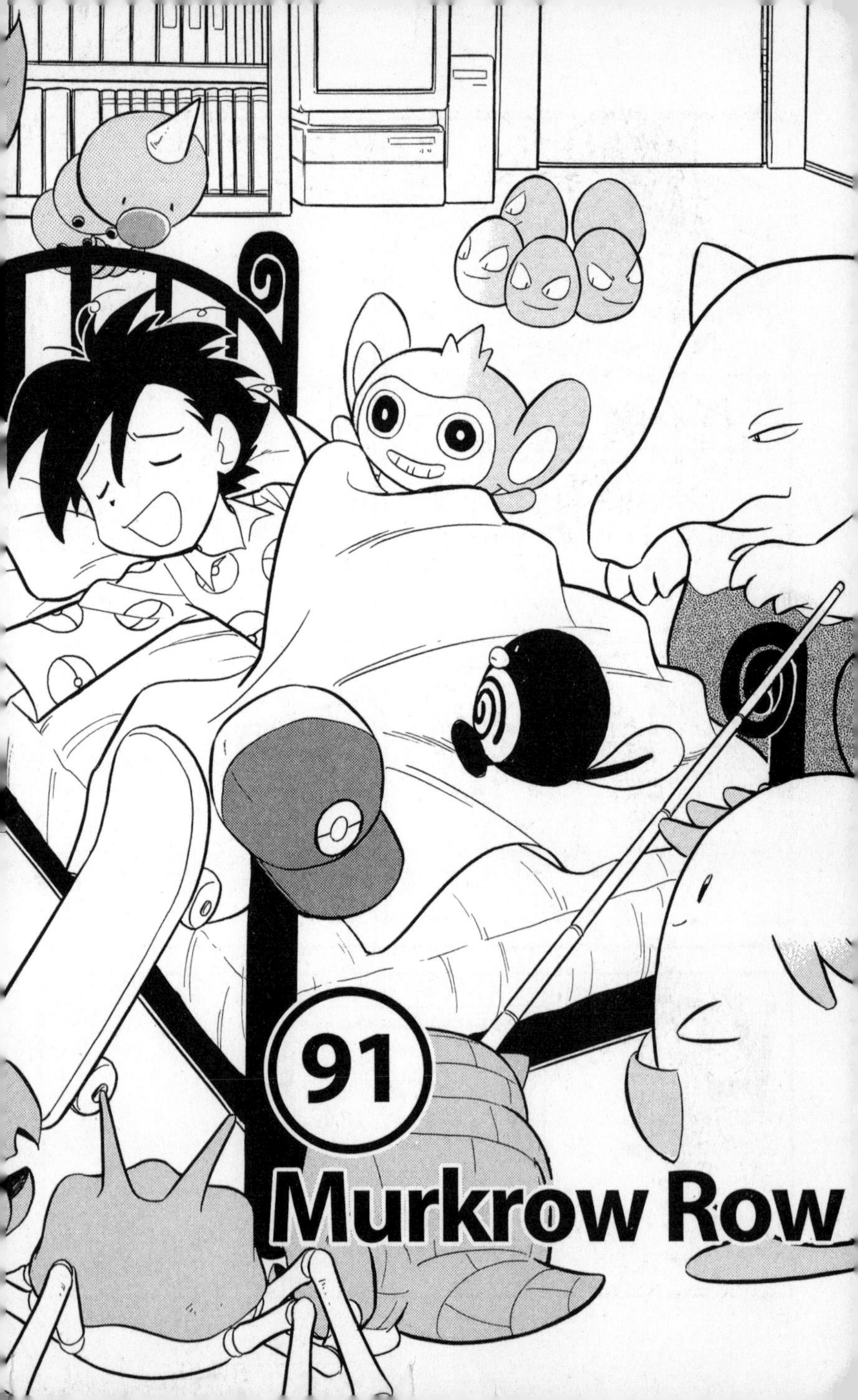
91
Murkrow Row

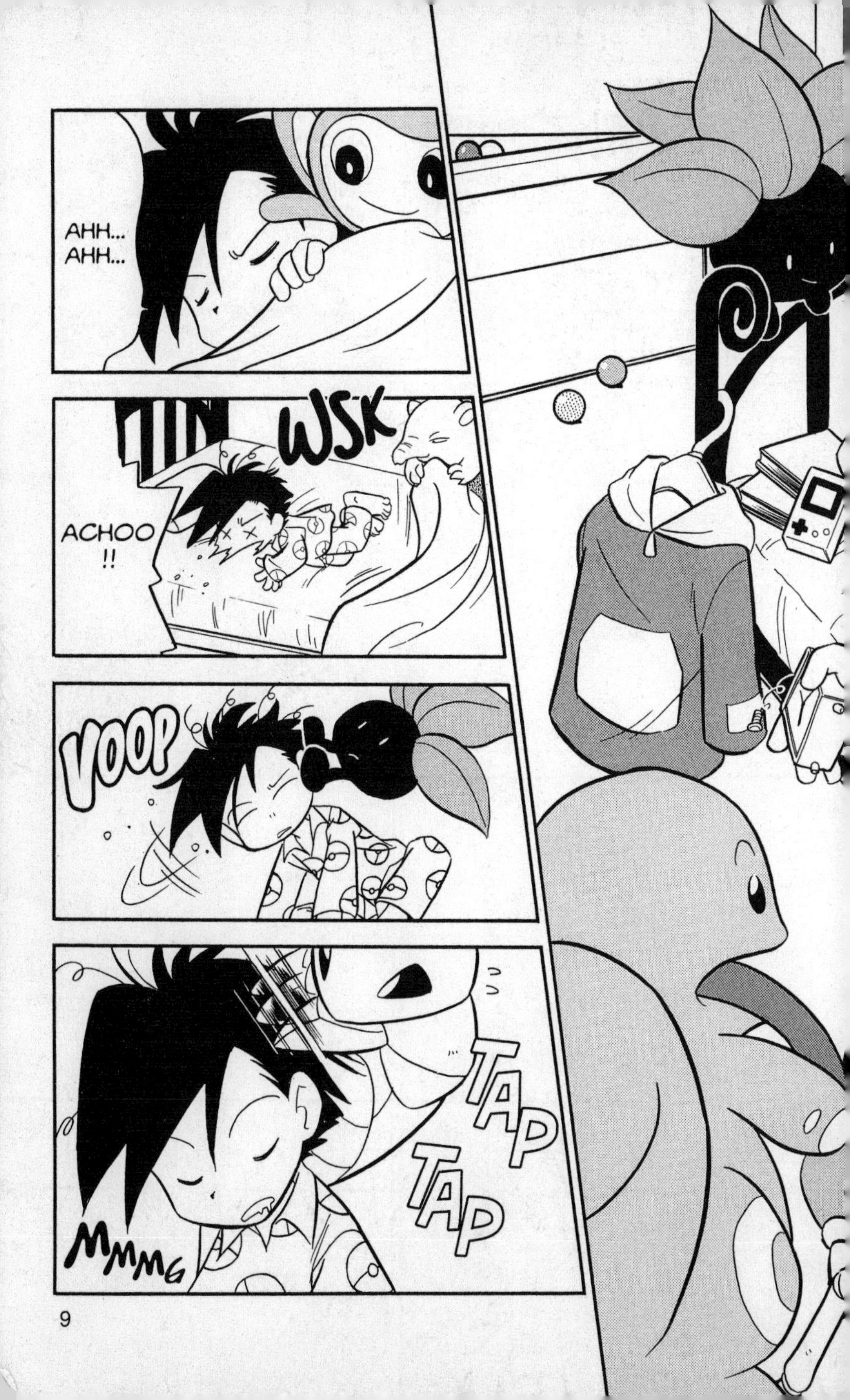
AHH... AHH...
WSK
ACHOO !!
VOOP
TAP TAP
MMMG

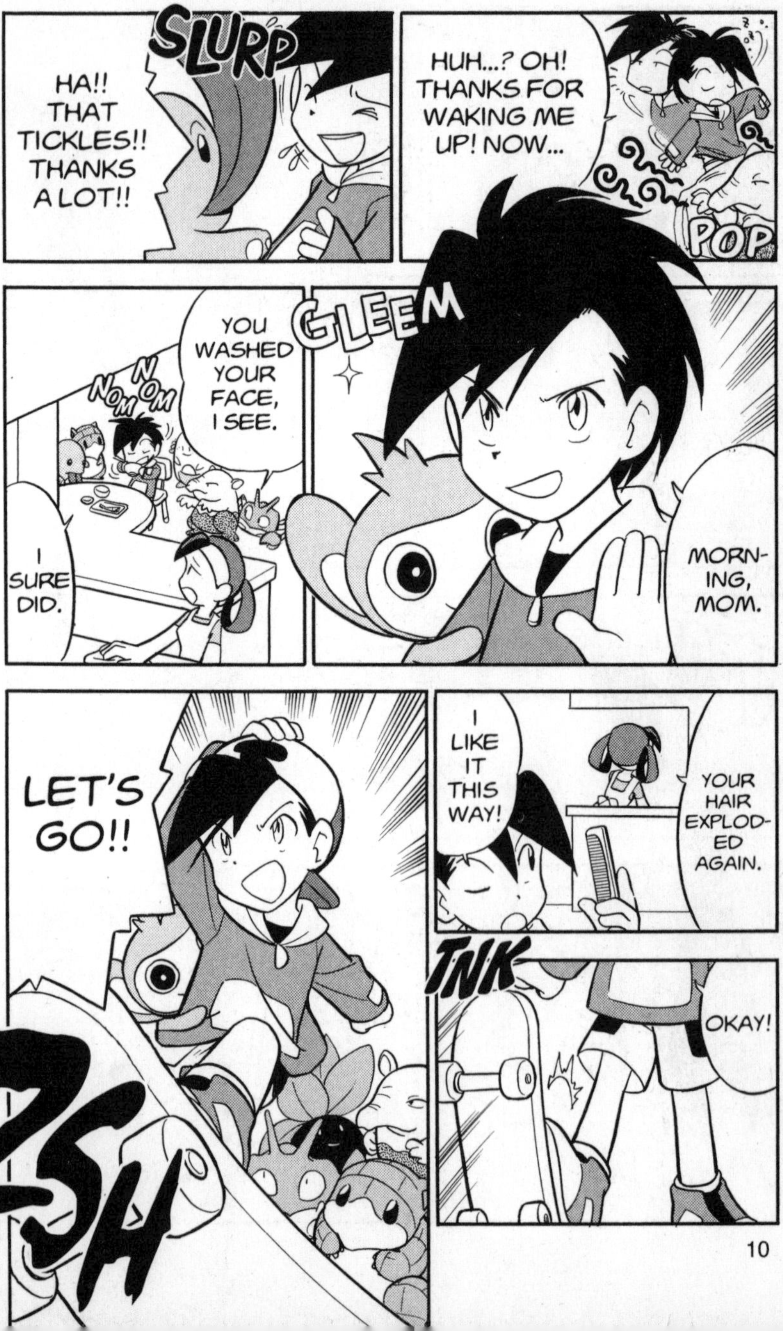
HUH...? OH! THANKS FOR WAKING ME UP! NOW...
POP
SLURP
HA!! THAT TICKLES!! THANKS A LOT!!
GLEEM
MORN-ING, MOM.
YOU WASHED YOUR FACE, I SEE.
NOM NOM
I SURE DID.
YOUR HAIR EXPLOD-ED AGAIN.
I LIKE IT THIS WAY!
TNK
OKAY!
LET'S GO!!
ZSH

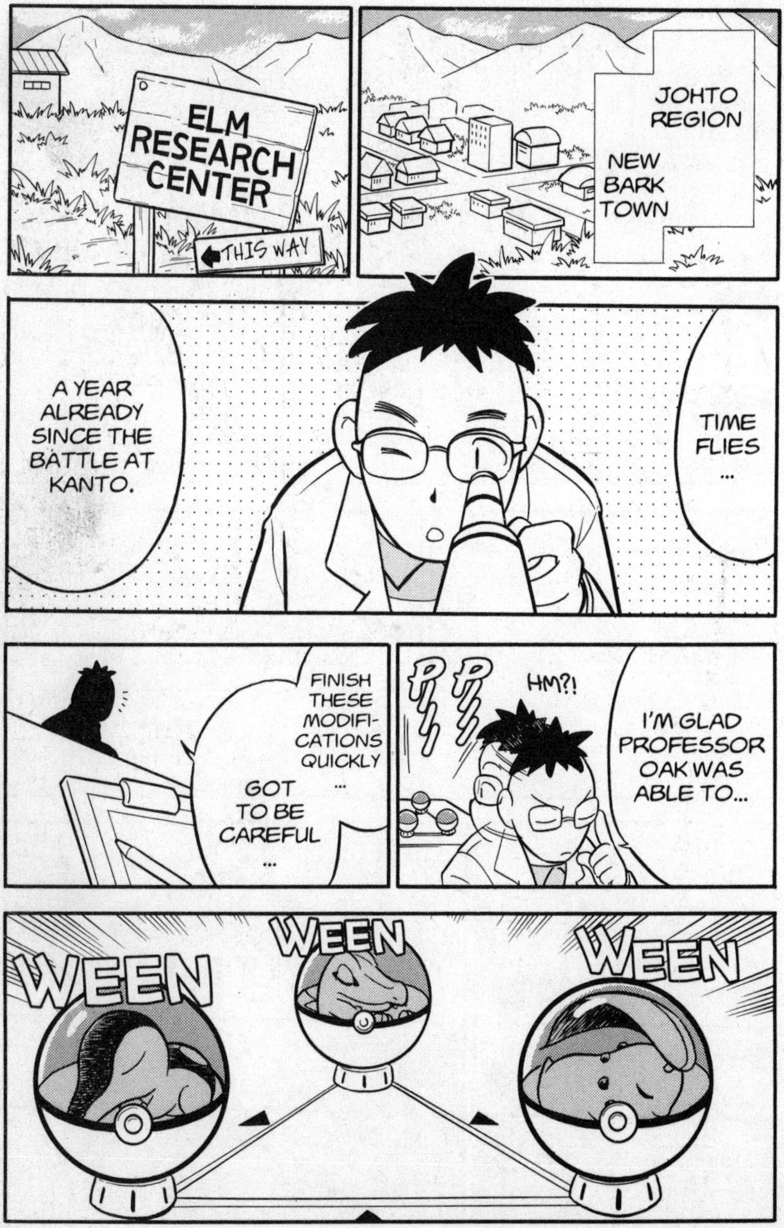
JOHTO REGION
NEW BARK TOWN
ELM RESEARCH CENTER
THIS WAY
TIME FLIES ...
A YEAR ALREADY SINCE THE BATTLE AT KANTO.
I'M GLAD PROFESSOR OAK WAS ABLE TO...
HM?!
PI PI
FINISH THESE MODIFI-CATIONS QUICKLY ...
GOT TO BE CAREFUL ...
WEEN
WEEN
WEEN

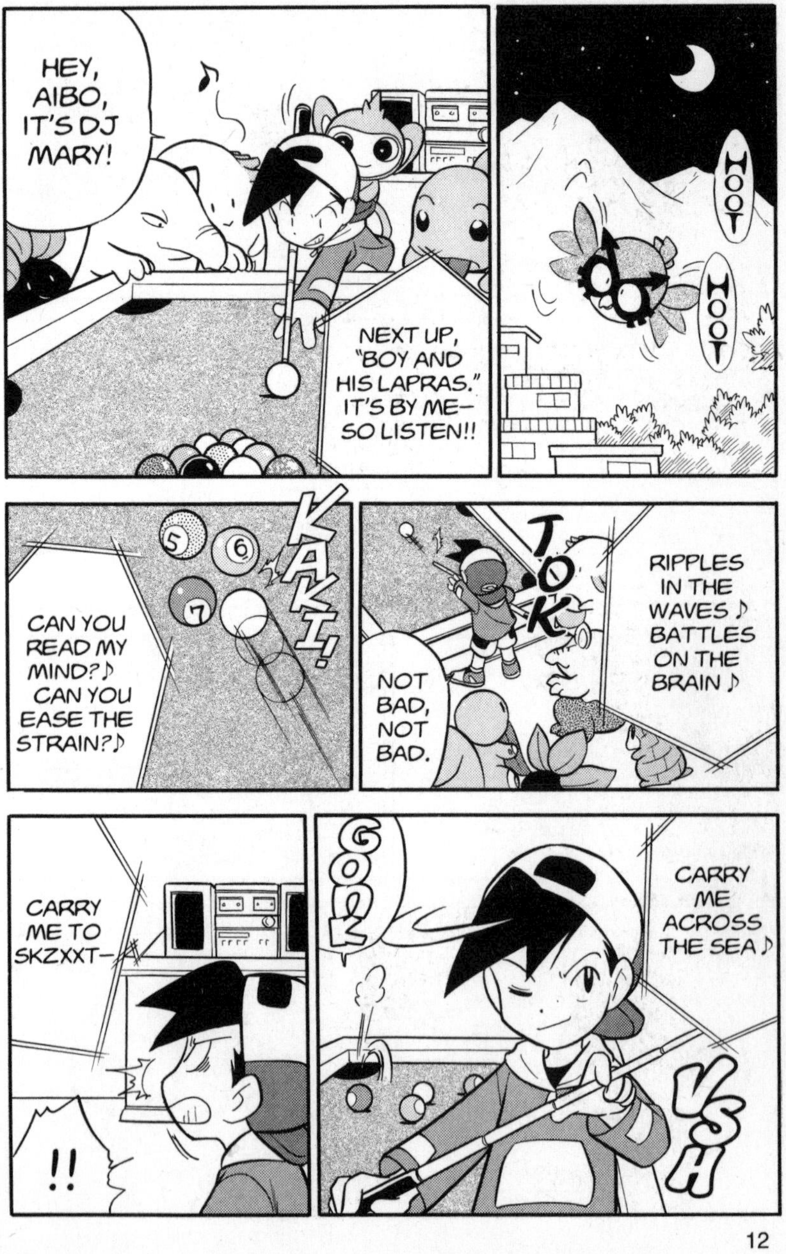
HOOT
HOOT
HEY, AIBO, IT'S DJ MARY!
♪
NEXT UP, "BOY AND HIS LAPRAS." IT'S BY ME— SO LISTEN!!
RIPPLES IN THE WAVES♪ BATTLES ON THE BRAIN♪
JOK
NOT BAD, NOT BAD.
KAKI!
CAN YOU READ MY MIND?♪ CAN YOU EASE THE STRAIN?♪
CARRY ME ACROSS THE SEA♪
GOOK
VSH
CARRY ME TO SKZXXT—
!!

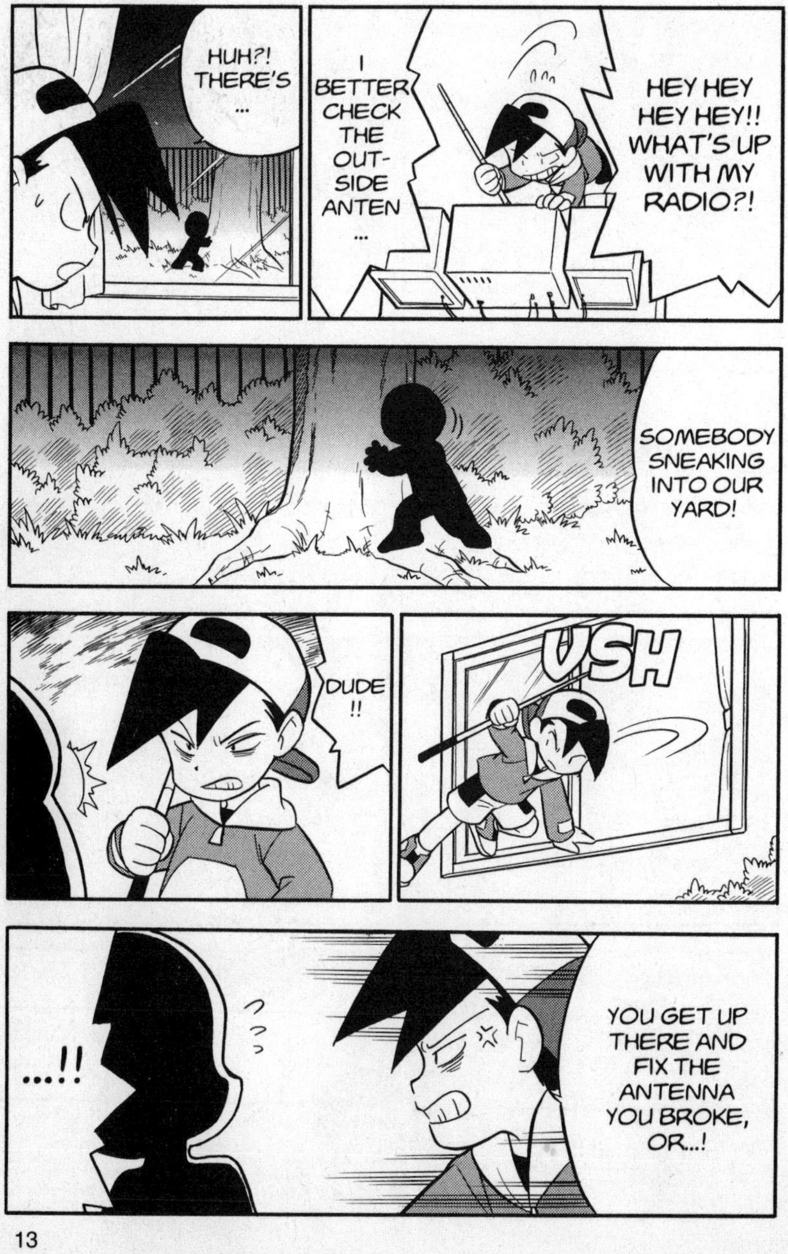
HEY HEY HEY HEY!! WHAT'S UP WITH MY RADIO?!
I BETTER CHECK THE OUT-SIDE ANTEN ...
HUH?! THERE'S ...
SOMEBODY SNEAKING INTO OUR YARD!
USH
DUDE !!
YOU GET UP THERE AND FIX THE ANTENNA YOU BROKE, OR...!
...!!

ASIDE FROM SNEAKING INTO MY YARD IN THE MIDDLE OF THE NIGHT?!

AIBO— SCRATCH!!

GYAAA!

W-WAIT! MY NAME'S JOEY! I DIDN'T DO ANYTHING WRONG!!

ZK ZK ZK

YOU'VE GOT IT ALL WRONG! LOOK UP THERE!!

A MURKROW! I WAS DELIVERING A PIECE OF LUGGAGE... AND THAT MURKROW JUST STOLE IT!

THAT'S...

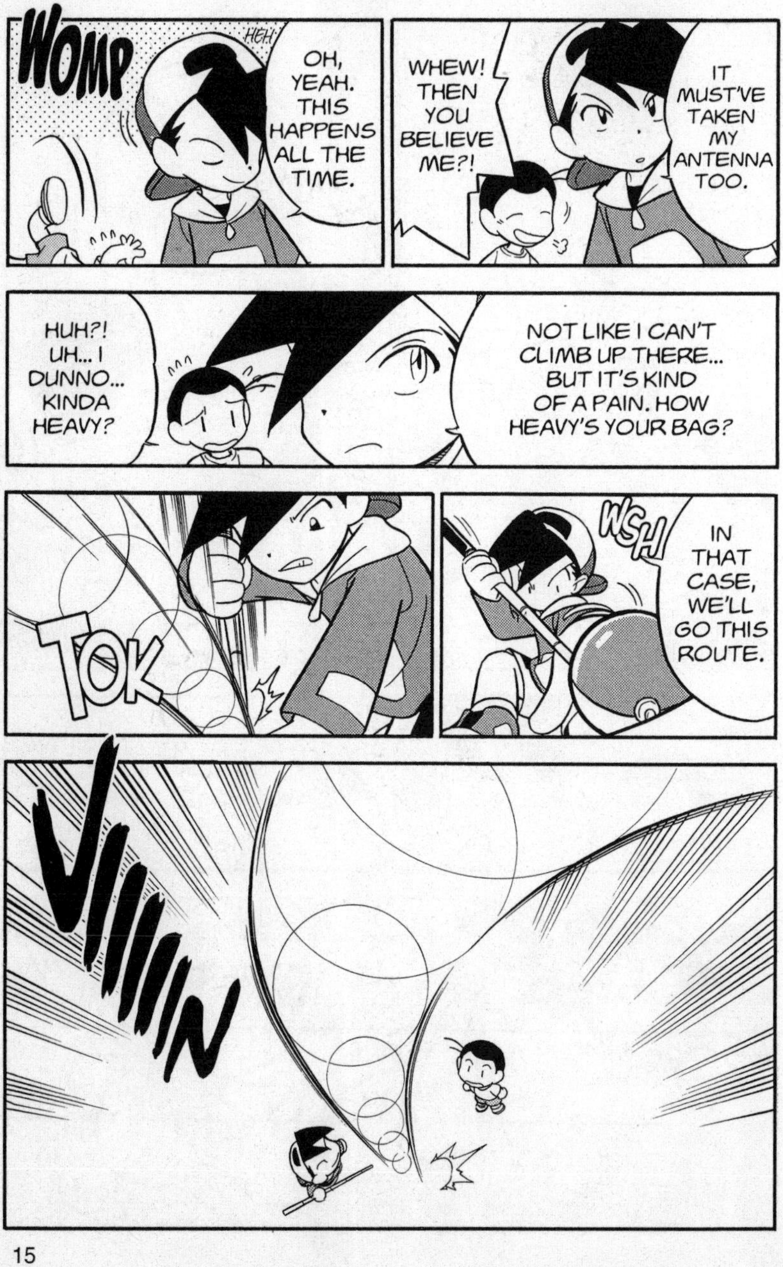
IT MUST'VE TAKEN MY ANTENNA TOO.
WHEW! THEN YOU BELIEVE ME?!
HEH
OH, YEAH. THIS HAPPENS ALL THE TIME.
WOMP
NOT LIKE I CAN'T CLIMB UP THERE... BUT IT'S KIND OF A PAIN. HOW HEAVY'S YOUR BAG?
HUH?! UH... I DUNNO... KINDA HEAVY?
WSH
IN THAT CASE, WE'LL GO THIS ROUTE.
TOK
VIIIIIN

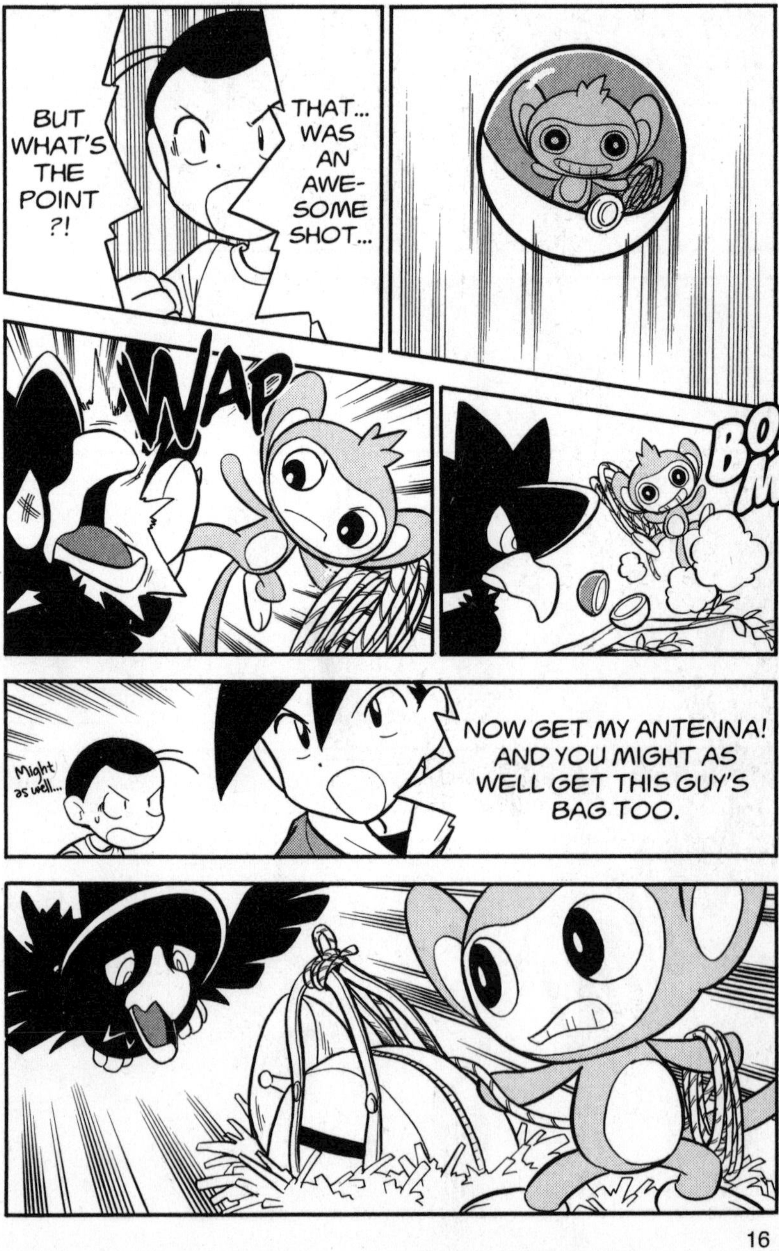
THAT... WAS AN AWESOME SHOT...
BUT WHAT'S THE POINT?!
BOOM
WAP
NOW GET MY ANTENNA! AND YOU MIGHT AS WELL GET THIS GUY'S BAG TOO.
Might as well...

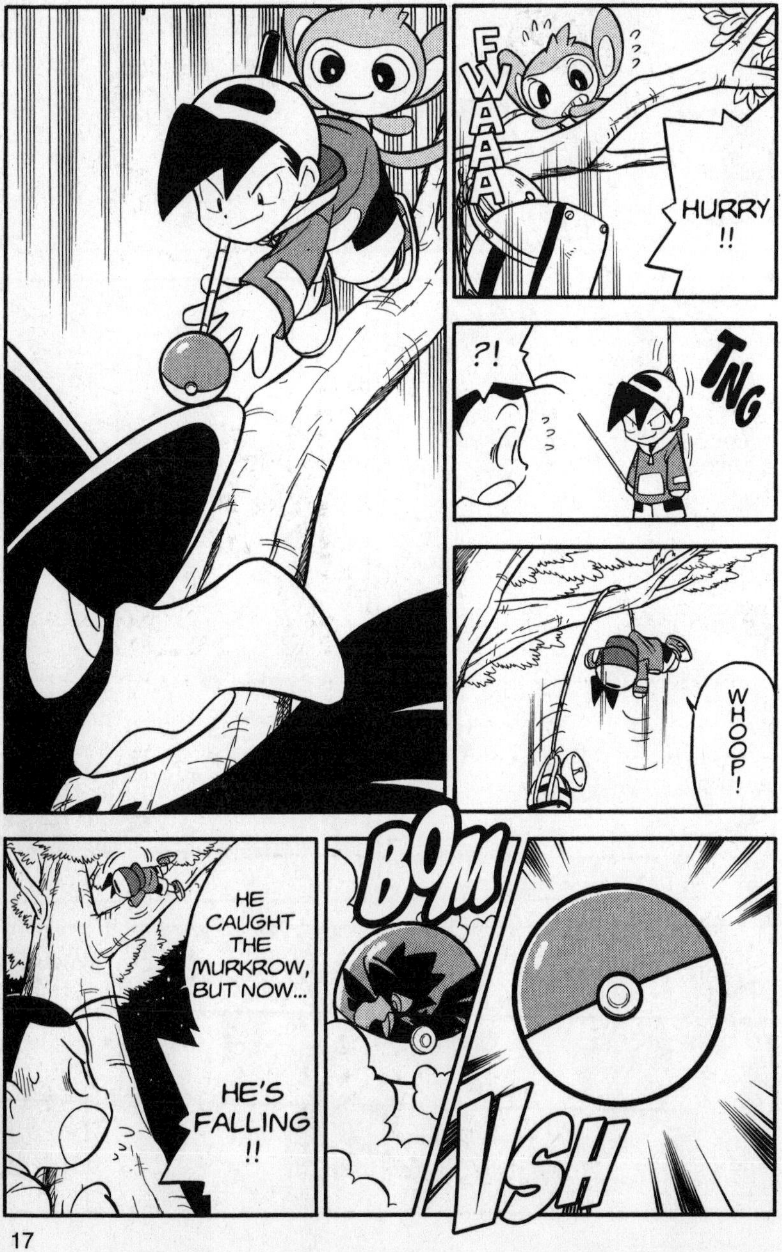
FWAAAA
HURRY !!
?!
TNG
WHOOP!
VISH
BOM
HE CAUGHT THE MURKROW, BUT NOW...
HE'S FALLING !!

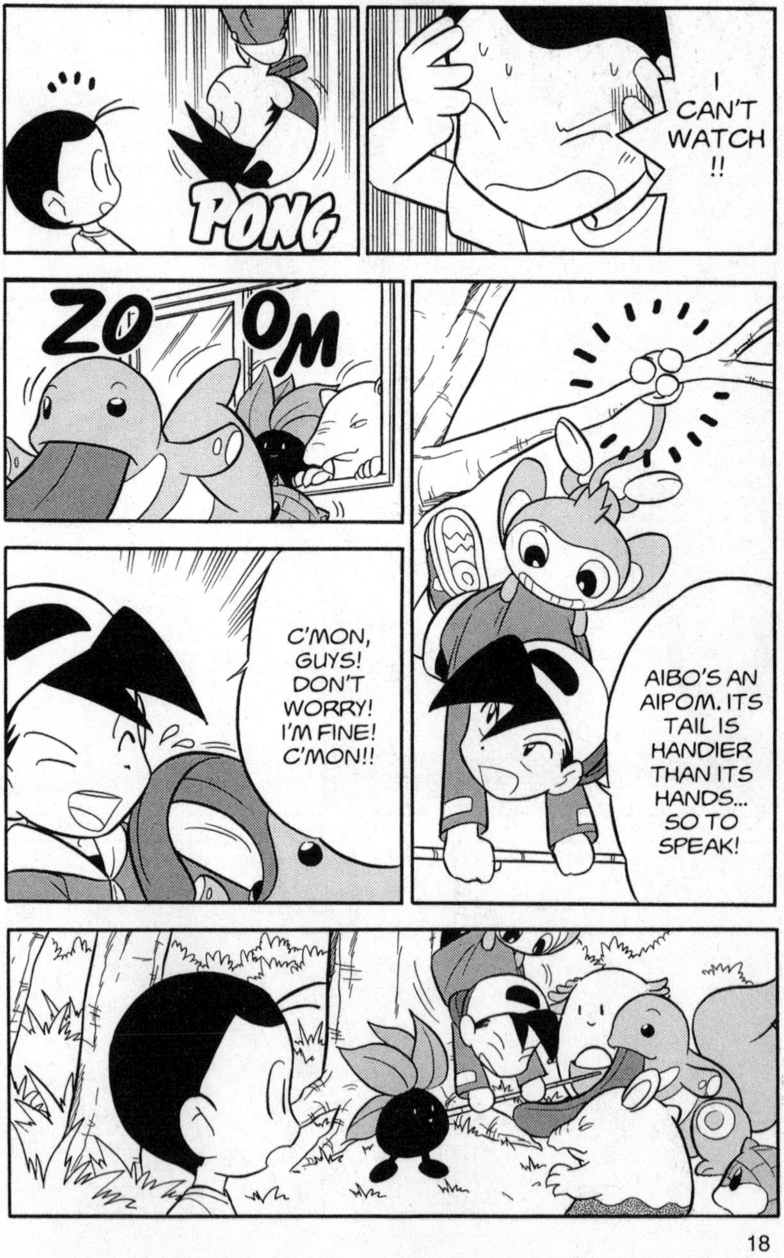
I CAN'T WATCH !!
...
PONG
AIBO'S AN AIPOM. ITS TAIL IS HANDIER THAN ITS HANDS... SO TO SPEAK!
ZOOM
C'MON, GUYS! DON'T WORRY! I'M FINE! C'MON!!

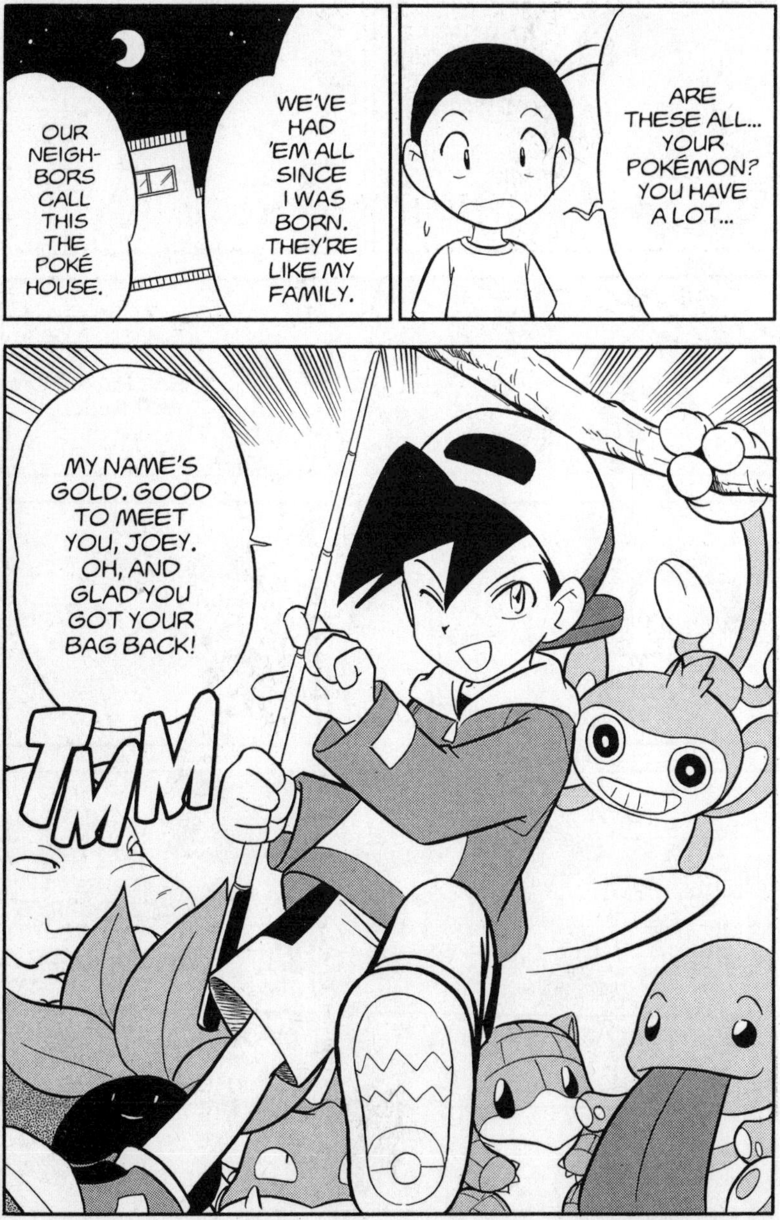
ARE THESE ALL... YOUR POKÉMON? YOU HAVE A LOT...
WE'VE HAD 'EM ALL SINCE I WAS BORN. THEY'RE LIKE MY FAMILY.
OUR NEIGHBORS CALL THIS THE POKÉ HOUSE.
MY NAME'S GOLD. GOOD TO MEET YOU, JOEY. OH, AND GLAD YOU GOT YOUR BAG BACK!
TMM

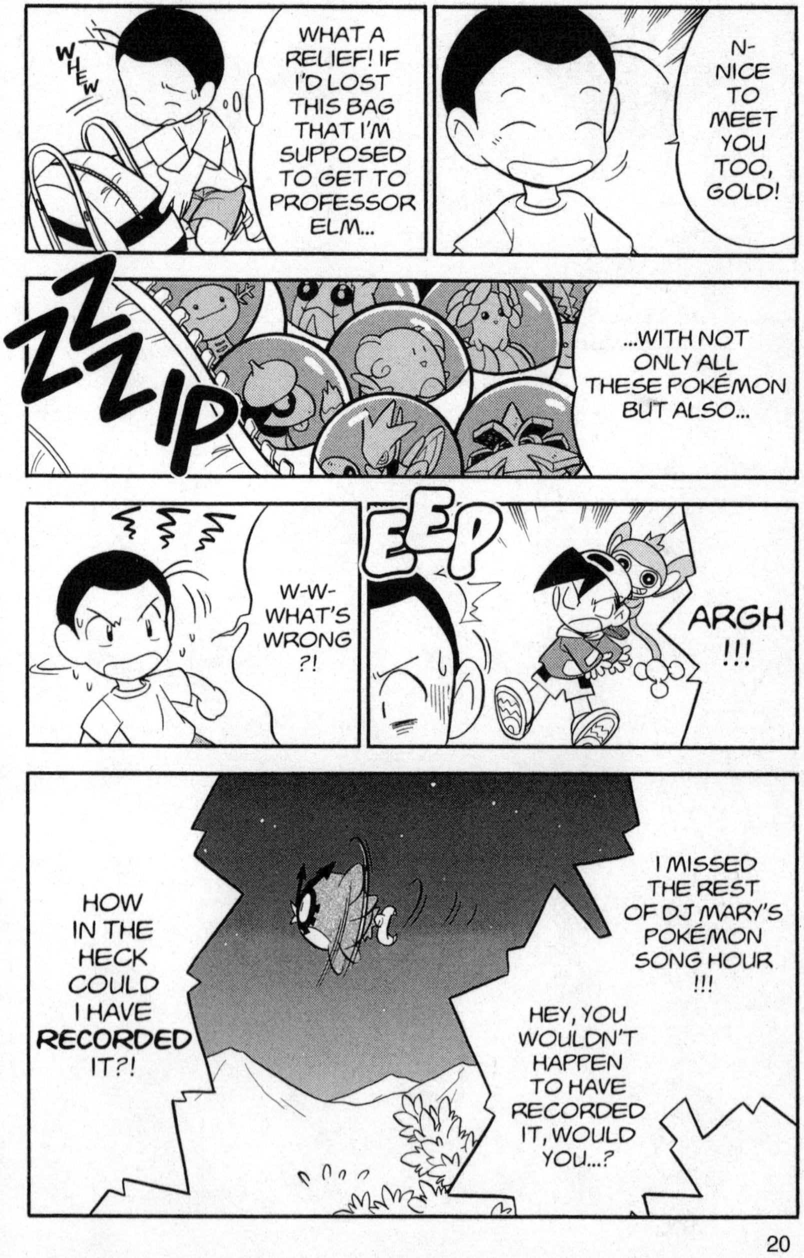
N- NICE TO MEET YOU TOO, GOLD!
WHEW
WHAT A RELIEF! IF I'D LOST THIS BAG THAT I'M SUPPOSED TO GET TO PROFESSOR ELM...
...WITH NOT ONLY ALL THESE POKÉMON BUT ALSO...
ZZZIP
EEP
ARGH!!!
W-W-WHAT'S WRONG?!
I MISSED THE REST OF DJ MARY'S POKÉMON SONG HOUR!!!
HEY, YOU WOULDN'T HAPPEN TO HAVE RECORDED IT, WOULD YOU...?
HOW IN THE HECK COULD I HAVE **RECORDED** IT?!

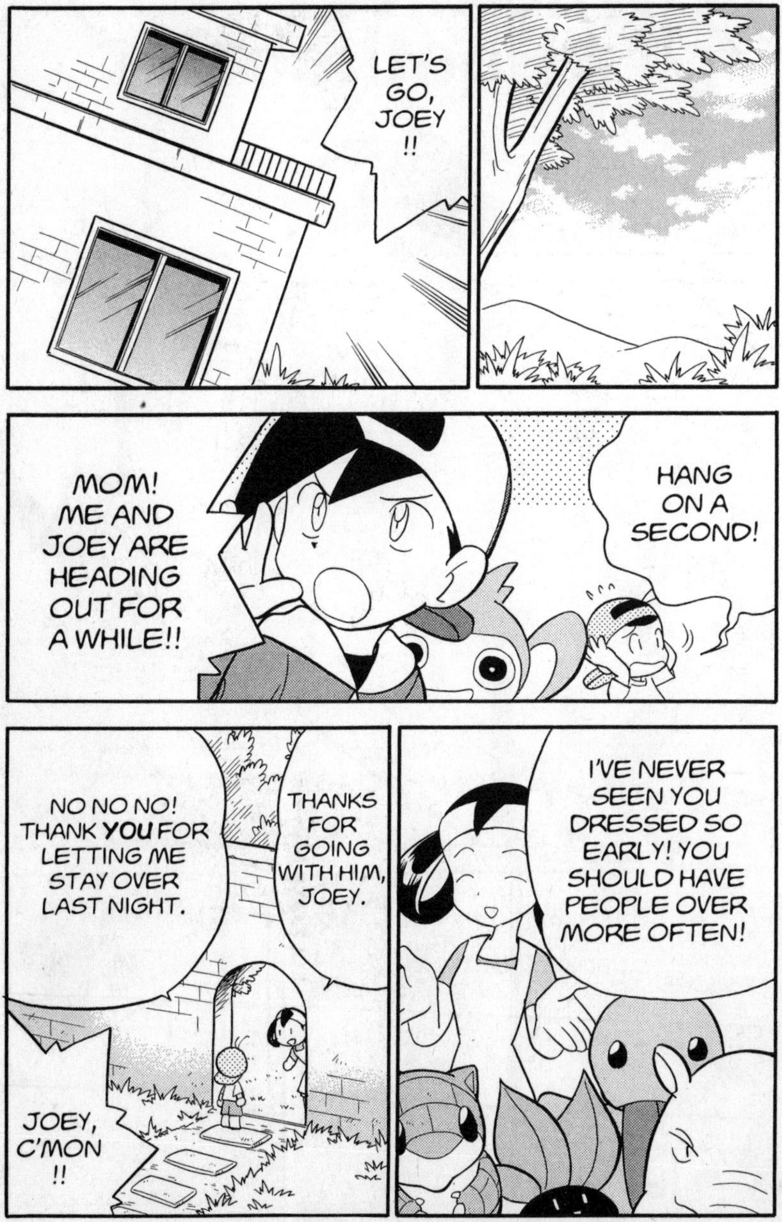
LET'S GO, JOEY !!
HANG ON A SECOND!
MOM! ME AND JOEY ARE HEADING OUT FOR A WHILE!!
I'VE NEVER SEEN YOU DRESSED SO EARLY! YOU SHOULD HAVE PEOPLE OVER MORE OFTEN!
THANKS FOR GOING WITH HIM, JOEY.
NO NO NO! THANK **YOU** FOR LETTING ME STAY OVER LAST NIGHT.
JOEY, C'MON !!

92 Who Gives a Hoothoot?

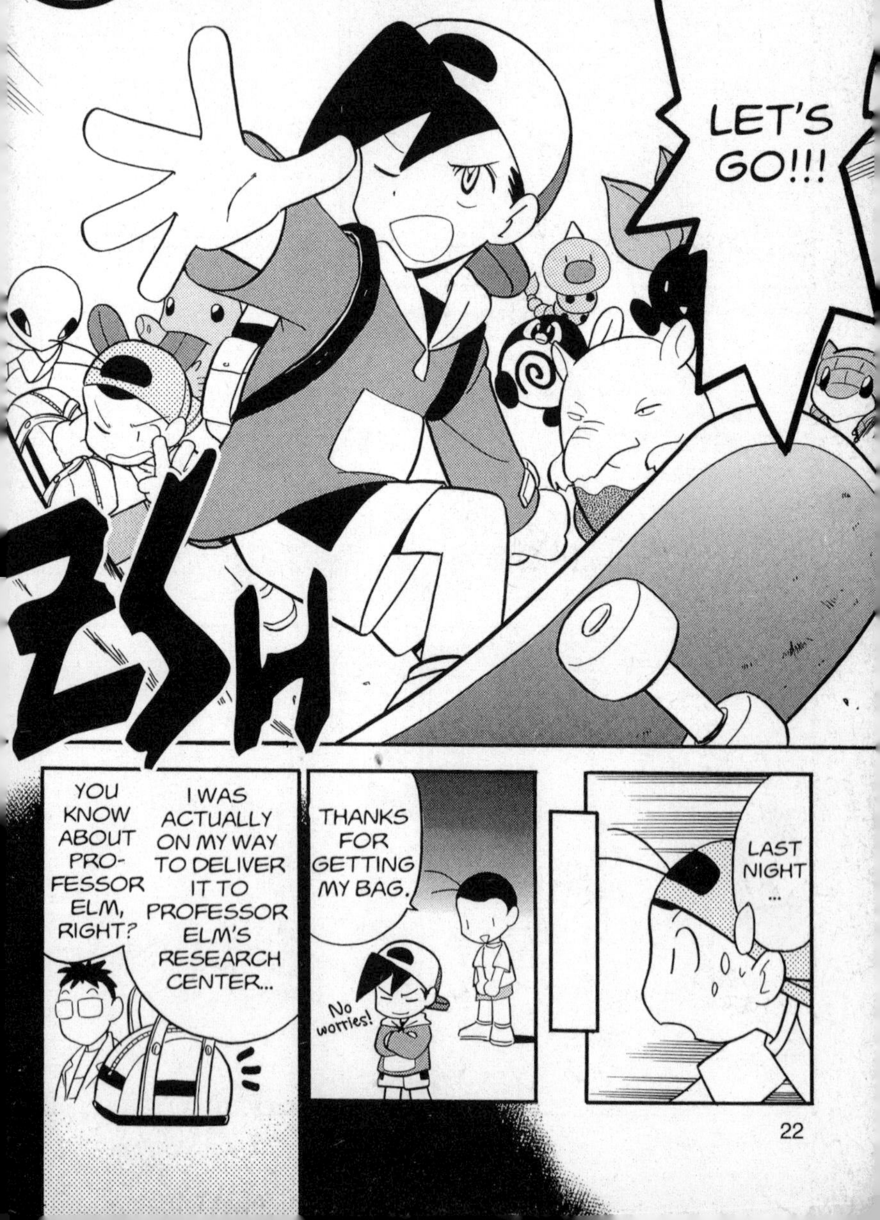
LET'S GO!!!
LAST NIGHT ...
THANKS FOR GETTING MY BAG.
No worries!
I WAS ACTUALLY ON MY WAY TO DELIVER IT TO PROFESSOR ELM'S RESEARCH CENTER...
YOU KNOW ABOUT PRO-FESSOR ELM, RIGHT?

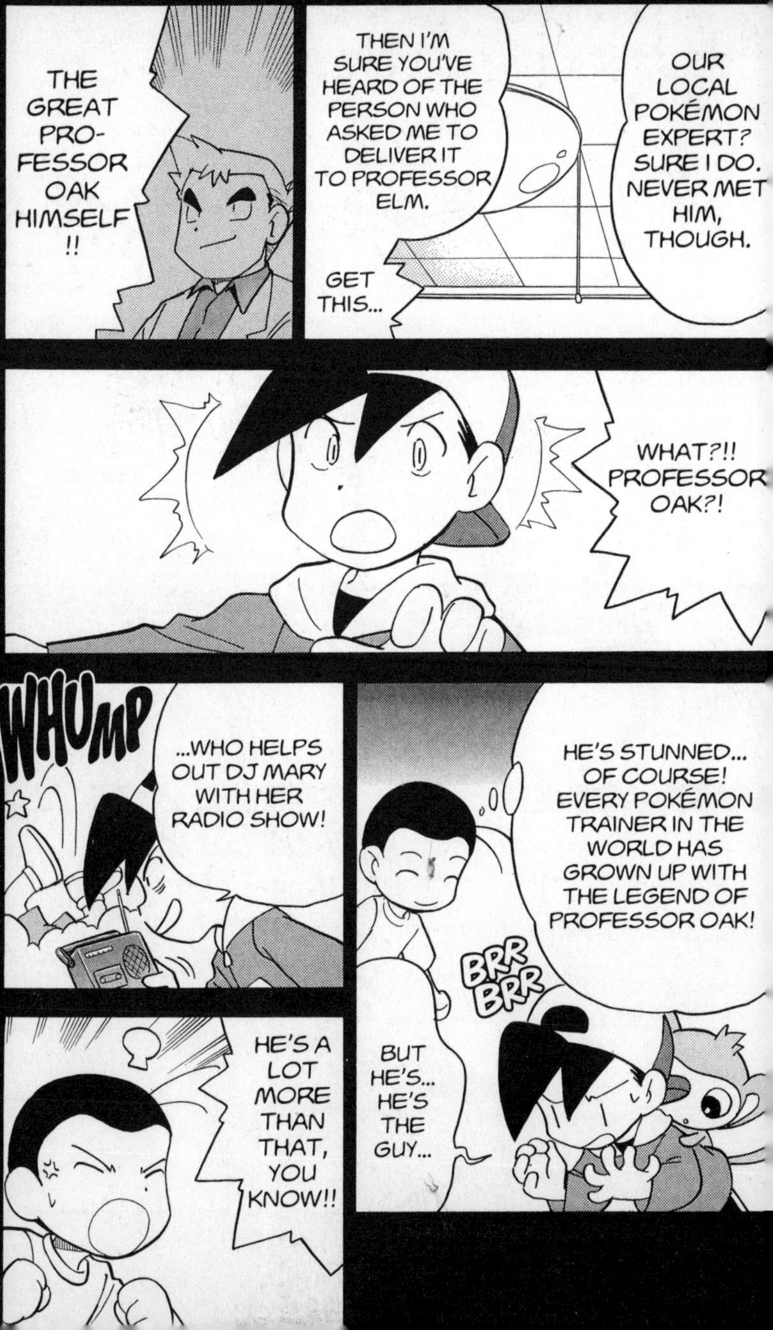
OUR LOCAL POKÉMON EXPERT? SURE I DO. NEVER MET HIM, THOUGH.
THEN I'M SURE YOU'VE HEARD OF THE PERSON WHO ASKED ME TO DELIVER IT TO PROFESSOR ELM.
GET THIS...
THE GREAT PRO-FESSOR OAK HIMSELF !!
WHAT?!! PROFESSOR OAK?!
HE'S STUNNED... OF COURSE! EVERY POKÉMON TRAINER IN THE WORLD HAS GROWN UP WITH THE LEGEND OF PROFESSOR OAK!
BRR BRR
BUT HE'S... HE'S THE GUY...
WHUMP
...WHO HELPS OUT DJ MARY WITH HER RADIO SHOW!
HE'S A LOT MORE THAN THAT, YOU KNOW!!

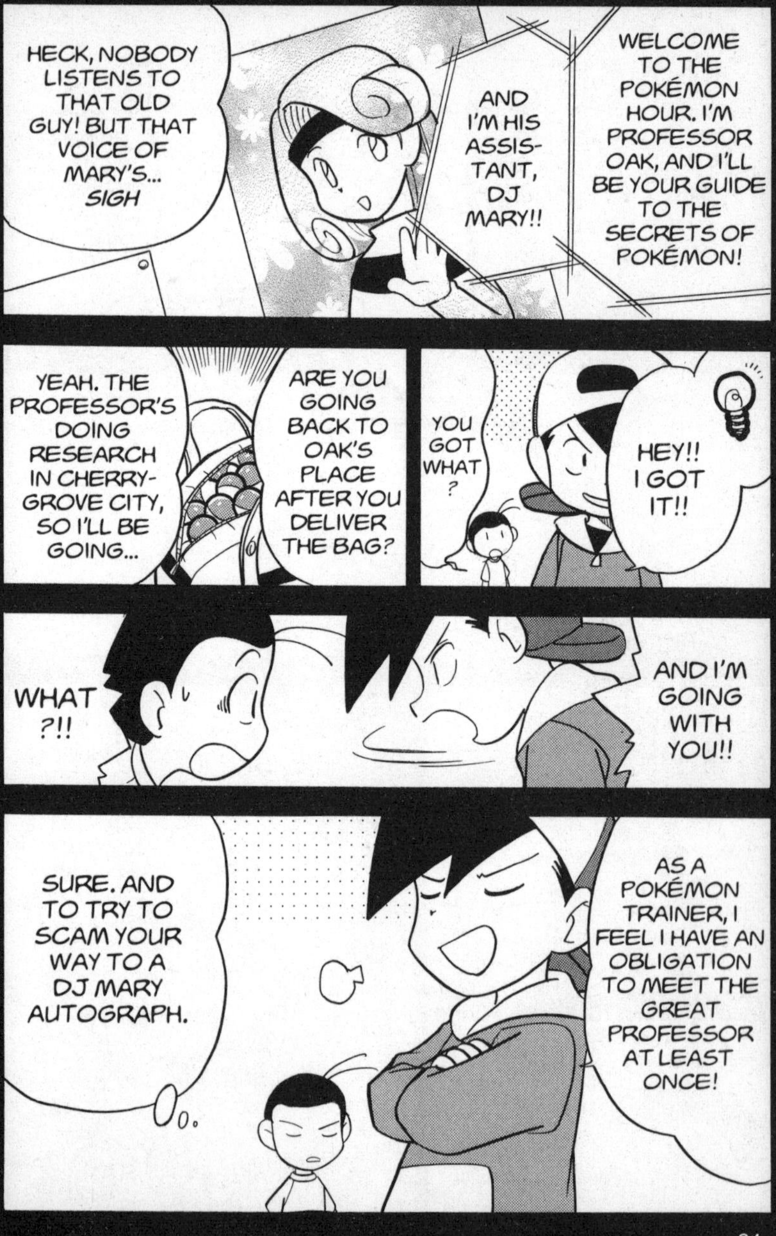
WELCOME TO THE POKÉMON HOUR. I'M PROFESSOR OAK, AND I'LL BE YOUR GUIDE TO THE SECRETS OF POKÉMON!
AND I'M HIS ASSISTANT, DJ MARY!!
HECK, NOBODY LISTENS TO THAT OLD GUY! BUT THAT VOICE OF MARY'S... *SIGH*
HEY!! I GOT IT!!
YOU GOT WHAT?
ARE YOU GOING BACK TO OAK'S PLACE AFTER YOU DELIVER THE BAG?
YEAH. THE PROFESSOR'S DOING RESEARCH IN CHERRYGROVE CITY, SO I'LL BE GOING...
AND I'M GOING WITH YOU!!
WHAT?!!
AS A POKÉMON TRAINER, I FEEL I HAVE AN OBLIGATION TO MEET THE GREAT PROFESSOR AT LEAST ONCE!
SURE. AND TO TRY TO SCAM YOUR WAY TO A DJ MARY AUTOGRAPH.

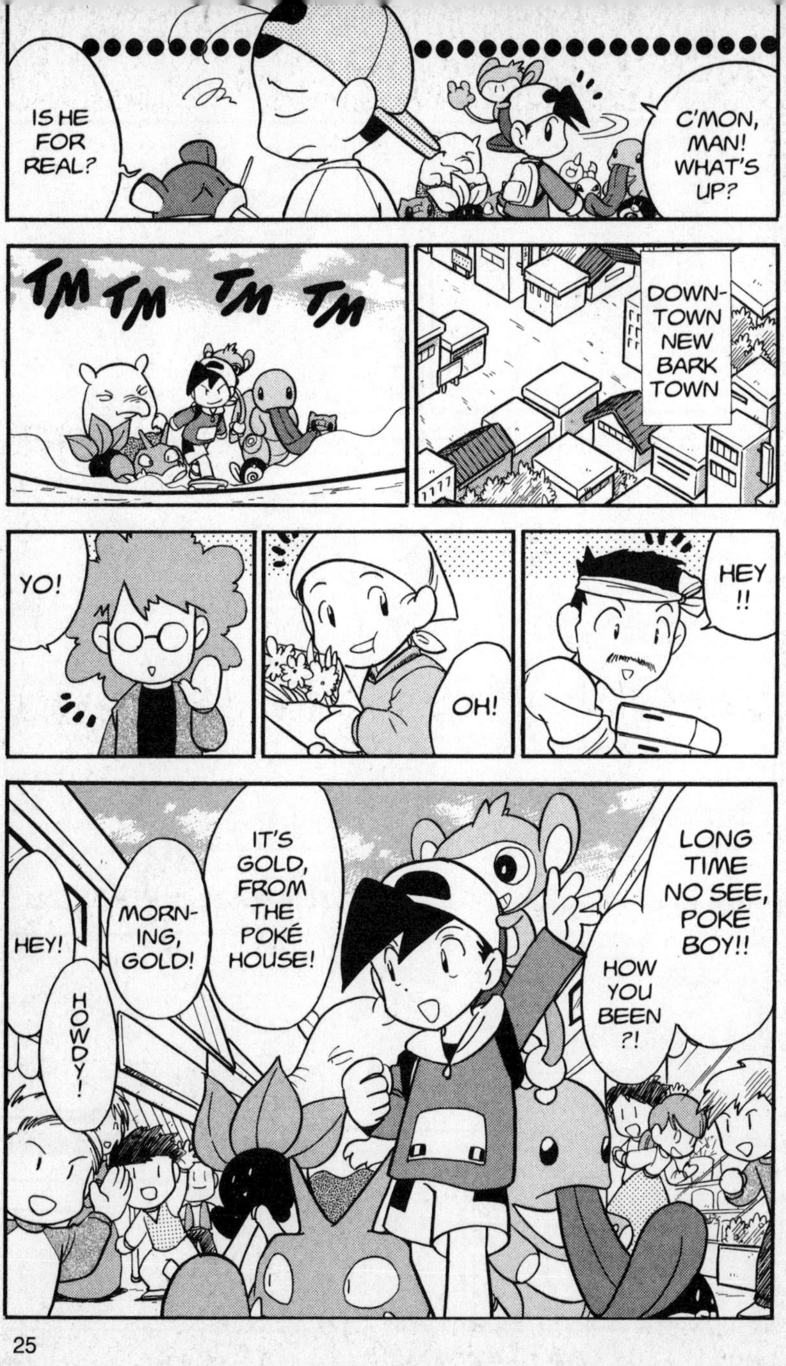
C'MON, MAN! WHAT'S UP?
IS HE FOR REAL?
DOWN-TOWN NEW BARK TOWN
TM TM TM TM
HEY !!
OH!
YO!
LONG TIME NO SEE, POKÉ BOY!!
HOW YOU BEEN ?!
IT'S GOLD, FROM THE POKÉ HOUSE!
MORN-ING, GOLD!
HEY!
HOWDY!

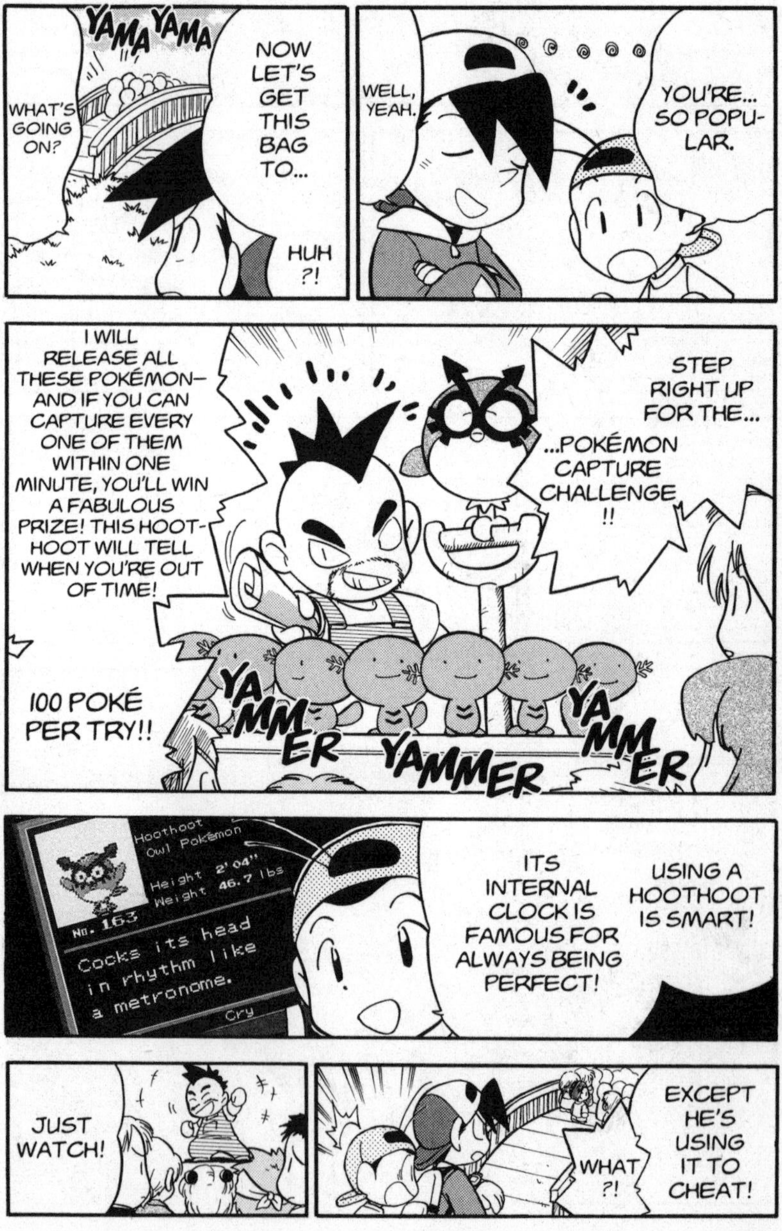
YOU'RE... SO POPU-LAR.
WELL, YEAH.
YAMA YAMA
NOW LET'S GET THIS BAG TO...
WHAT'S GOING ON?
HUH ?!
STEP RIGHT UP FOR THE...
...POKÉMON CAPTURE CHALLENGE !!
I WILL RELEASE ALL THESE POKÉMON—AND IF YOU CAN CAPTURE EVERY ONE OF THEM WITHIN ONE MINUTE, YOU'LL WIN A FABULOUS PRIZE! THIS HOOT-HOOT WILL TELL WHEN YOU'RE OUT OF TIME!
YAMMER
YAMMER
YAMMER
100 POKÉ PER TRY!!
USING A HOOTHOOT IS SMART!
ITS INTERNAL CLOCK IS FAMOUS FOR ALWAYS BEING PERFECT!
Hoothoot
Owl Pokémon
Height 2' 04"
Weight 46.7 lbs
No. 163
Cocks its head in rhythm like a metronome.
Cry
EXCEPT HE'S USING IT TO CHEAT!
WHAT ?!
JUST WATCH!

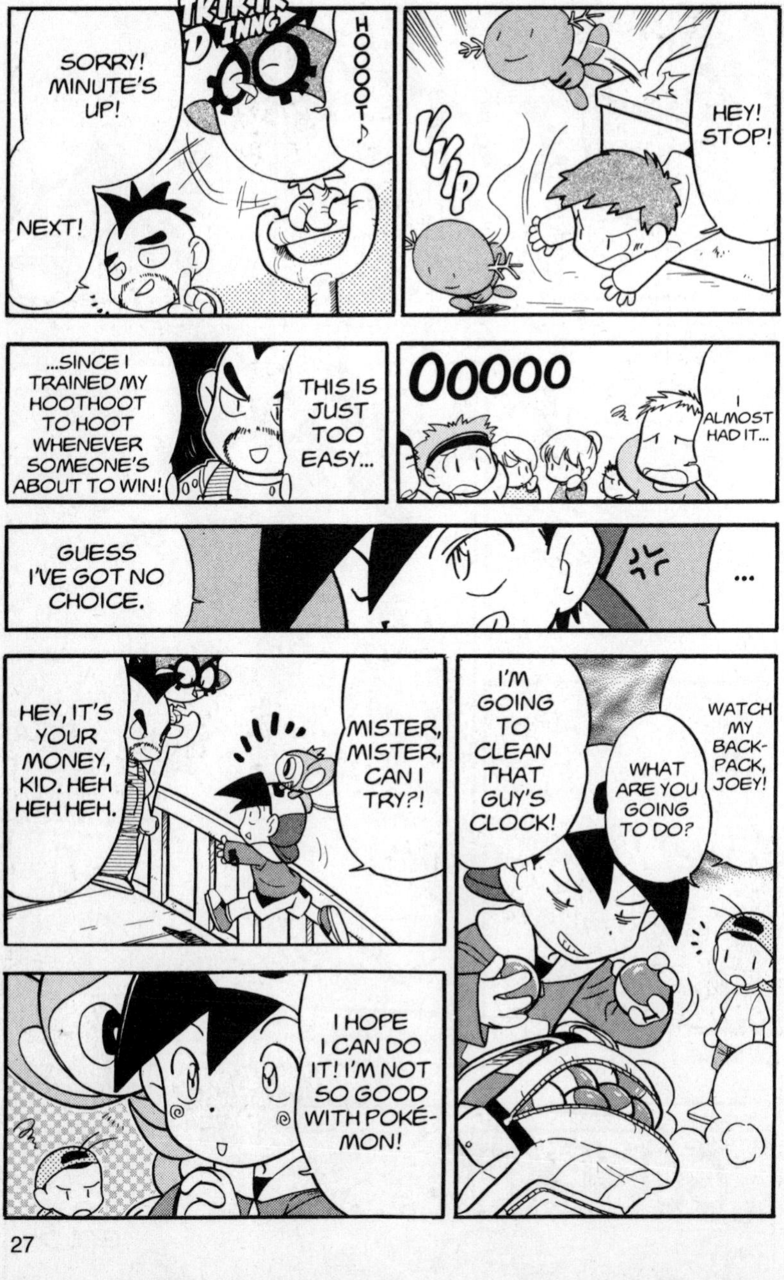
HEY! STOP!
VVIP
HOOOOOT♪
TKTKTK DINNG
SORRY! MINUTE'S UP!
NEXT!
I ALMOST HAD IT...
OOOOO
THIS IS JUST TOO EASY...
...SINCE I TRAINED MY HOOTHOOT TO HOOT WHENEVER SOMEONE'S ABOUT TO WIN!
...
GUESS I'VE GOT NO CHOICE.
WATCH MY BACK-PACK, JOEY!
WHAT ARE YOU GOING TO DO?
I'M GOING TO CLEAN THAT GUY'S CLOCK!
MISTER, MISTER, CAN I TRY?!
HEY, IT'S YOUR MONEY, KID. HEH HEH HEH HEH.
I HOPE I CAN DO IT! I'M NOT SO GOOD WITH POKÉ-MON!

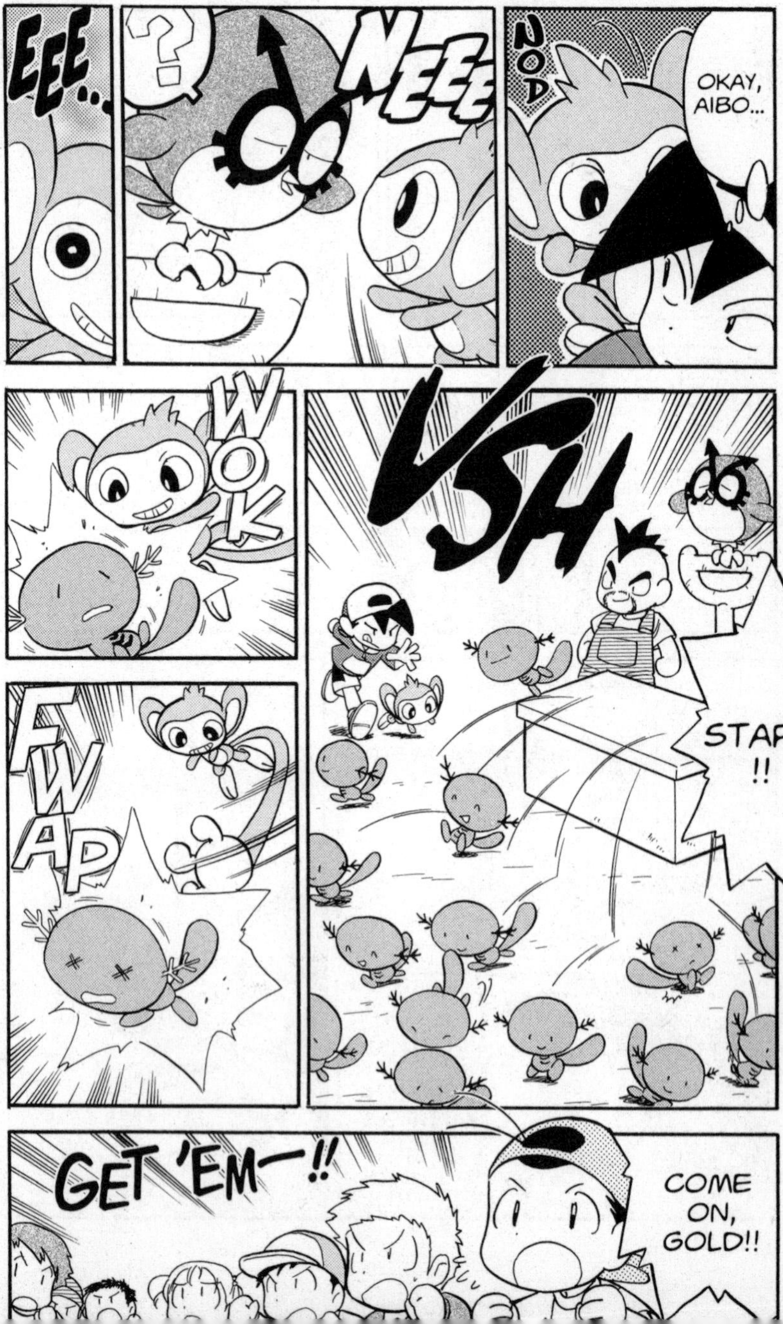
NOD
OKAY, AIBO...
?
NEEE
EEE...
VSH
START!!
WOK
FWAP
COME ON, GOLD!!
GET 'EM—!!

BON
BON
HMM ...
THIS KID'S PRETTY GOOD...
OKAY, HOOT-HOOT!
TIME FOR A LITTLE PREMATURE HOOTING!
TWEET TWEET
DUHH
UHH
?!
FWAP
FWAP
H-HEY!! WHAT'RE YOU DOING ?!!
HEH

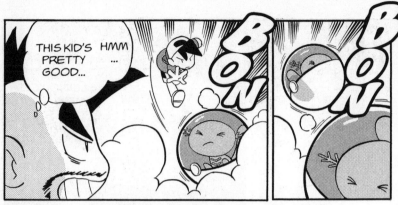

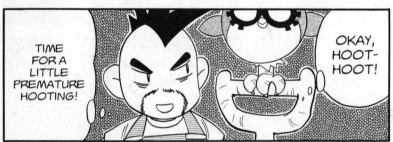

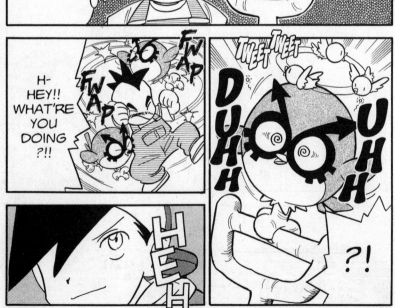

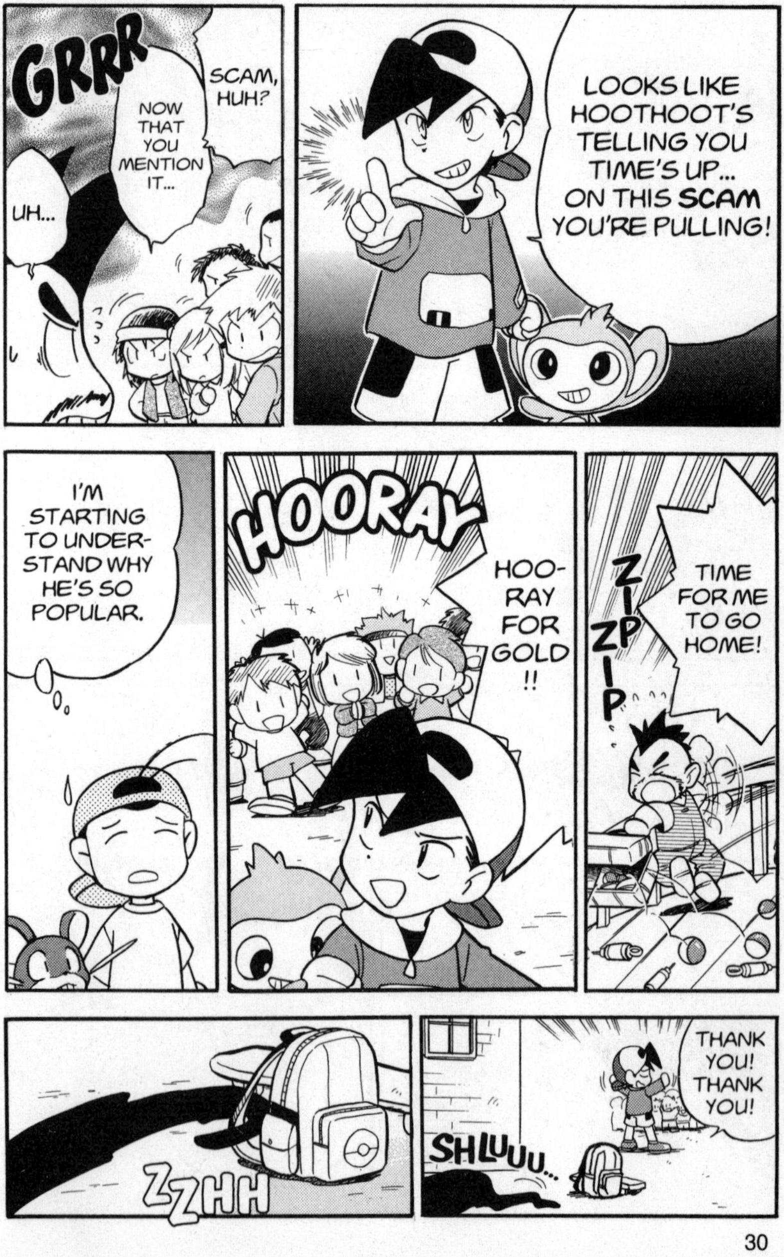
LOOKS LIKE HOOTHOOT'S TELLING YOU TIME'S UP... ON THIS SCAM YOU'RE PULLING!
GRRR
SCAM, HUH?
NOW THAT YOU MENTION IT...
UH...
TIME FOR ME TO GO HOME!
ZIP ZIP ZIP
HOORAY
HOORAY FOR GOLD!!
I'M STARTING TO UNDERSTAND WHY HE'S SO POPULAR.
THANK YOU! THANK YOU!
SHLUUU...
ZZHH

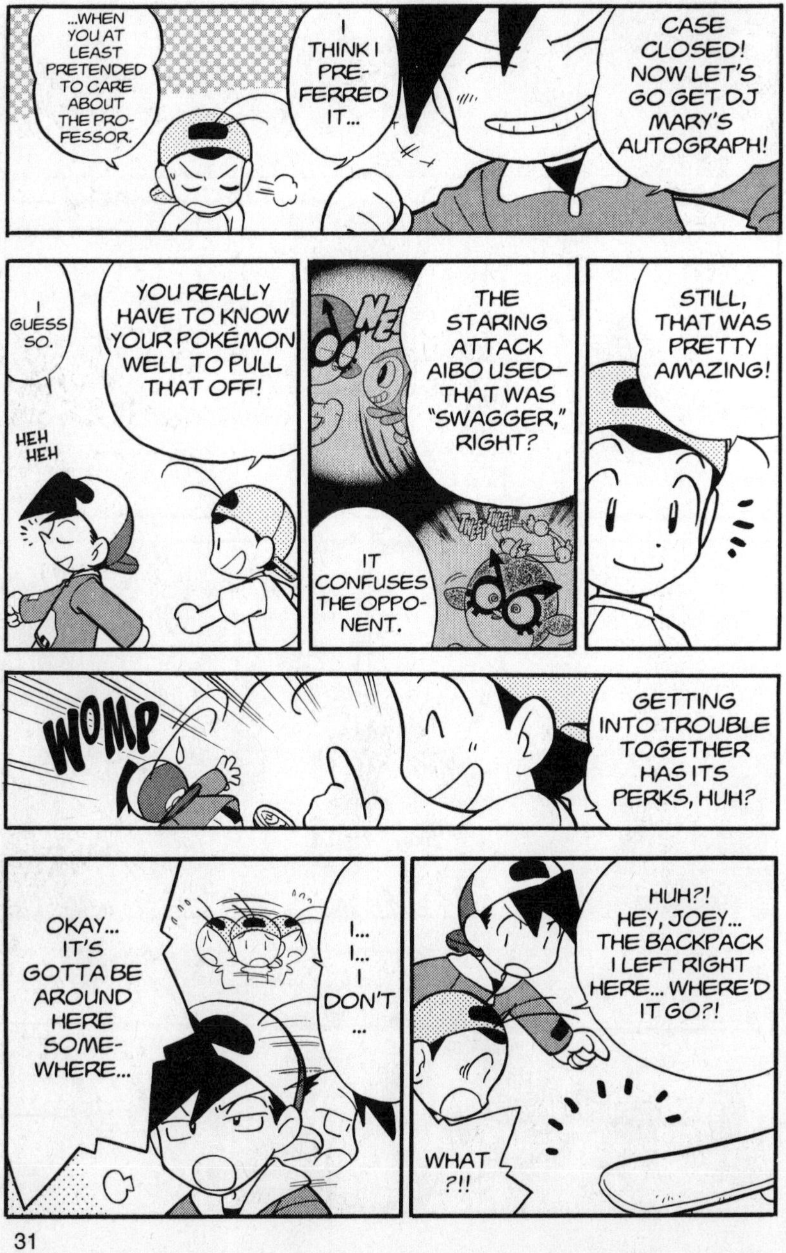
CASE CLOSED! NOW LET'S GO GET DJ MARY'S AUTOGRAPH!
I THINK I PREFERRED IT...
...WHEN YOU AT LEAST PRETENDED TO CARE ABOUT THE PROFESSOR.
STILL, THAT WAS PRETTY AMAZING!
THE STARING ATTACK AIBO USED—THAT WAS "SWAGGER," RIGHT?
IT CONFUSES THE OPPONENT.
YOU REALLY HAVE TO KNOW YOUR POKÉMON WELL TO PULL THAT OFF!
I GUESS SO.
HEH HEH
GETTING INTO TROUBLE TOGETHER HAS ITS PERKS, HUH?
WOMP
HUH?! HEY, JOEY... THE BACKPACK I LEFT RIGHT HERE... WHERE'D IT GO?!
WHAT?!!
I... I... I DON'T ...
OKAY... IT'S GOTTA BE AROUND HERE SOMEWHERE...

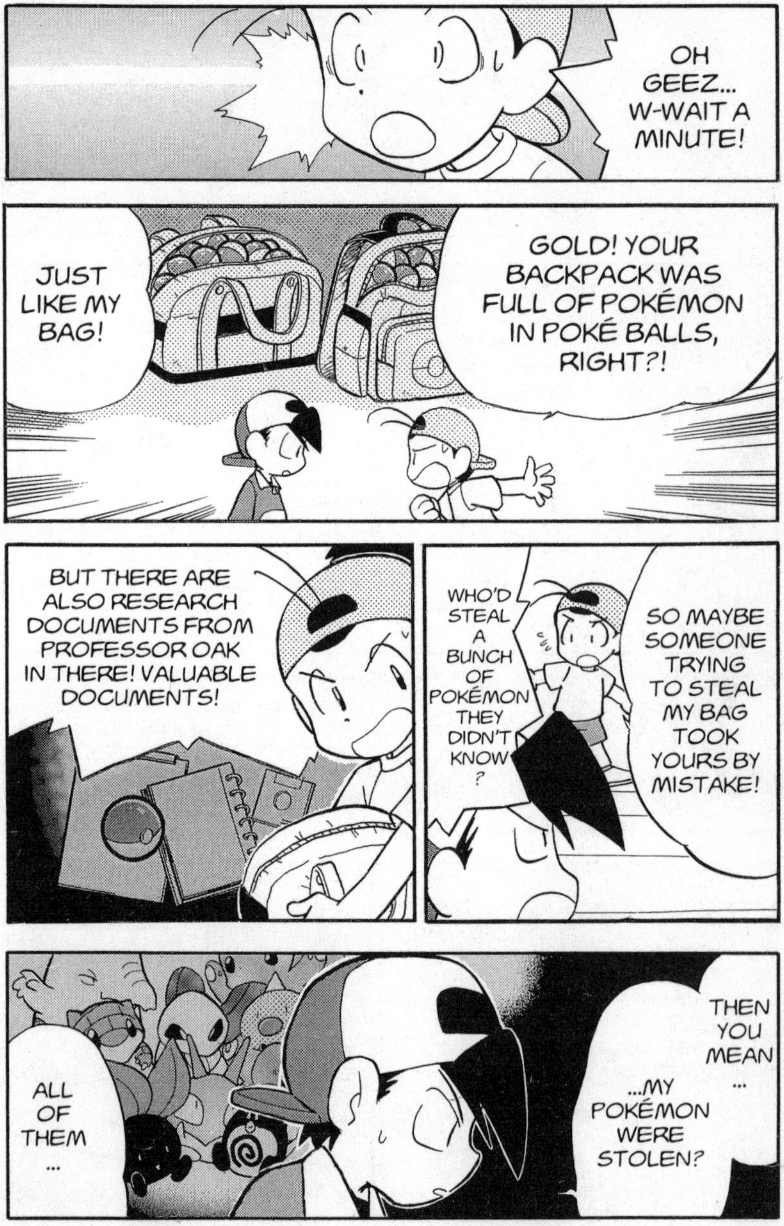
OH GEEZ... W-WAIT A MINUTE!
GOLD! YOUR BACKPACK WAS FULL OF POKÉMON IN POKÉ BALLS, RIGHT?!
JUST LIKE MY BAG!
SO MAYBE SOMEONE TRYING TO STEAL MY BAG TOOK YOURS BY MISTAKE!
WHO'D STEAL A BUNCH OF POKÉMON THEY DIDN'T KNOW?
BUT THERE ARE ALSO RESEARCH DOCUMENTS FROM PROFESSOR OAK IN THERE! VALUABLE DOCUMENTS!
THEN YOU MEAN ...
...MY POKÉMON WERE STOLEN?
ALL OF THEM ...

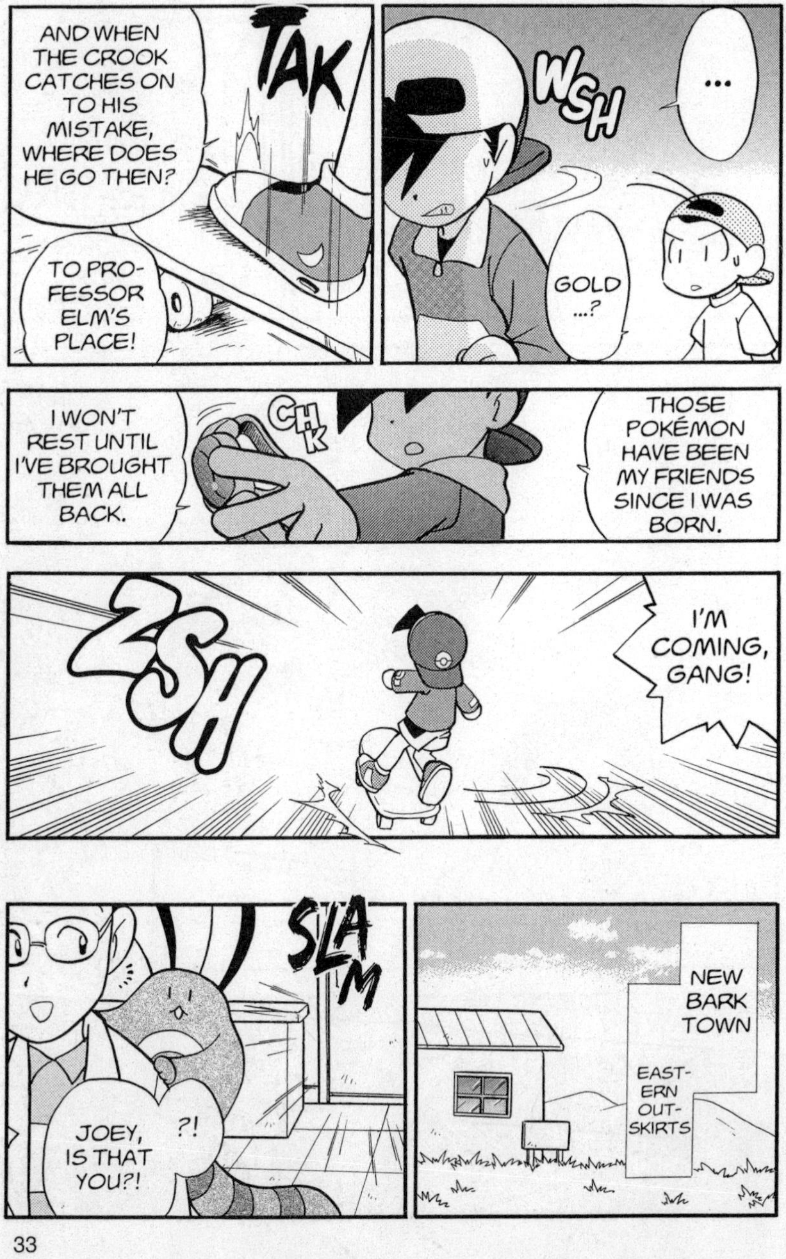
...
WSH
GOLD ...?
TAK
AND WHEN THE CROOK CATCHES ON TO HIS MISTAKE, WHERE DOES HE GO THEN?
TO PRO-FESSOR ELM'S PLACE!
THOSE POKÉMON HAVE BEEN MY FRIENDS SINCE I WAS BORN.
CHK
I WON'T REST UNTIL I'VE BROUGHT THEM ALL BACK.
I'M COMING, GANG!
ZSH
NEW BARK TOWN
EAST-ERN OUT-SKIRTS
SLAM
?!
JOEY, IS THAT YOU?!

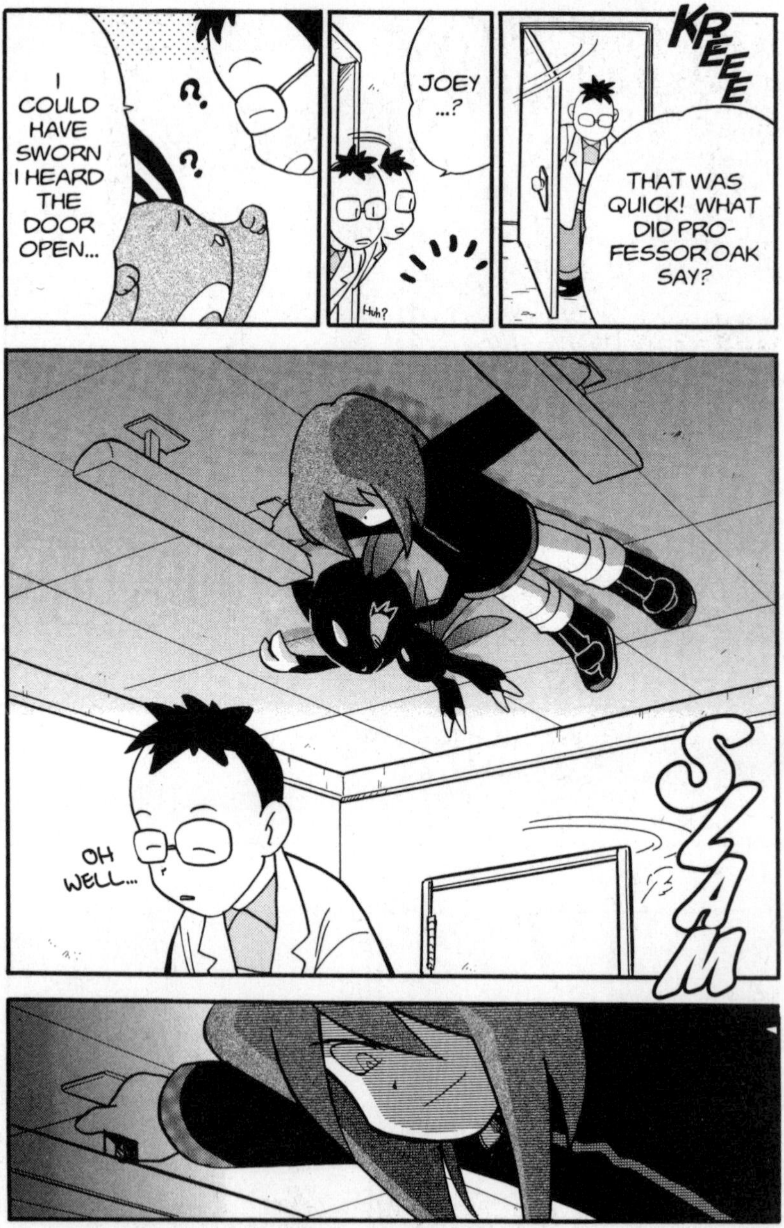
KREEE
THAT WAS QUICK! WHAT DID PRO-FESSOR OAK SAY?
JOEY ...?
Huh?
I COULD HAVE SWORN I HEARD THE DOOR OPEN...
SLAM
OH WELL...

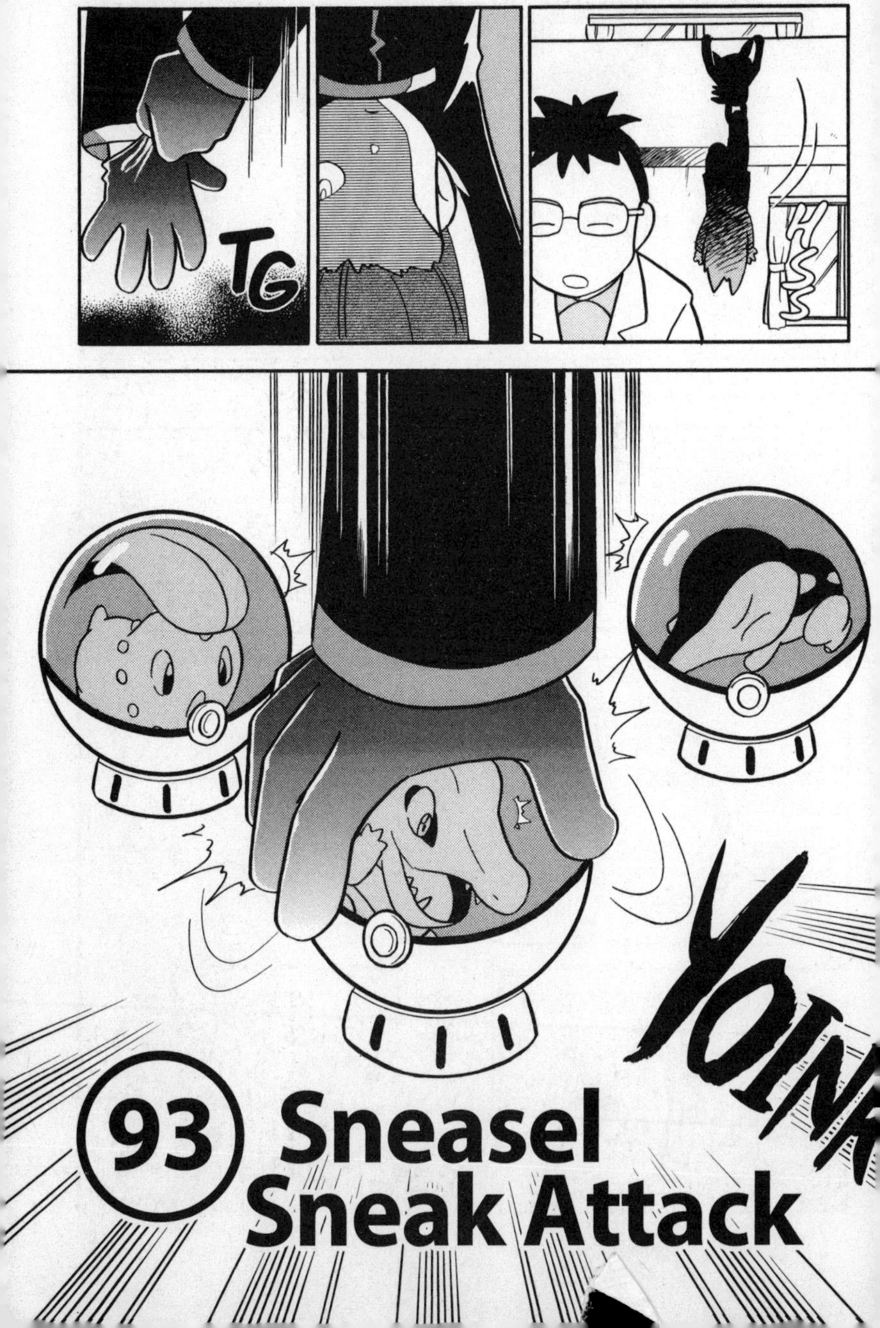
HISS
TG
YOINK
93 Sneasel Sneak Attack

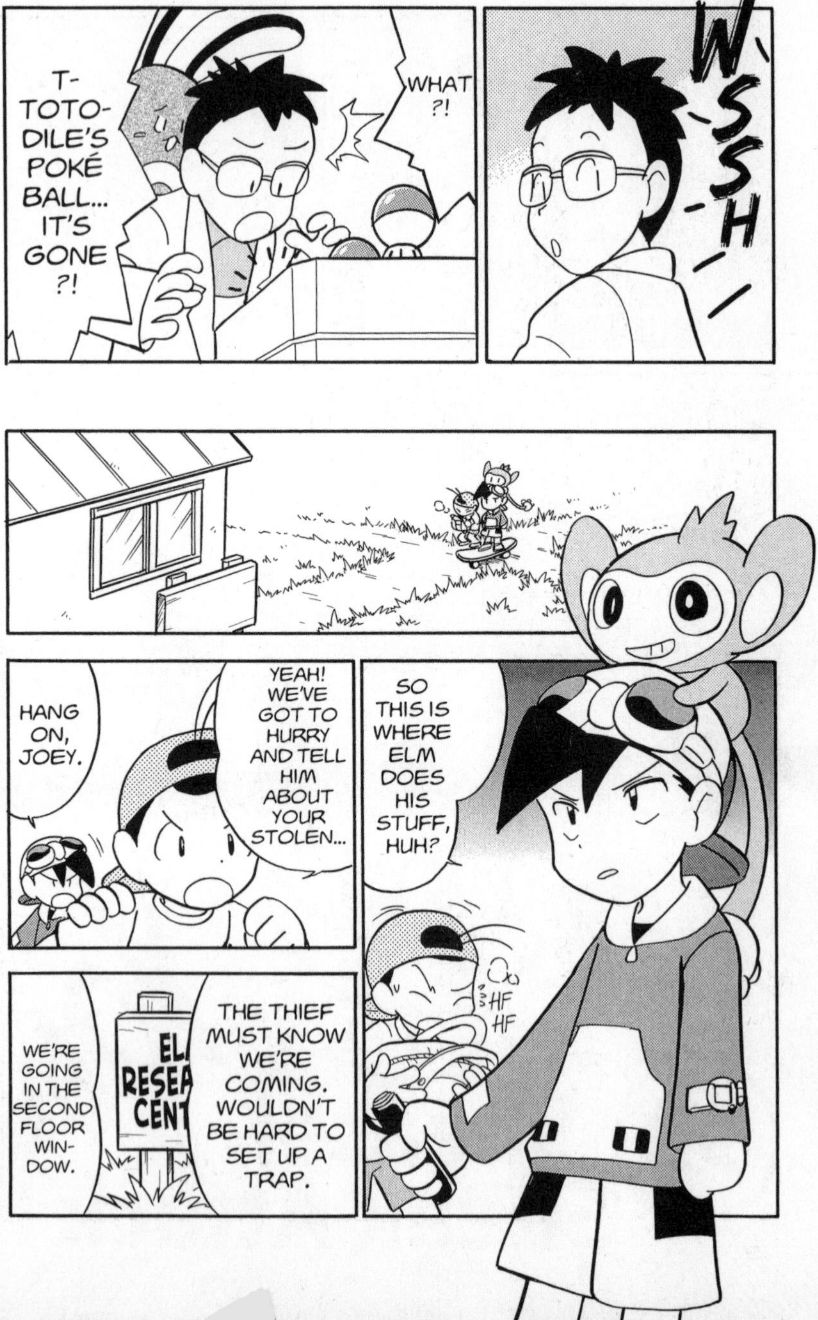
WSSH
WHAT?!
T-TOTODILE'S POKÉ BALL... IT'S GONE?!
SO THIS IS WHERE ELM DOES HIS STUFF, HUH?
HF HF
YEAH! WE'VE GOT TO HURRY AND TELL HIM ABOUT YOUR STOLEN...
HANG ON, JOEY.
THE THIEF MUST KNOW WE'RE COMING. WOULDN'T BE HARD TO SET UP A TRAP.
WE'RE GOING IN THE SECOND FLOOR WINDOW.

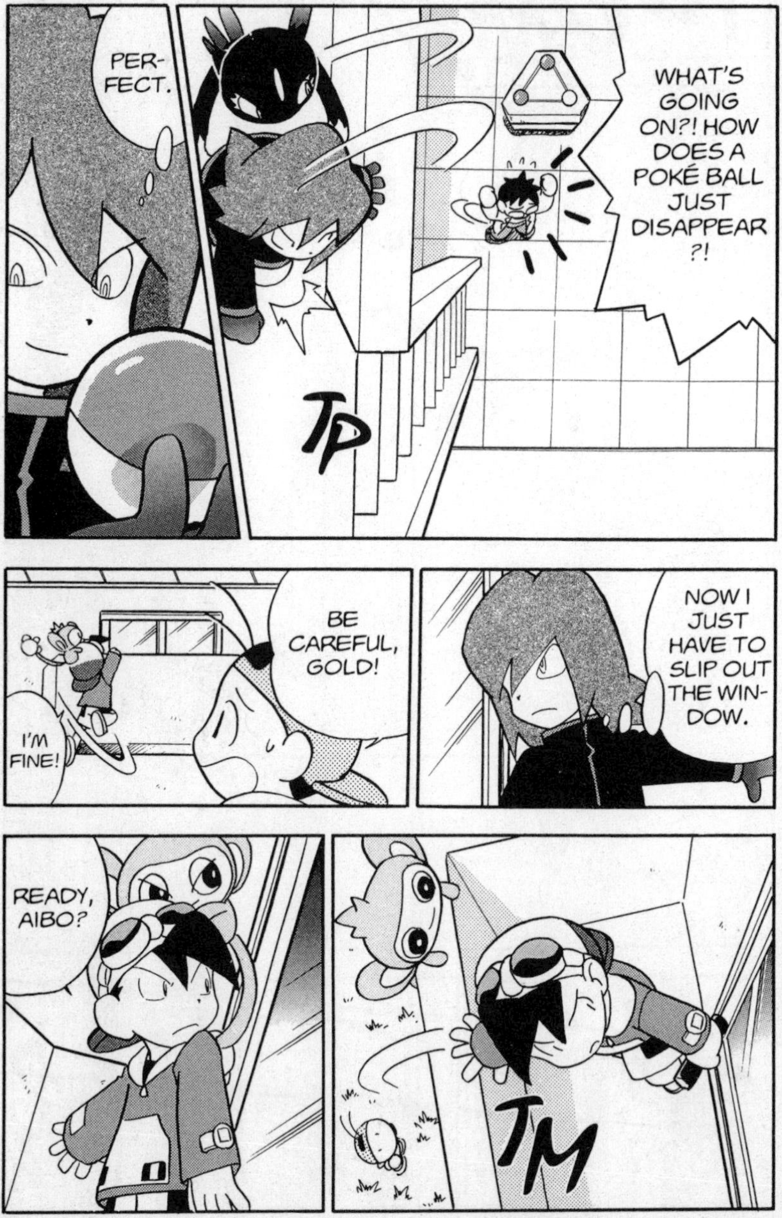
WHAT'S GOING ON?! HOW DOES A POKÉ BALL JUST DISAPPEAR?!
TP
PER-FECT.
NOW I JUST HAVE TO SLIP OUT THE WIN-DOW.
BE CAREFUL, GOLD!
I'M FINE!
TM
READY, AIBO?

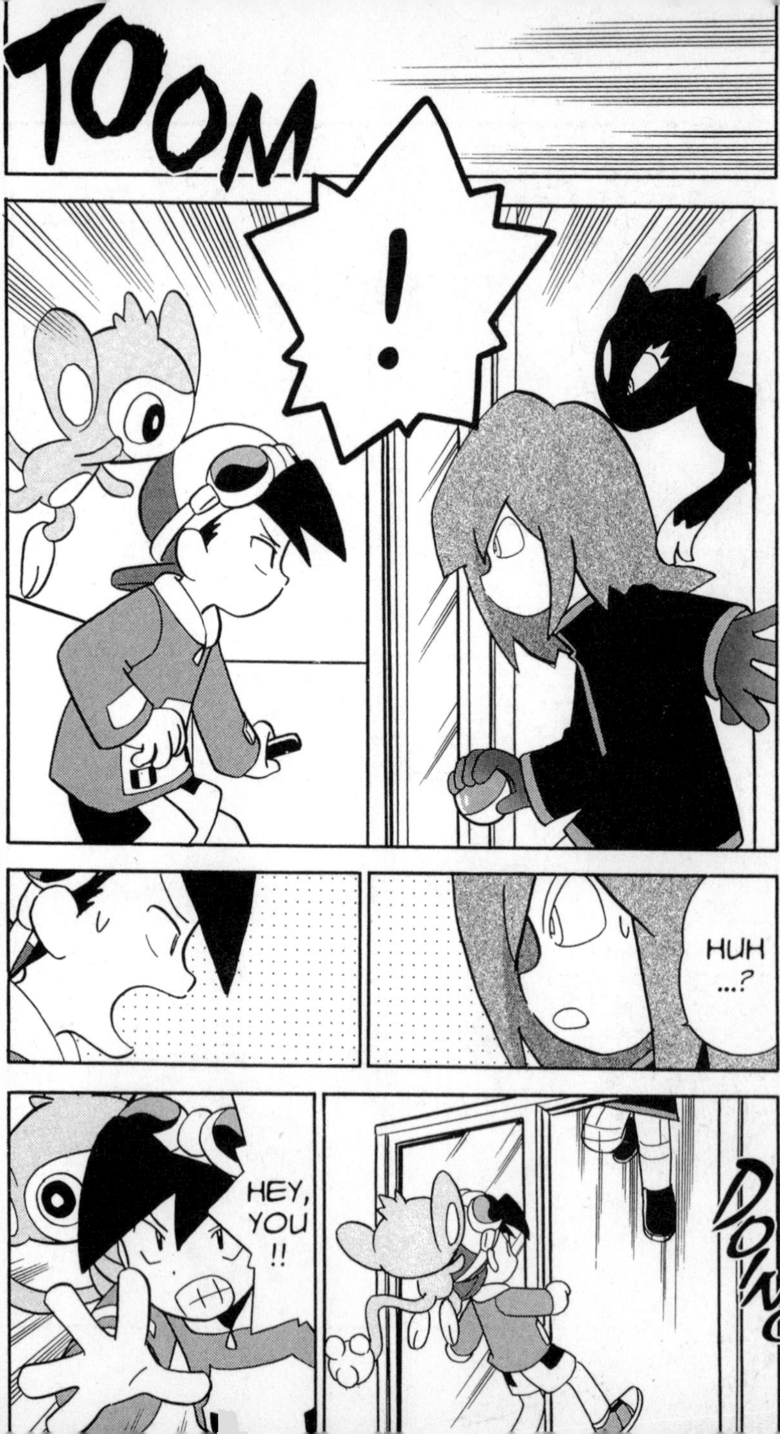
TOOM
!
HUH ...?
DOING
HEY, YOU !!

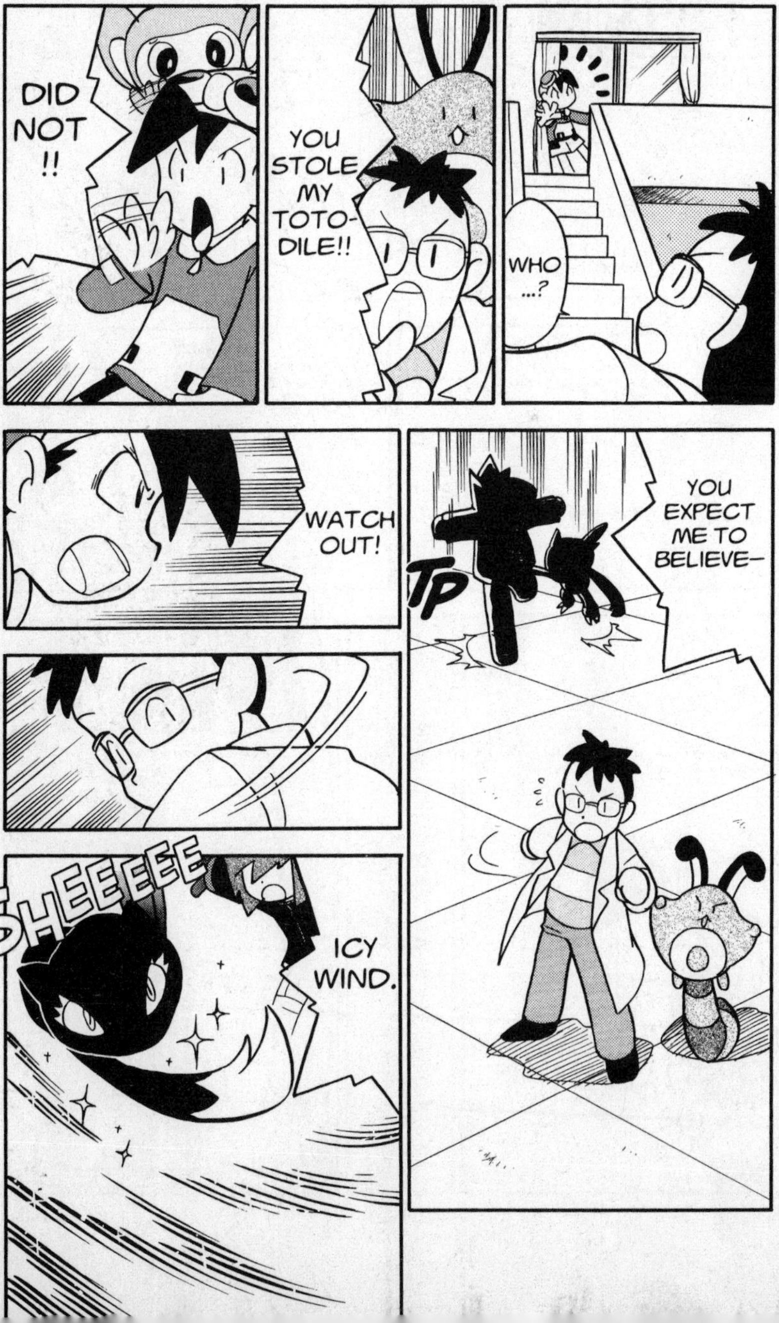
WHO ...?
YOU STOLE MY TOTO-DILE!!
DID NOT !!
YOU EXPECT ME TO BELIEVE—
TP
WATCH OUT!
SHEEEEE
ICY WIND.

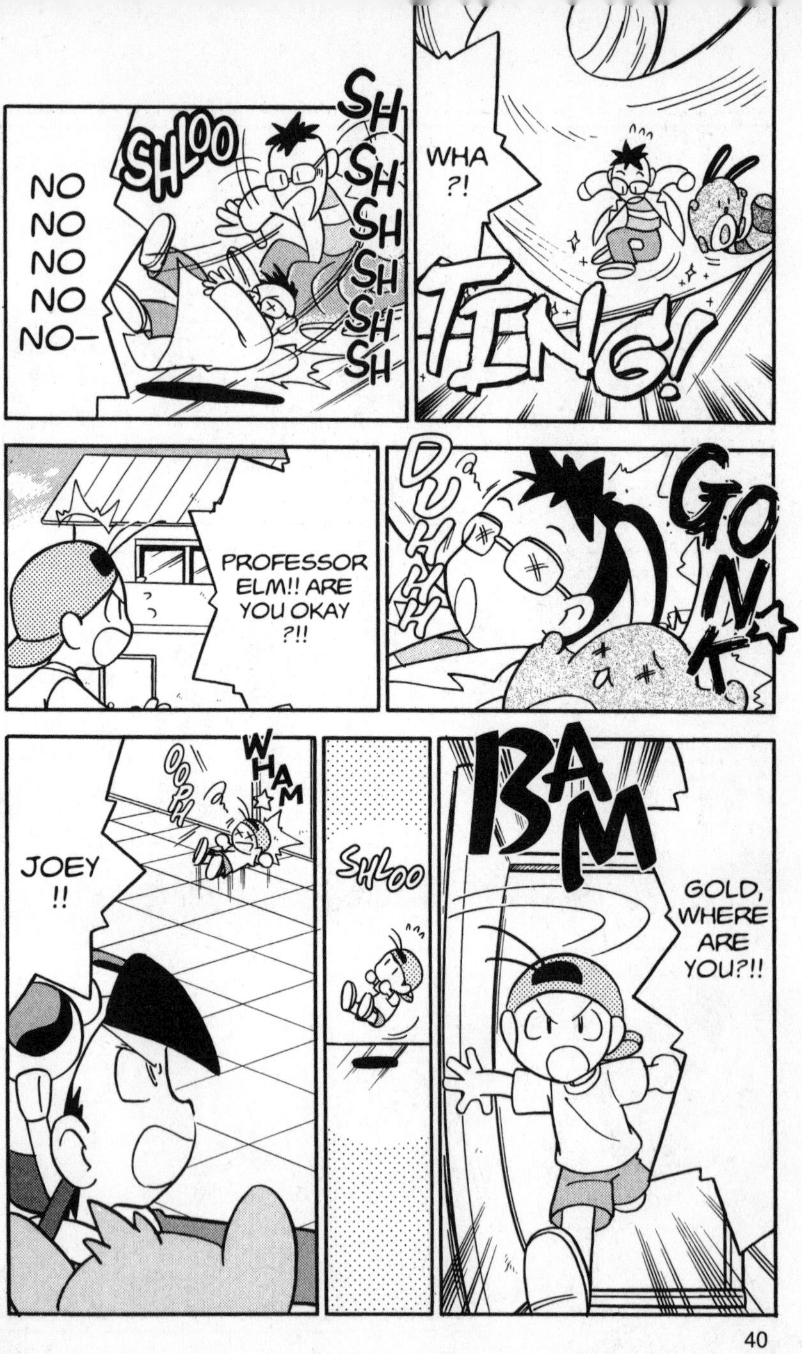
WHA ?!
TING!
SHLOO
SH SH SH SH SH SH
NO NO NO NO NO—
DUHHHH
GONK
PROFESSOR ELM!! ARE YOU OKAY ?!!
BAM
GOLD, WHERE ARE YOU?!!
SHLOO
WHAM
OOPH
JOEY !!

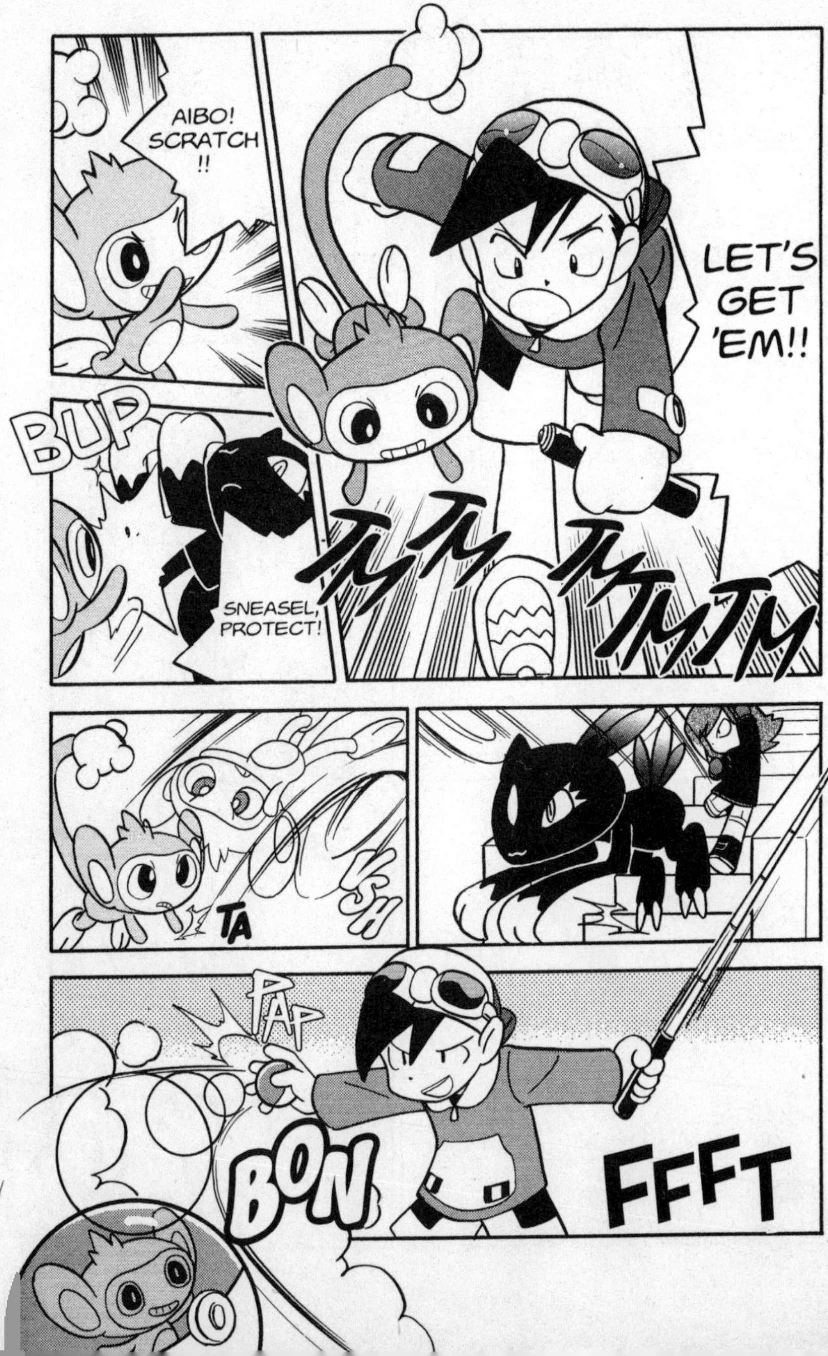
LET'S GET 'EM!!
TMTM TMTMTM
AIBO! SCRATCH!!
BUP
SNEASEL, PROTECT!
VSH
TA
PAP
FFFT
BON

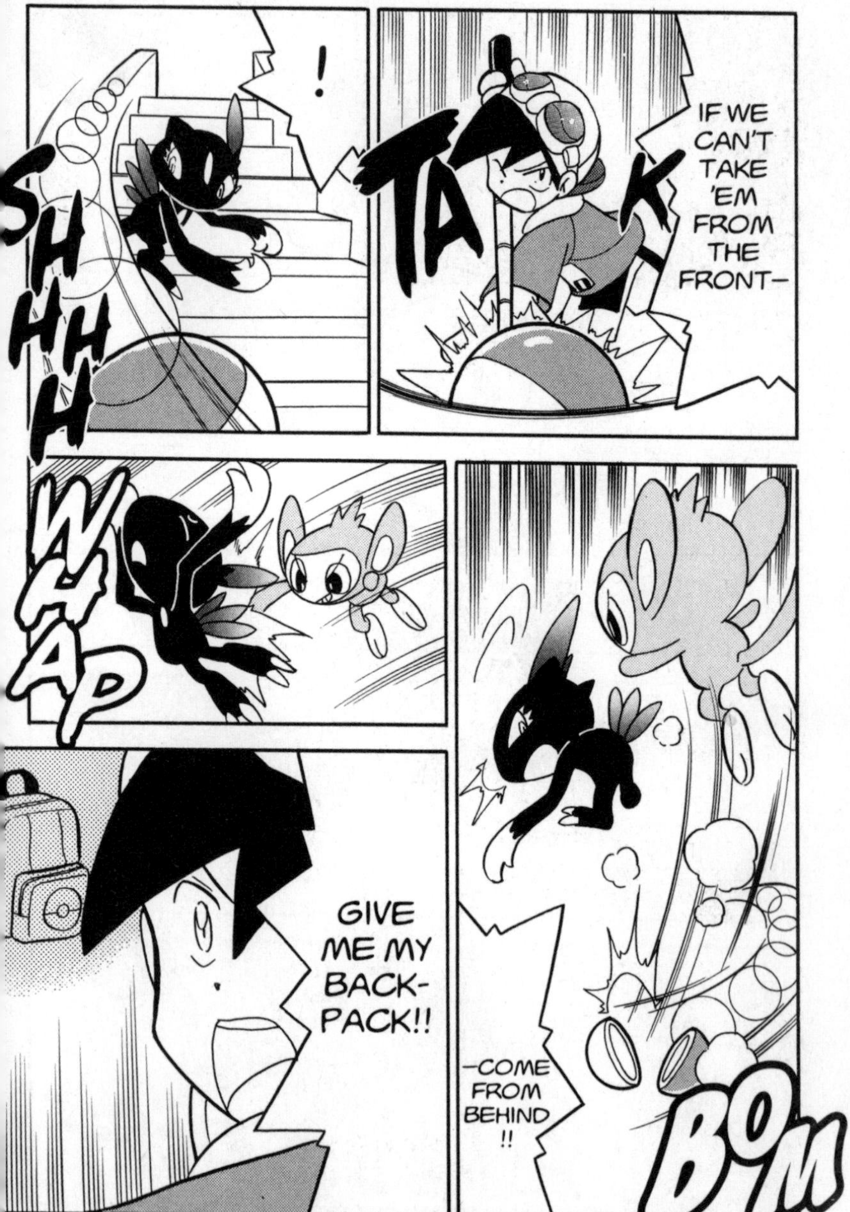
TAK
IF WE CAN'T TAKE 'EM FROM THE FRONT—
!
SHHHHH
—COME FROM BEHIND!!
BOOM
WHAP
GIVE ME MY BACK-PACK!!

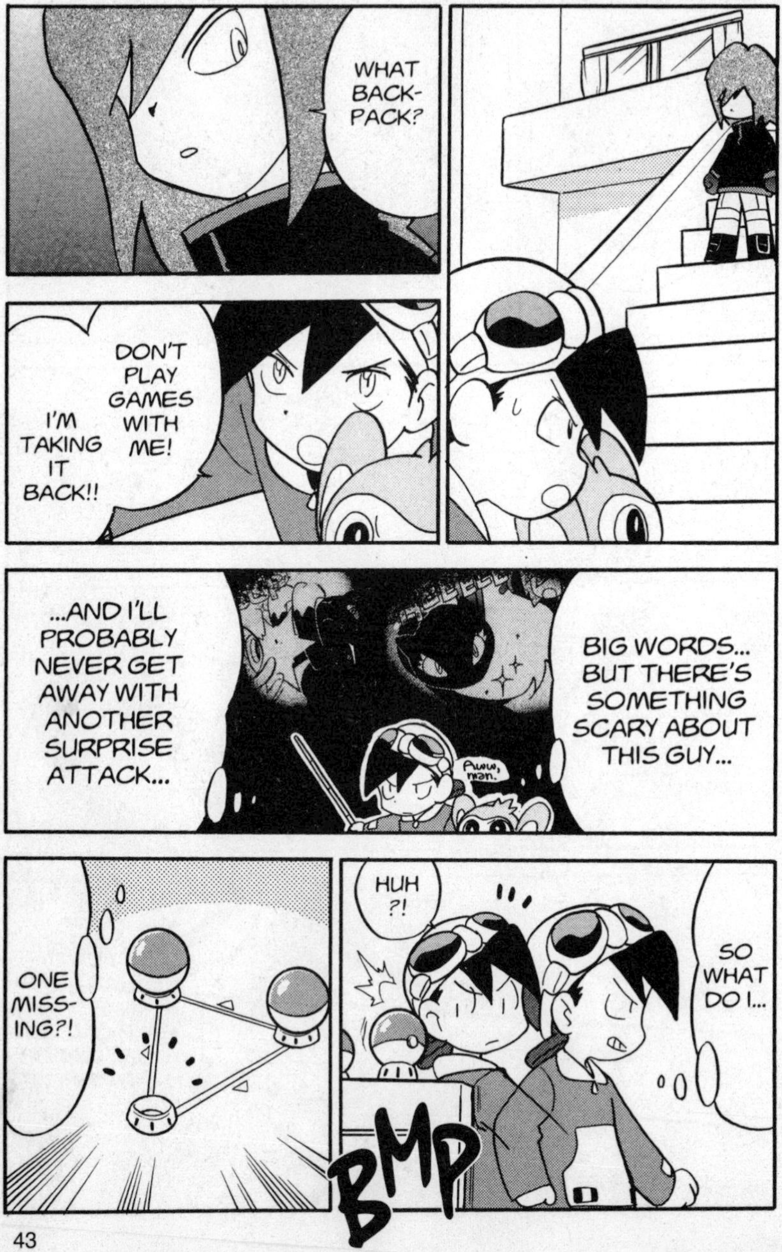
WHAT BACK-PACK?
DON'T PLAY GAMES WITH ME!
I'M TAKING IT BACK!!
BIG WORDS... BUT THERE'S SOMETHING SCARY ABOUT THIS GUY...
Aww, man.
...AND I'LL PROBABLY NEVER GET AWAY WITH ANOTHER SURPRISE ATTACK...
SO WHAT DO I...
HUH ?!
BMP
ONE MISS-ING?!

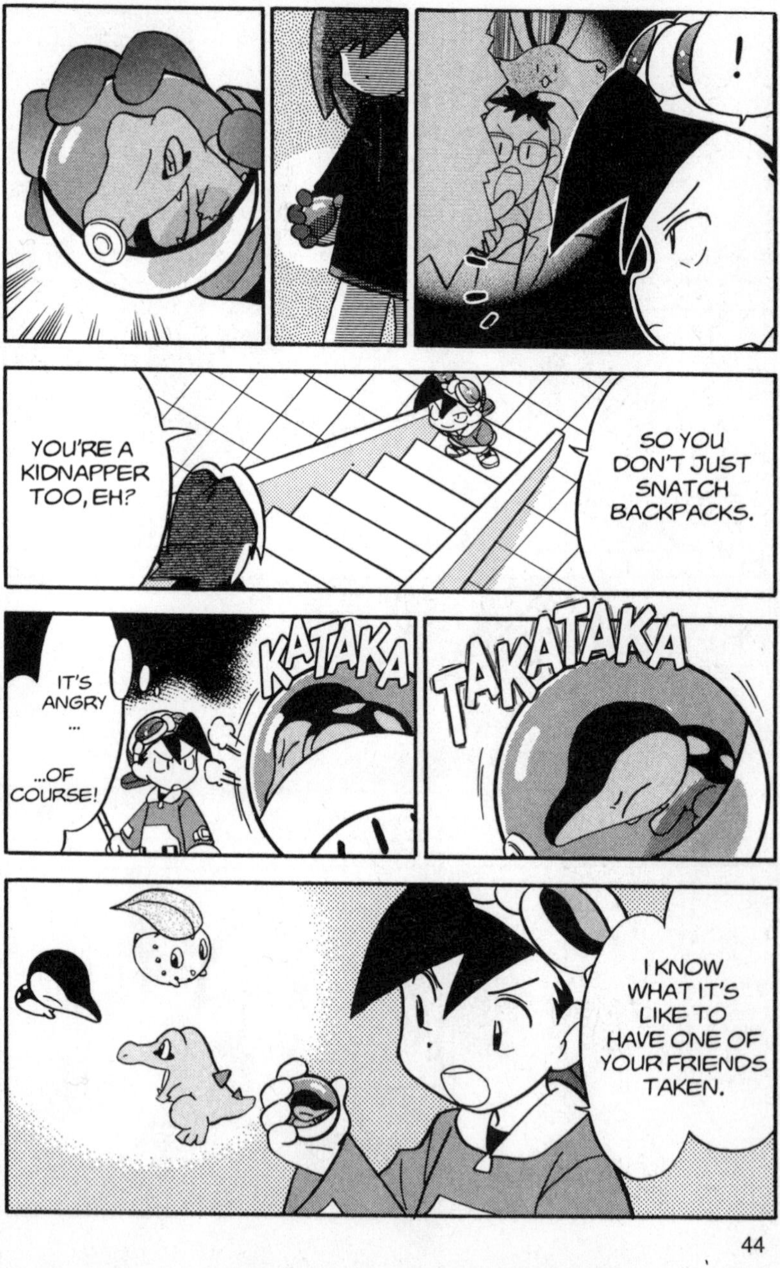
!
SO YOU DON'T JUST SNATCH BACKPACKS.
YOU'RE A KIDNAPPER TOO, EH?
TAKATAKA
KATAKA
IT'S ANGRY ...
...OF COURSE!
I KNOW WHAT IT'S LIKE TO HAVE ONE OF YOUR FRIENDS TAKEN.

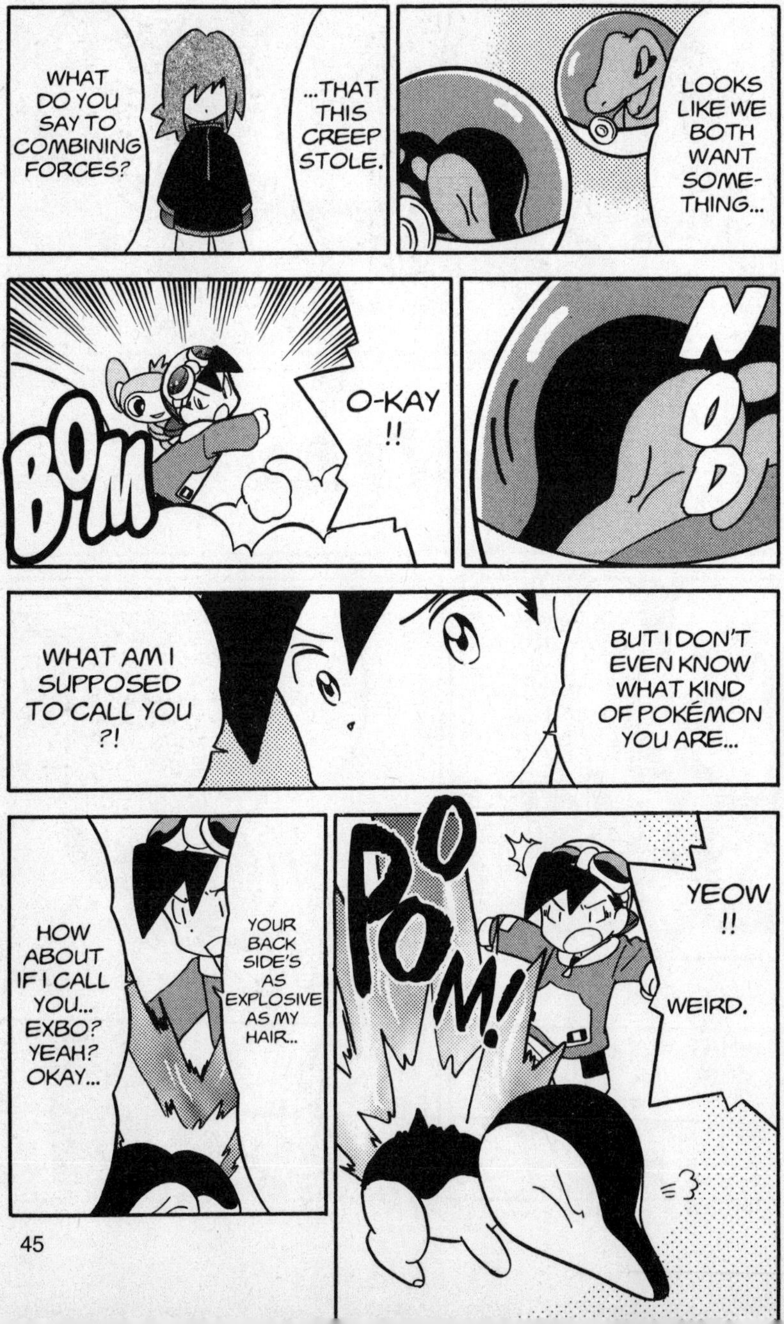
LOOKS LIKE WE BOTH WANT SOME-THING...
...THAT THIS CREEP STOLE.
WHAT DO YOU SAY TO COMBINING FORCES?
NOD
O-KAY!!
BOOM
BUT I DON'T EVEN KNOW WHAT KIND OF POKÉMON YOU ARE...
WHAT AM I SUPPOSED TO CALL YOU?!
YEOW!!
POOM!
WEIRD.
YOUR BACK SIDE'S AS EXPLOSIVE AS MY HAIR..
HOW ABOUT IF I CALL YOU... EXBO? YEAH? OKAY...

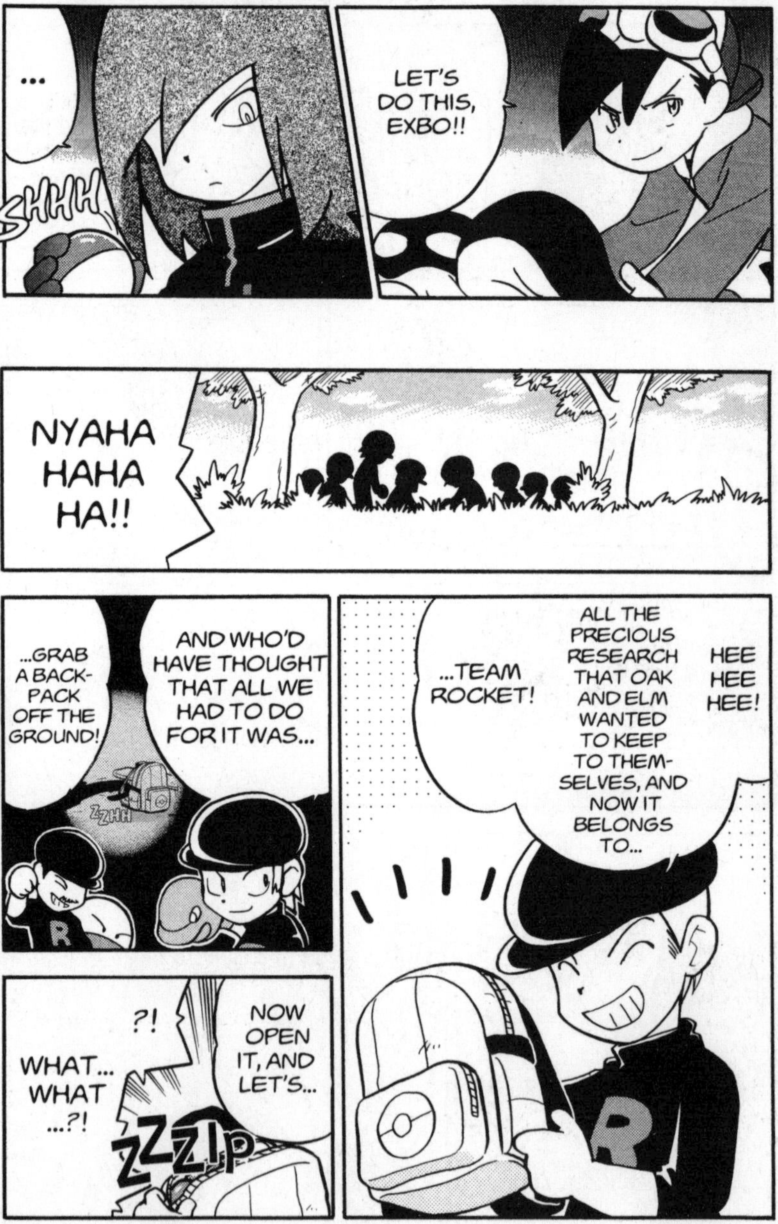
LET'S DO THIS, EXBO!!
...
SHHH
NYAHA HAHA HA!!
HEE HEE HEE!
ALL THE PRECIOUS RESEARCH THAT OAK AND ELM WANTED TO KEEP TO THEMSELVES, AND NOW IT BELONGS TO...
...TEAM ROCKET!
AND WHO'D HAVE THOUGHT THAT ALL WE HAD TO DO FOR IT WAS...
...GRAB A BACKPACK OFF THE GROUND!
ZZHH
NOW OPEN IT, AND LET'S...
?!
WHAT... WHAT ...?!
ZZZIP

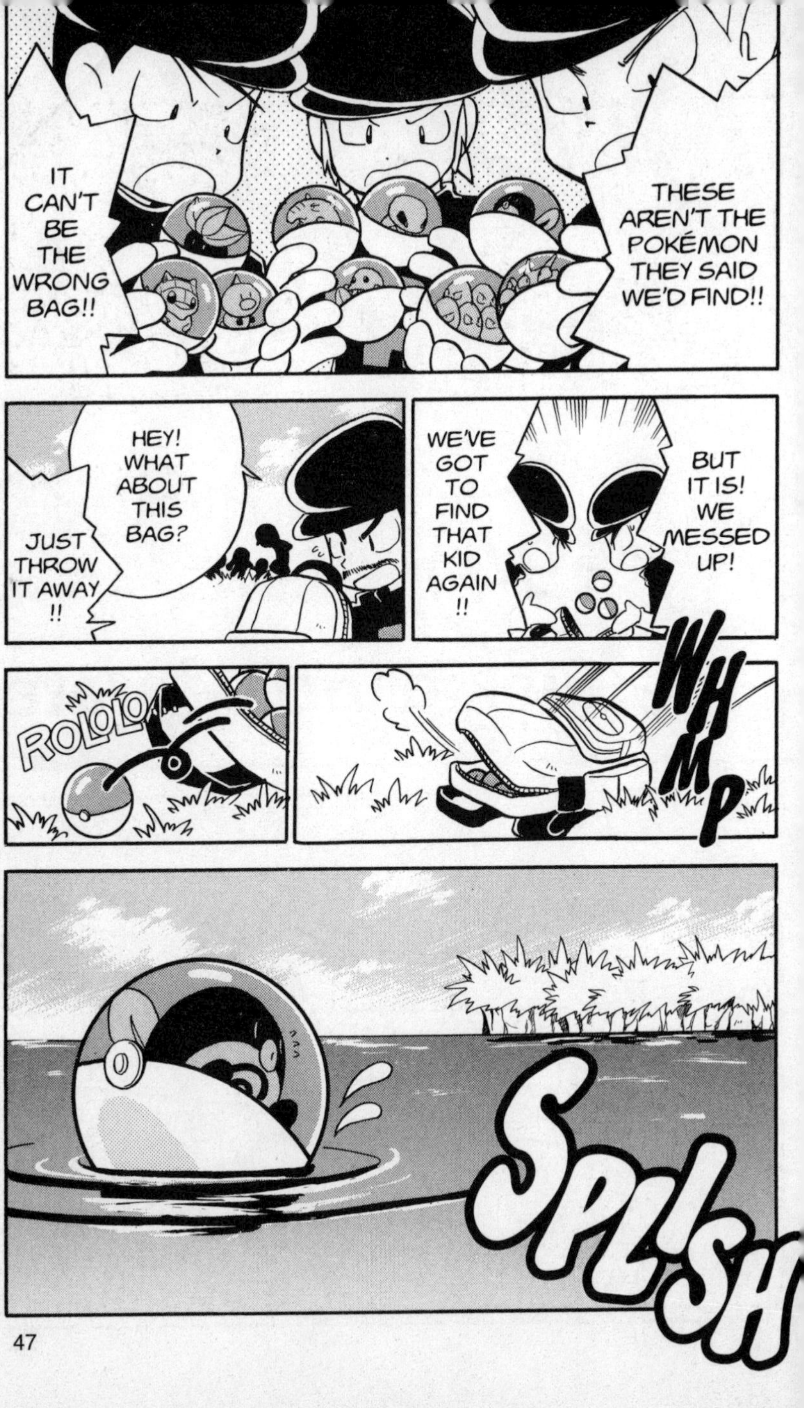
THESE AREN'T THE POKÉMON THEY SAID WE'D FIND!!
IT CAN'T BE THE WRONG BAG!!
BUT IT IS! WE MESSED UP!
WE'VE GOT TO FIND THAT KID AGAIN!!
HEY! WHAT ABOUT THIS BAG?
JUST THROW IT AWAY!!
WHMP
ROLOLO
SPLSH

94 Elekid Incorporated

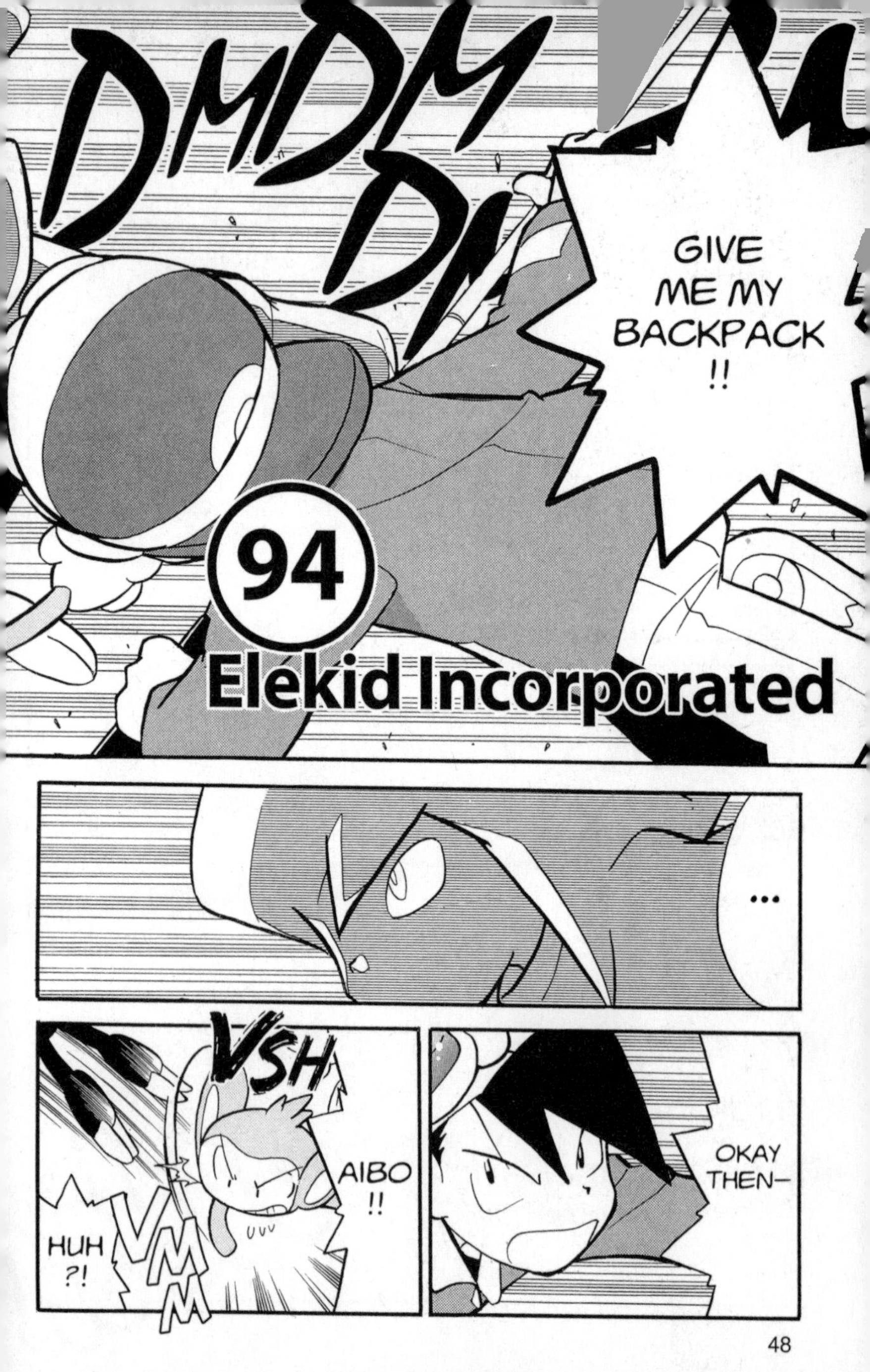
DMDM
DM
GIVE ME MY BACKPACK !!
...
OKAY THEN—
VSH
AIBO !!
HUH ?!
VMMM

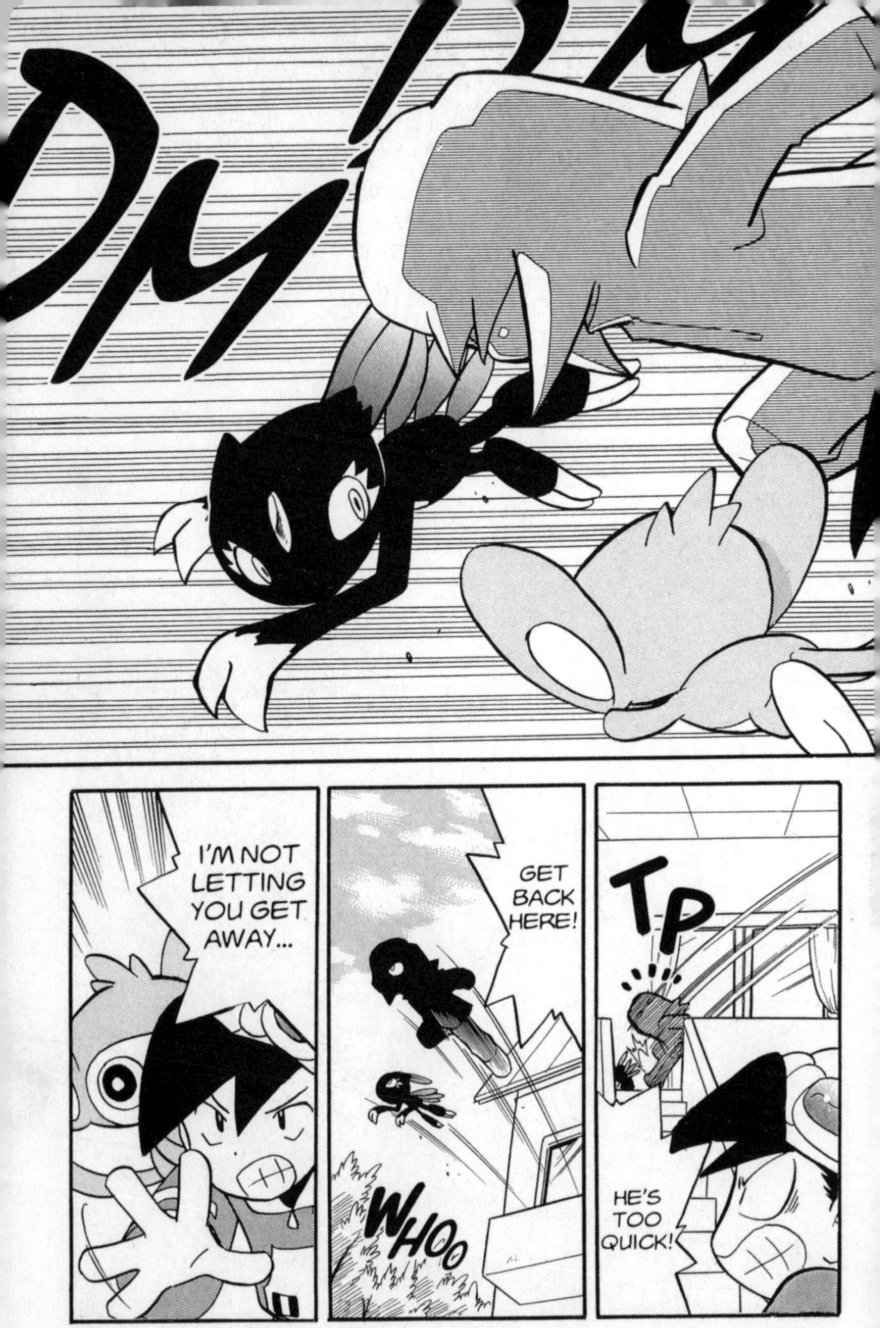
TP
HE'S TOO QUICK!
GET BACK HERE!
WHOO
I'M NOT LETTING YOU GET AWAY...

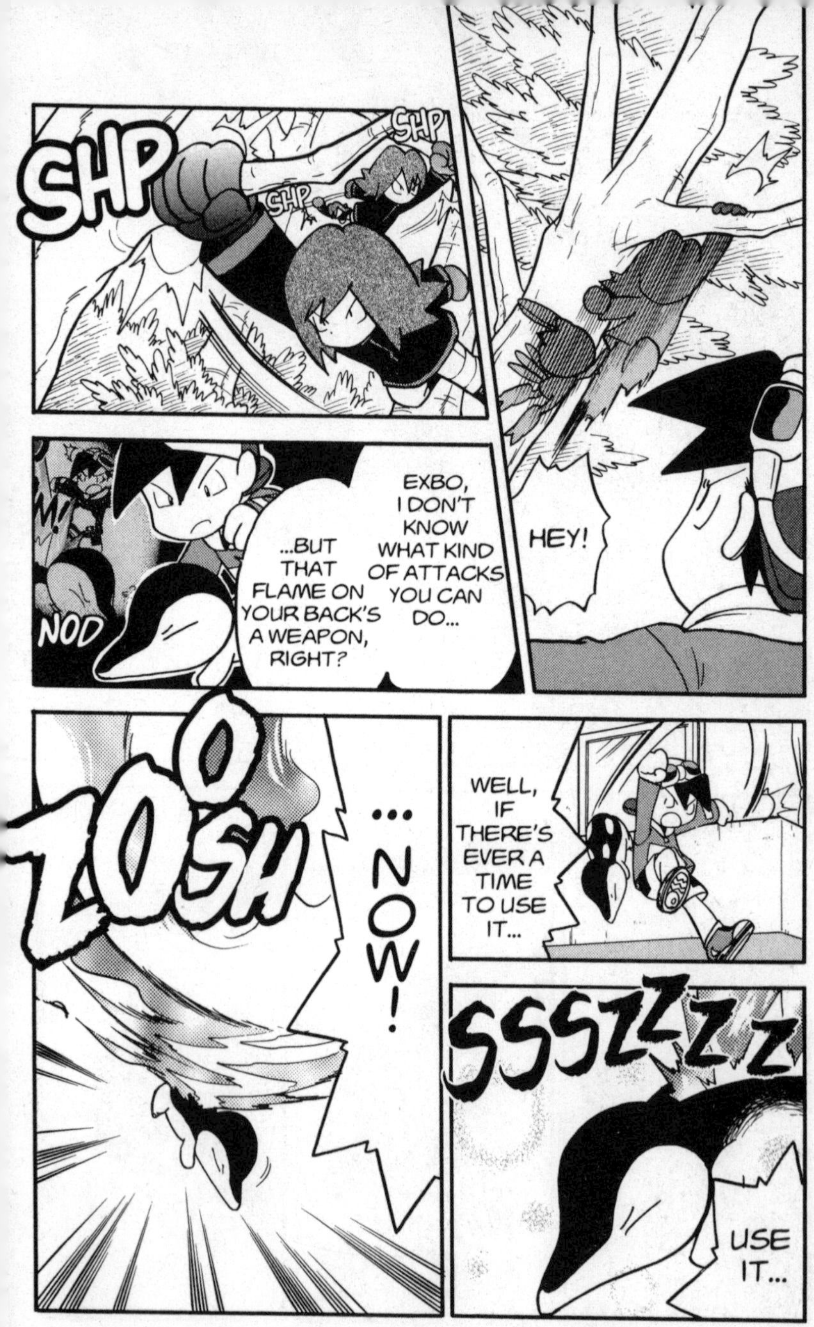
HEY!
SHP
SHP
SHP
EXBO, I DON'T KNOW WHAT KIND OF ATTACKS YOU CAN DO...
...BUT THAT FLAME ON YOUR BACK'S A WEAPON, RIGHT?
NOD
WELL, IF THERE'S EVER A TIME TO USE IT...
SSSZZZZ
USE IT...
ZOOSH
...NOW!

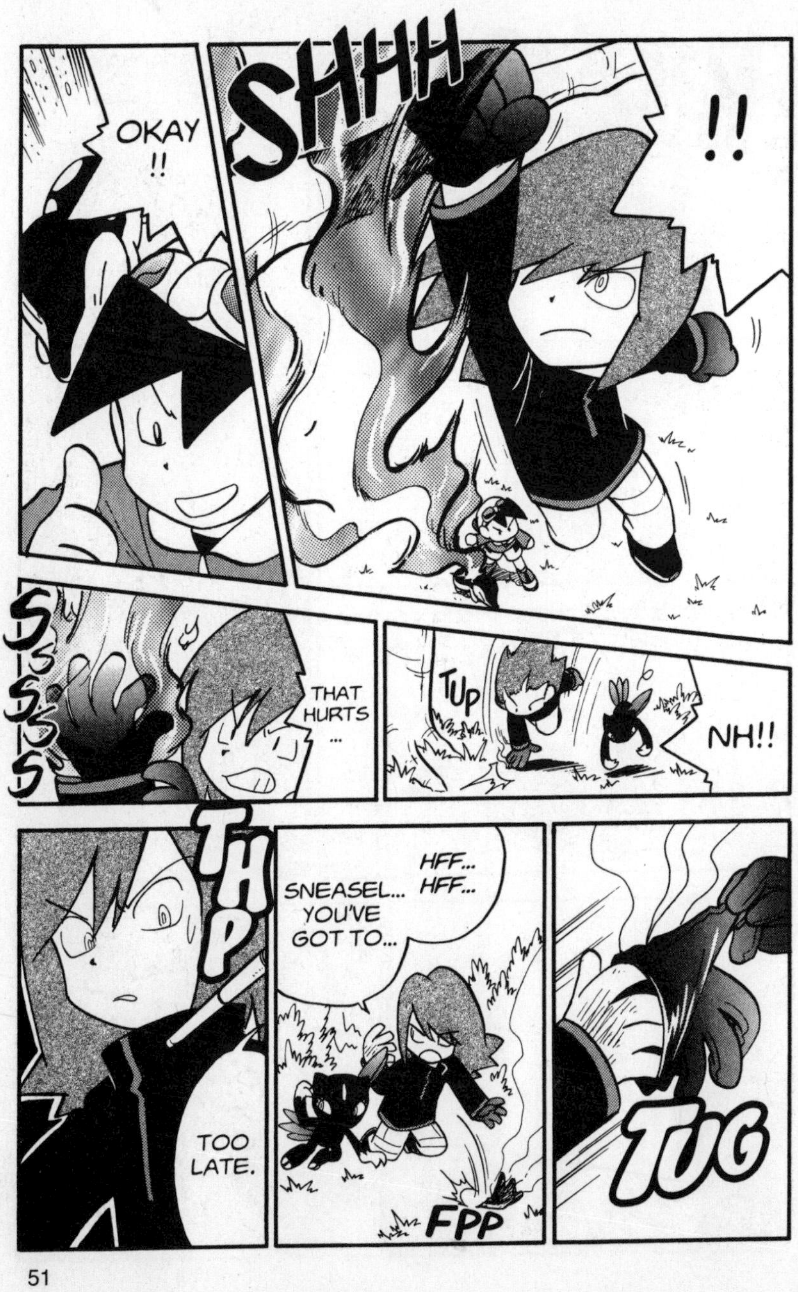
SHHH
!!
OKAY !!
TUP
NH!!
SSSSS
THAT HURTS ...
TUG
HFF... HFF...
SNEASEL... YOU'VE GOT TO...
FPP
THP
TOO LATE.

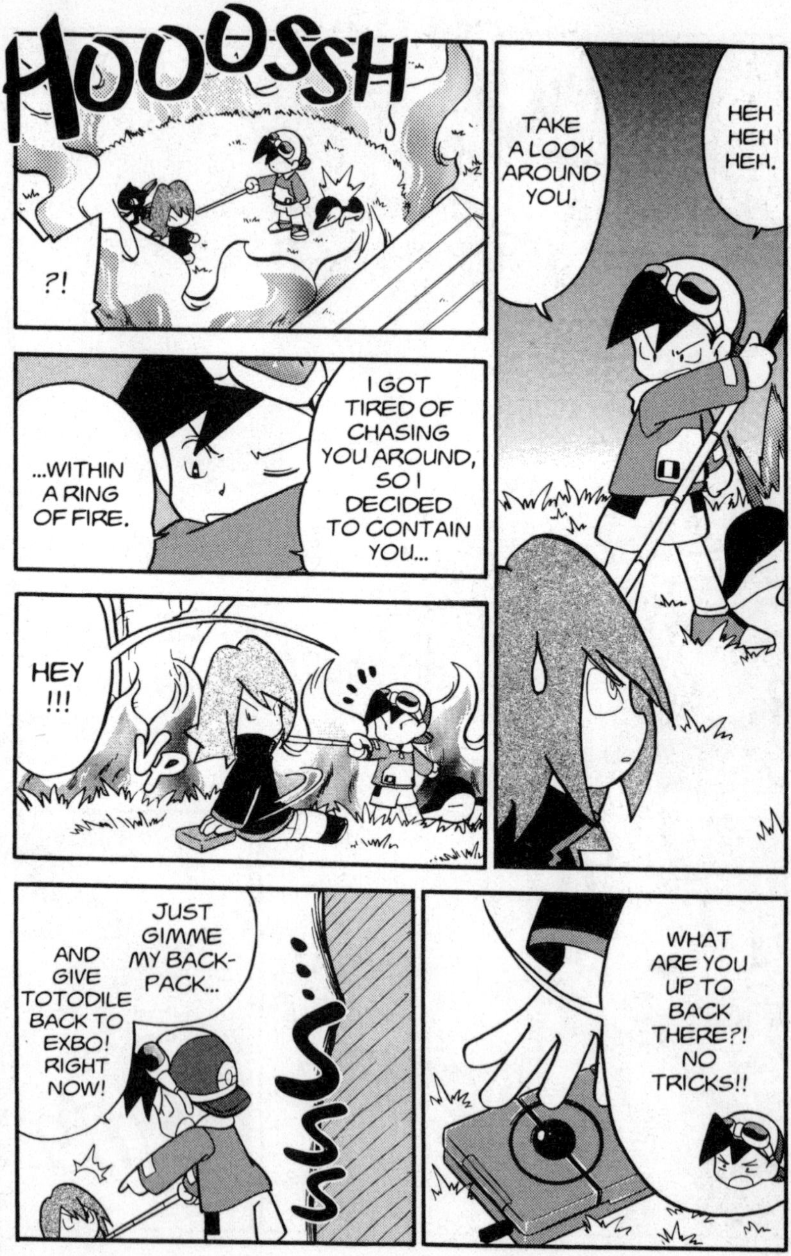
HEH HEH HEH.
TAKE A LOOK AROUND YOU.
HOOOSSH
?!
I GOT TIRED OF CHASING YOU AROUND, SO I DECIDED TO CONTAIN YOU...
...WITHIN A RING OF FIRE.
HEY !!!
WHAT ARE YOU UP TO BACK THERE?! NO TRICKS!!
SSS...
JUST GIMME MY BACK-PACK...
AND GIVE TOTODILE BACK TO EXBO! RIGHT NOW!

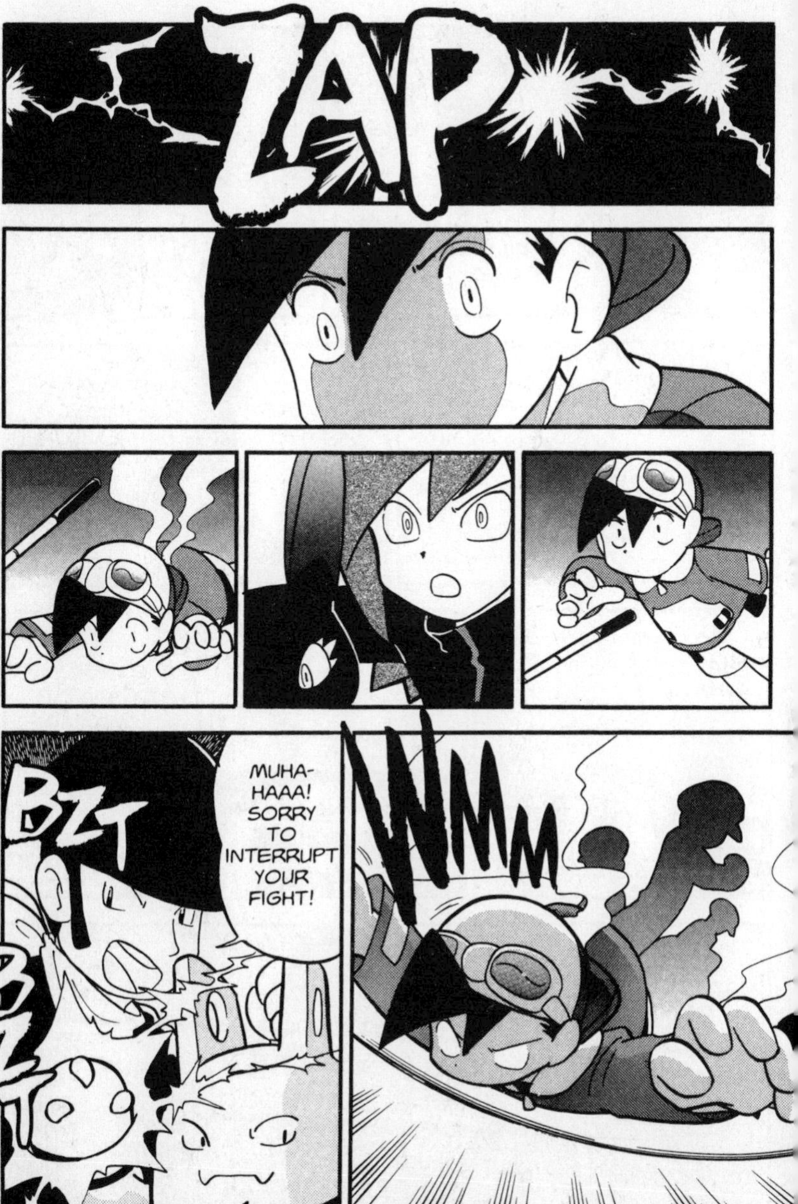
ZAP
WMMM
MUHA-HAAA! SORRY TO INTERRUPT YOUR FIGHT!
BZT
BZT

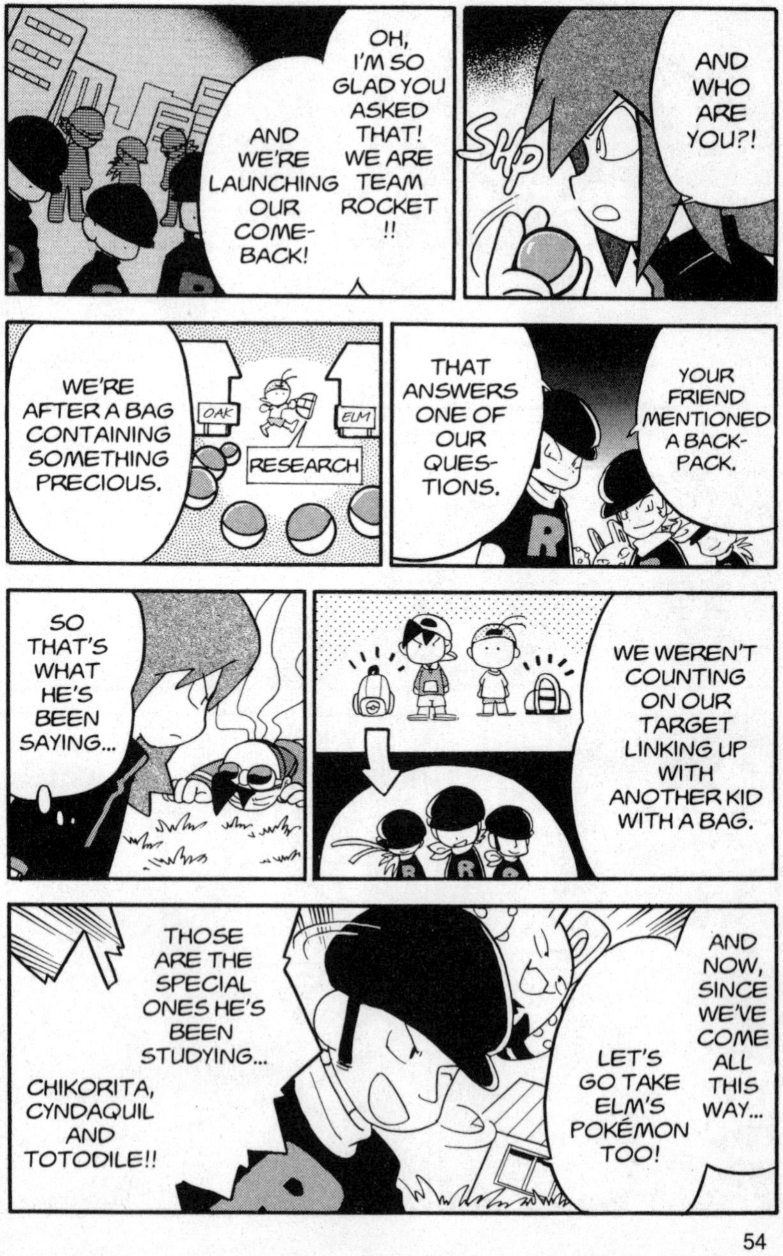
AND WHO ARE YOU?!
SHP
OH, I'M SO GLAD YOU ASKED THAT! WE ARE TEAM ROCKET!!
AND WE'RE LAUNCHING OUR COME-BACK!
YOUR FRIEND MENTIONED A BACK-PACK.
THAT ANSWERS ONE OF OUR QUES-TIONS.
WE'RE AFTER A BAG CONTAINING SOMETHING PRECIOUS.
OAK
ELM
RESEARCH
WE WEREN'T COUNTING ON OUR TARGET LINKING UP WITH ANOTHER KID WITH A BAG.
SO THAT'S WHAT HE'S BEEN SAYING...
AND NOW, SINCE WE'VE COME ALL THIS WAY...
LET'S GO TAKE ELM'S POKÉMON TOO!
THOSE ARE THE SPECIAL ONES HE'S BEEN STUDYING...
CHIKORITA, CYNDAQUIL AND TOTODILE!!

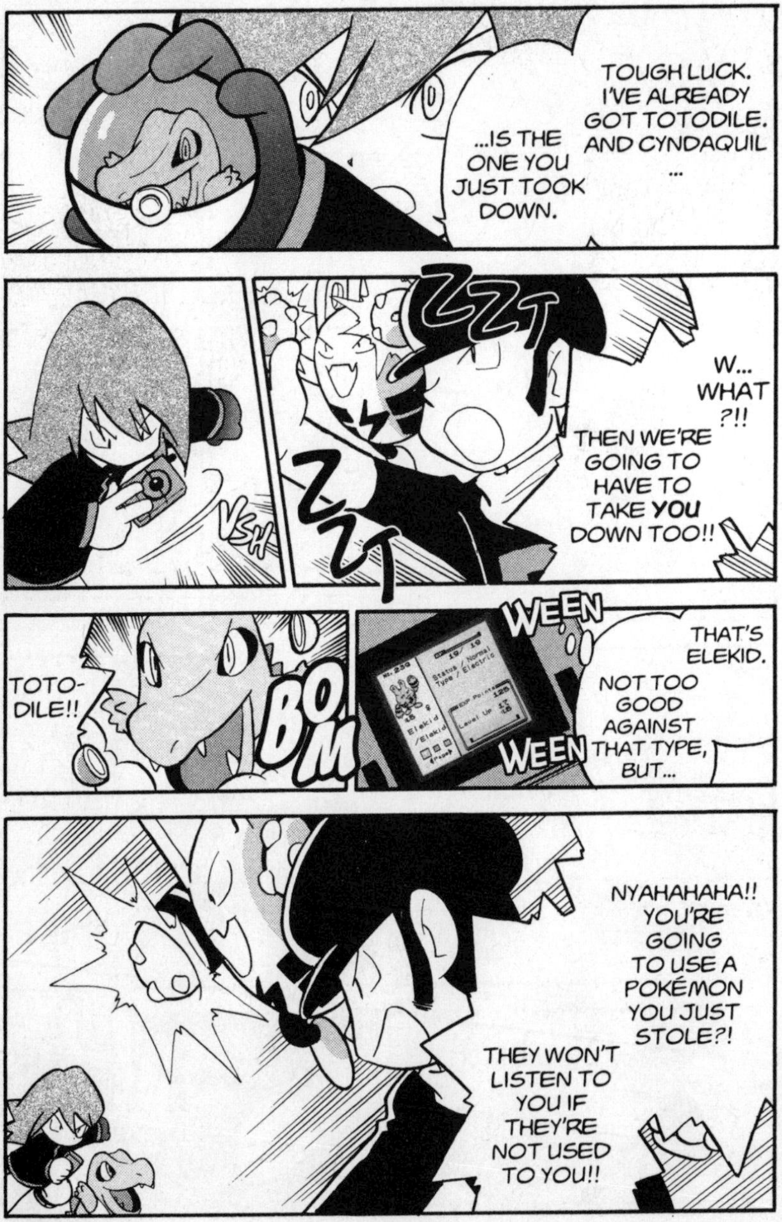
TOUGH LUCK. I'VE ALREADY GOT TOTODILE. AND CYNDAQUIL ...
...IS THE ONE YOU JUST TOOK DOWN.
ZZZT
W... WHAT ?!!
THEN WE'RE GOING TO HAVE TO TAKE **YOU** DOWN TOO!!
ZZZT
VSH
WEEN
THAT'S ELEKID.
NOT TOO GOOD AGAINST THAT TYPE, BUT...
WEEN
BOOM
TOTO-DILE!!
NYAHAHAHA!! YOU'RE GOING TO USE A POKÉMON YOU JUST STOLE?!
THEY WON'T LISTEN TO YOU IF THEY'RE NOT USED TO YOU!!

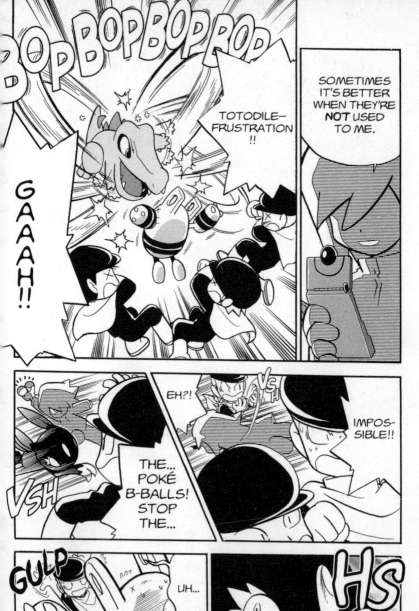

SOMETIMES IT'S BETTER WHEN THEY'RE **NOT** USED TO ME.
BOPBOPBOPBOPBOP
TOTODILE-FRUSTRATION !!
GAAAAH!!
EH?!
VSH
IMPOSSIBLE!!
THE... POKÉ B-BALLS! STOP THE...
VSH
HSSS
GULP
UH...

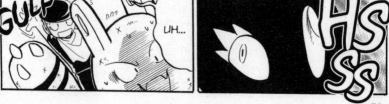

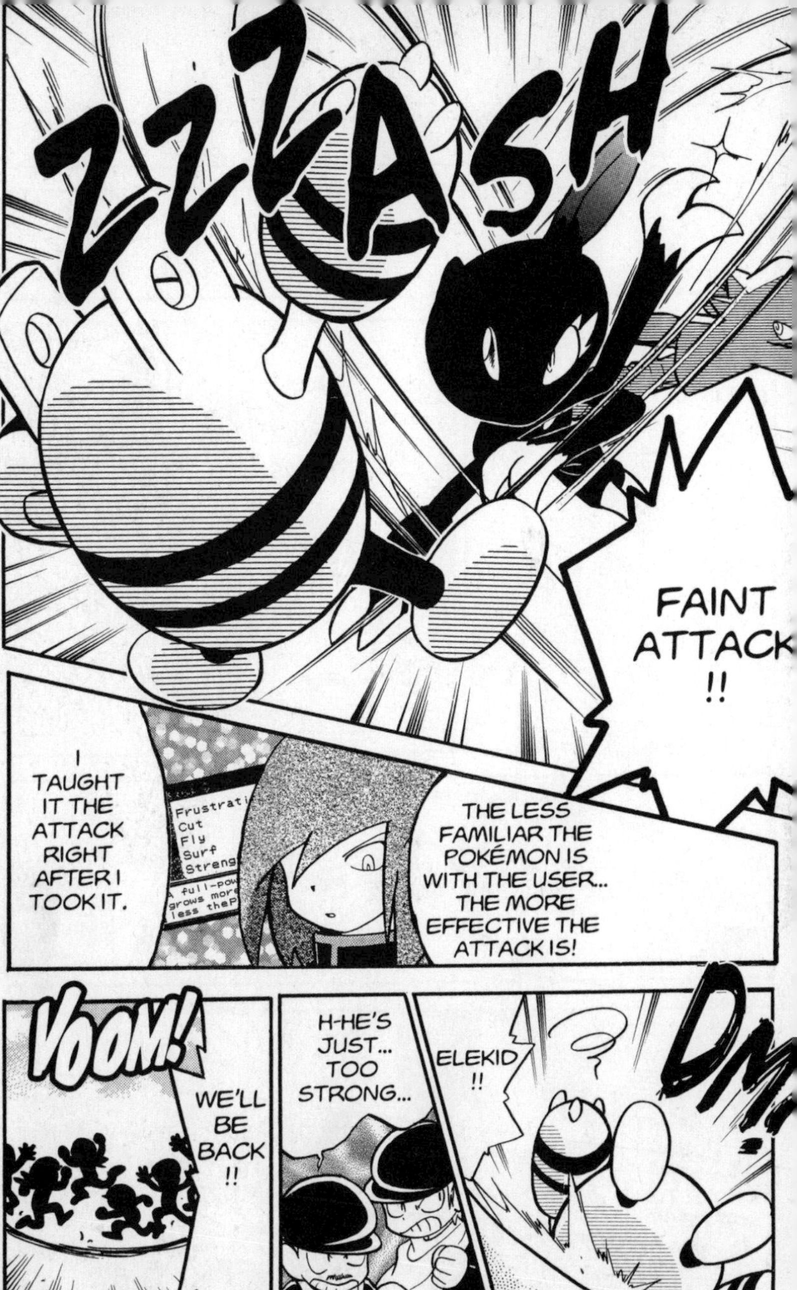
ZZZASH
FAINT ATTACK !!
THE LESS FAMILIAR THE POKÉMON IS WITH THE USER... THE MORE EFFECTIVE THE ATTACK IS!
I TAUGHT IT THE ATTACK RIGHT AFTER I TOOK IT.
Frustrati
Cut
Fly
Surf
Streng
ELEKID !!
H-HE'S JUST... TOO STRONG...
WE'LL BE BACK !!
VOOM!

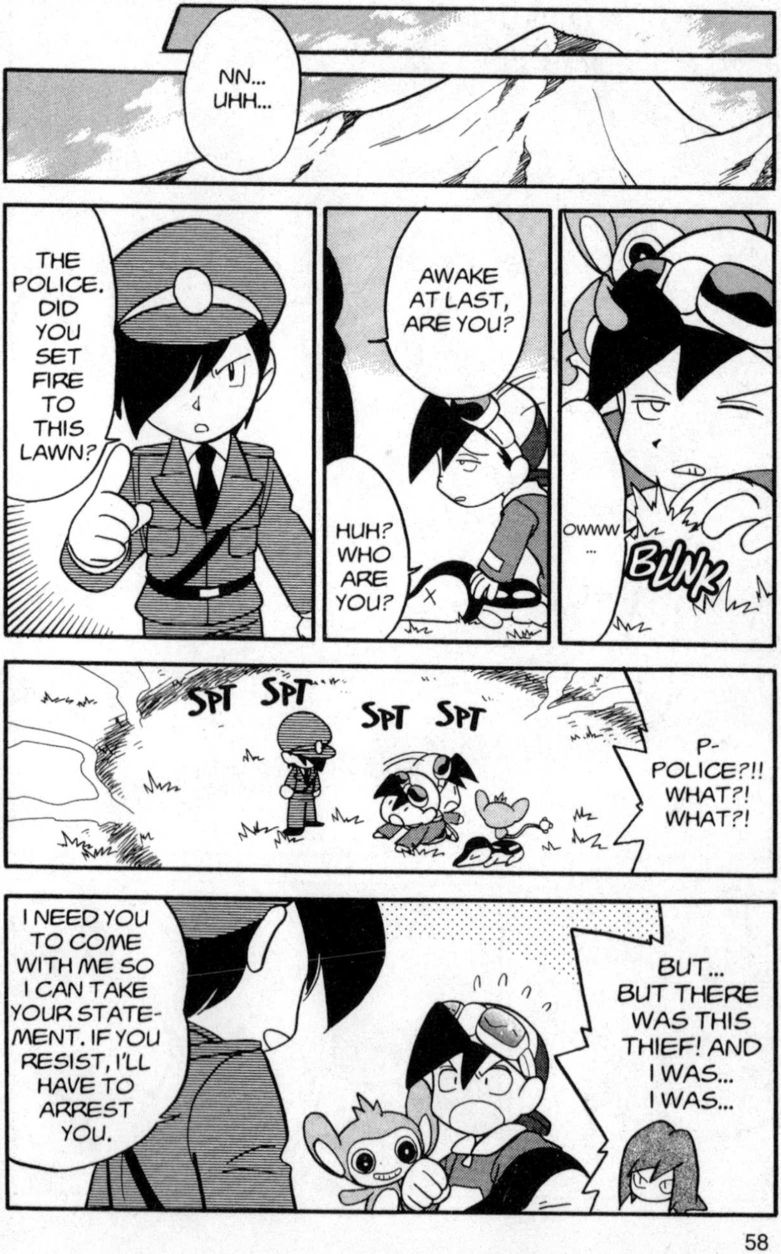
NN... UHH...
OWWW...
BLNK
AWAKE AT LAST, ARE YOU?
HUH? WHO ARE YOU?
THE POLICE. DID YOU SET FIRE TO THIS LAWN?
P- POLICE?!! WHAT?! WHAT?!
SPT SPT
SPT SPT
BUT... BUT THERE WAS THIS THIEF! AND I WAS... I WAS...
I NEED YOU TO COME WITH ME SO I CAN TAKE YOUR STATEMENT. IF YOU RESIST, I'LL HAVE TO ARREST YOU.

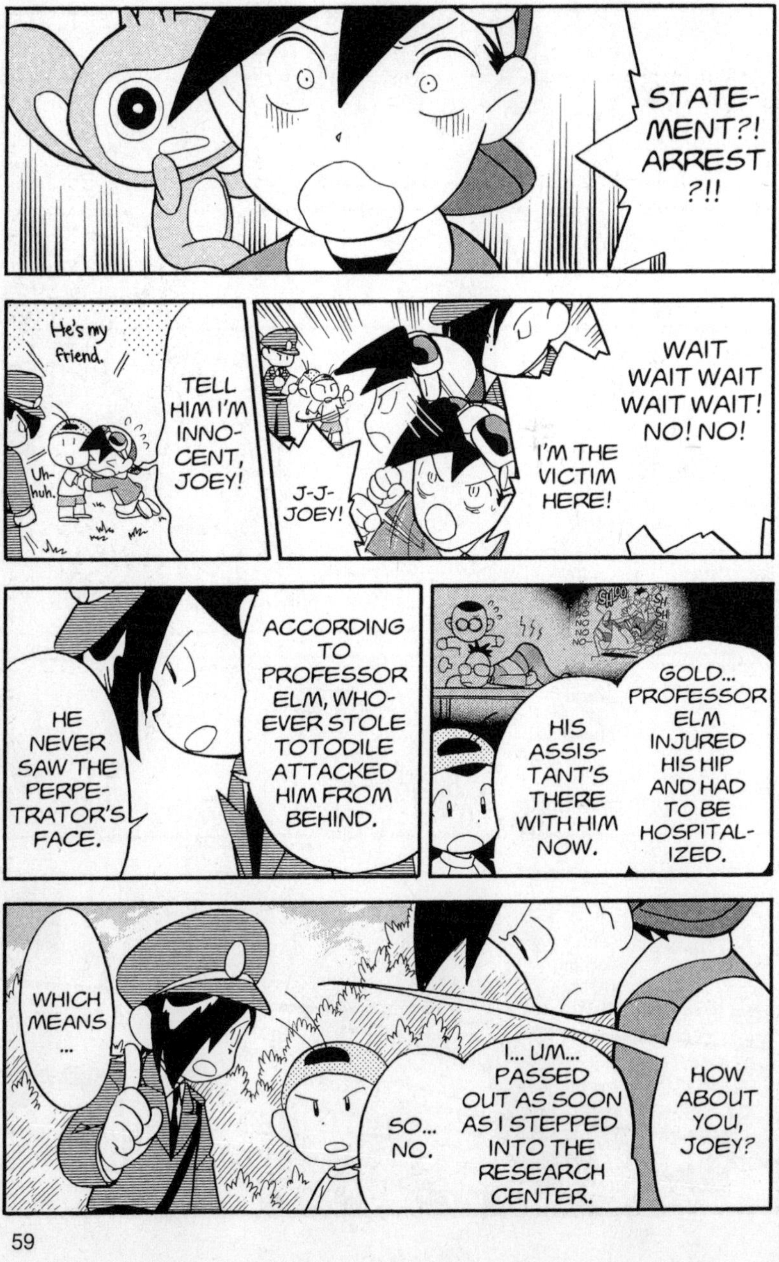
STATEMENT?! ARREST?!!
WAIT WAIT WAIT WAIT WAIT! NO! NO!
I'M THE VICTIM HERE!
J-J-JOEY!
TELL HIM I'M INNOCENT, JOEY!
He's my friend.
Uh-huh.
GOLD... PROFESSOR ELM INJURED HIS HIP AND HAD TO BE HOSPITALIZED.
HIS ASSISTANT'S THERE WITH HIM NOW.
ACCORDING TO PROFESSOR ELM, WHOEVER STOLE TOTODILE ATTACKED HIM FROM BEHIND.
HE NEVER SAW THE PERPETRATOR'S FACE.
HOW ABOUT YOU, JOEY?
I... UM... PASSED OUT AS SOON AS I STEPPED INTO THE RESEARCH CENTER.
SO... NO.
WHICH MEANS ...

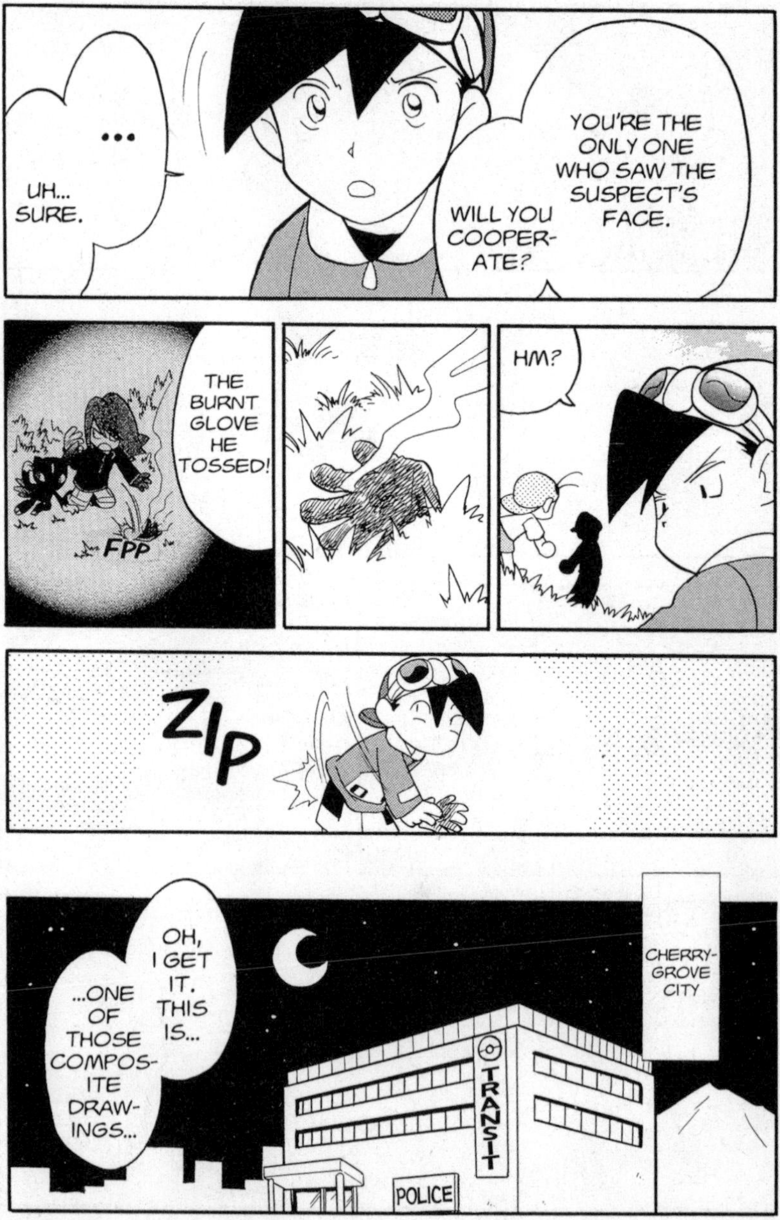
YOU'RE THE ONLY ONE WHO SAW THE SUSPECT'S FACE.
WILL YOU COOPER-ATE?
...
UH... SURE.
HM?
THE BURNT GLOVE HE TOSSED!
FPP
ZIP
CHERRY-GROVE CITY
OH, I GET IT. THIS IS...
...ONE OF THOSE COMPOS-ITE DRAW-INGS...
TRANSIT
POLICE

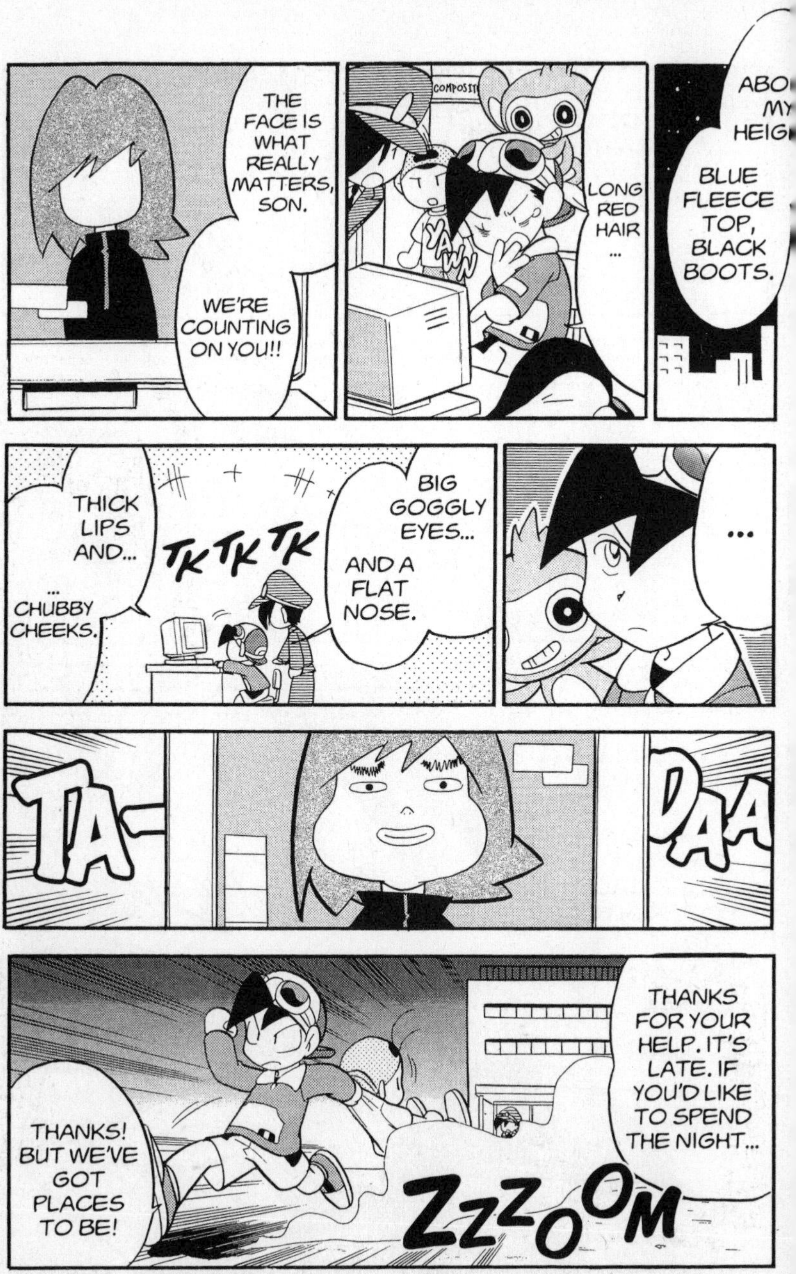
ABO MY HEIG
BLUE FLEECE TOP, BLACK BOOTS.
LONG RED HAIR ...
YAWN
THE FACE IS WHAT REALLY MATTERS, SON.
WE'RE COUNTING ON YOU!!
...
BIG GOGGLY EYES...
AND A FLAT NOSE.
TK TK TK
THICK LIPS AND...
... CHUBBY CHEEKS.
TA-
DAA
THANKS FOR YOUR HELP. IT'S LATE. IF YOU'D LIKE TO SPEND THE NIGHT...
ZZZOOM
THANKS! BUT WE'VE GOT PLACES TO BE!

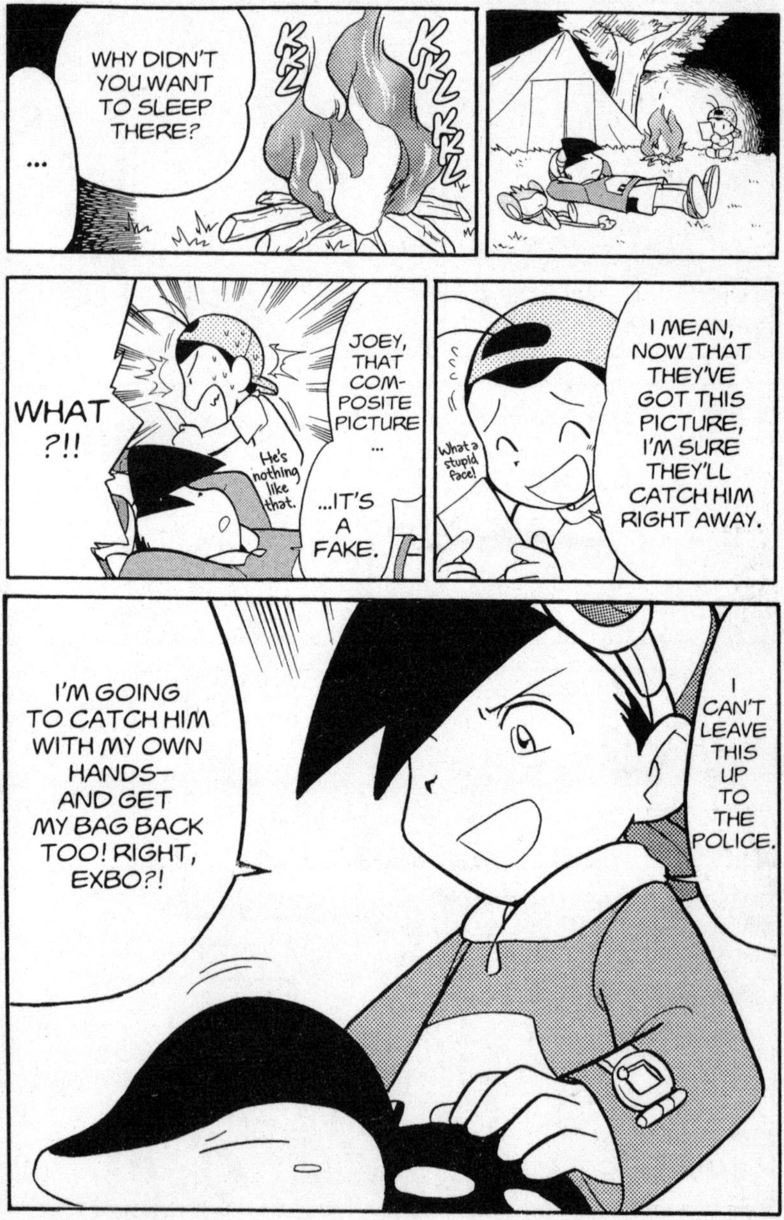
WHY DIDN'T YOU WANT TO SLEEP THERE?
...
I MEAN, NOW THAT THEY'VE GOT THIS PICTURE, I'M SURE THEY'LL CATCH HIM RIGHT AWAY.
What a stupid face!
JOEY, THAT COMPOSITE PICTURE ...
...IT'S A FAKE.
He's nothing like that.
WHAT?!!
I CAN'T LEAVE THIS UP TO THE POLICE.
I'M GOING TO CATCH HIM WITH MY OWN HANDS— AND GET MY BAG BACK TOO! RIGHT, EXBO?!

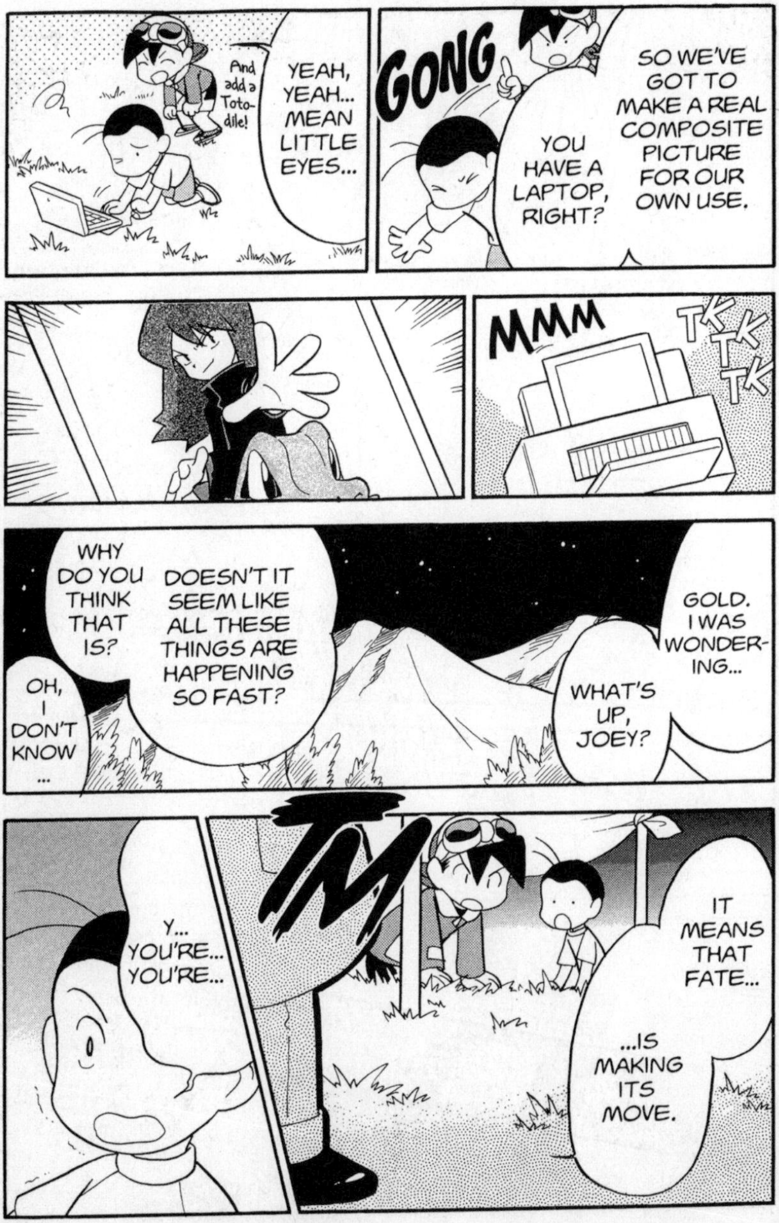
GONG
SO WE'VE GOT TO MAKE A REAL COMPOSITE PICTURE FOR OUR OWN USE.
YOU HAVE A LAPTOP, RIGHT?
YEAH, YEAH... MEAN LITTLE EYES...
And add a Totodile!
MMM
TK TK TK
GOLD. I WAS WONDERING...
WHAT'S UP, JOEY?
DOESN'T IT SEEM LIKE ALL THESE THINGS ARE HAPPENING SO FAST?
WHY DO YOU THINK THAT IS?
OH, I DON'T KNOW...
TM
IT MEANS THAT FATE...
...IS MAKING ITS MOVE.
Y... YOU'RE... YOU'RE...

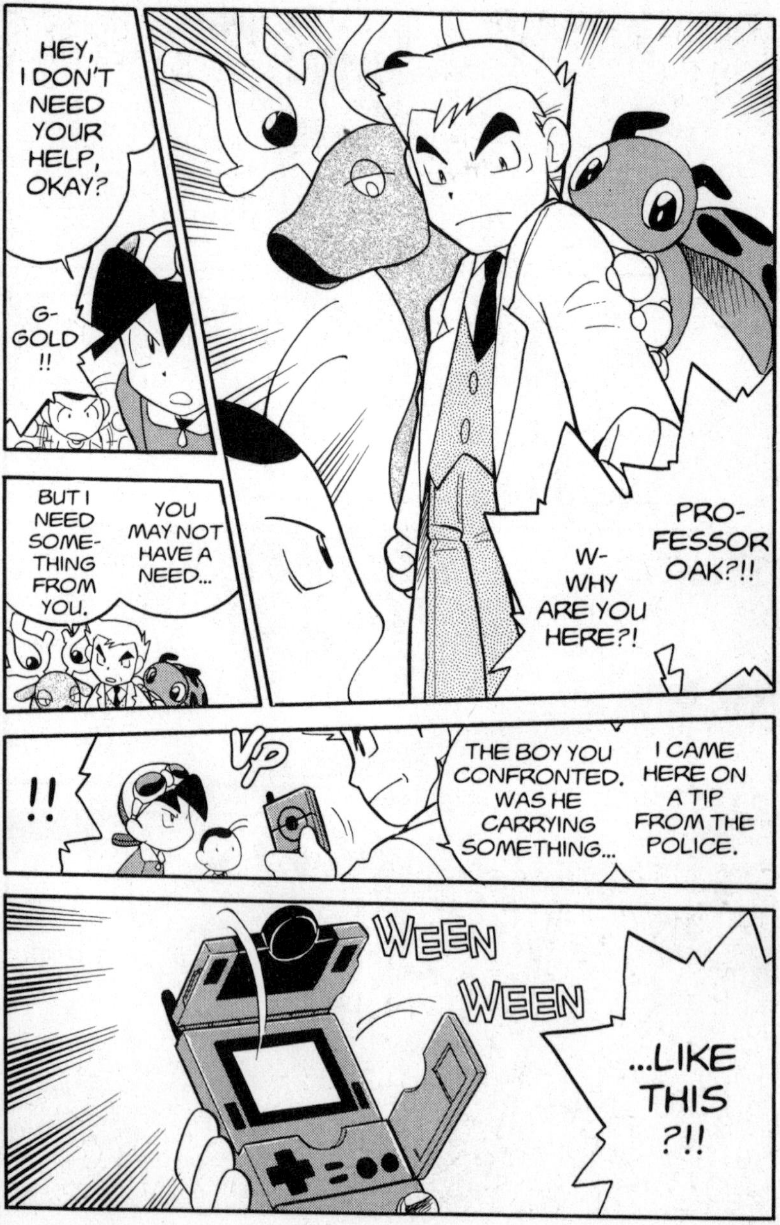
PRO-FESSOR OAK?!!
W-WHY ARE YOU HERE?!
HEY, I DON'T NEED YOUR HELP, OKAY?
G-GOLD !!
YOU MAY NOT HAVE A NEED...
BUT I NEED SOME-THING FROM YOU.
I CAME HERE ON A TIP FROM THE POLICE.
THE BOY YOU CONFRONTED. WAS HE CARRYING SOMETHING...
VP
!!
WEEN
WEEN
...LIKE THIS ?!!

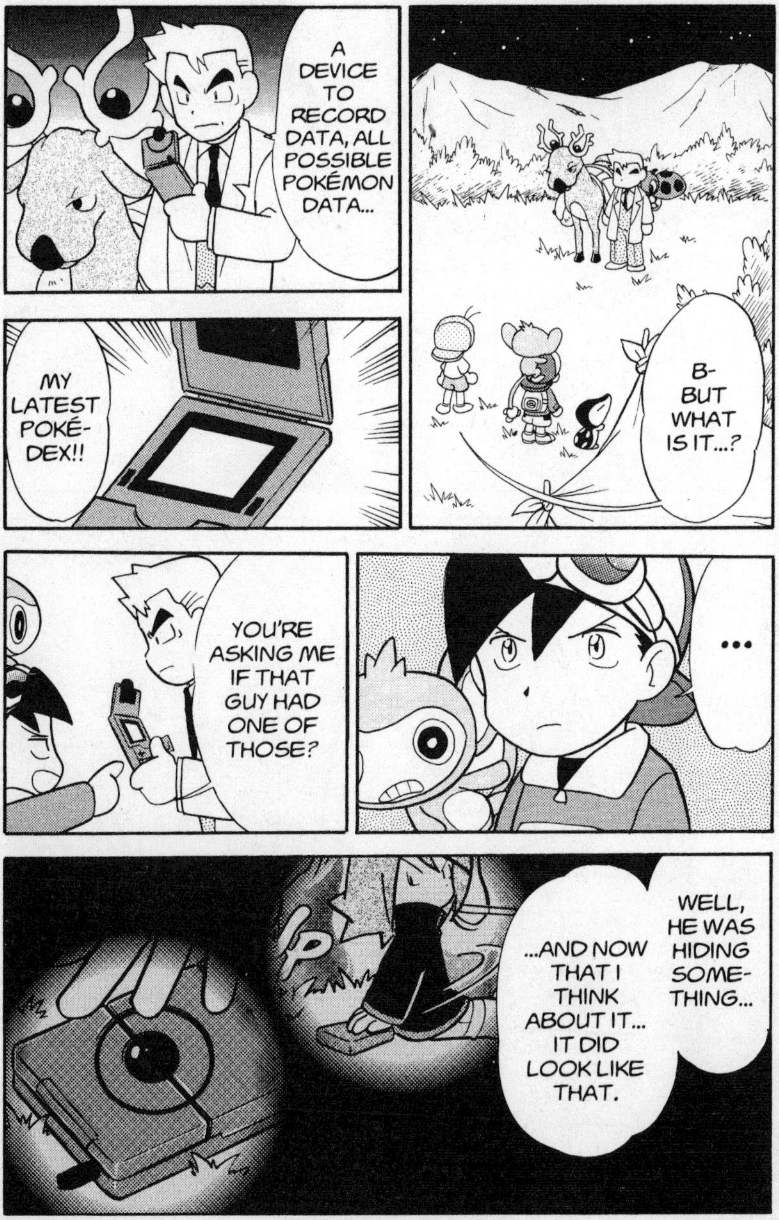
B-BUT WHAT IS IT...?
A DEVICE TO RECORD DATA, ALL POSSIBLE POKÉMON DATA...
MY LATEST POKÉ-DEX!!
...
YOU'RE ASKING ME IF THAT GUY HAD ONE OF THOSE?
WELL, HE WAS HIDING SOME-THING...
...AND NOW THAT I THINK ABOUT IT... IT DID LOOK LIKE THAT.

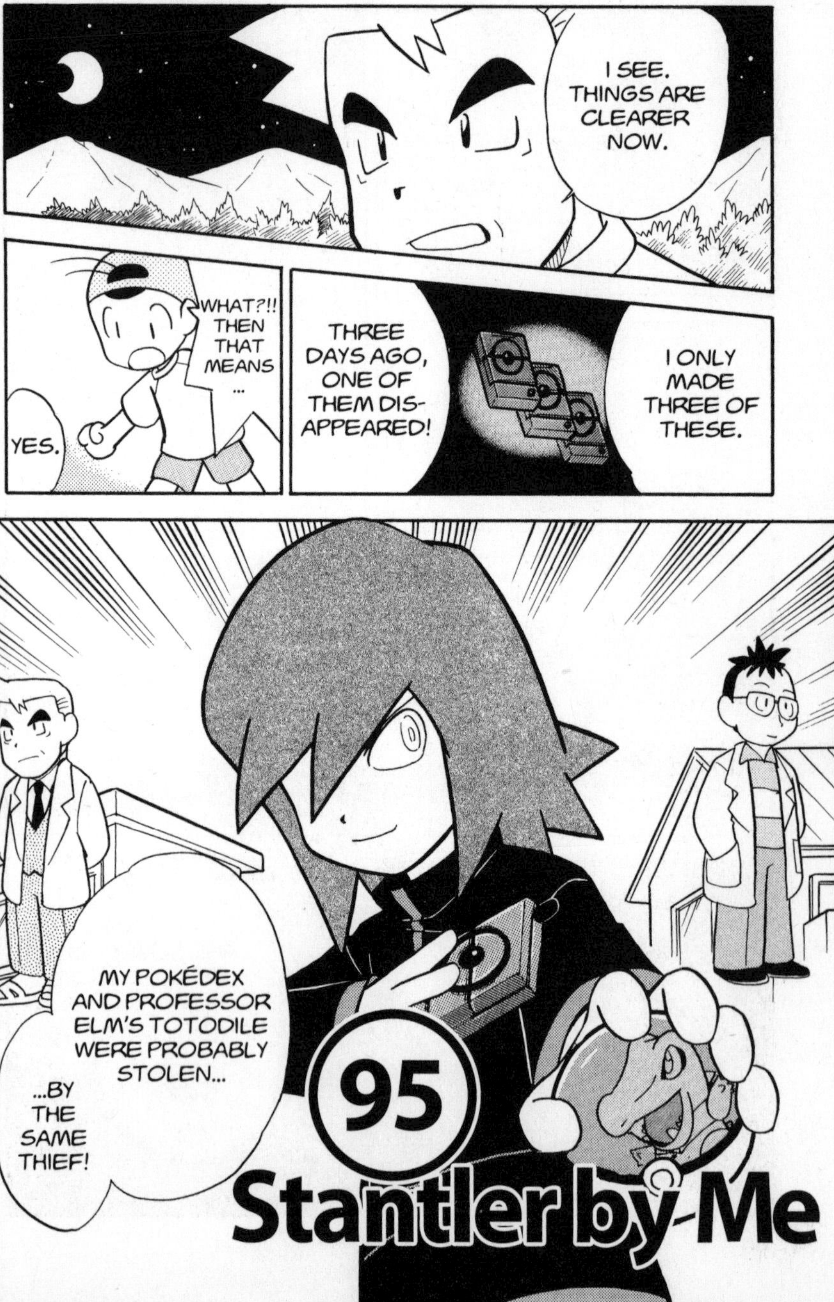
I SEE. THINGS ARE CLEARER NOW.
I ONLY MADE THREE OF THESE.
THREE DAYS AGO, ONE OF THEM DIS-APPEARED!
WHAT?!! THEN THAT MEANS ...
YES.
MY POKÉDEX AND PROFESSOR ELM'S TOTODILE WERE PROBABLY STOLEN...
...BY THE SAME THIEF!
95
Stantler by Me

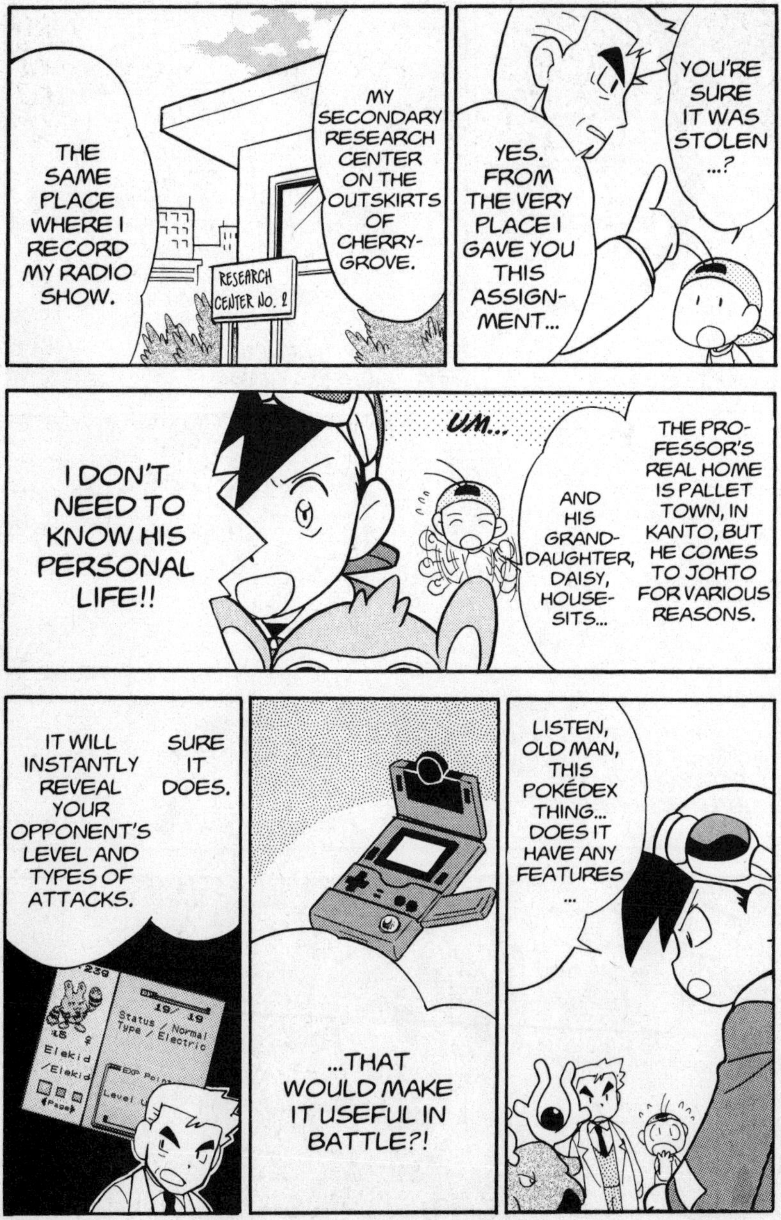
YOU'RE SURE IT WAS STOLEN ...?
YES. FROM THE VERY PLACE I GAVE YOU THIS ASSIGN-MENT...
MY SECONDARY RESEARCH CENTER ON THE OUTSKIRTS OF CHERRY-GROVE.
RESEARCH CENTER No. 2
THE SAME PLACE WHERE I RECORD MY RADIO SHOW.
UM...
THE PRO-FESSOR'S REAL HOME IS PALLET TOWN, IN KANTO, BUT HE COMES TO JOHTO FOR VARIOUS REASONS.
AND HIS GRAND-DAUGHTER, DAISY, HOUSE-SITS...
I DON'T NEED TO KNOW HIS PERSONAL LIFE!!
LISTEN, OLD MAN, THIS POKÉDEX THING... DOES IT HAVE ANY FEATURES ...
...THAT WOULD MAKE IT USEFUL IN BATTLE?!
SURE IT DOES.
IT WILL INSTANTLY REVEAL YOUR OPPONENT'S LEVEL AND TYPES OF ATTACKS.
Status / Normal
Type / Electric
Elekid
/Elekid

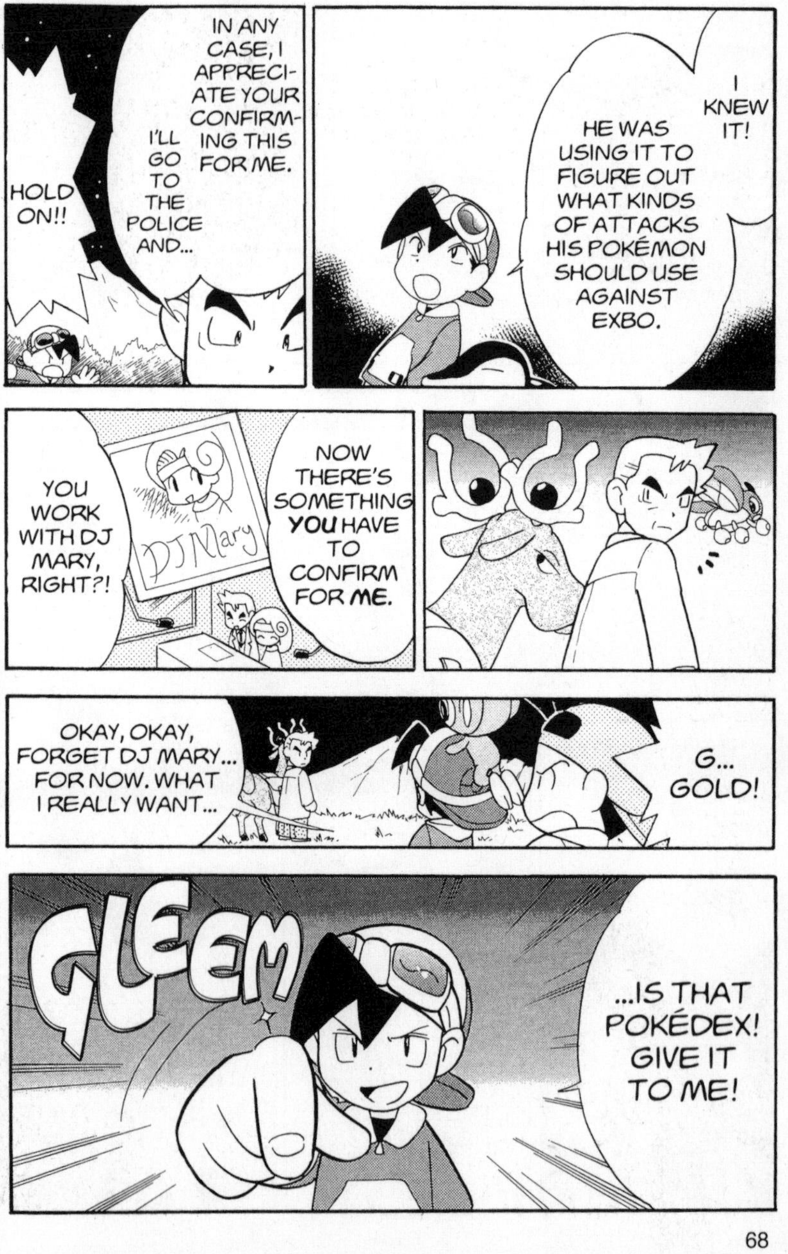
I KNEW IT!
HE WAS USING IT TO FIGURE OUT WHAT KINDS OF ATTACKS HIS POKÉMON SHOULD USE AGAINST EXBO.
IN ANY CASE, I APPRECIATE YOUR CONFIRMING THIS FOR ME.
I'LL GO TO THE POLICE AND...
HOLD ON!!
...
NOW THERE'S SOMETHING **YOU** HAVE TO CONFIRM FOR **ME**.
DJ Mary
YOU WORK WITH DJ MARY, RIGHT?!
G... GOLD!
OKAY, OKAY, FORGET DJ MARY... FOR NOW. WHAT I REALLY WANT...
...IS THAT POKÉDEX! GIVE IT TO ME!
GLEEM

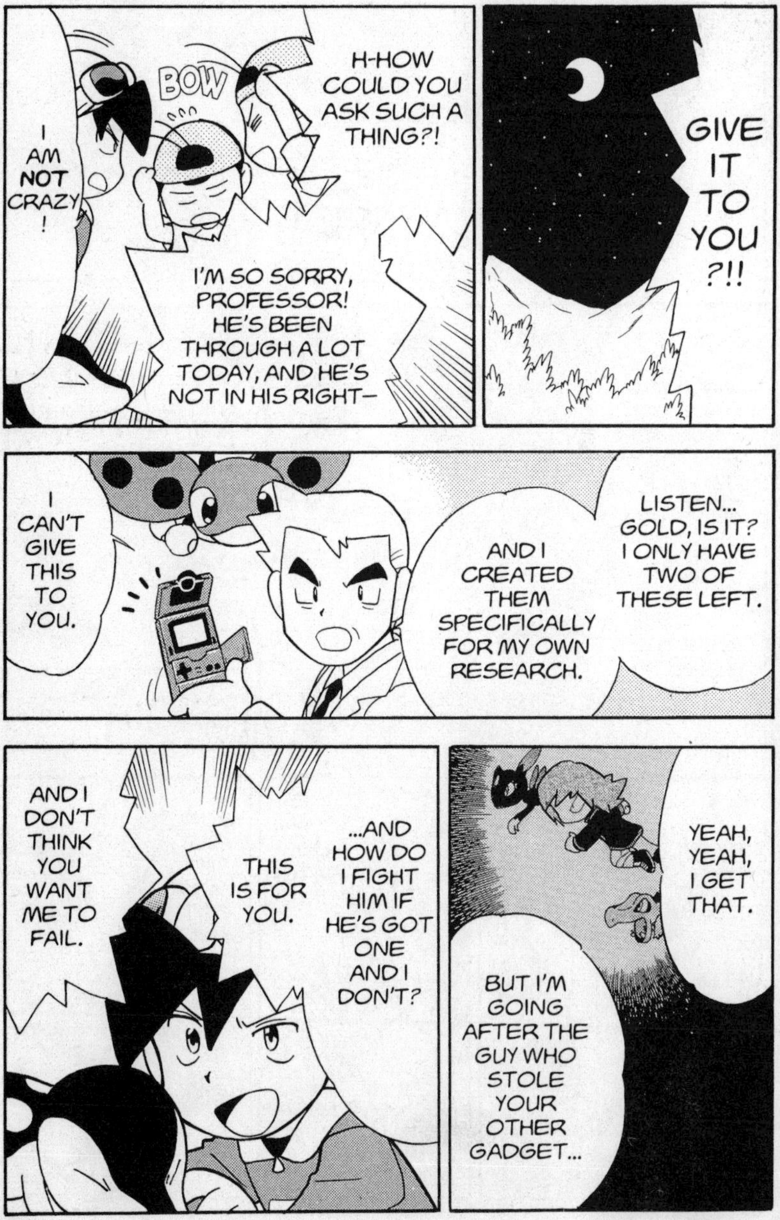
GIVE IT TO YOU?!!
H-HOW COULD YOU ASK SUCH A THING?!
BOW
I AM **NOT** CRAZY!
I'M SO SORRY, PROFESSOR! HE'S BEEN THROUGH A LOT TODAY, AND HE'S NOT IN HIS RIGHT—
LISTEN... GOLD, IS IT? I ONLY HAVE TWO OF THESE LEFT.
AND I CREATED THEM SPECIFICALLY FOR MY OWN RESEARCH.
I CAN'T GIVE THIS TO YOU.
YEAH, YEAH, I GET THAT.
BUT I'M GOING AFTER THE GUY WHO STOLE YOUR OTHER GADGET...
...AND HOW DO I FIGHT HIM IF HE'S GOT ONE AND I DON'T?
THIS IS FOR YOU.
AND I DON'T THINK YOU WANT ME TO FAIL.

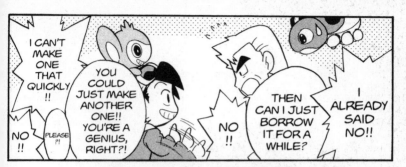

I ALREADY SAID NO!!
THEN CAN I JUST BORROW IT FOR A WHILE?
NO !!
YOU COULD JUST MAKE ANOTHER ONE!! YOU'RE A GENIUS, RIGHT?!
I CAN'T MAKE ONE THAT QUICKLY !!
PLEASE ?!
NO !!
PANT PANT... TRY TO UNDER-STAND THIS...
I'VE ONLY GIVEN POKÉDEXES TO TRAINERS I TRUST TO GATHER THOROUGH AND ACCURATE DATA FOR MY RESEARCH...
...**AND** WHO HAVE THE CHARACTER AND SKILLS TO HELP OTHERS.
I DON'T GIVE THEM TO PEOPLE I DON'T KNOW.
SKILLS, HUH?
YOU'RE FINE IF YOU'VE GOT SKILLS, HUH?!
OKAY THEN ...
AIBO, SCRATCH !!
VAP
N-NO! THAT'S NOT WHAT I'M...
MMG
STOP THAT!! STANT-LER! LEDYBA!

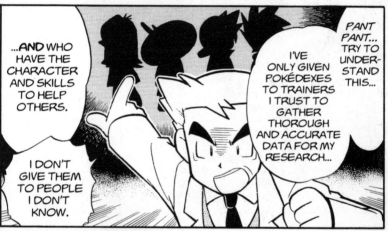

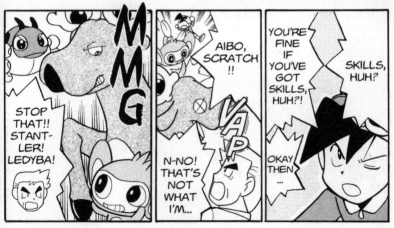

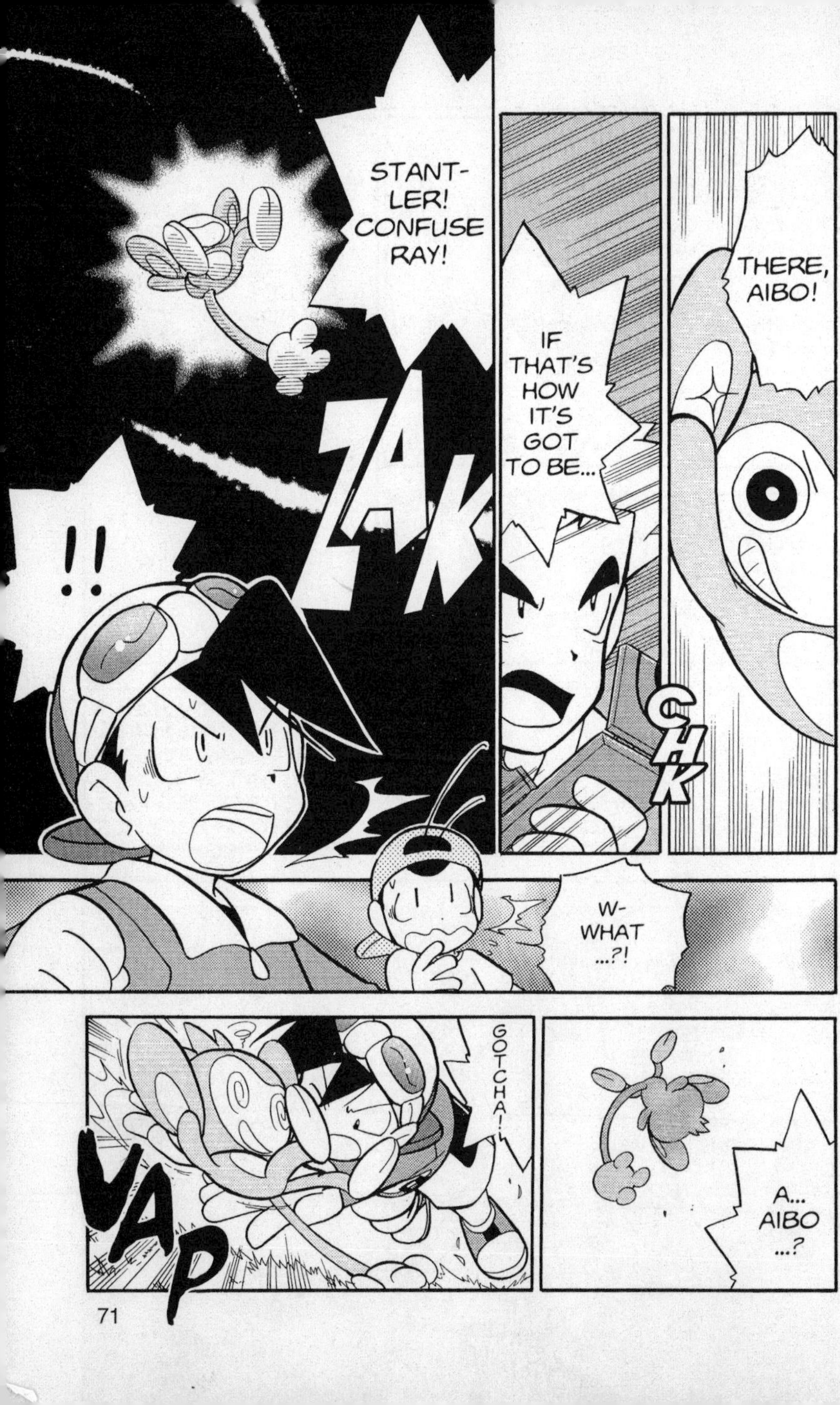
THERE, AIBO!
CHK
IF THAT'S HOW IT'S GOT TO BE...
STANTLER! CONFUSE RAY!
ZAK
!!
W-WHAT ...?!
A... AIBO ...?
GOTCHA!
VAP

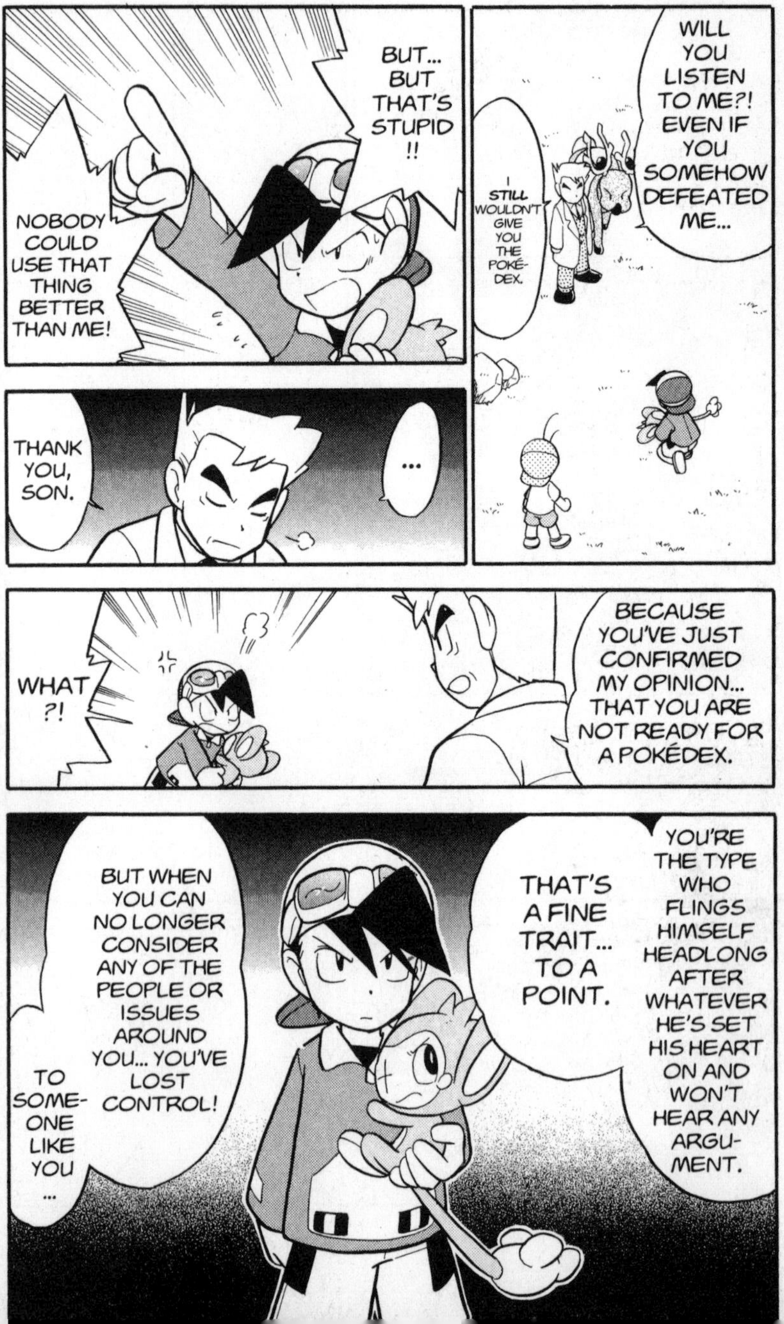
WILL YOU LISTEN TO ME?! EVEN IF YOU SOMEHOW DEFEATED ME...
I STILL WOULDN'T GIVE YOU THE POKÉDEX.
BUT... BUT THAT'S STUPID!!
NOBODY COULD USE THAT THING BETTER THAN ME!
...
THANK YOU, SON.
BECAUSE YOU'VE JUST CONFIRMED MY OPINION... THAT YOU ARE NOT READY FOR A POKÉDEX.
WHAT?!
YOU'RE THE TYPE WHO FLINGS HIMSELF HEADLONG AFTER WHATEVER HE'S SET HIS HEART ON AND WON'T HEAR ANY ARGUMENT.
THAT'S A FINE TRAIT... TO A POINT.
BUT WHEN YOU CAN NO LONGER CONSIDER ANY OF THE PEOPLE OR ISSUES AROUND YOU... YOU'VE LOST CONTROL!
TO SOMEONE LIKE YOU...

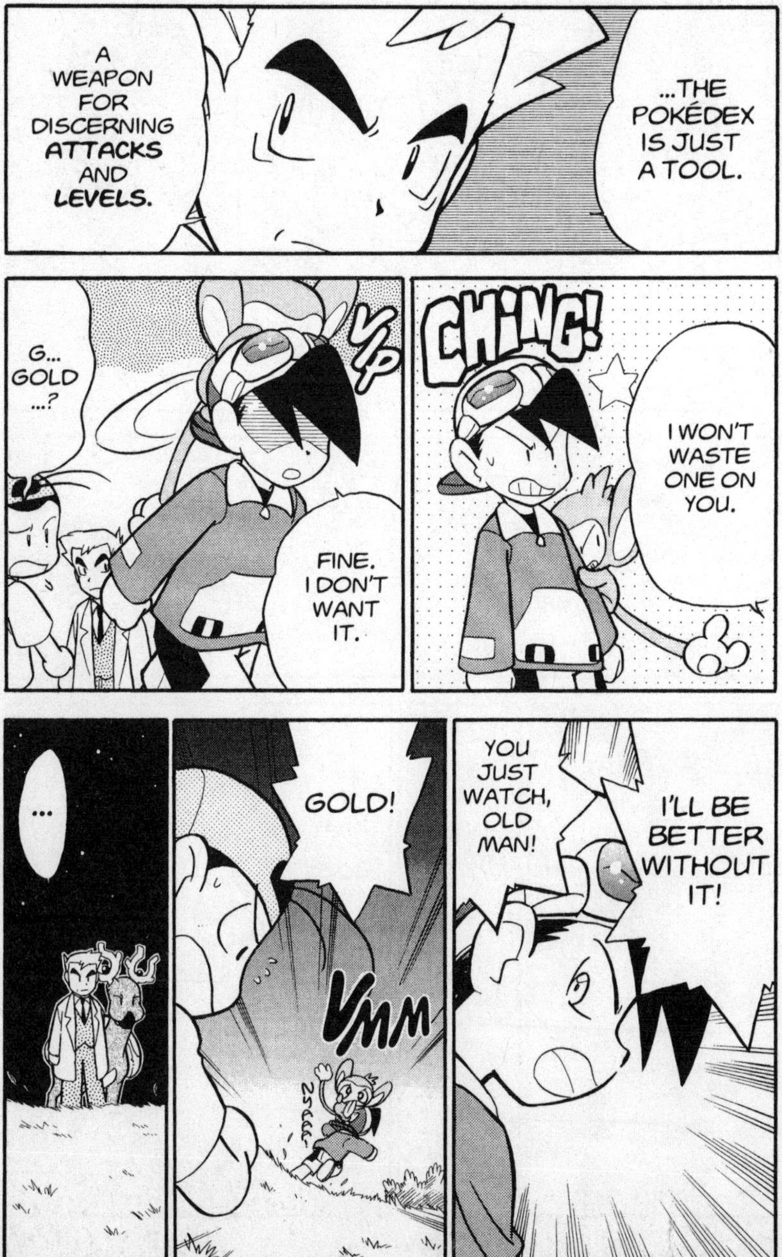
...THE POKÉDEX IS JUST A TOOL.
A WEAPON FOR DISCERNING **ATTACKS** AND **LEVELS.**
CHING!
I WON'T WASTE ONE ON YOU.
VIP
G... GOLD ...?
FINE. I DON'T WANT IT.
YOU JUST WATCH, OLD MAN!
I'LL BE BETTER WITHOUT IT!
GOLD!
VMM
NYAAA!
...

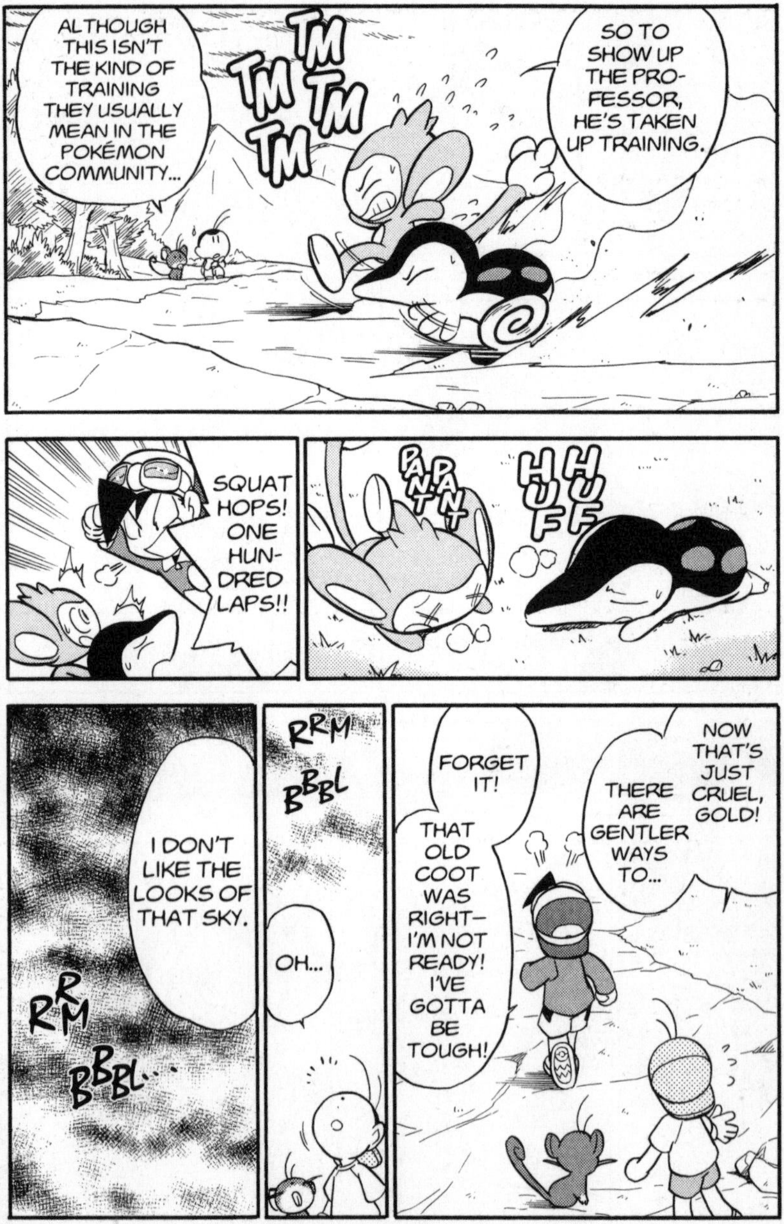
SO TO SHOW UP THE PRO-FESSOR, HE'S TAKEN UP TRAINING.
TM TM TM TM TM
ALTHOUGH THIS ISN'T THE KIND OF TRAINING THEY USUALLY MEAN IN THE POKÉMON COMMUNITY...
HUFF HUFF
PANT PANT
SQUAT HOPS! ONE HUN-DRED LAPS!!
NOW THAT'S JUST CRUEL, GOLD!
THERE ARE GENTLER WAYS TO...
FORGET IT!
THAT OLD COOT WAS RIGHT— I'M NOT READY! I'VE GOTTA BE TOUGH!
RRM
BBBL
OH...
I DON'T LIKE THE LOOKS OF THAT SKY.
RRM
BBBL...

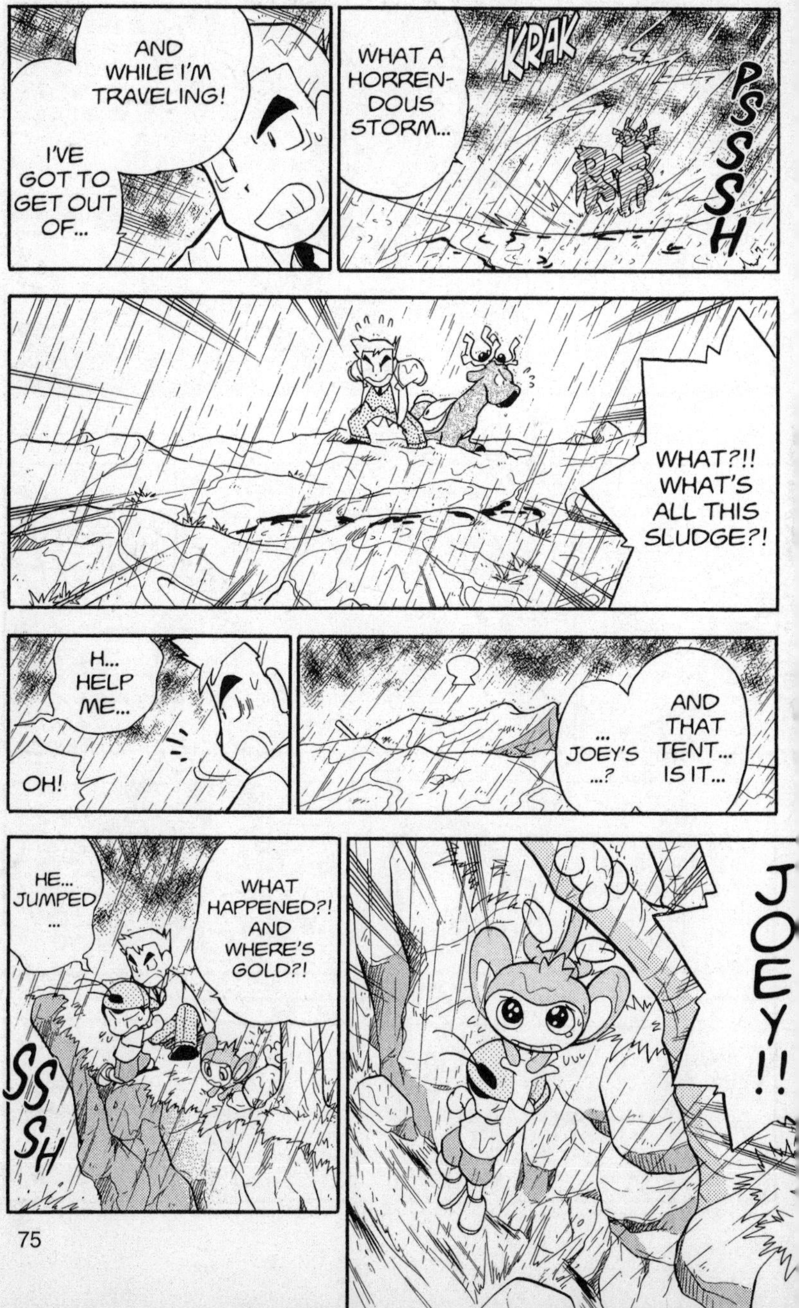

WHAT A HORREN-DOUS STORM...
KRAK
PSSSH
AND WHILE I'M TRAVELING!
I'VE GOT TO GET OUT OF...
WHAT?!! WHAT'S ALL THIS SLUDGE?!
AND THAT TENT... IS IT...
... JOEY'S ...?
H... HELP ME...
OH!
JOEY!!
WHAT HAPPENED?! AND WHERE'S GOLD?!
HE... JUMPED ...
SSSH

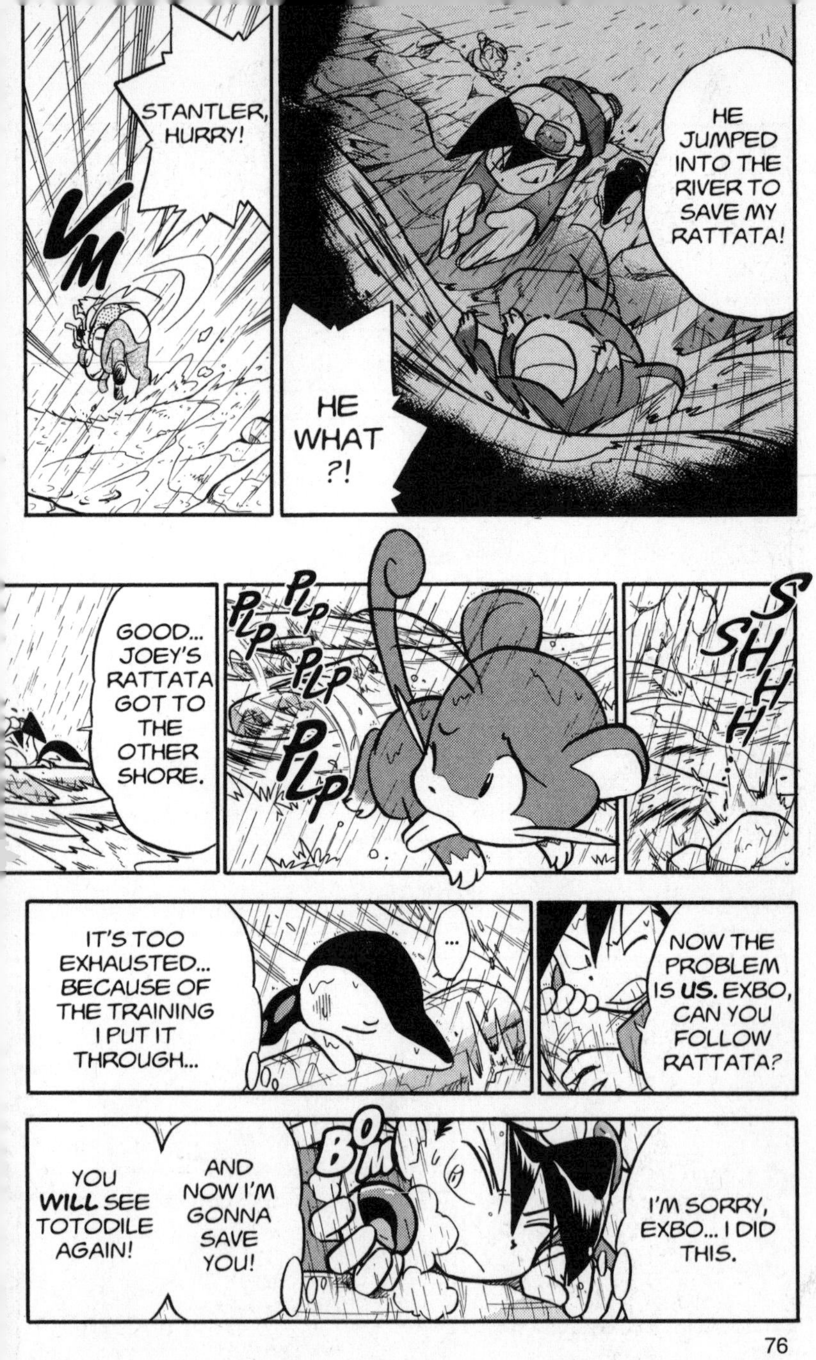
HE JUMPED INTO THE RIVER TO SAVE MY RATTATA!
HE WHAT ?!
STANTLER, HURRY!
VM
SSHHH...
PLP PLP PLP PLP PLP
GOOD... JOEY'S RATTATA GOT TO THE OTHER SHORE.
NOW THE PROBLEM IS **US.** EXBO, CAN YOU FOLLOW RATTATA?
...
IT'S TOO EXHAUSTED... BECAUSE OF THE TRAINING I PUT IT THROUGH...
I'M SORRY, EXBO... I DID THIS.
BOM
AND NOW I'M GONNA SAVE YOU!
YOU **WILL** SEE TOTODILE AGAIN!

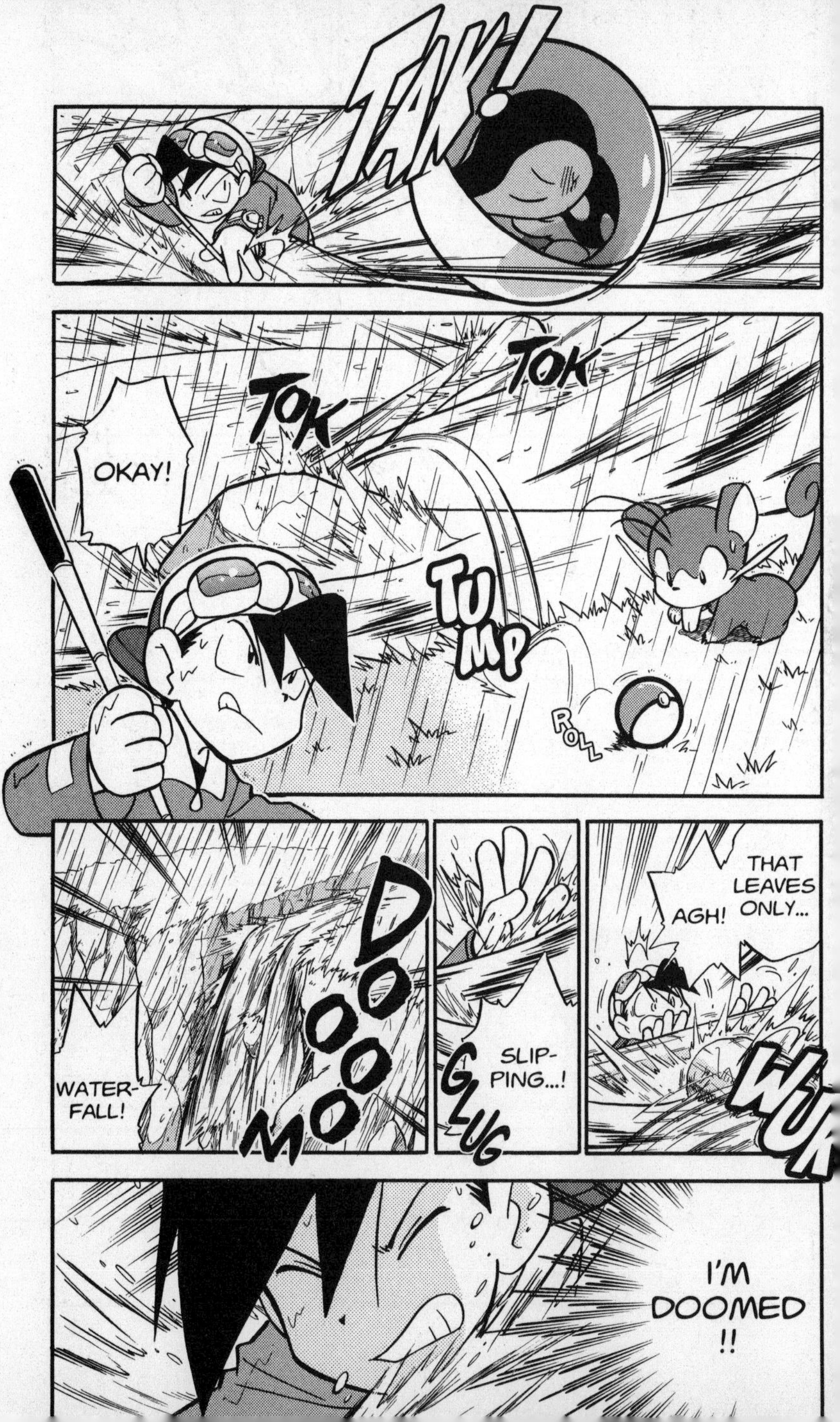
TAK!
TOK
TOK
OKAY!
TUMP
ROLL
THAT LEAVES ONLY...
AGH!
WUK
SLIP-PING...!
GLUG
DOOOOOM
WATER-FALL!
I'M DOOMED !!

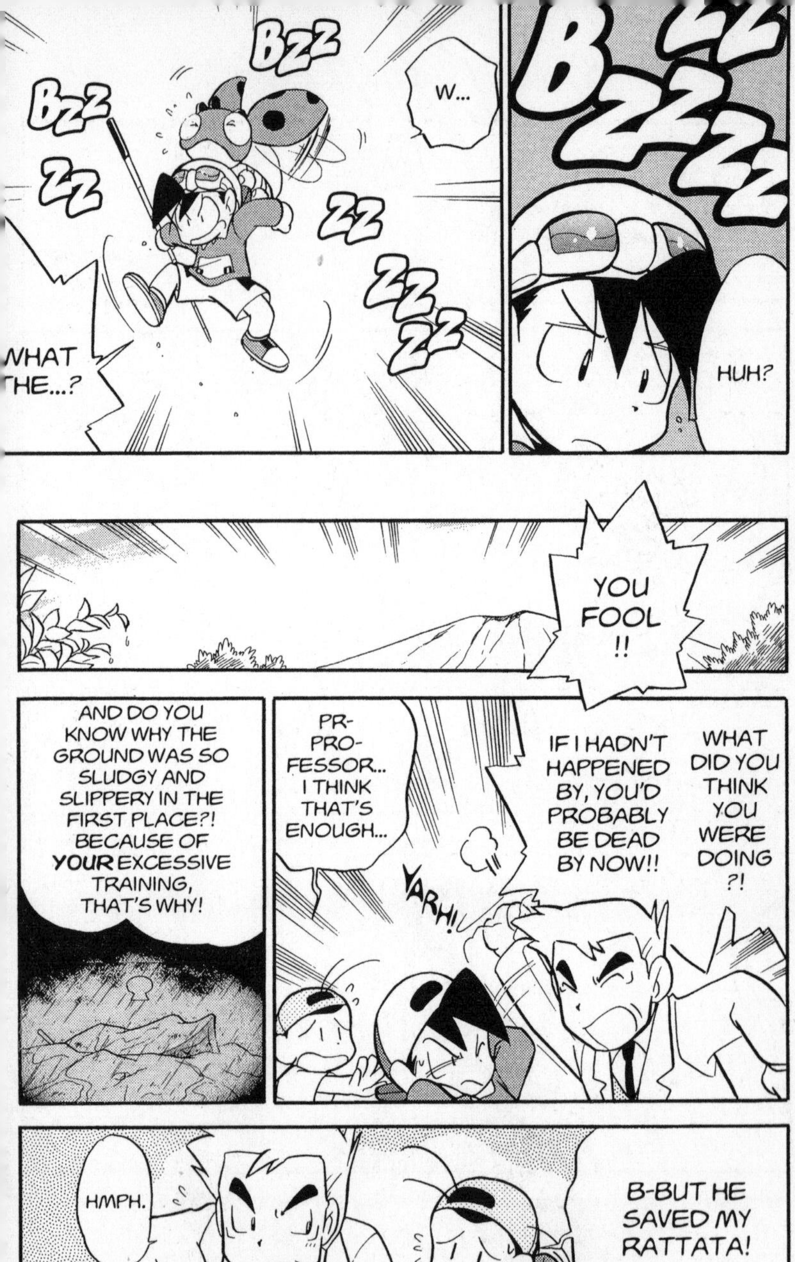
BZZZZZZ
HUH?
W...
Bzz
Bzz
ZZ
ZZ
ZZZZ
WHAT THE...?
YOU FOOL!!
WHAT DID YOU THINK YOU WERE DOING?!
IF I HADN'T HAPPENED BY, YOU'D PROBABLY BE DEAD BY NOW!!
YARH!
PR-PRO-FESSOR... I THINK THAT'S ENOUGH...
AND DO YOU KNOW WHY THE GROUND WAS SO SLUDGY AND SLIPPERY IN THE FIRST PLACE?! BECAUSE OF **YOUR** EXCESSIVE TRAINING, THAT'S WHY!
B-BUT HE SAVED MY RATTATA!
HMPH.

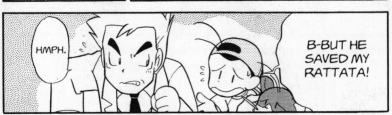

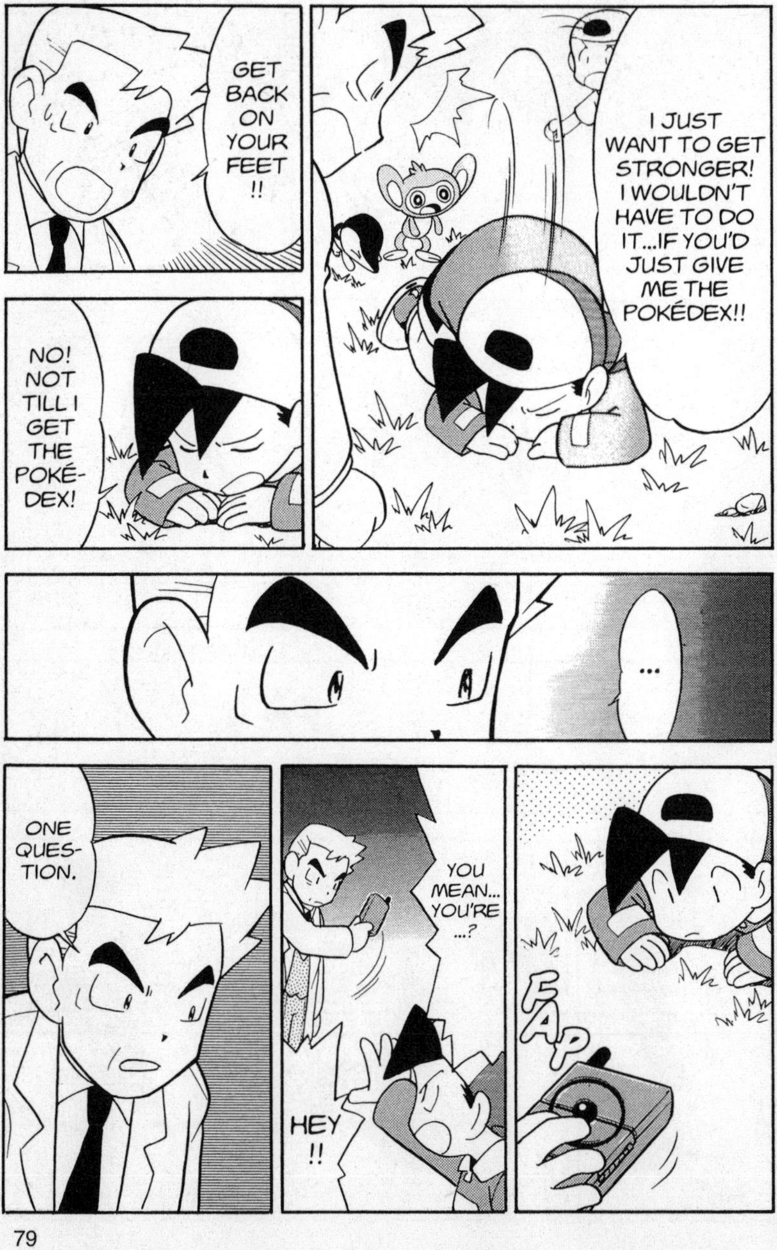
I JUST WANT TO GET STRONGER! I WOULDN'T HAVE TO DO IT...IF YOU'D JUST GIVE ME THE POKÉDEX!!
GET BACK ON YOUR FEET !!
NO! NOT TILL I GET THE POKÉ-DEX!
...
FAP
YOU MEAN... YOU'RE ...?
HEY !!
ONE QUES-TION.

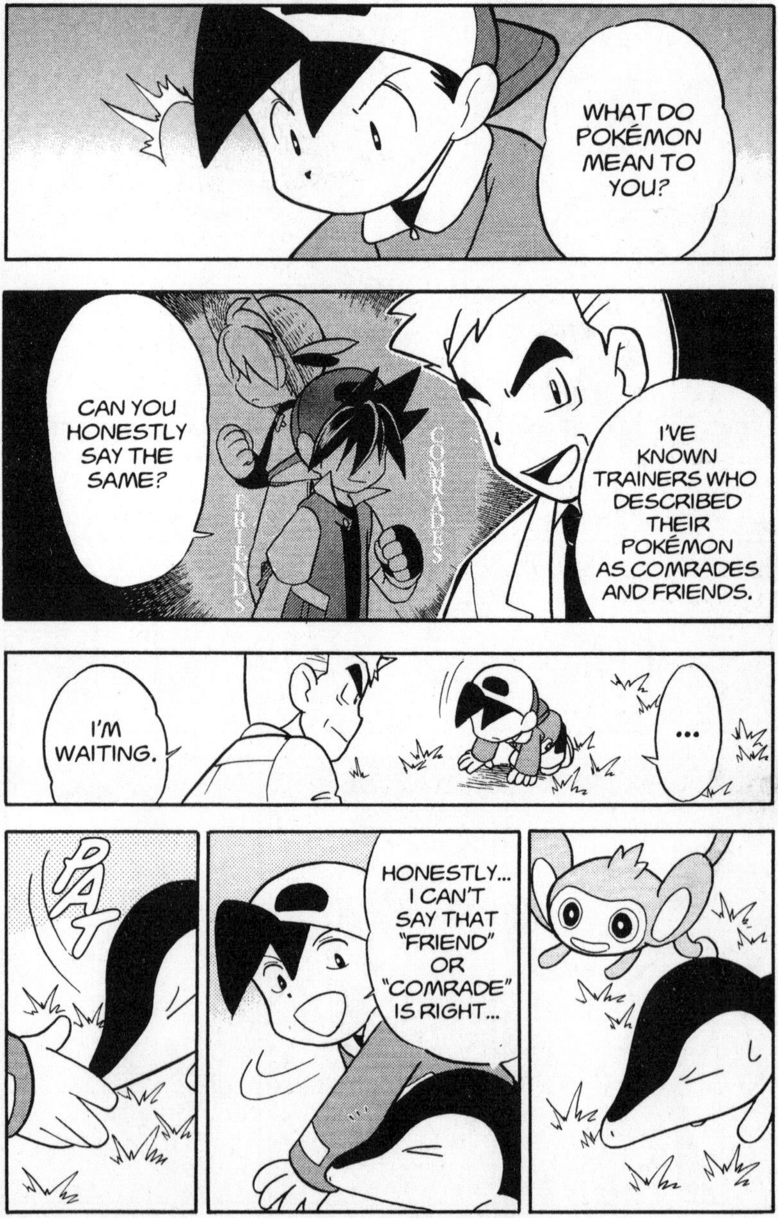
WHAT DO POKÉMON MEAN TO YOU?
I'VE KNOWN TRAINERS WHO DESCRIBED THEIR POKÉMON AS COMRADES AND FRIENDS.
COMRADES
FRIENDS
CAN YOU HONESTLY SAY THE SAME?
...
I'M WAITING.
HONESTLY... I CAN'T SAY THAT "FRIEND" OR "COMRADE" IS RIGHT...
PAT

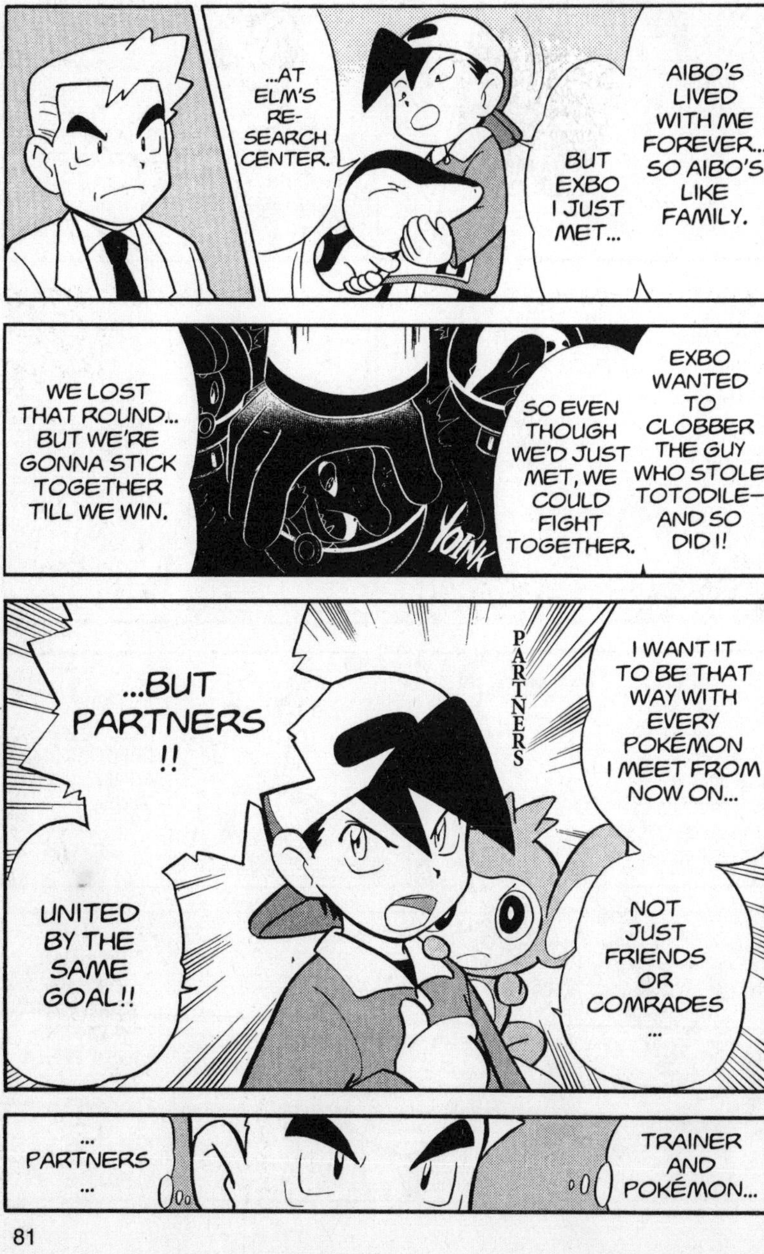
AIBO'S LIVED WITH ME FOREVER... SO AIBO'S LIKE FAMILY.
BUT EXBO I JUST MET...
...AT ELM'S RE-SEARCH CENTER.
EXBO WANTED TO CLOBBER THE GUY WHO STOLE TOTODILE— AND SO DID I!
SO EVEN THOUGH WE'D JUST MET, WE COULD FIGHT TOGETHER.
YOINK
WE LOST THAT ROUND... BUT WE'RE GONNA STICK TOGETHER TILL WE WIN.
I WANT IT TO BE THAT WAY WITH EVERY POKÉMON I MEET FROM NOW ON...
NOT JUST FRIENDS OR COMRADES ...
PARTNERS
...BUT PARTNERS !!
UNITED BY THE SAME GOAL!!
TRAINER AND POKÉMON...
... PARTNERS ...

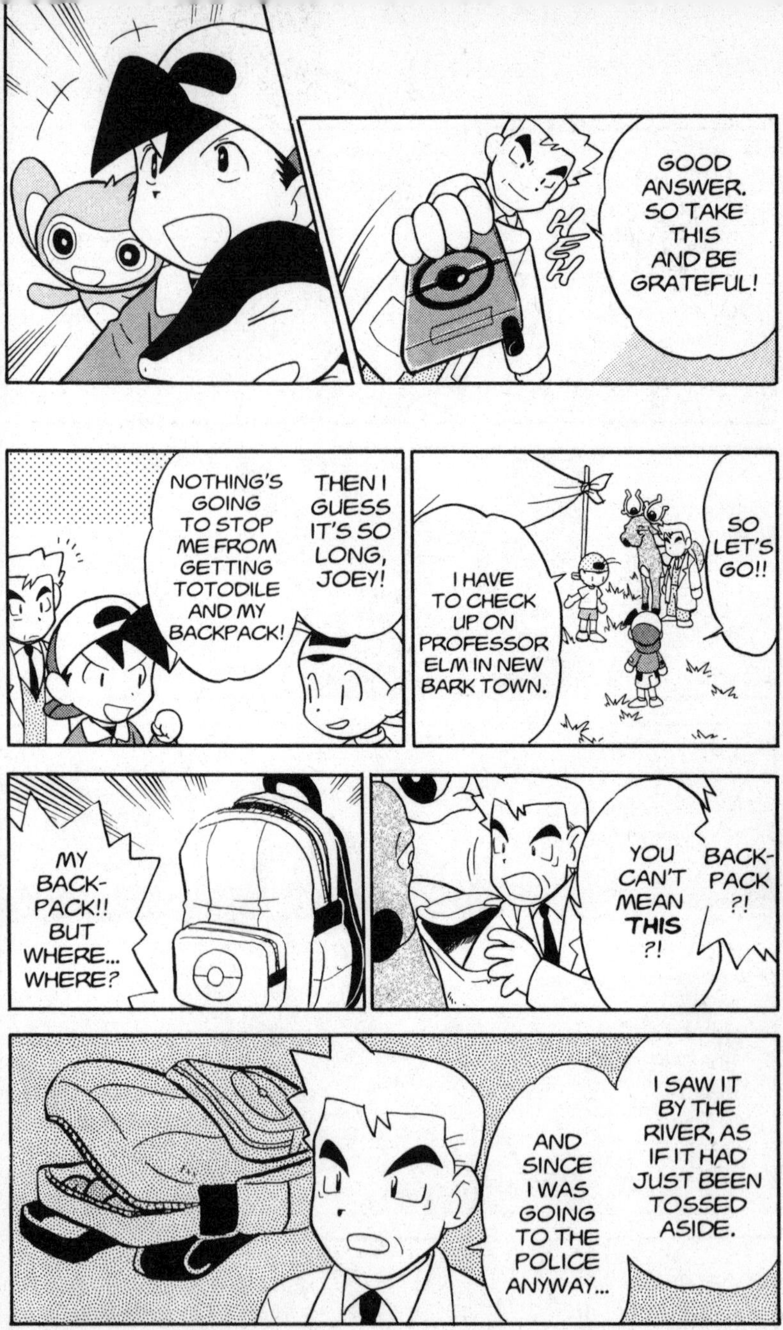
GOOD ANSWER. SO TAKE THIS AND BE GRATEFUL!
HEH
SO LET'S GO!!
I HAVE TO CHECK UP ON PROFESSOR ELM IN NEW BARK TOWN.
THEN I GUESS IT'S SO LONG, JOEY!
NOTHING'S GOING TO STOP ME FROM GETTING TOTODILE AND MY BACKPACK!
BACK-PACK?!
YOU CAN'T MEAN **THIS**?!
MY BACK-PACK!! BUT WHERE... WHERE?
I SAW IT BY THE RIVER, AS IF IT HAD JUST BEEN TOSSED ASIDE.
AND SINCE I WAS GOING TO THE POLICE ANYWAY...

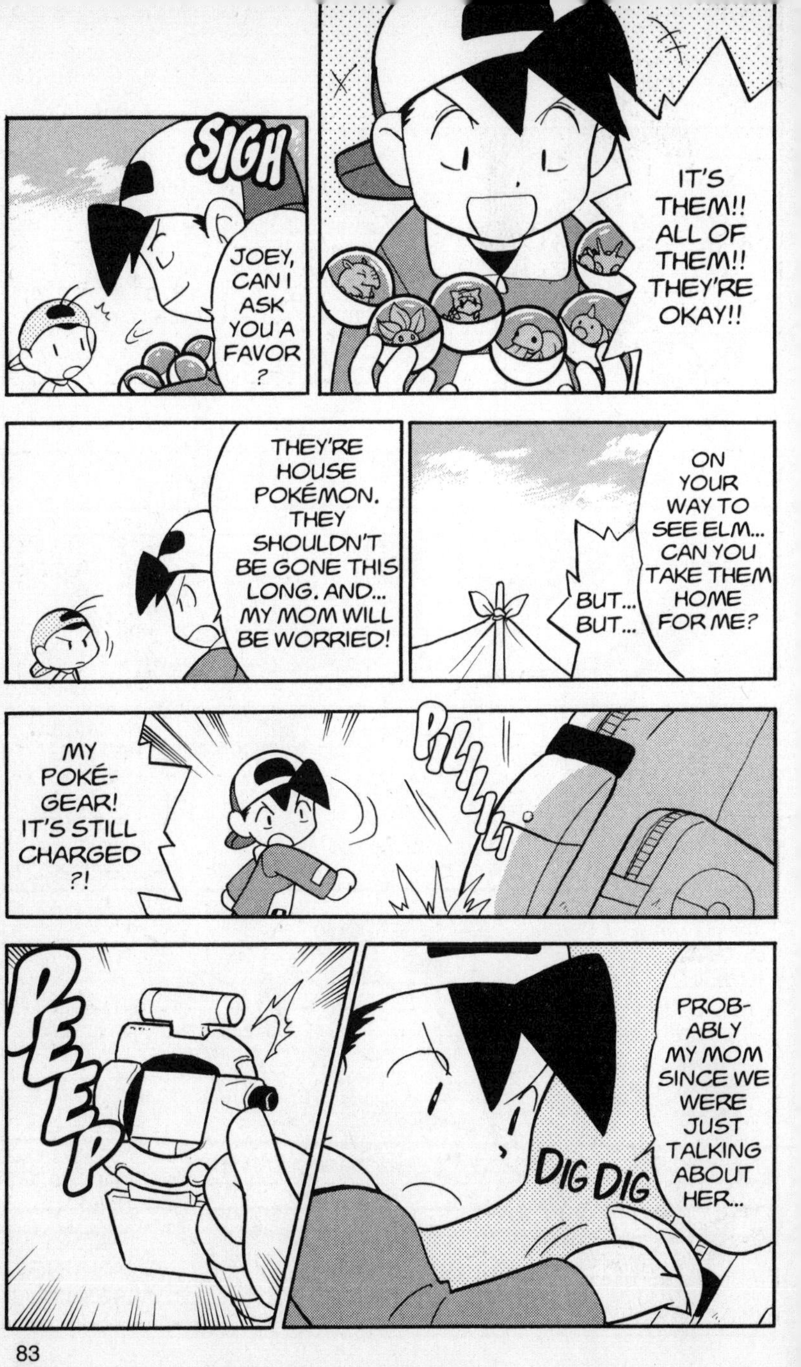
IT'S THEM!! ALL OF THEM!! THEY'RE OKAY!!
SIGH
JOEY, CAN I ASK YOU A FAVOR?
ON YOUR WAY TO SEE ELM... CAN YOU TAKE THEM HOME FOR ME?
BUT... BUT...
THEY'RE HOUSE POKÉMON. THEY SHOULDN'T BE GONE THIS LONG. AND... MY MOM WILL BE WORRIED!
PILILILI
MY POKÉ-GEAR! IT'S STILL CHARGED?!
PROB-ABLY MY MOM SINCE WE WERE JUST TALKING ABOUT HER...
DIG DIG
PEEP

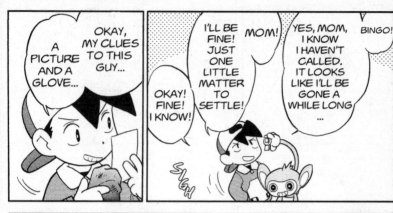

BINGO!
YES, MOM, I KNOW I HAVEN'T CALLED. IT LOOKS LIKE I'LL BE GONE A WHILE LONG ...
MOM!
I'LL BE FINE! JUST ONE LITTLE MATTER TO SETTLE!
OKAY! FINE! I KNOW!
SIGH
OKAY, MY CLUES TO THIS GUY...
A PICTURE AND A GLOVE...
!
SILVE
WHY WOULD HE HAVE "SILVER" STITCHED INTO THE INSIDE OF HIS GLOVE...
...UNLESS THAT'S HIS NAME!!
OKAY, THEN! I'M OFF!!
SEE YOU, JOEY! AND YOU TOO, OAK!
HE'S CHANGING ALREADY.
HEH
SUDDENLY I'M "OAK"...INSTEAD OF JUST "OLD MAN."

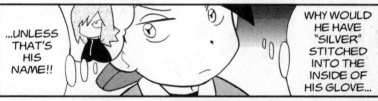

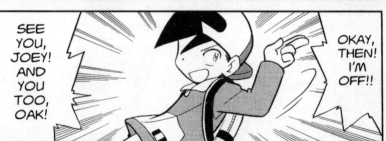

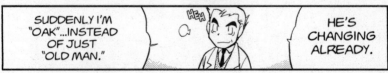

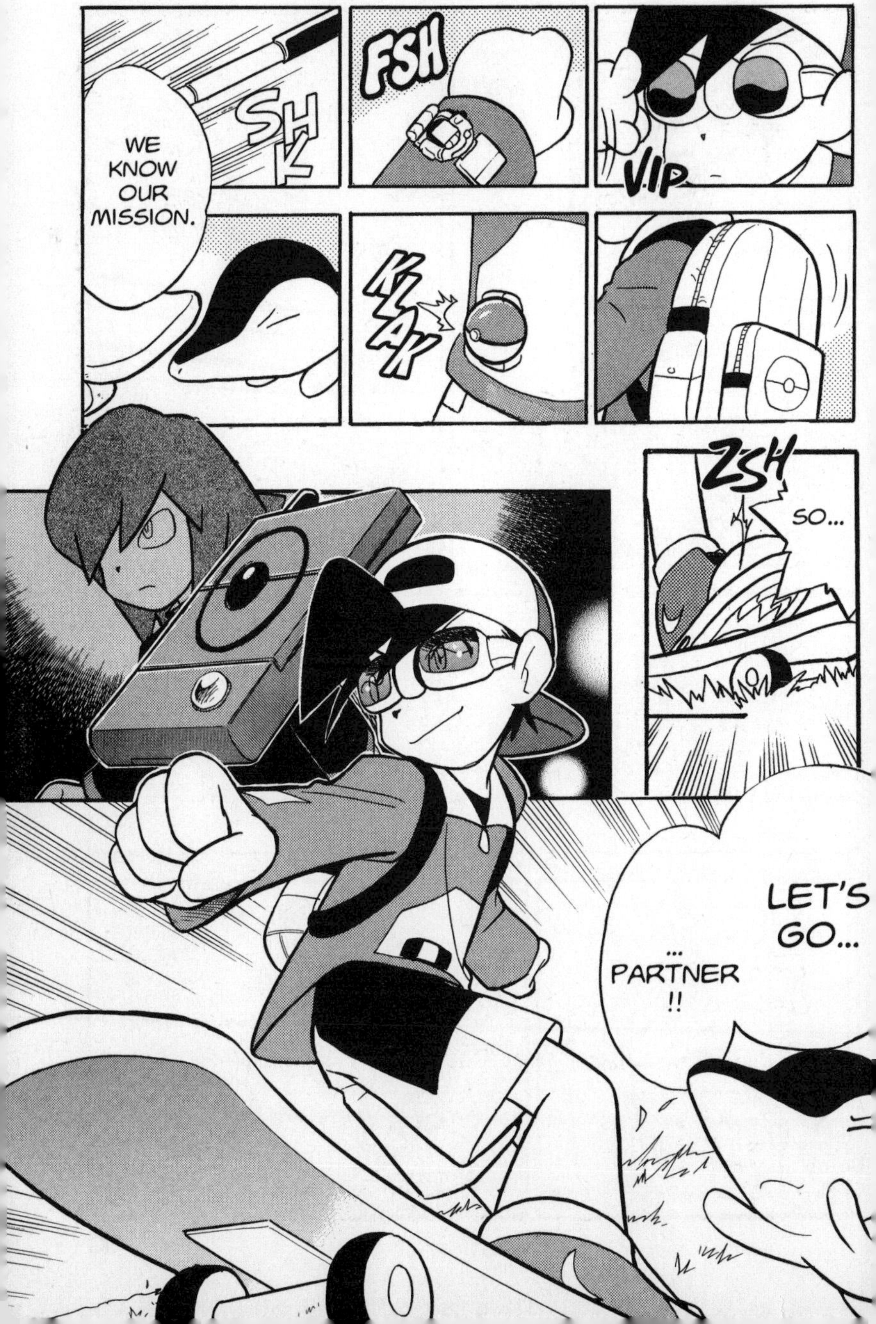
VIP
FSH
SHK
WE KNOW OUR MISSION.
KLAK
ZSH
SO...
LET'S GO...
... PARTNER !!

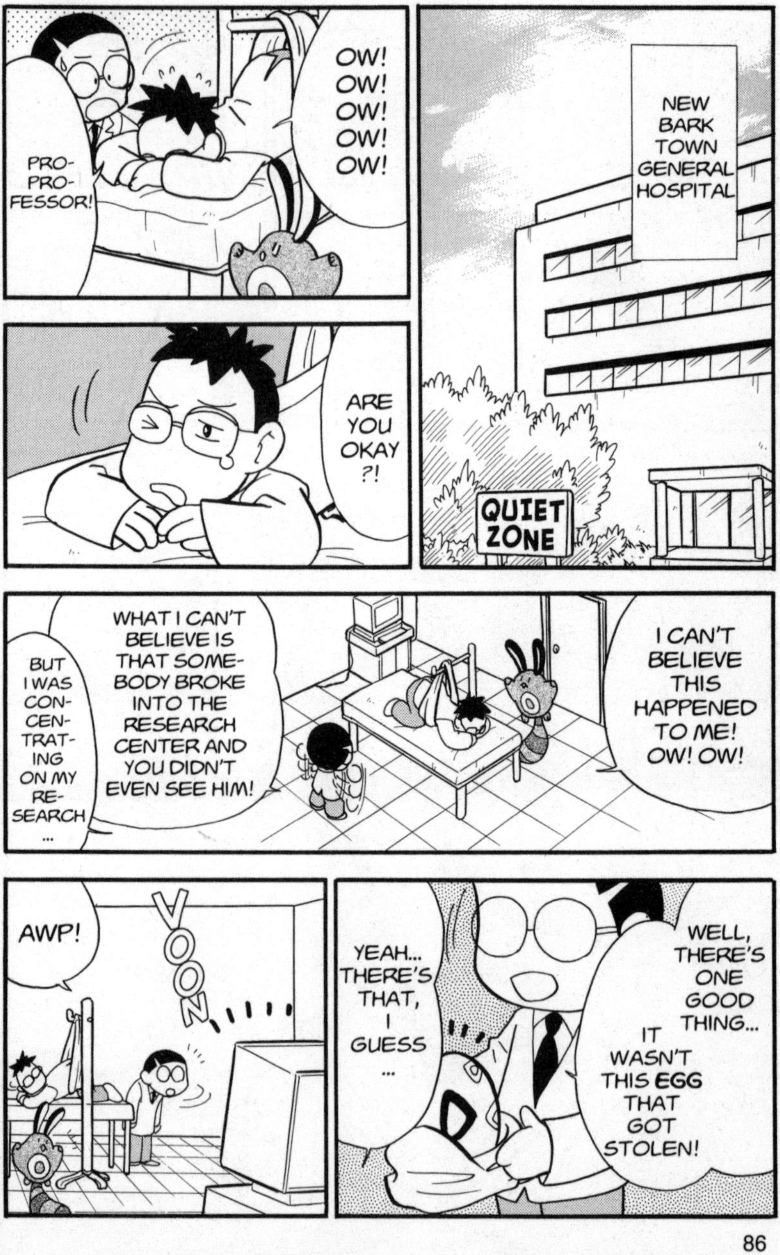
NEW BARK TOWN GENERAL HOSPITAL
QUIET ZONE
OW! OW! OW! OW! OW!
PRO-PRO-FESSOR!
ARE YOU OKAY?!
I CAN'T BELIEVE THIS HAPPENED TO ME! OW! OW!
WHAT I CAN'T BELIEVE IS THAT SOMEBODY BROKE INTO THE RESEARCH CENTER AND YOU DIDN'T EVEN SEE HIM!
BUT I WAS CONCENTRATING ON MY RESEARCH...
WELL, THERE'S ONE GOOD THING...
IT WASN'T THIS EGG THAT GOT STOLEN!
YEAH... THERE'S THAT, I GUESS...
VOON
AWP!

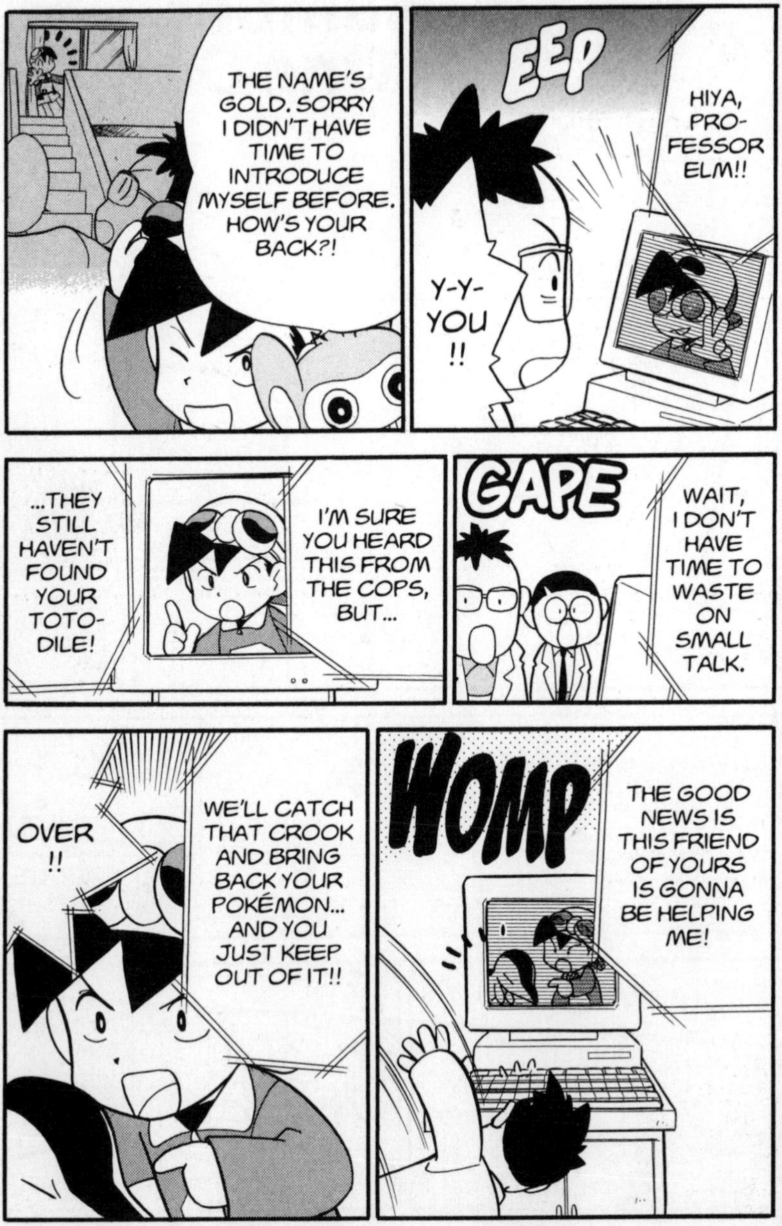
EEP
HIYA, PRO-FESSOR ELM!!
Y-Y-YOU!!
THE NAME'S GOLD. SORRY I DIDN'T HAVE TIME TO INTRODUCE MYSELF BEFORE. HOW'S YOUR BACK?!
GAPE
WAIT, I DON'T HAVE TIME TO WASTE ON SMALL TALK.
I'M SURE YOU HEARD THIS FROM THE COPS, BUT...
...THEY STILL HAVEN'T FOUND YOUR TOTO-DILE!
WOMP
THE GOOD NEWS IS THIS FRIEND OF YOURS IS GONNA BE HELPING ME!
WE'LL CATCH THAT CROOK AND BRING BACK YOUR POKÉMON... AND YOU JUST KEEP OUT OF IT!!
OVER!!

96 Number One Donphan

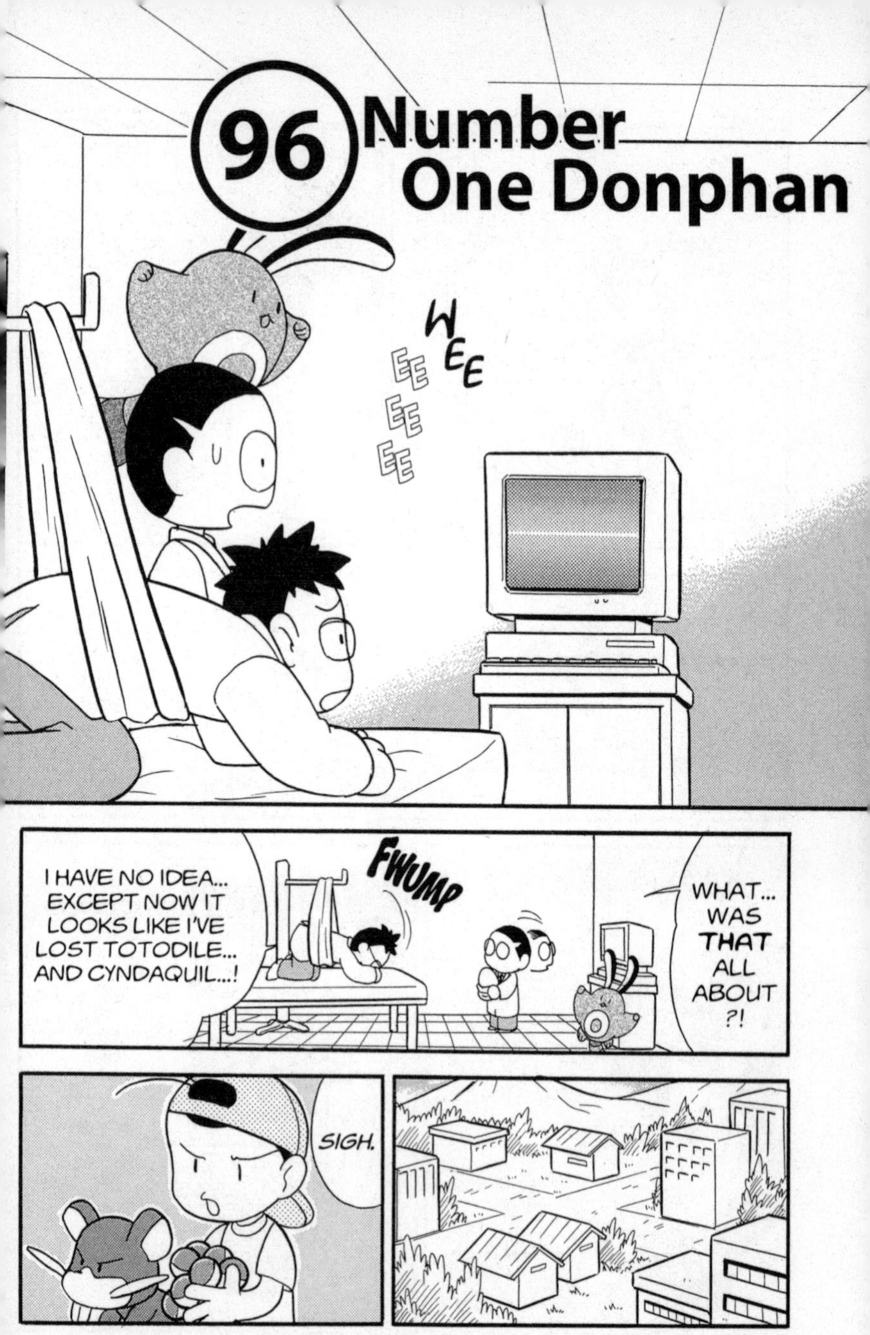
WEEEEEEE
WHAT... WAS THAT ALL ABOUT?!
FWUMP
I HAVE NO IDEA... EXCEPT NOW IT LOOKS LIKE I'VE LOST TOTODILE... AND CYNDAQUIL...!
SIGH.

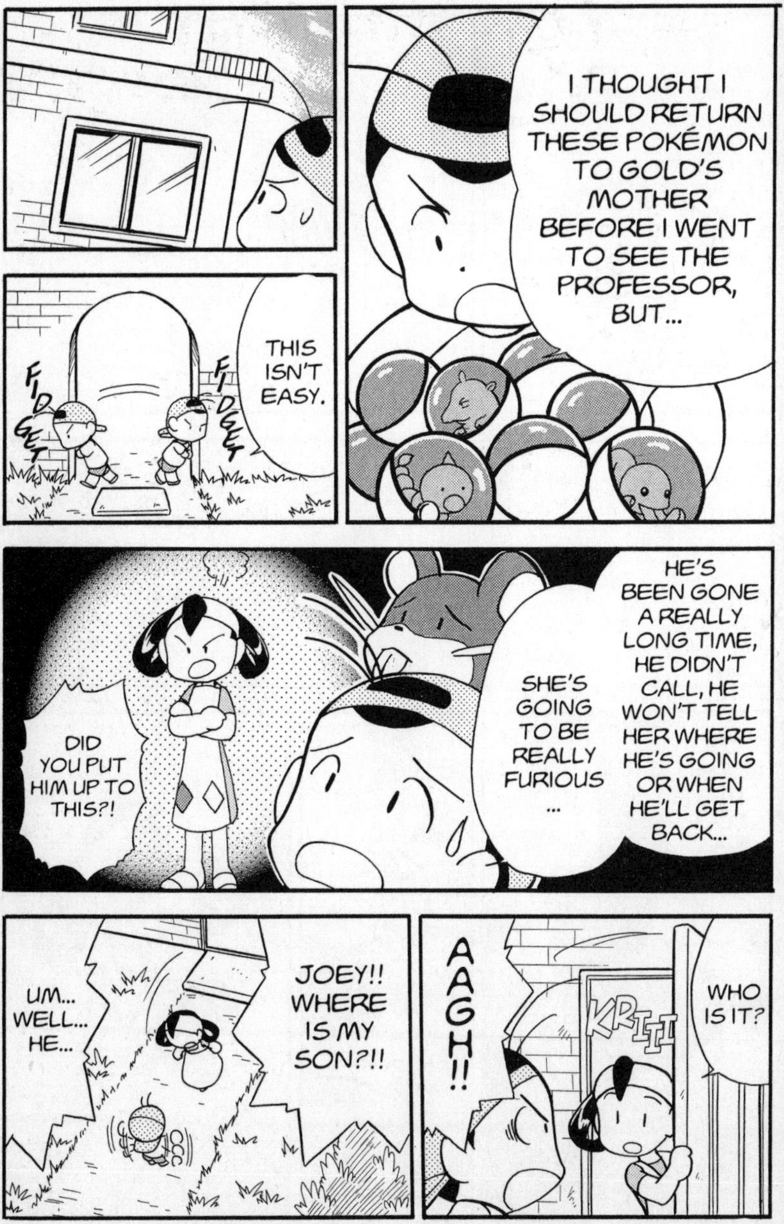
I THOUGHT I SHOULD RETURN THESE POKÉMON TO GOLD'S MOTHER BEFORE I WENT TO SEE THE PROFESSOR, BUT...
THIS ISN'T EASY.
FIDGET
FIDGET
HE'S BEEN GONE A REALLY LONG TIME, HE DIDN'T CALL, HE WON'T TELL HER WHERE HE'S GOING OR WHEN HE'LL GET BACK...
SHE'S GOING TO BE REALLY FURIOUS ...
DID YOU PUT HIM UP TO THIS?!
WHO IS IT?
KRIII
AAGH!!
JOEY!! WHERE IS MY SON?!!
UM... WELL... HE...

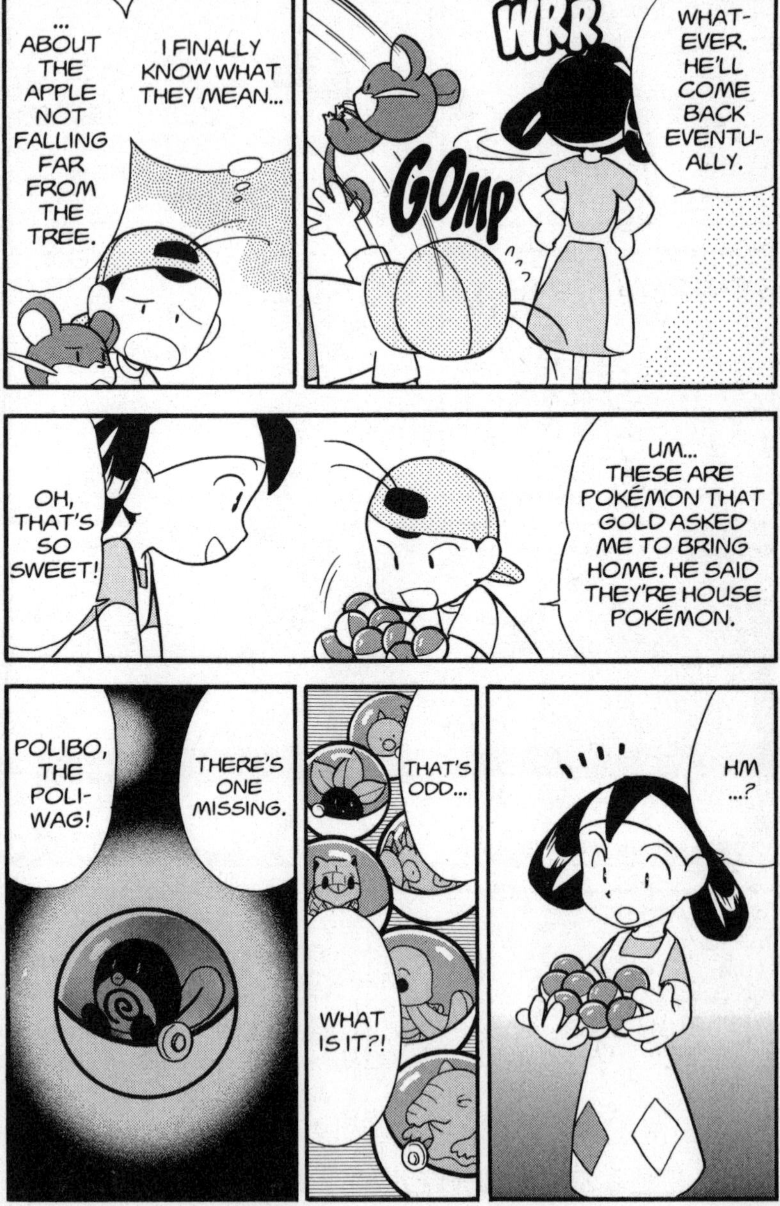
WRR
WHATEVER. HE'LL COME BACK EVENTUALLY.
GOMP
I FINALLY KNOW WHAT THEY MEAN...
... ABOUT THE APPLE NOT FALLING FAR FROM THE TREE.
UM... THESE ARE POKÉMON THAT GOLD ASKED ME TO BRING HOME. HE SAID THEY'RE HOUSE POKÉMON.
OH, THAT'S SO SWEET!
HM ...?
THAT'S ODD...
WHAT IS IT?!
THERE'S ONE MISSING.
POLIBO, THE POLIWAG!

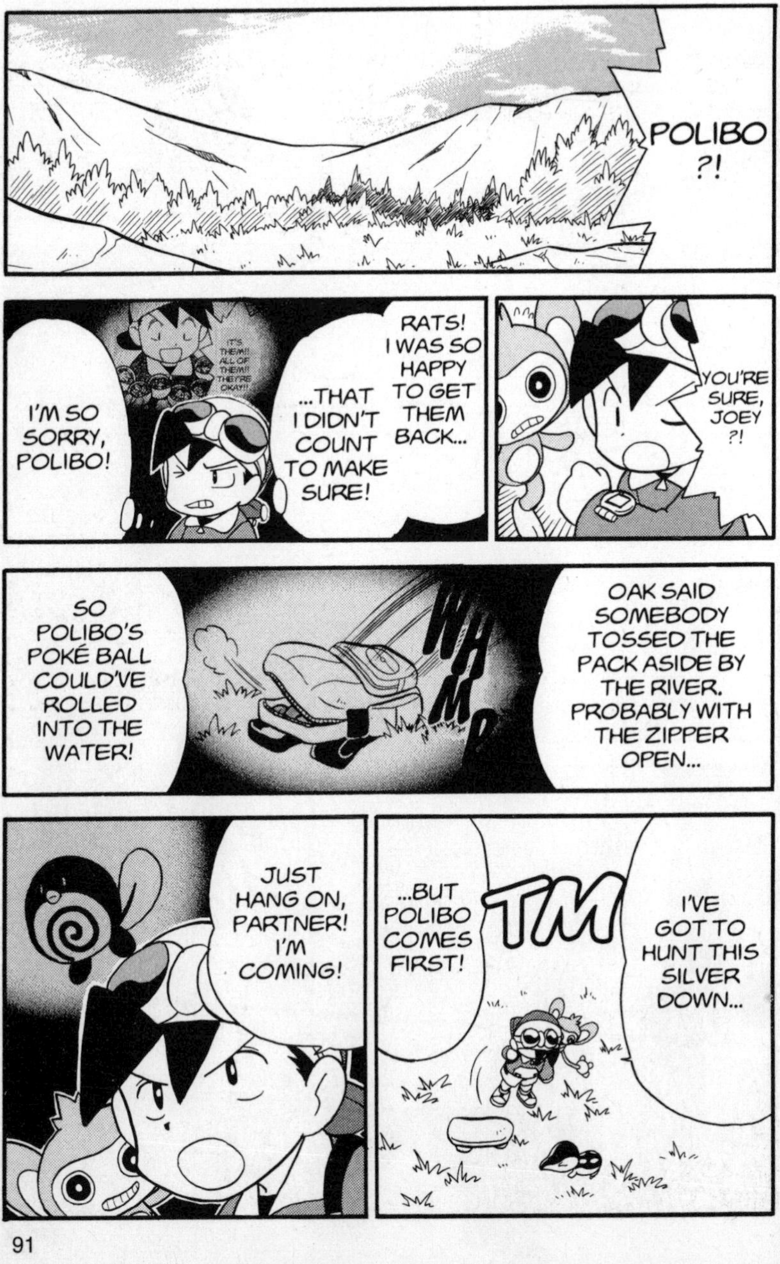
POLIBO ?!
YOU'RE SURE, JOEY ?!
RATS! I WAS SO HAPPY TO GET THEM BACK...
...THAT I DIDN'T COUNT TO MAKE SURE!
IT'S THEM!! ALL OF THEM!! THEY'RE OKAY!!!
I'M SO SORRY, POLIBO!
OAK SAID SOMEBODY TOSSED THE PACK ASIDE BY THE RIVER. PROBABLY WITH THE ZIPPER OPEN...
WHUMP
SO POLIBO'S POKÉ BALL COULD'VE ROLLED INTO THE WATER!
I'VE GOT TO HUNT THIS SILVER DOWN...
TM
...BUT POLIBO COMES FIRST!
JUST HANG ON, PARTNER! I'M COMING!

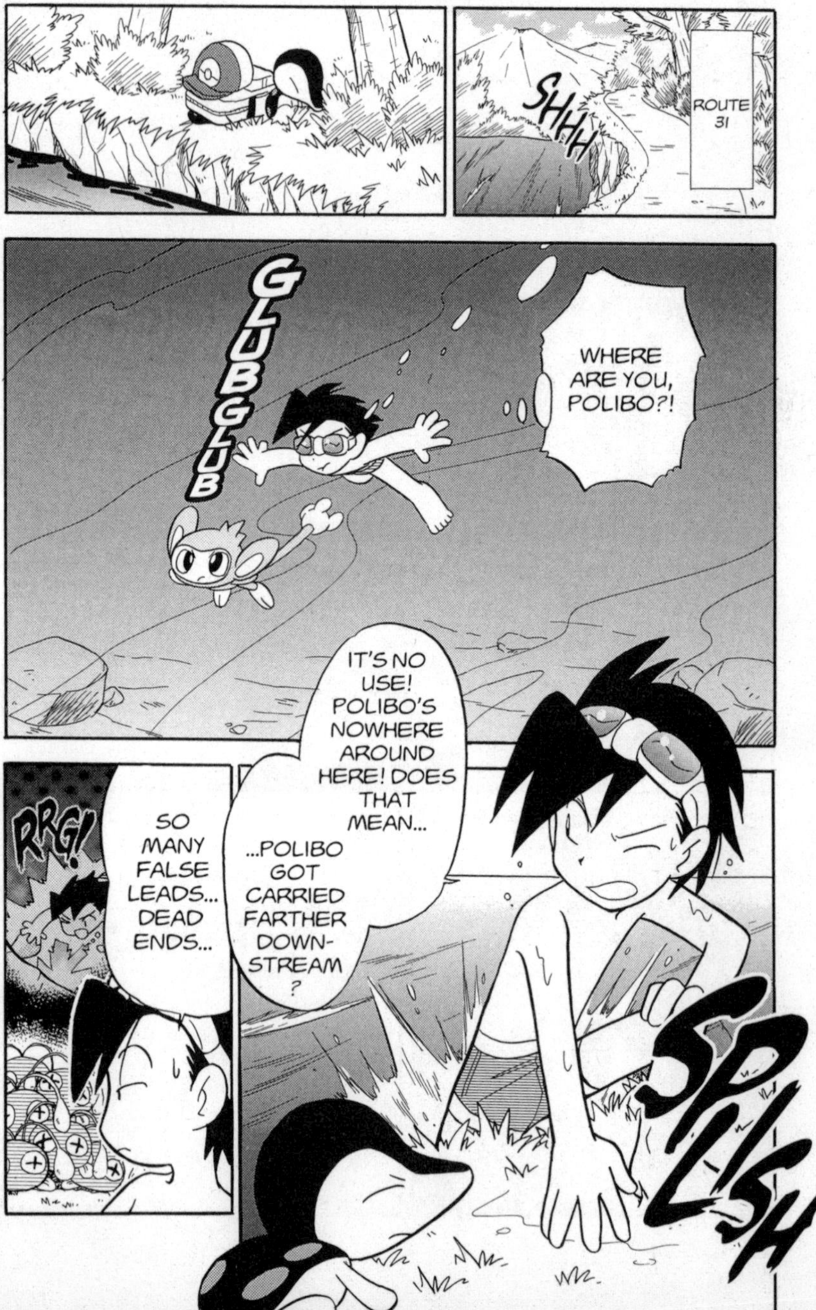
SHHH
ROUTE 31
WHERE ARE YOU, POLIBO?!
GLUBGLUB
IT'S NO USE! POLIBO'S NOWHERE AROUND HERE! DOES THAT MEAN...
...POLIBO GOT CARRIED FARTHER DOWN-STREAM?
SPLISH
RRG!
SO MANY FALSE LEADS... DEAD ENDS...

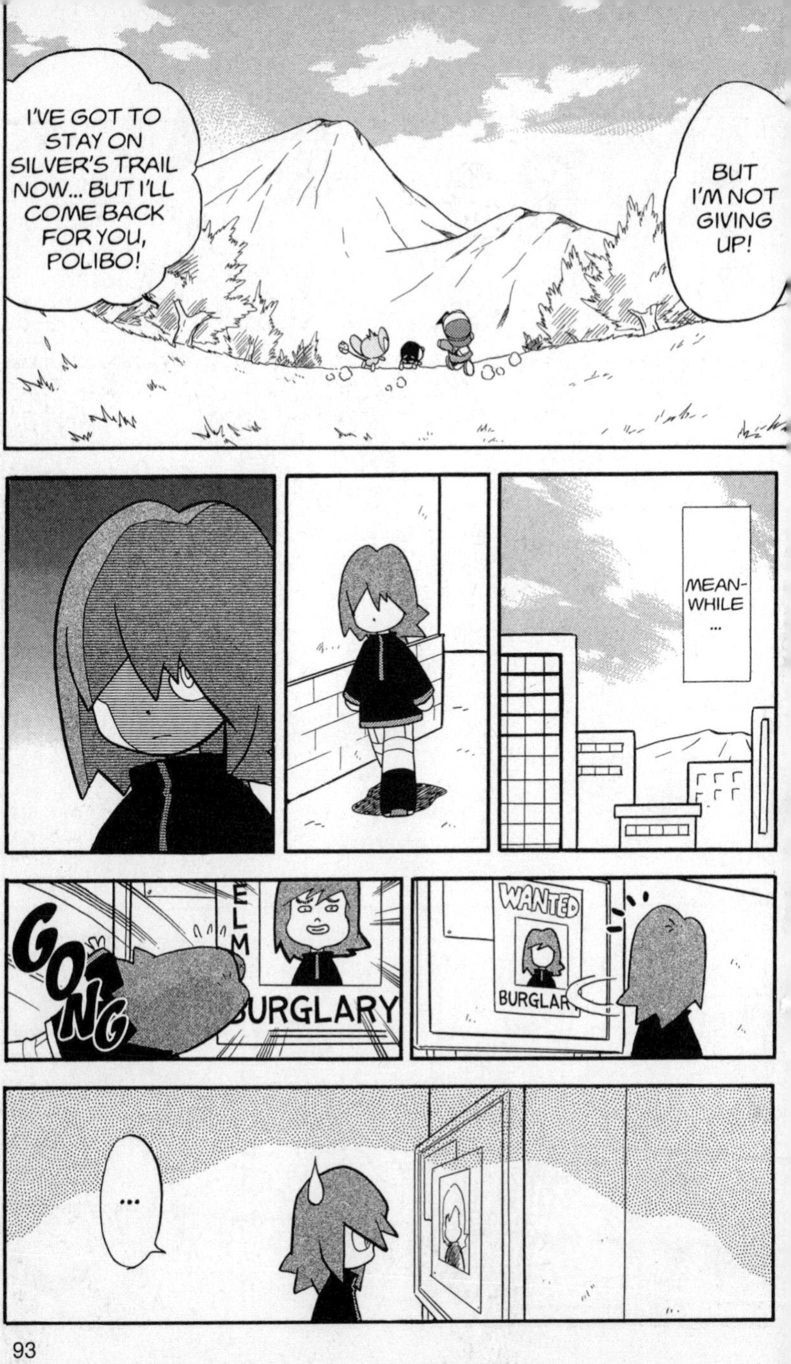
I'VE GOT TO STAY ON SILVER'S TRAIL NOW... BUT I'LL COME BACK FOR YOU, POLIBO!
BUT I'M NOT GIVING UP!
MEAN-WHILE ...
WANTED
BURGLARY
ELM
BURGLARY
GONG
...

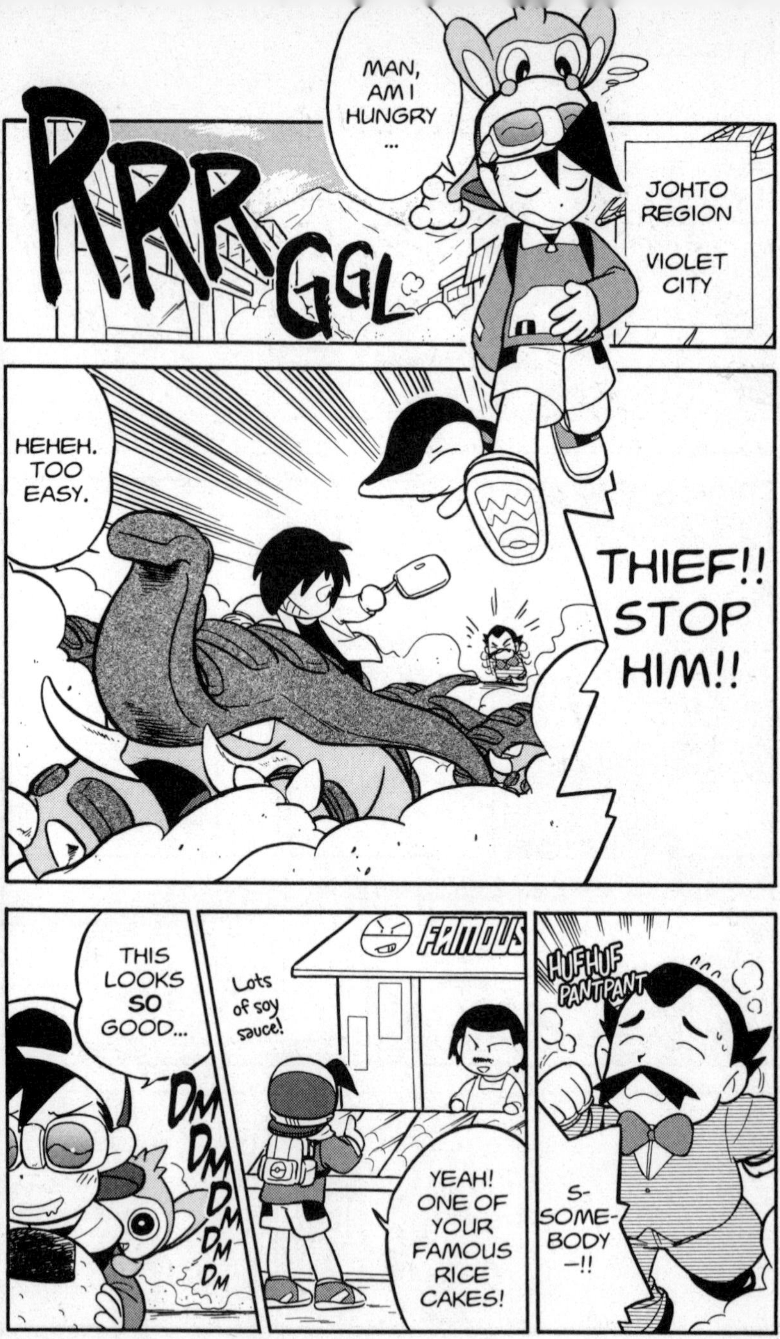
JOHTO REGION
VIOLET CITY
MAN, AM I HUNGRY ...
RRRGGL
THIEF!! STOP HIM!!
HEHEH. TOO EASY.
HUFHUF PANTPANT
S-SOMEBODY—!!
FAMOUS
YEAH! ONE OF YOUR FAMOUS RICE CAKES!
Lots of soy sauce!
THIS LOOKS SO GOOD...
DMDMDMDMDMDMDM

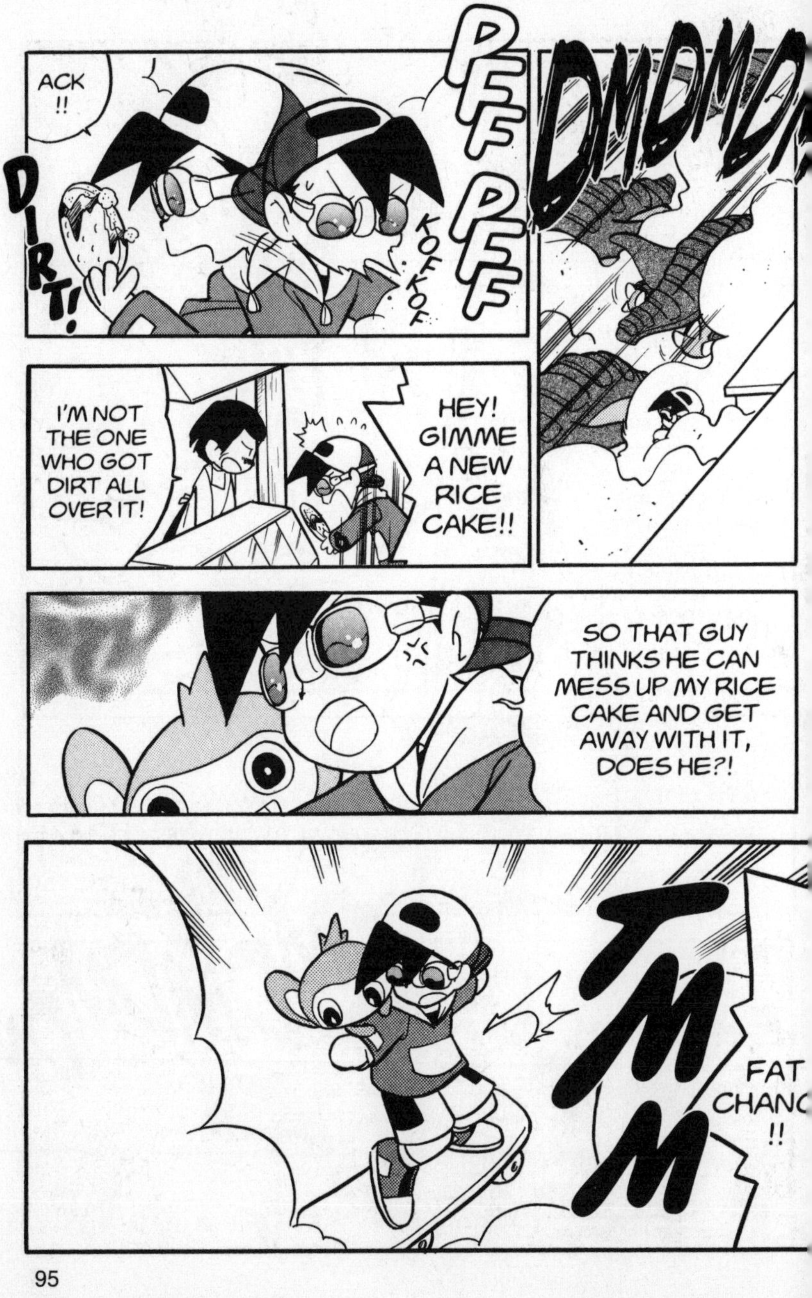
DMDMDM
ACK !!
PFF PFF
KOF KOF
DIRT!
HEY! GIMME A NEW RICE CAKE!!
I'M NOT THE ONE WHO GOT DIRT ALL OVER IT!
SO THAT GUY THINKS HE CAN MESS UP MY RICE CAKE AND GET AWAY WITH IT, DOES HE?!
TMM
FAT CHANC !!

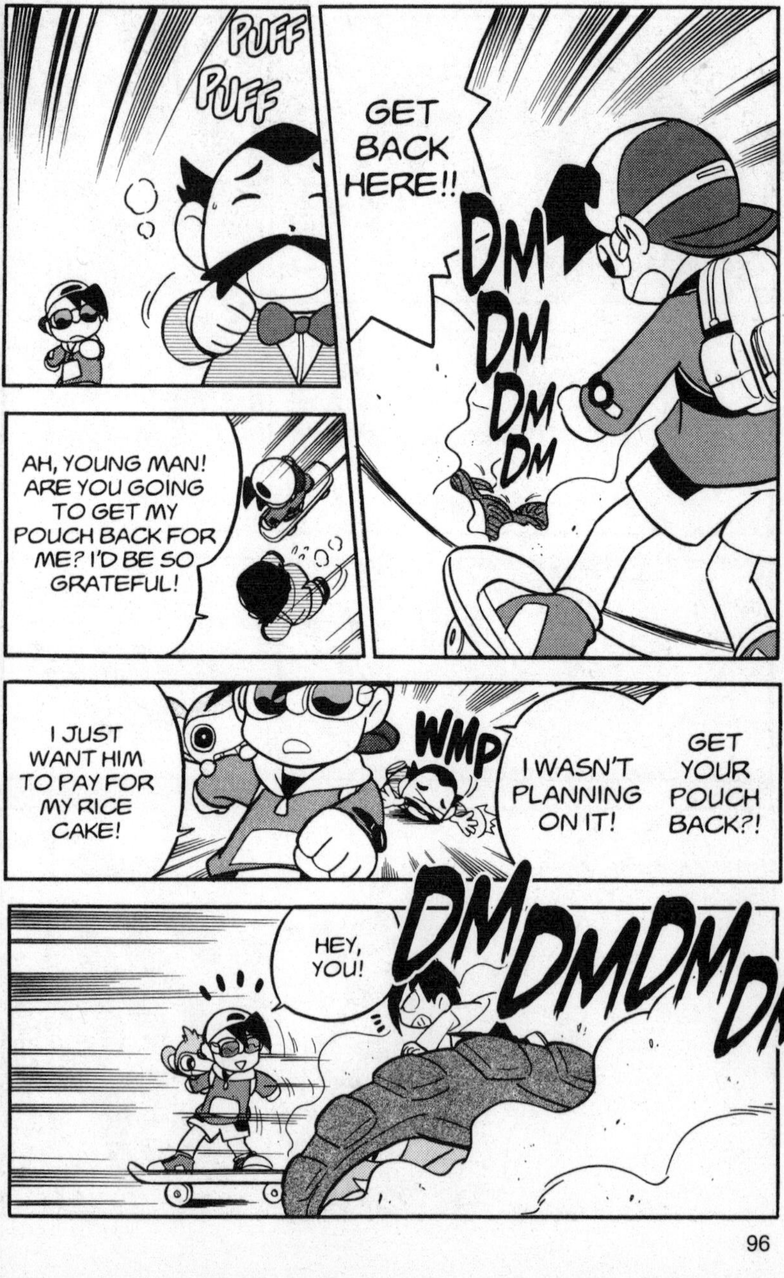
GET BACK HERE!!
DM DM DM DM
PUFF PUFF
AH, YOUNG MAN! ARE YOU GOING TO GET MY POUCH BACK FOR ME? I'D BE SO GRATEFUL!
GET YOUR POUCH BACK?!
I WASN'T PLANNING ON IT!
WMP
I JUST WANT HIM TO PAY FOR MY RICE CAKE!
DMDMDMDM
HEY, YOU!

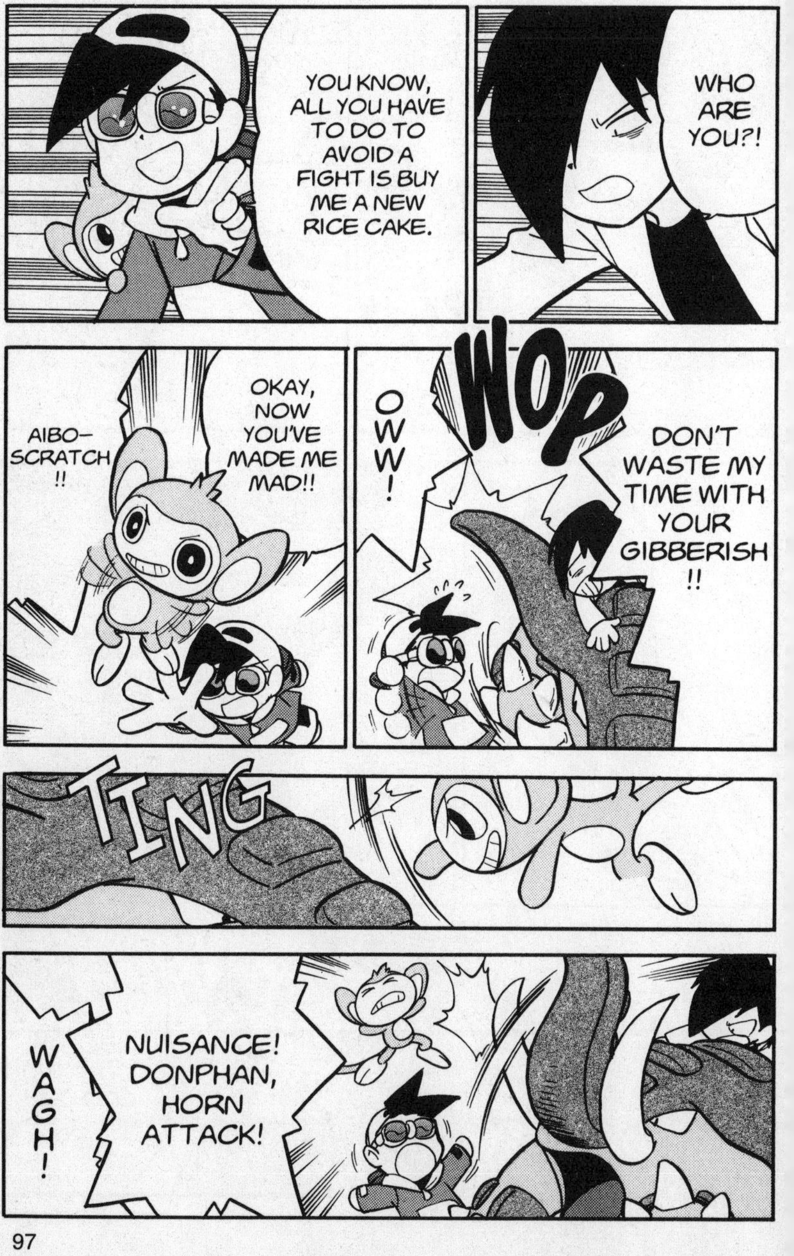
WHO ARE YOU?!
YOU KNOW, ALL YOU HAVE TO DO TO AVOID A FIGHT IS BUY ME A NEW RICE CAKE.
WOP
DON'T WASTE MY TIME WITH YOUR GIBBERISH!!
OWW!
OKAY, NOW YOU'VE MADE ME MAD!!
AIBO-SCRATCH!!
TING
NUISANCE! DONPHAN, HORN ATTACK!
WAGH!

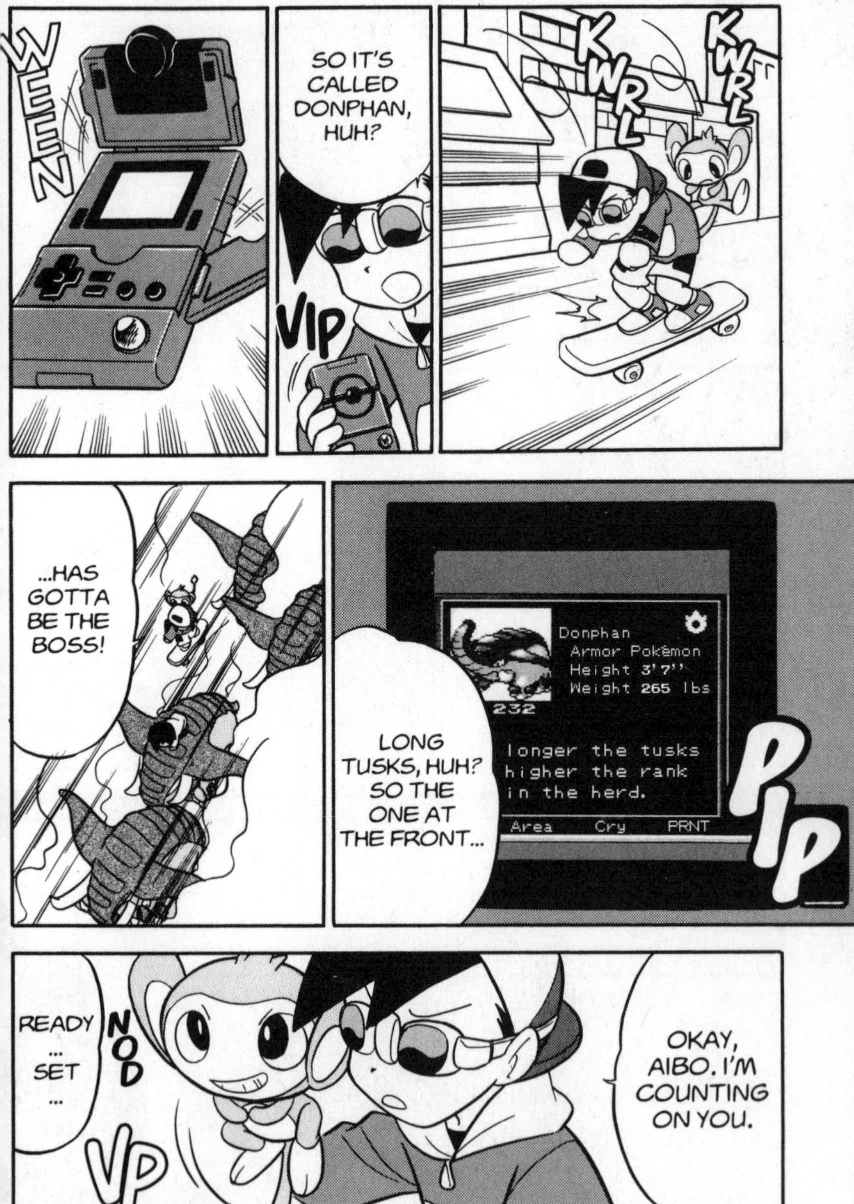
KWRL
KWRL
SO IT'S CALLED DONPHAN, HUH?
VIP
WEEN
Donphan
Armor Pokémon
Height 3'7''
Weight 265 lbs
232
longer the tusks
higher the rank
in the herd.
Area Cry PRNT
LONG TUSKS, HUH? SO THE ONE AT THE FRONT...
PIP
...HAS GOTTA BE THE BOSS!
OKAY, AIBO. I'M COUNTING ON YOU.
NOD
VP
READY ... SET ...

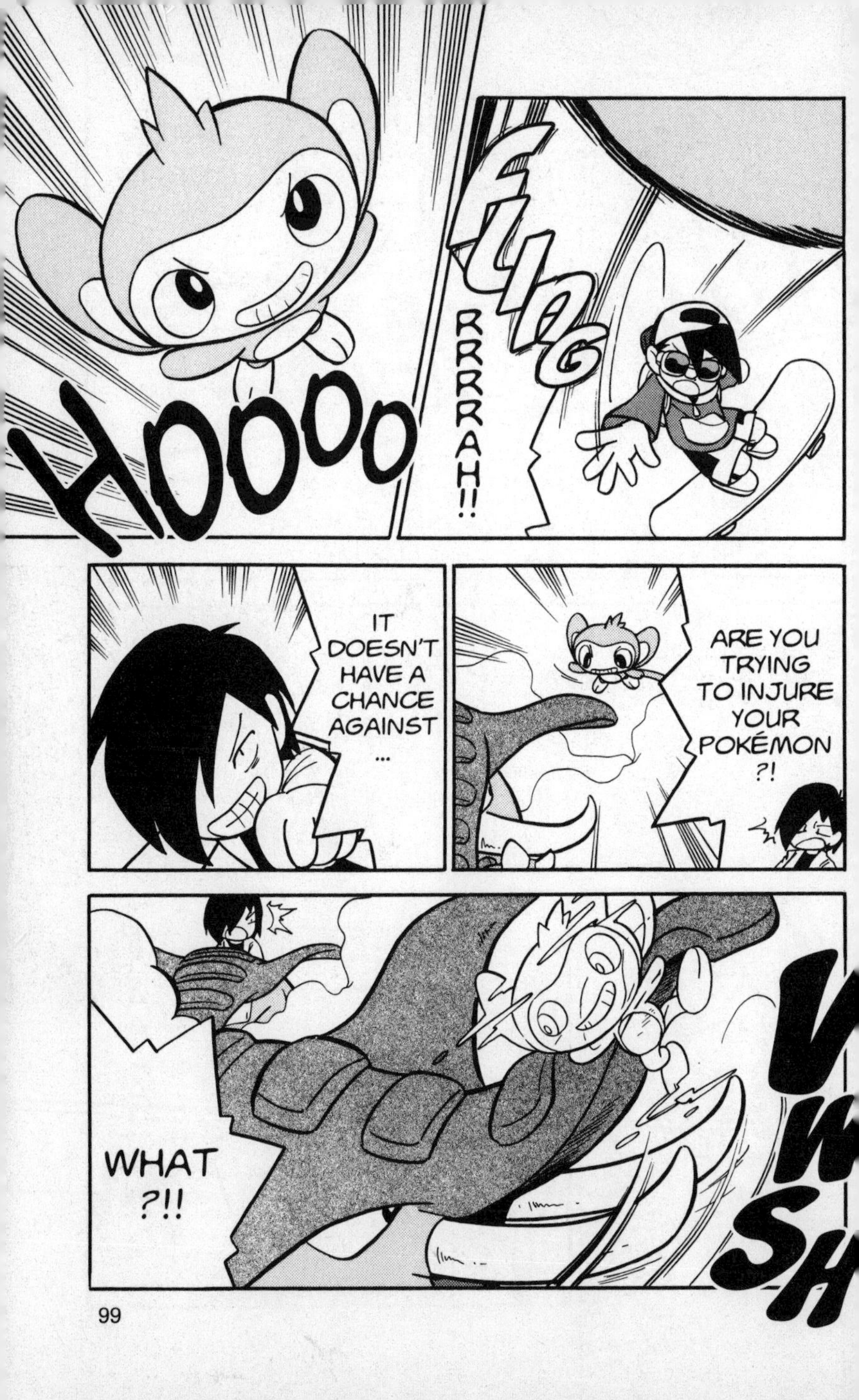
FLING
RRRRAH!!
HOOOO
ARE YOU TRYING TO INJURE YOUR POKÉMON ?!
IT DOESN'T HAVE A CHANCE AGAINST ...
WHAT ?!!

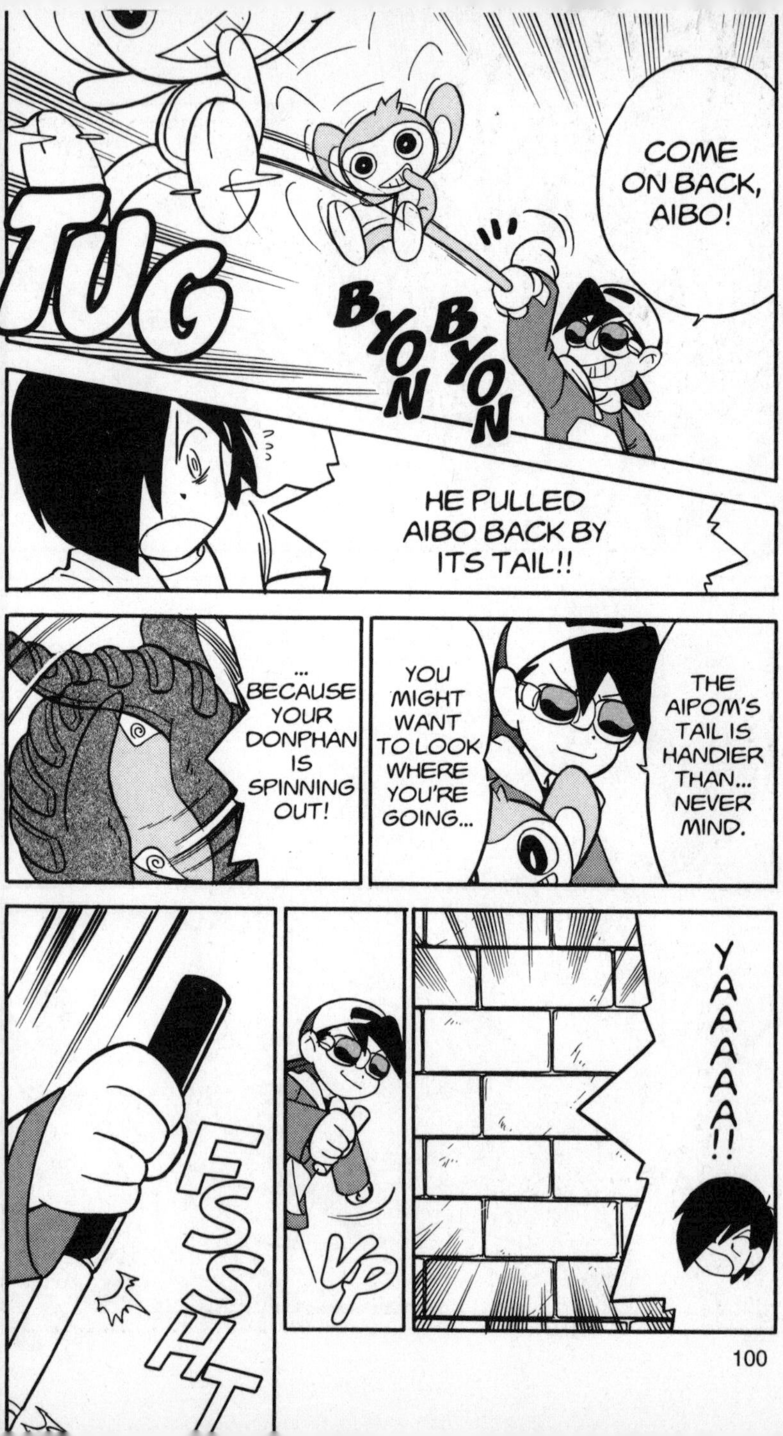
COME ON BACK, AIBO!
BYON BYON
TUG
HE PULLED AIBO BACK BY ITS TAIL!!
THE AIPOM'S TAIL IS HANDIER THAN... NEVER MIND.
YOU MIGHT WANT TO LOOK WHERE YOU'RE GOING...
...BECAUSE YOUR DONPHAN IS SPINNING OUT!
YAAAAAA!!
VP
FSSHT

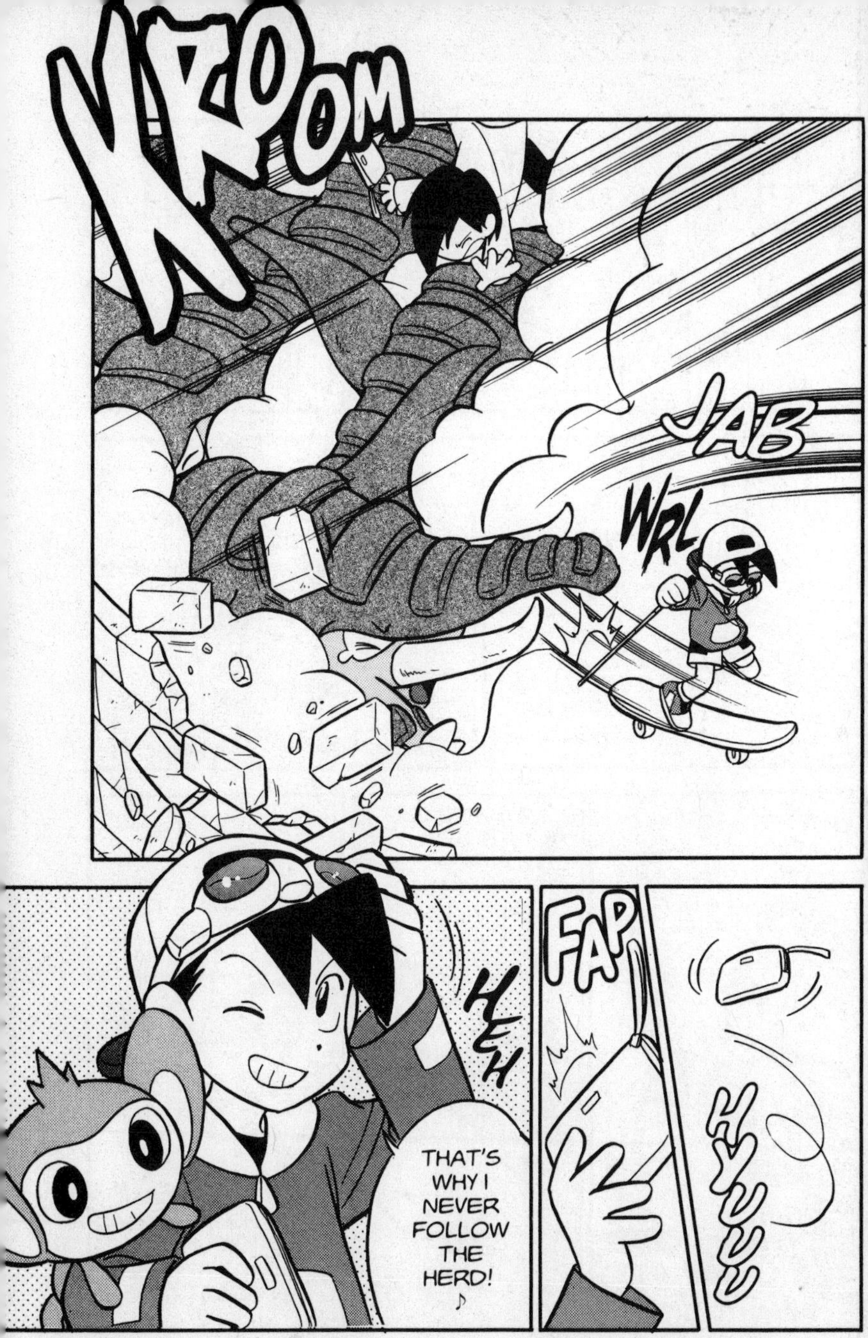
KROOM
JAB
WRL
HYUUUU
FAP
HEH
THAT'S WHY I NEVER FOLLOW THE HERD! ♪

AH AH AHA!
NOMNOM NOMNOM
YOU'RE TOO GENER-OUS!
NOMNOM
I REALLY DON'T DESERVE THIS!
IT'S REWARD ENOUGH JUST KNOWING THAT I DID THE RIGHT THING AND BROUGHT A CRIMINAL TO JUSTICE! HO HO HO...
LIAR.
LIAR.
STILL... I'M PLEASED THAT THIS POUCH IS SAFE.
MY NAME IS EARL, AND I RUN A POKÉMON ACADEMY HERE IN VIOLET CITY.
I'M SUPPOSED TO GIVE THE DOCUMENTS IN THIS POUCH TO SOMEONE TODAY... PROFESSOR ELM'S ASSISTANT.
PUH.
PRO-FESSOR ELM'S ASSISTANT IS GONNA BE HERE ?!
WHAT-WHAT-WHAT?
WRRRRL

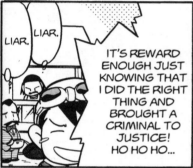

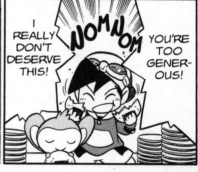

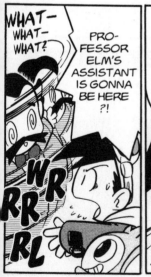

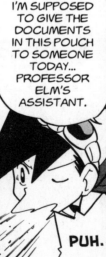

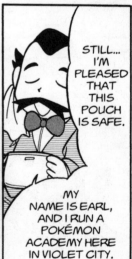

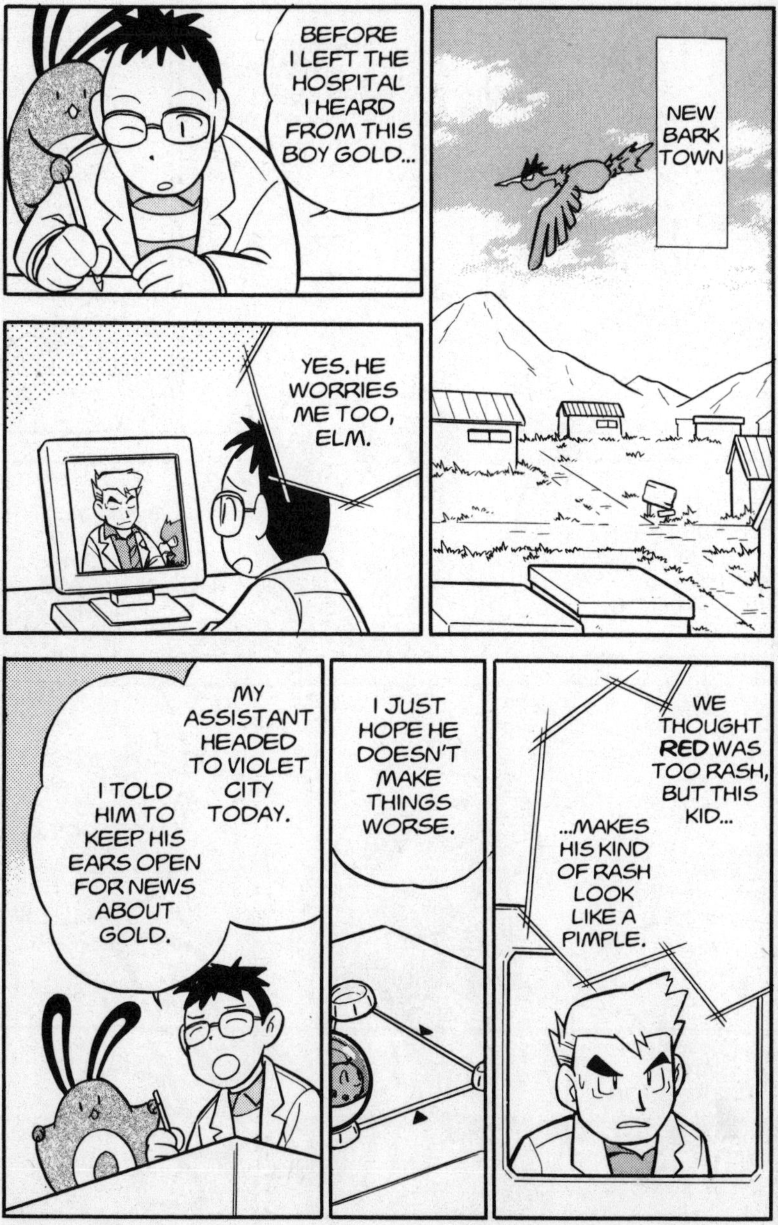
NEW BARK TOWN
BEFORE I LEFT THE HOSPITAL I HEARD FROM THIS BOY GOLD...
YES. HE WORRIES ME TOO, ELM.
WE THOUGHT RED WAS TOO RASH, BUT THIS KID...
...MAKES HIS KIND OF RASH LOOK LIKE A PIMPLE.
I JUST HOPE HE DOESN'T MAKE THINGS WORSE.
MY ASSISTANT HEADED TO VIOLET CITY TODAY.
I TOLD HIM TO KEEP HIS EARS OPEN FOR NEWS ABOUT GOLD.

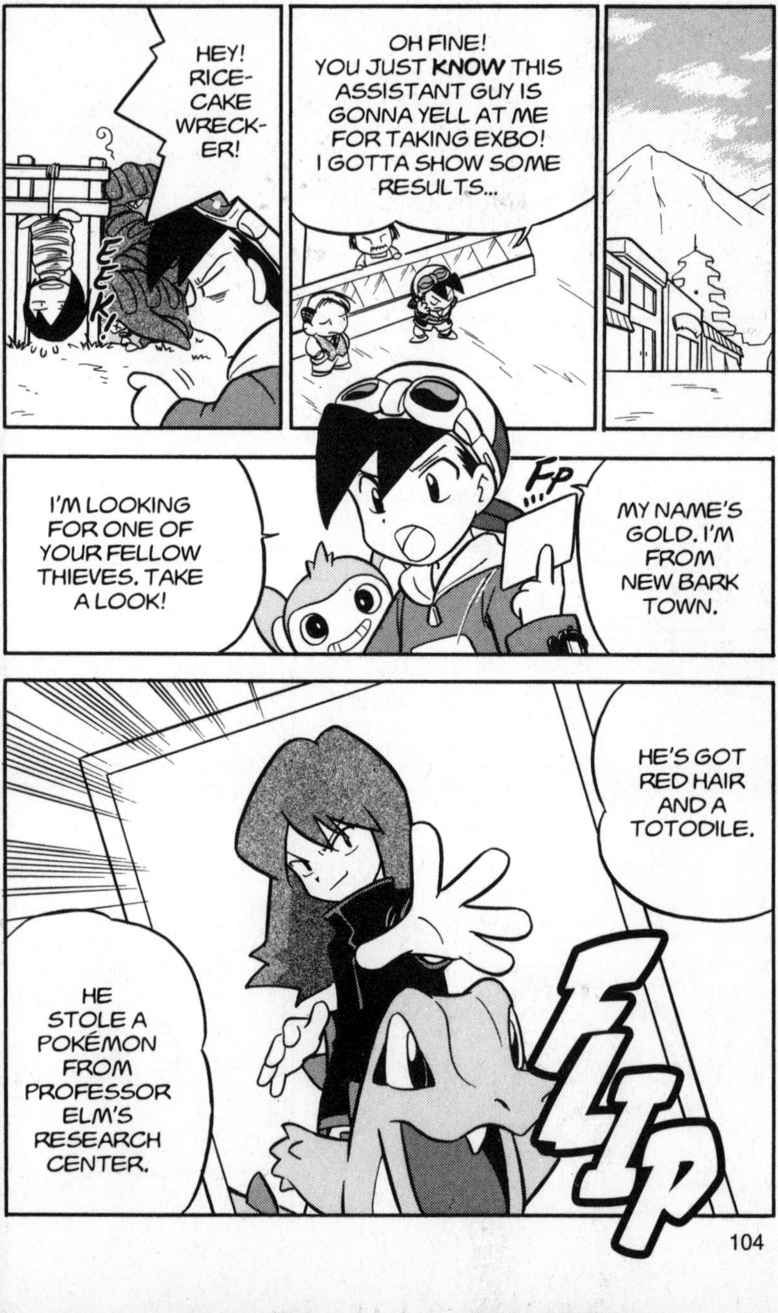
OH FINE!
YOU JUST **KNOW** THIS ASSISTANT GUY IS GONNA YELL AT ME FOR TAKING EXBO! I GOTTA SHOW SOME RESULTS...
HEY! RICE-CAKE WRECK-ER!
EEK!
MY NAME'S GOLD. I'M FROM NEW BARK TOWN.
FP
I'M LOOKING FOR ONE OF YOUR FELLOW THIEVES. TAKE A LOOK!
HE'S GOT RED HAIR AND A TOTODILE.
HE STOLE A POKéMON FROM PROFESSOR ELM'S RESEARCH CENTER.
FLIP

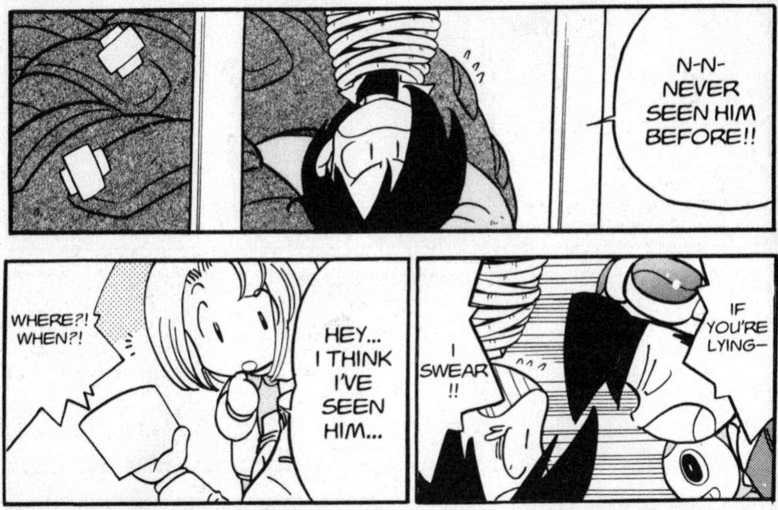
N-N-NEVER SEEN HIM BEFORE!!
IF YOU'RE LYING—
I SWEAR!!
HEY... I THINK I'VE SEEN HIM...
WHERE?! WHEN?!

97 Bellsprout Rout

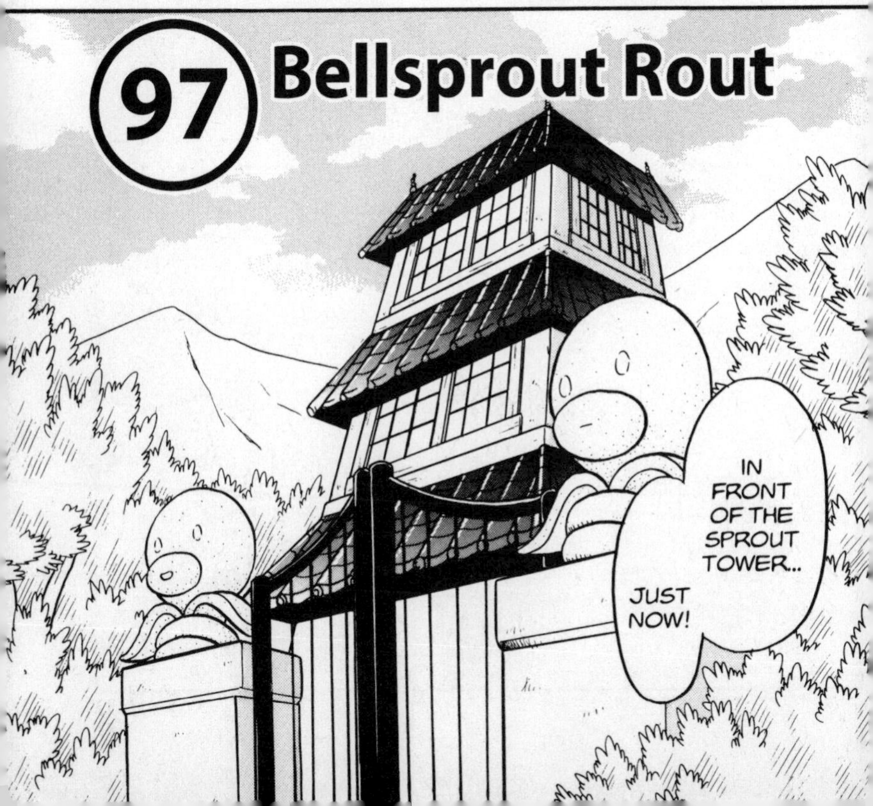
IN FRONT OF THE SPROUT TOWER...
JUST NOW!

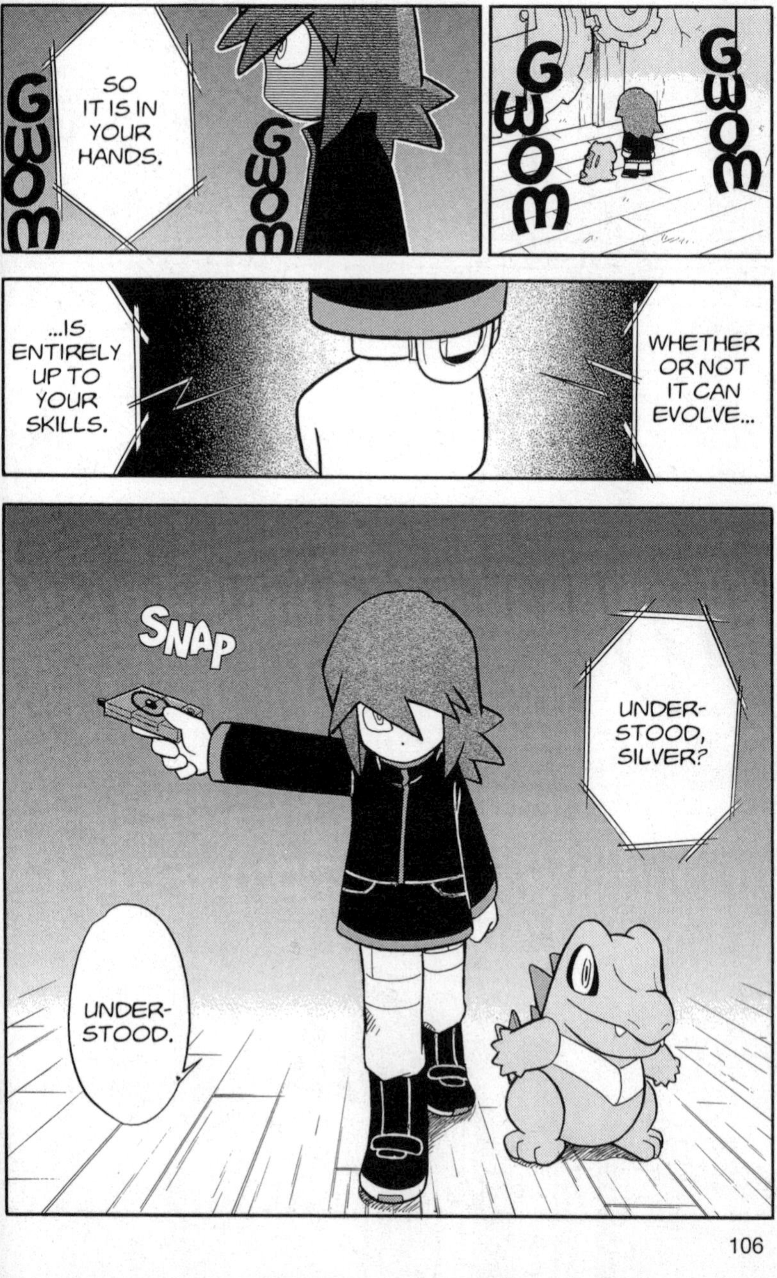
GWOM
GWOM
SO IT IS IN YOUR HANDS.
GWOM
GWOM
WHETHER OR NOT IT CAN EVOLVE...
...IS ENTIRELY UP TO YOUR SKILLS.
UNDER-STOOD, SILVER?
SNAP
UNDER-STOOD.

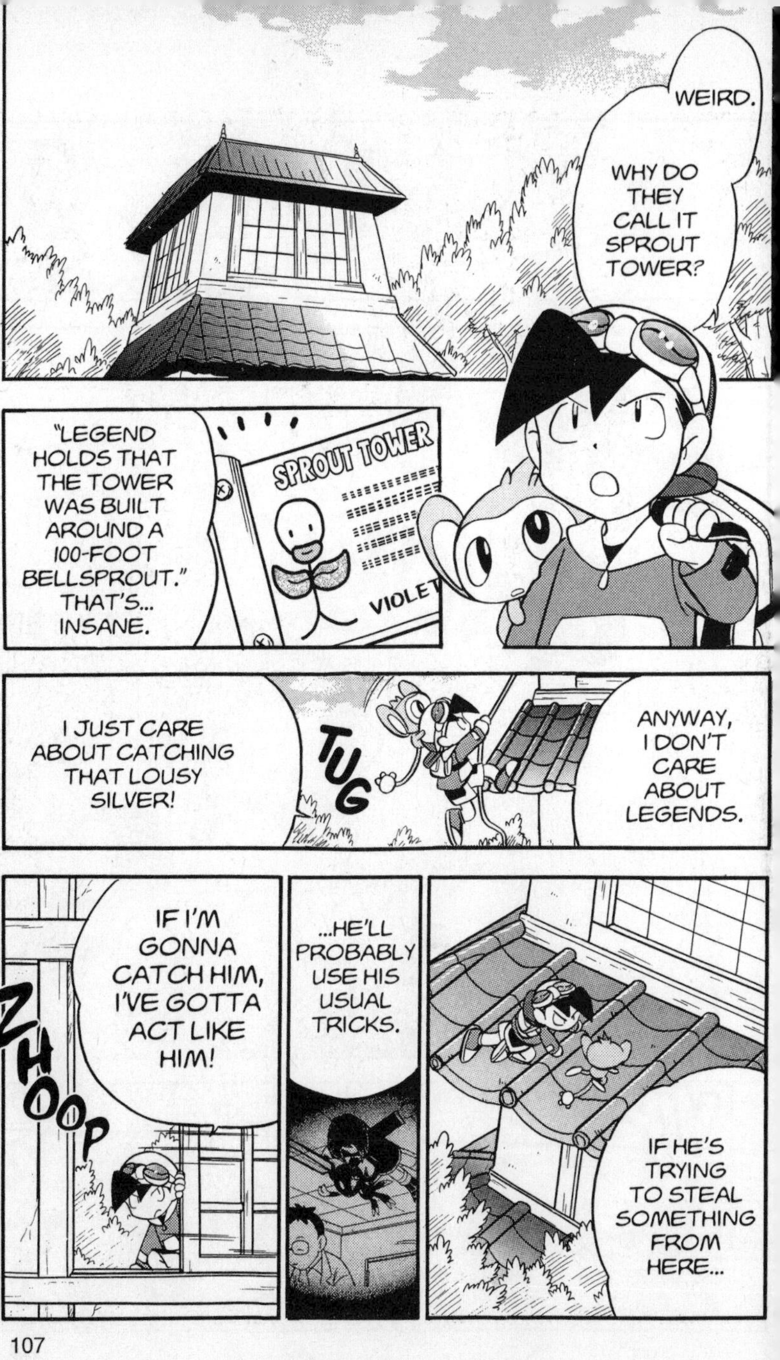
WEIRD.
WHY DO THEY CALL IT SPROUT TOWER?
SPROUT TOWER
VIOLET
"LEGEND HOLDS THAT THE TOWER WAS BUILT AROUND A 100-FOOT BELLSPROUT." THAT'S... INSANE.
ANYWAY, I DON'T CARE ABOUT LEGENDS.
TUG
I JUST CARE ABOUT CATCHING THAT LOUSY SILVER!
IF HE'S TRYING TO STEAL SOMETHING FROM HERE...
...HE'LL PROBABLY USE HIS USUAL TRICKS.
IF I'M GONNA CATCH HIM, I'VE GOTTA ACT LIKE HIM!
ZHOOP

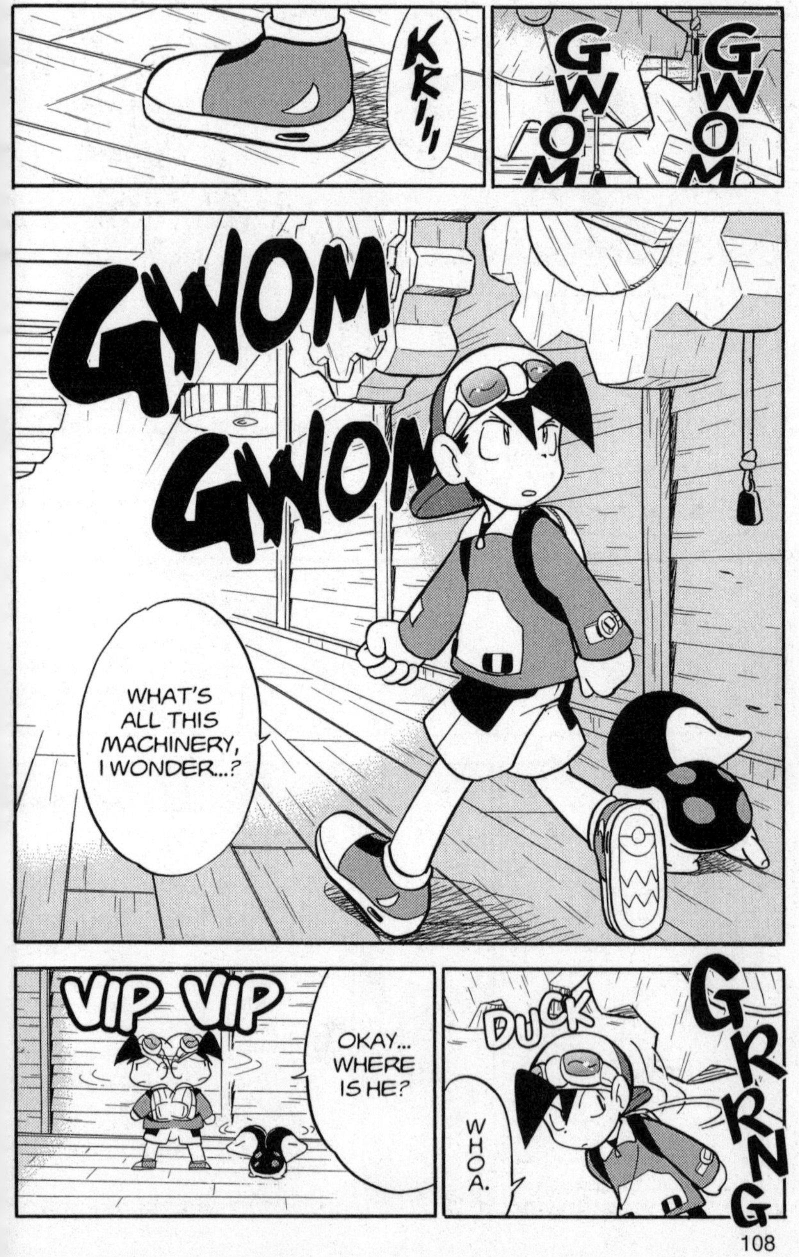
GWOM.
GWOM.
KRIII
GWOM
GWOM
WHAT'S ALL THIS MACHINERY, I WONDER...?
DUCK
GRRRNG
WHOA.
VIP VIP
OKAY... WHERE IS HE?

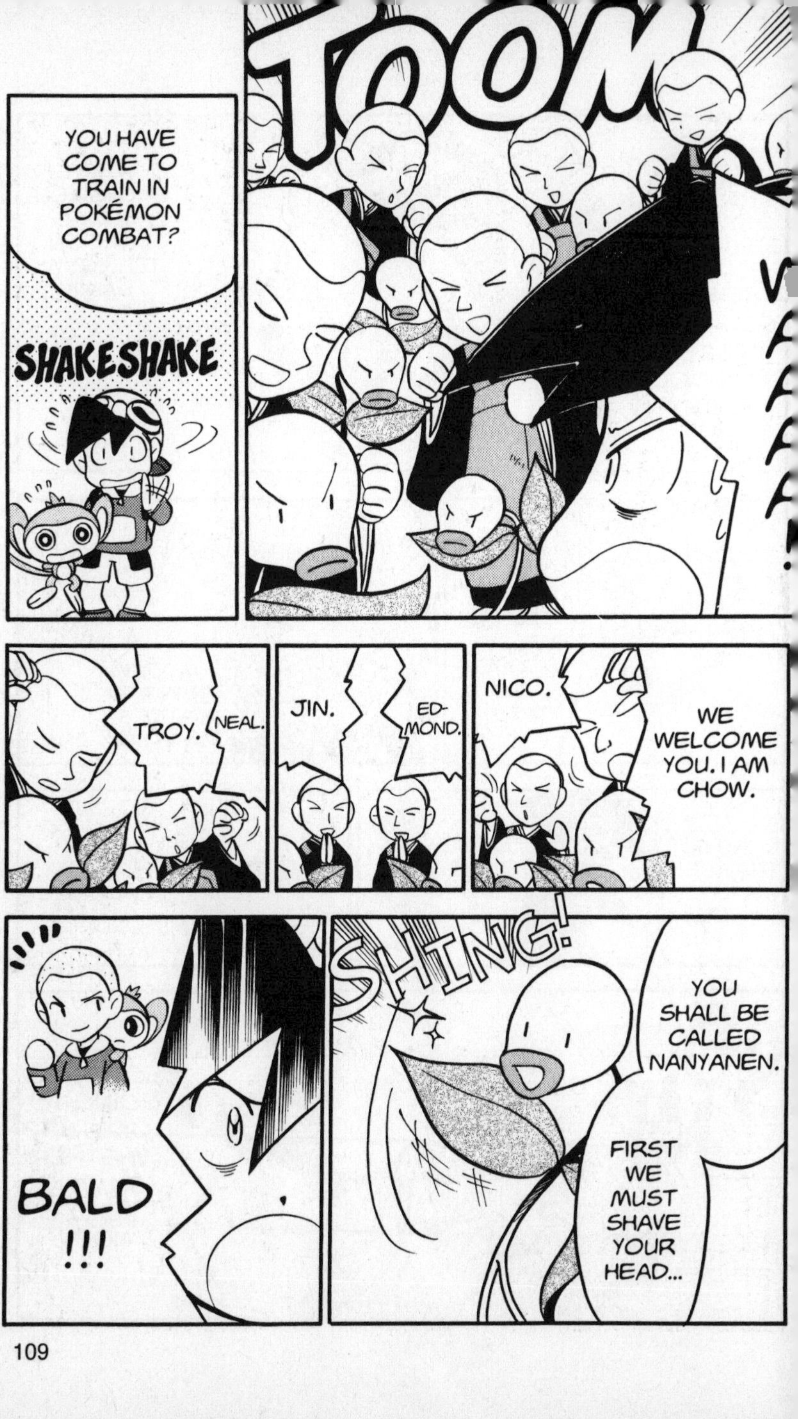

TOOM
VAAAA!
YOU HAVE COME TO TRAIN IN POKÉMON COMBAT?
SHAKESHAKE
WE WELCOME YOU. I AM CHOW.
NICO.
ED-MOND.
JIN.
NEAL.
TROY.
SHING!
YOU SHALL BE CALLED NANYANEN.
FIRST WE MUST SHAVE YOUR HEAD...
BALD !!!

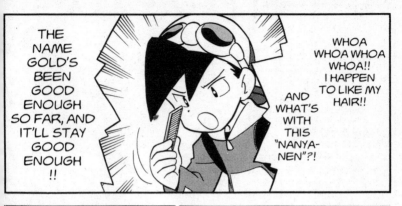

WHOA WHOA WHOA WHOA!! I HAPPEN TO LIKE MY HAIR!!
AND WHAT'S WITH THIS "NANYA-NEN"?!
THE NAME GOLD'S BEEN GOOD ENOUGH SO FAR, AND IT'LL STAY GOOD ENOUGH!!
AND WHY WOULD I WANT TO JOIN YOU ANYWAY?!
GASP
I'M JUST TRYING TO CATCH A BURGLAR!!
YOU MEAN... YOU DID NOT COME TO TRAIN?!
YES! EXACTLY! PRECISELY THAT!
BUT THE SPROUT TOWER IS DEVOTED TO OUR ORDER!
NONE BUT TRAINEES MAY STEP INSIDE!
SO YOU'RE GOING TO JOIN US WHETHER YOU WANT TO OR NOT!!
NOMP

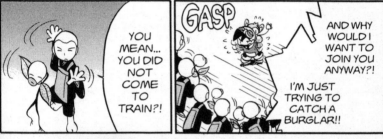

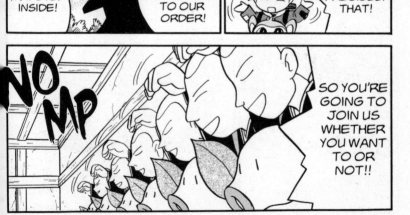

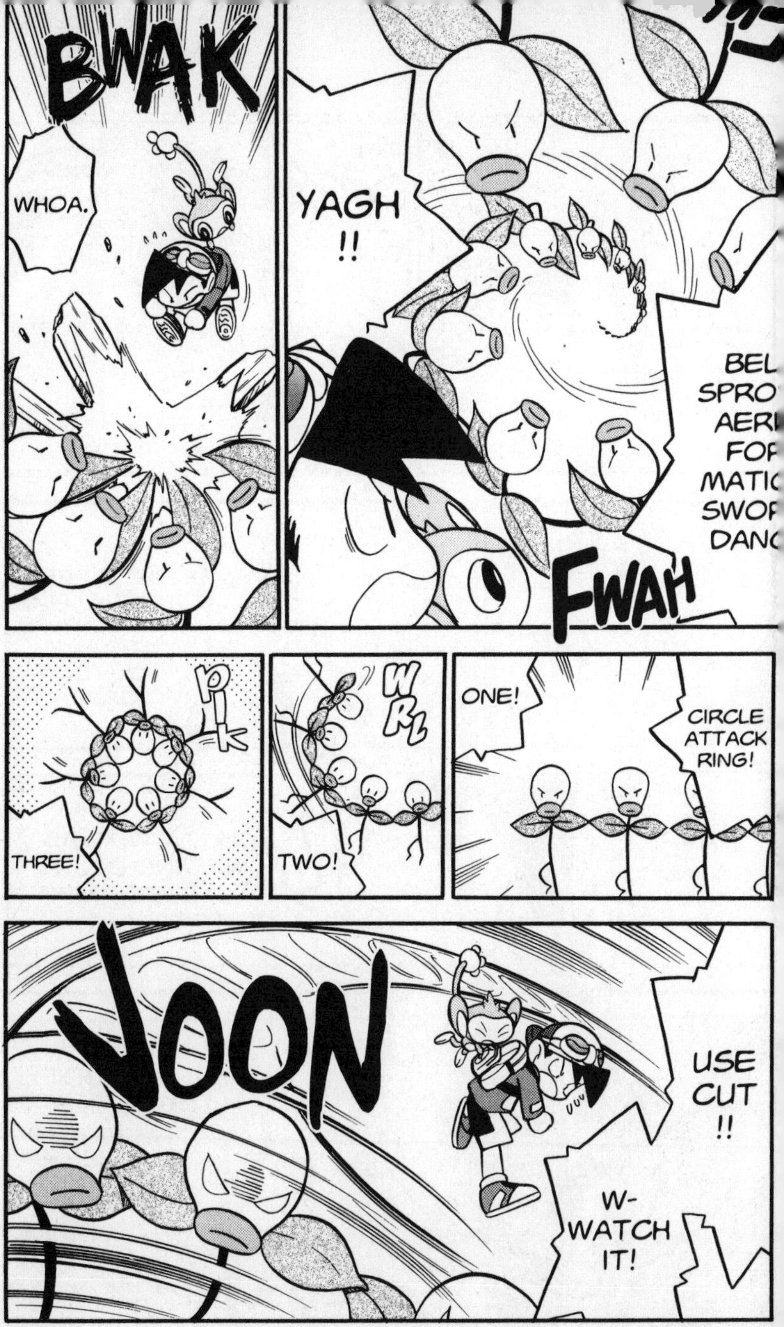

YAGH !!
BEL SPRO AERI FOR MATIC SWOR DANC
FWAH
BWAK
WHOA.
CIRCLE ATTACK RING!
ONE!
WRL
TWO!
PIK
THREE!
USE CUT !!
W-WATCH IT!
VOON

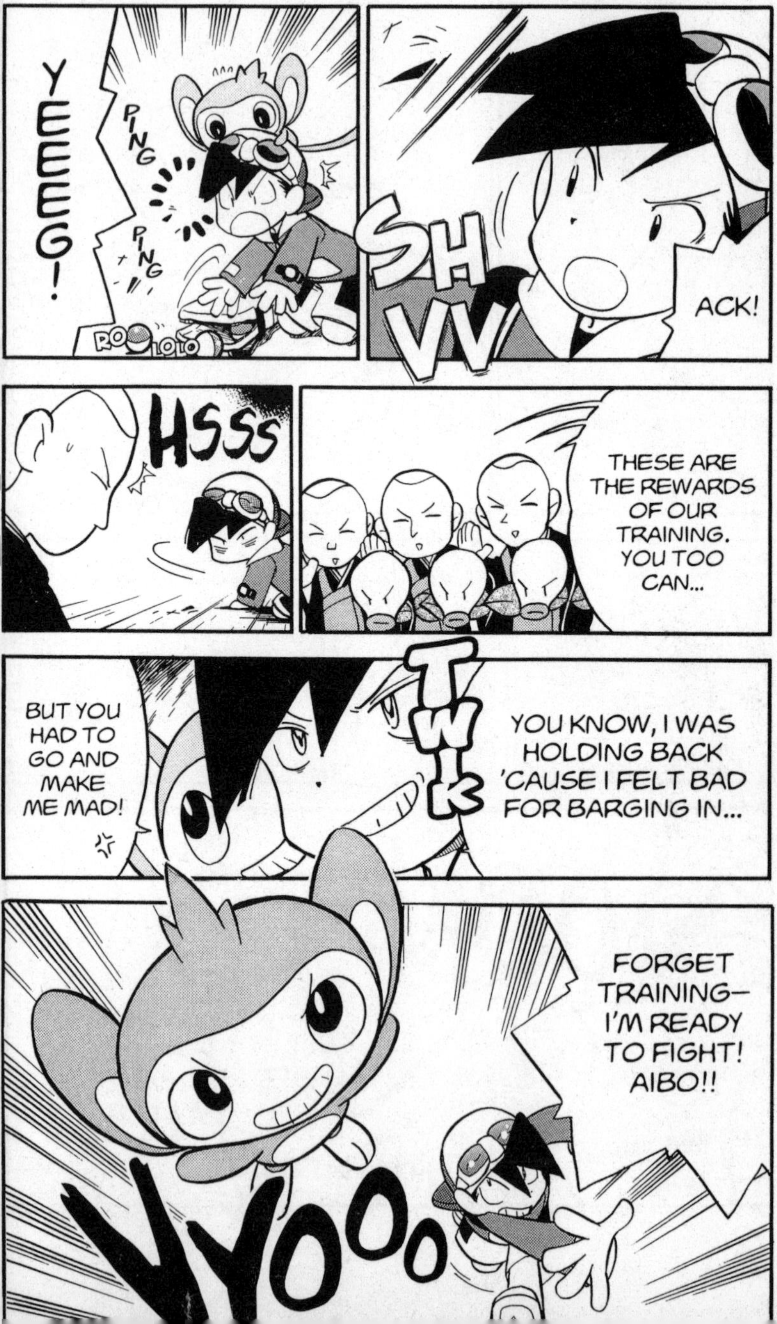
SHVV
ACK!
YEEEEG!
PING
PING
ROLOLO
THESE ARE THE REWARDS OF OUR TRAINING. YOU TOO CAN...
HSSS
TWIK
YOU KNOW, I WAS HOLDING BACK 'CAUSE I FELT BAD FOR BARGING IN...
BUT YOU HAD TO GO AND MAKE ME MAD!
FORGET TRAINING— I'M READY TO FIGHT! AIBO!!
YYOOOO

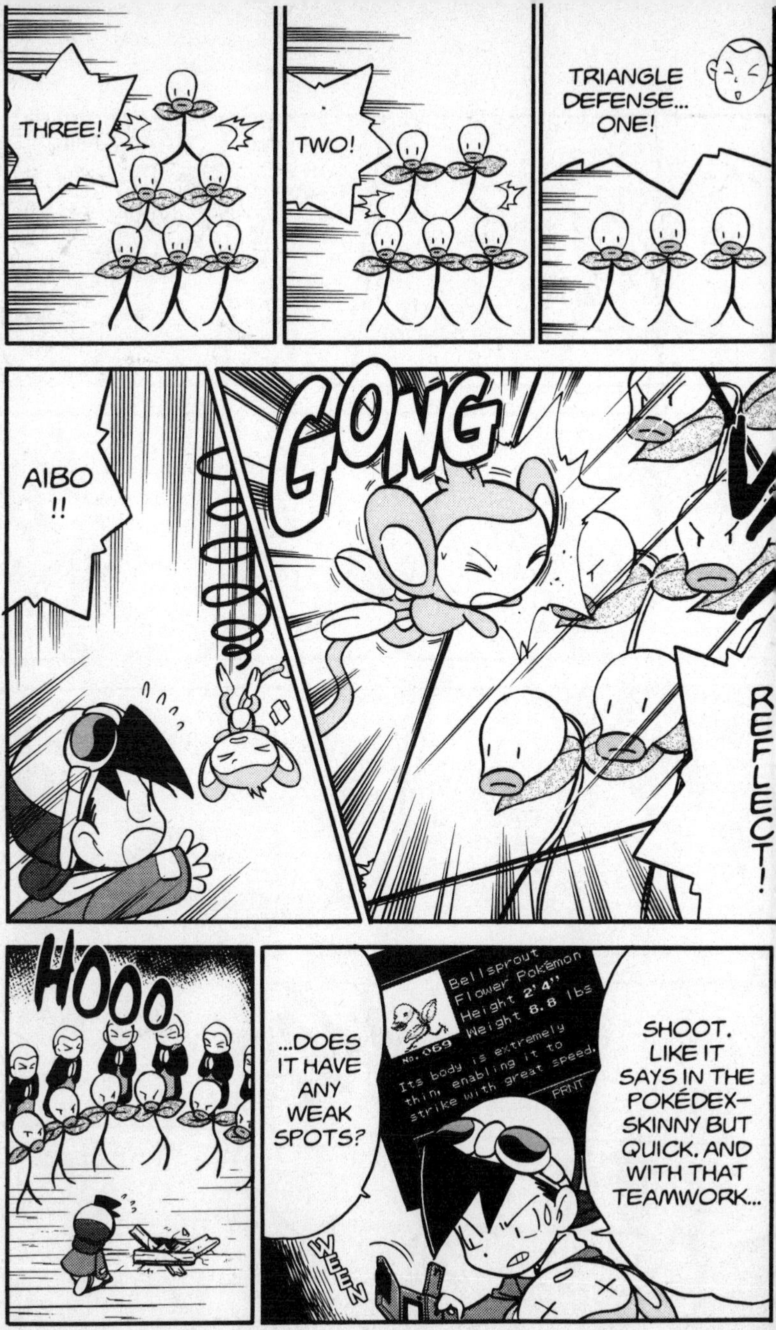
TRIANGLE DEFENSE... ONE!
TWO!
THREE!
GONG
REFLECT!
AIBO !!
Bellsprout Flower Pokémon Height 2'4" Weight 8.8 lbs
No. 069
Its body is extremely thin, enabling it to strike with great speed.
PRNT
SHOOT. LIKE IT SAYS IN THE POKÉDEX— SKINNY BUT QUICK. AND WITH THAT TEAMWORK...
...DOES IT HAVE ANY WEAK SPOTS?
WEEN
HOOO

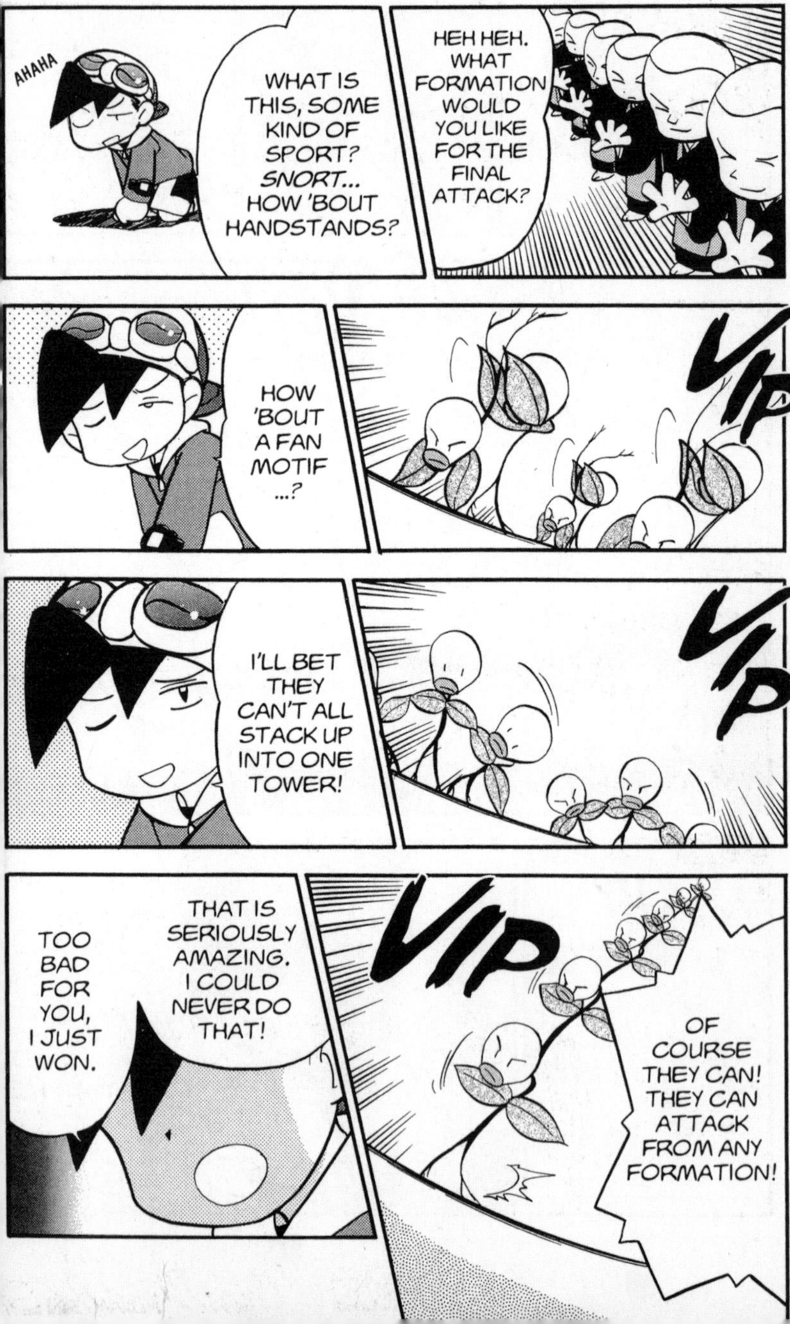
HEH HEH. WHAT FORMATION WOULD YOU LIKE FOR THE FINAL ATTACK?
WHAT IS THIS, SOME KIND OF SPORT? *SNORT...* HOW 'BOUT HANDSTANDS?
AHAHA
VIP
HOW 'BOUT A FAN MOTIF ...?
VIP
I'LL BET THEY CAN'T ALL STACK UP INTO ONE TOWER!
VIP
OF COURSE THEY CAN! THEY CAN ATTACK FROM ANY FORMATION!
THAT IS SERIOUSLY AMAZING. I COULD NEVER DO THAT!
TOO BAD FOR YOU, I JUST WON.

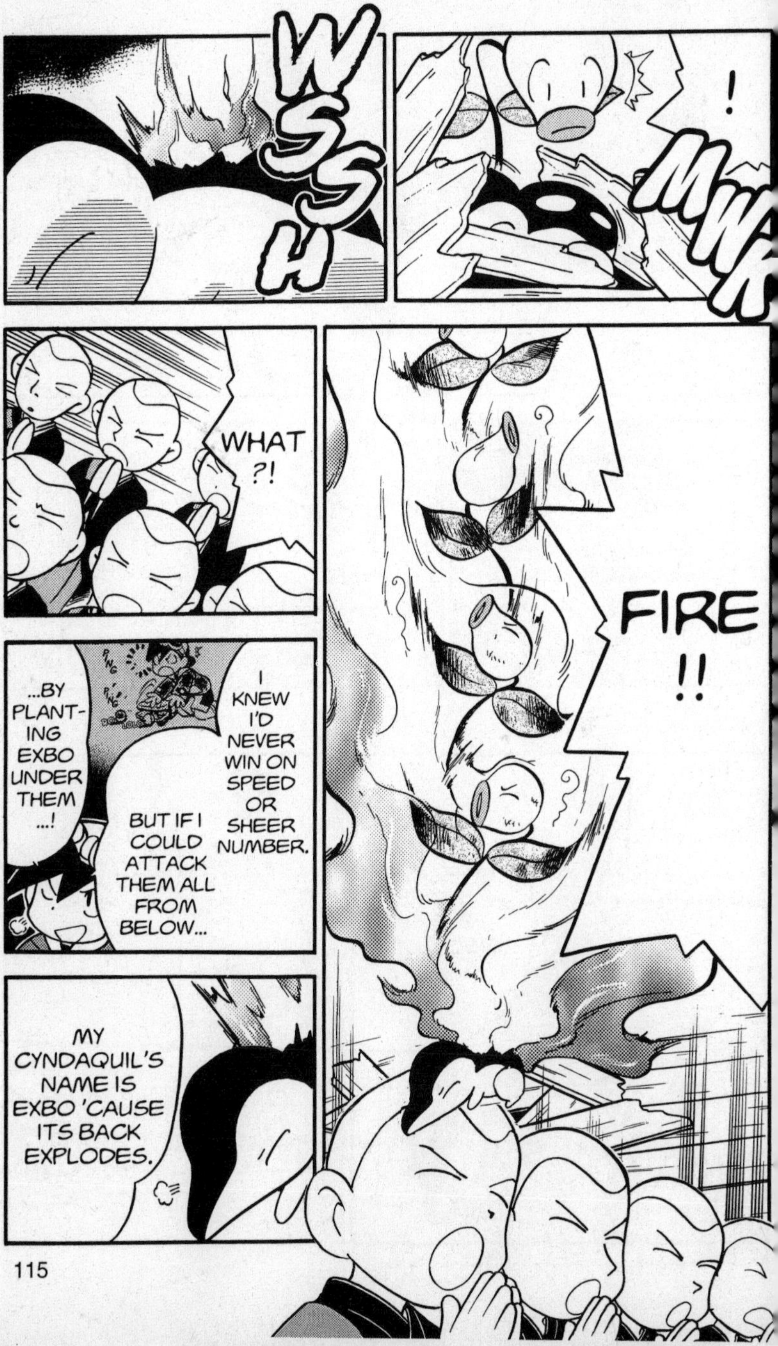
!
MWK
WSSH
FIRE !!
WHAT ?!
I KNEW I'D NEVER WIN ON SPEED OR SHEER NUMBER.
BUT IF I COULD ATTACK THEM ALL FROM BELOW...
...BY PLANTING EXBO UNDER THEM ...!
MY CYNDAQUIL'S NAME IS EXBO 'CAUSE ITS BACK EXPLODES.

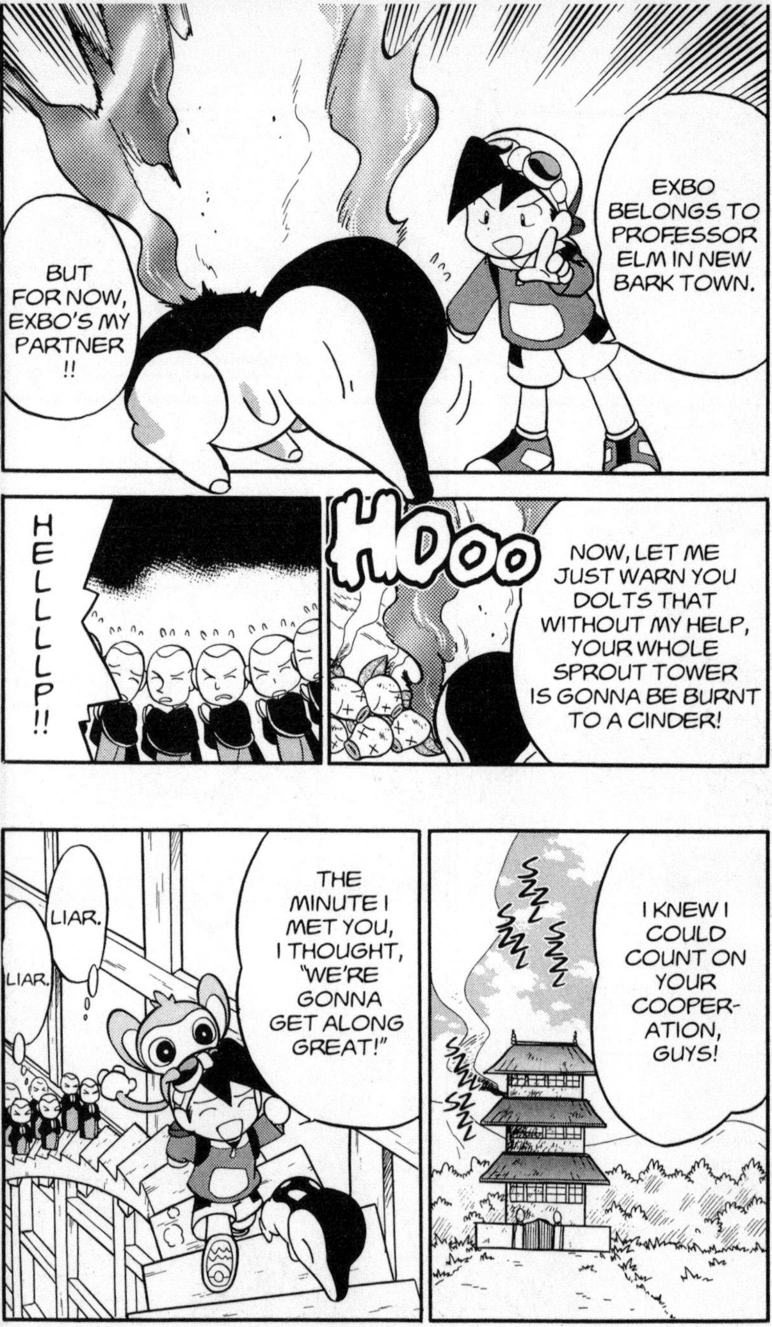
EXBO BELONGS TO PROFESSOR ELM IN NEW BARK TOWN.
BUT FOR NOW, EXBO'S MY PARTNER !!
NOW, LET ME JUST WARN YOU DOLTS THAT WITHOUT MY HELP, YOUR WHOLE SPROUT TOWER IS GONNA BE BURNT TO A CINDER!
HOOO
HELLLLLP!!
I KNEW I COULD COUNT ON YOUR COOPER-ATION, GUYS!
THE MINUTE I MET YOU, I THOUGHT, "WE'RE GONNA GET ALONG GREAT!"
LIAR.
LIAR.

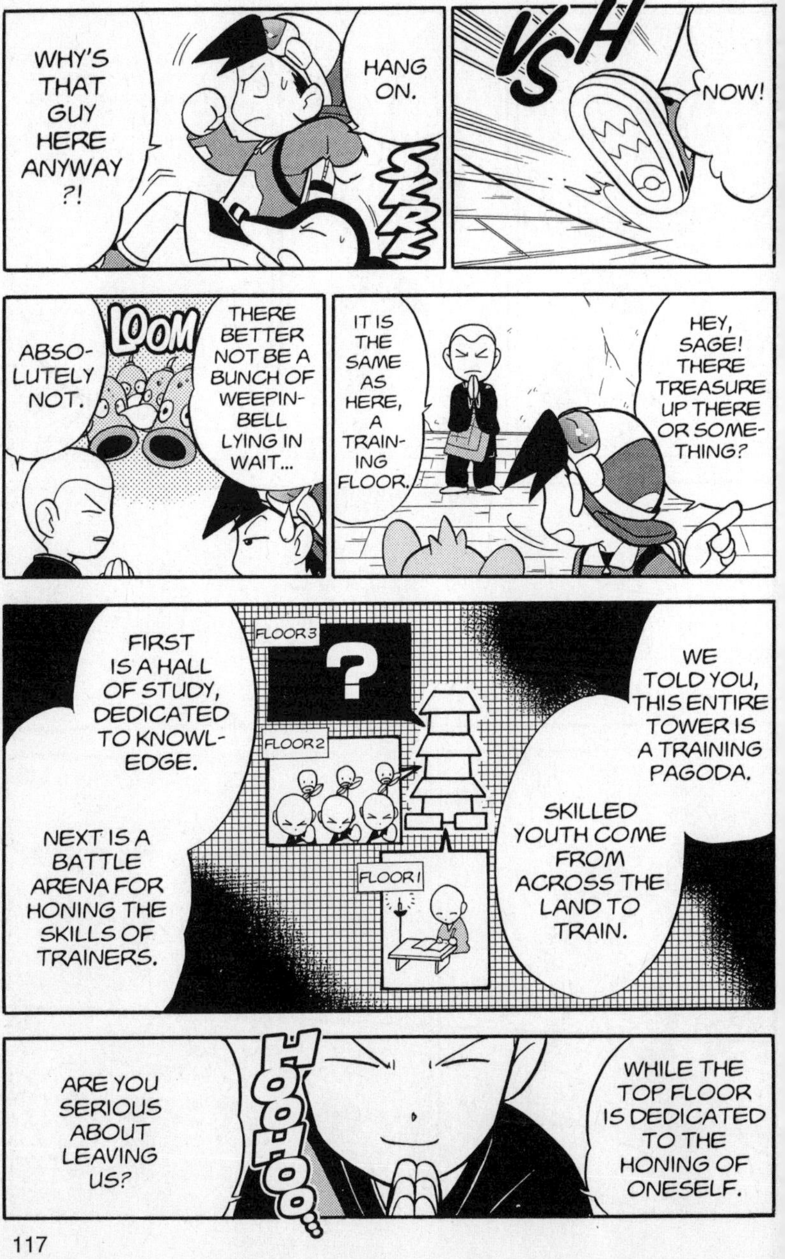
VSH
NOW!
HANG ON.
WHY'S THAT GUY HERE ANYWAY?!
HEY, SAGE! THERE TREASURE UP THERE OR SOMETHING?
IT IS THE SAME AS HERE, A TRAINING FLOOR.
THERE BETTER NOT BE A BUNCH OF WEEPINBELL LYING IN WAIT...
LOOM
ABSOLUTELY NOT.
WE TOLD YOU, THIS ENTIRE TOWER IS A TRAINING PAGODA.
SKILLED YOUTH COME FROM ACROSS THE LAND TO TRAIN.
FLOOR 3
?
FLOOR 2
FLOOR 1
FIRST IS A HALL OF STUDY, DEDICATED TO KNOWLEDGE.
NEXT IS A BATTLE ARENA FOR HONING THE SKILLS OF TRAINERS.
WHILE THE TOP FLOOR IS DEDICATED TO THE HONING OF ONESELF.
HOHOHO...
ARE YOU SERIOUS ABOUT LEAVING US?

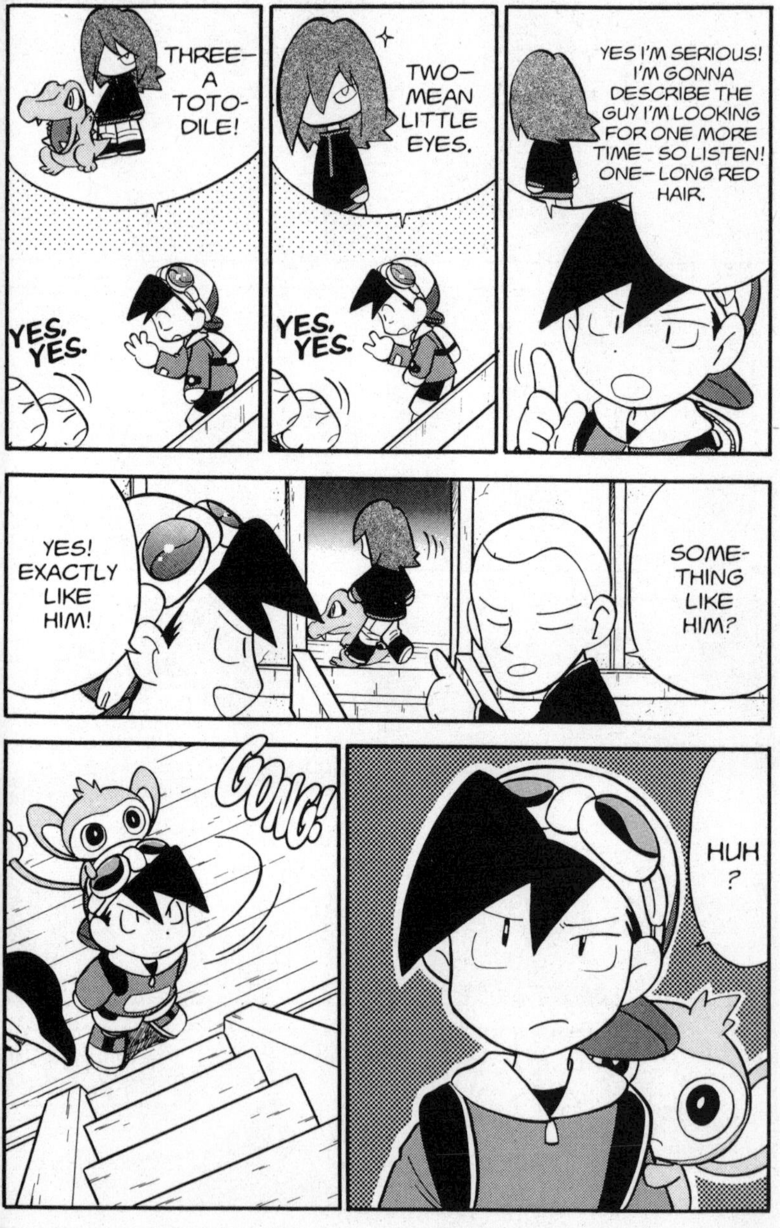
YES I'M SERIOUS! I'M GONNA DESCRIBE THE GUY I'M LOOKING FOR ONE MORE TIME— SO LISTEN! ONE— LONG RED HAIR.
TWO— MEAN LITTLE EYES.
YES, YES.
THREE— A TOTO-DILE!
YES, YES.
SOME-THING LIKE HIM?
YES! EXACTLY LIKE HIM!
HUH ?
GONG!

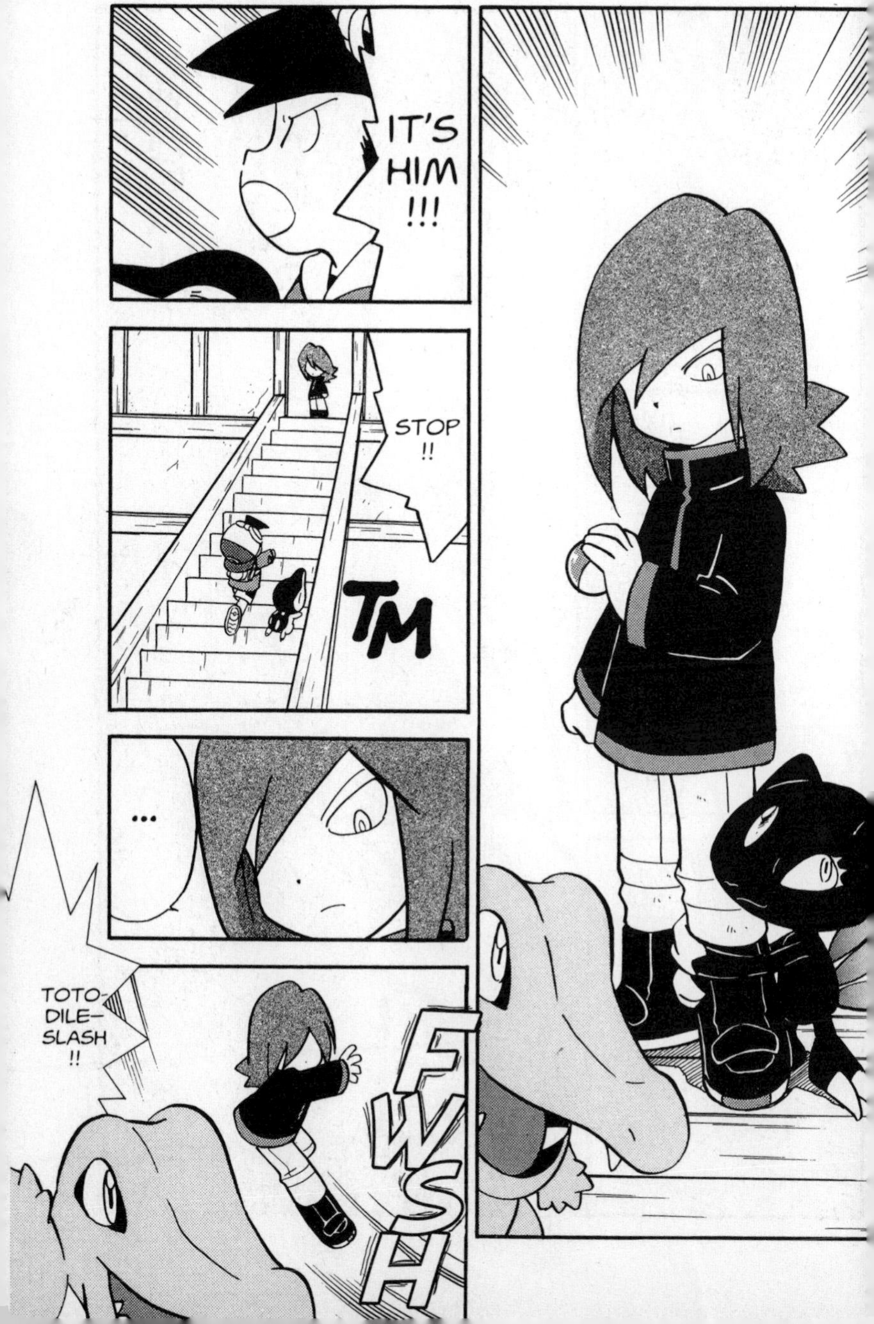
IT'S HIM !!!
STOP !!
TM
...
TOTO-DILE-SLASH !!
FWSH

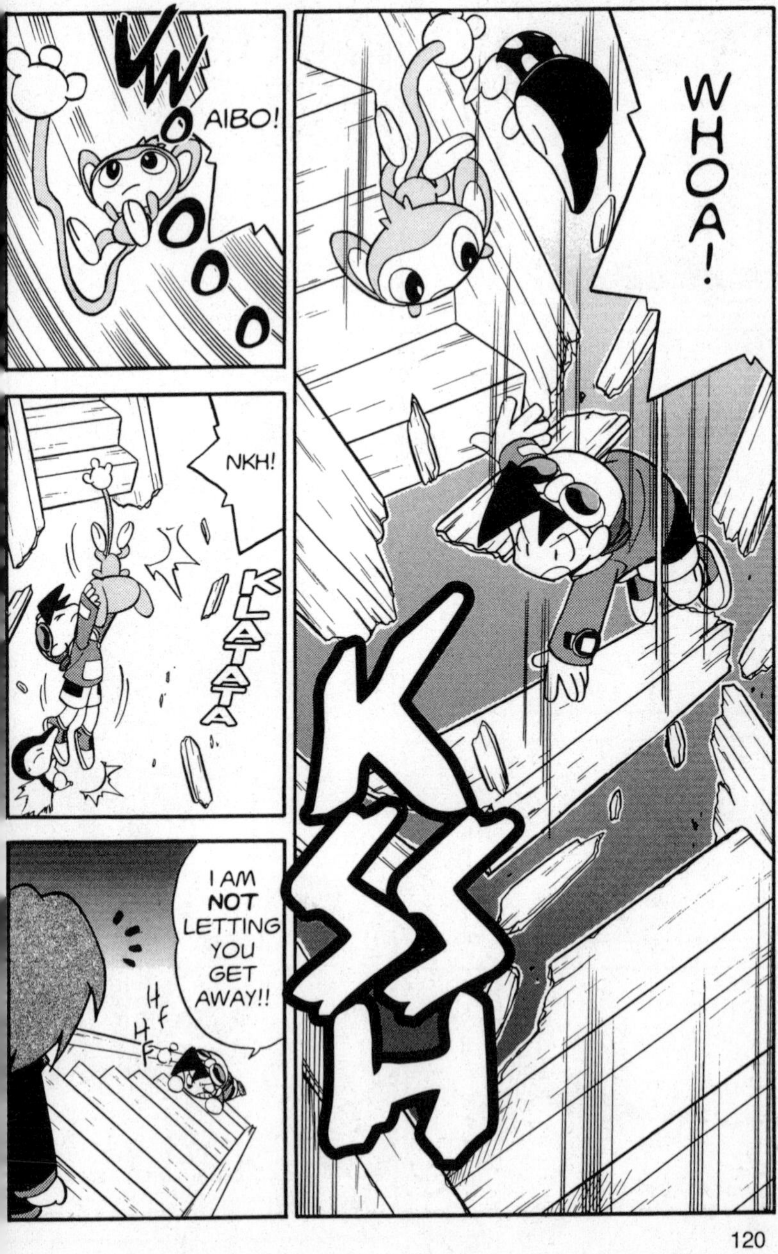
WHOA!
KSSH
WOOOO
AIBO!
NKH!
KLATATA
I AM **NOT** LETTING YOU GET AWAY!!
HF HF

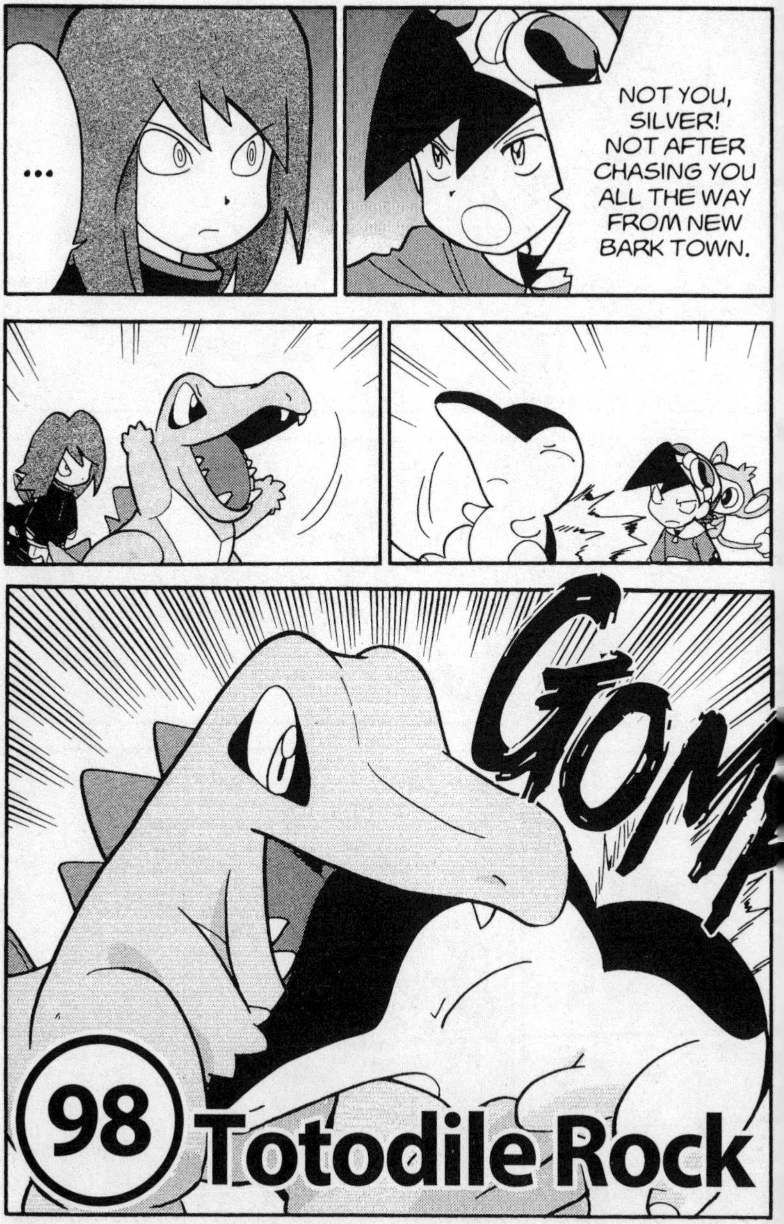
NOT YOU, SILVER! NOT AFTER CHASING YOU ALL THE WAY FROM NEW BARK TOWN.
...
GOM
98 Totodile Rock

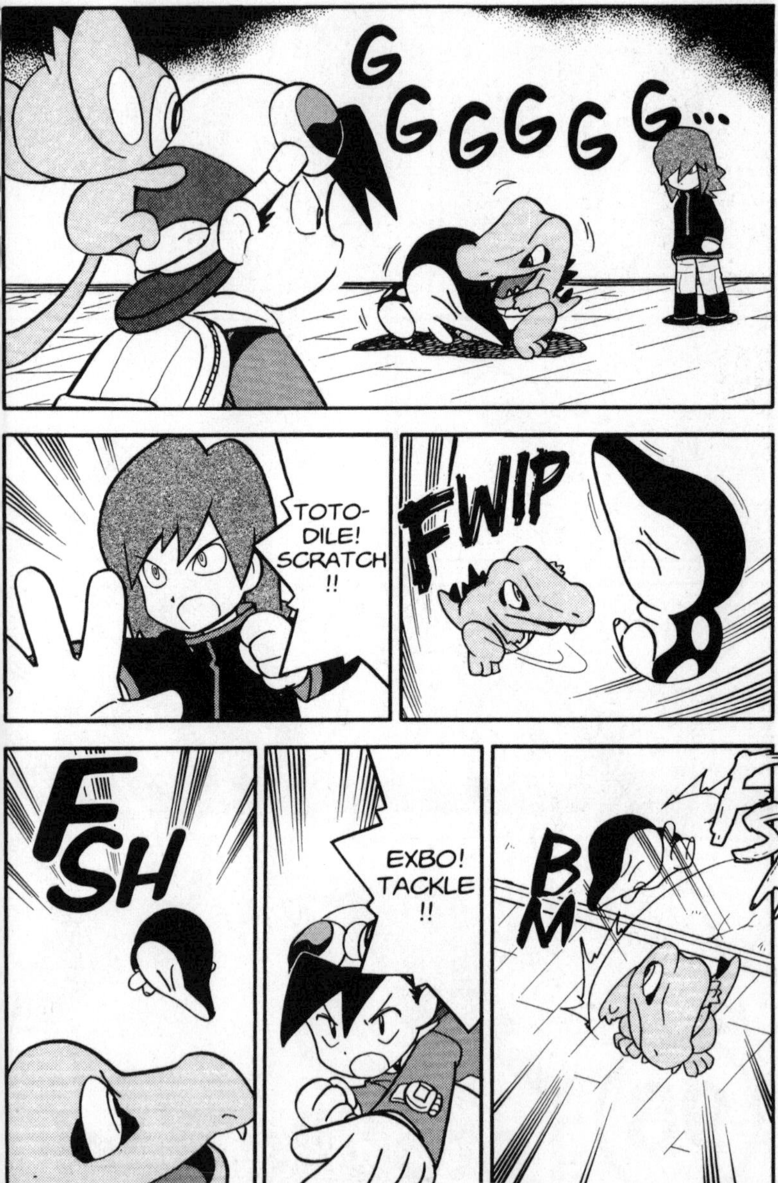
GGGGGG...
FWIP
TOTO-DILE! SCRATCH !!
BM
FSH
EXBO! TACKLE !!
FSH

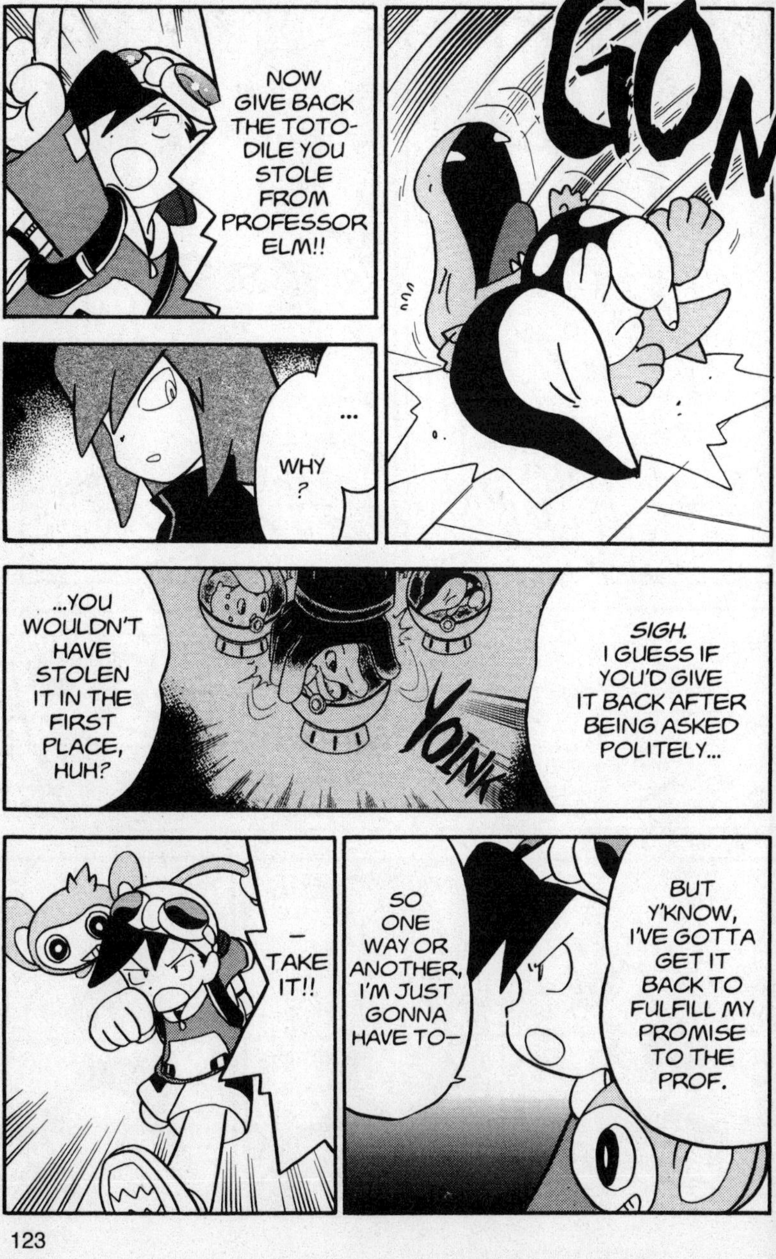
GON
NOW GIVE BACK THE TOTO-DILE YOU STOLE FROM PROFESSOR ELM!!
... WHY?
SIGH. I GUESS IF YOU'D GIVE IT BACK AFTER BEING ASKED POLITELY...
YOINK
...YOU WOULDN'T HAVE STOLEN IT IN THE FIRST PLACE, HUH?
BUT Y'KNOW, I'VE GOTTA GET IT BACK TO FULFILL MY PROMISE TO THE PROF.
SO ONE WAY OR ANOTHER, I'M JUST GONNA HAVE TO—
—TAKE IT!!

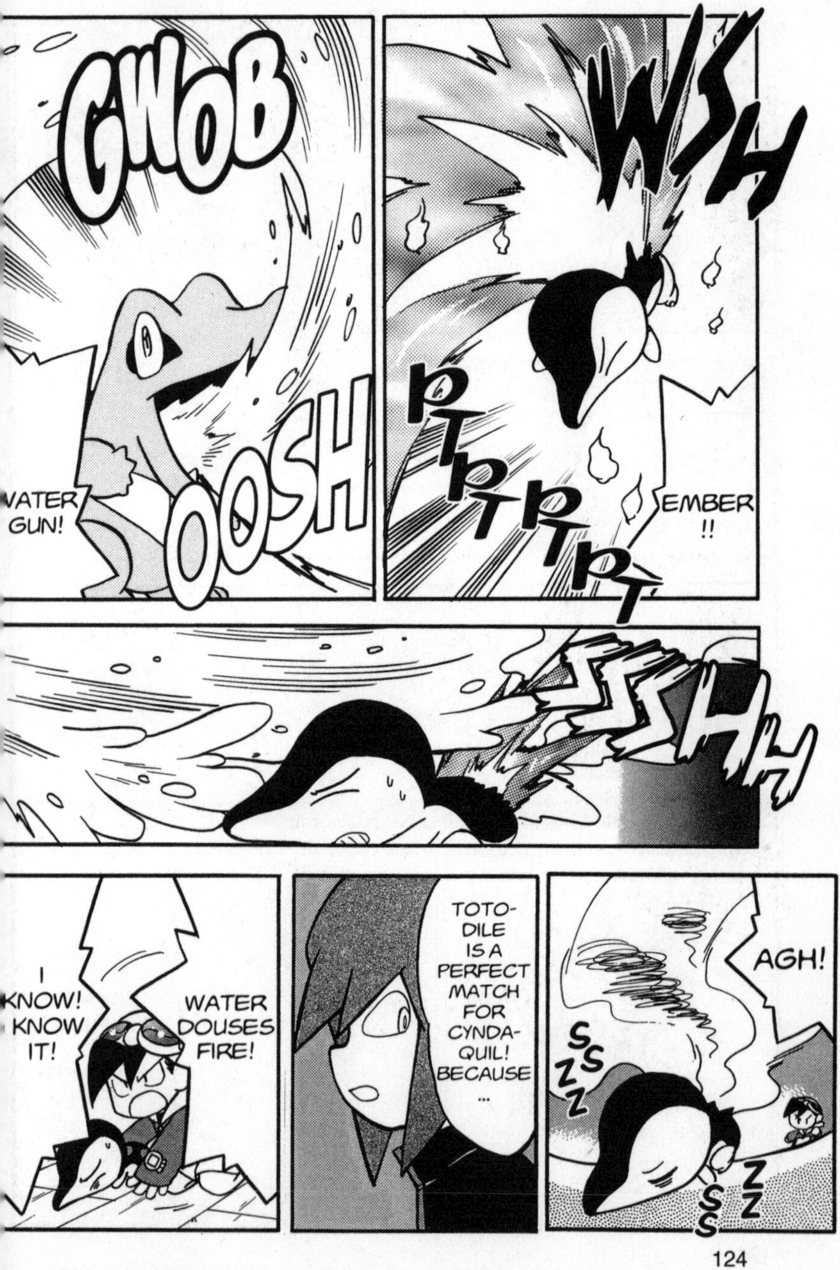
WSH
PTPTPTPT
EMBER !!
GWOB
WATER GUN!
OOSH
SSHH
AGH!
SSZZ
ZZSS
TOTO-DILE IS A PERFECT MATCH FOR CYNDA-QUIL! BECAUSE ...
WATER DOUSES FIRE!
I KNOW! KNOW IT!

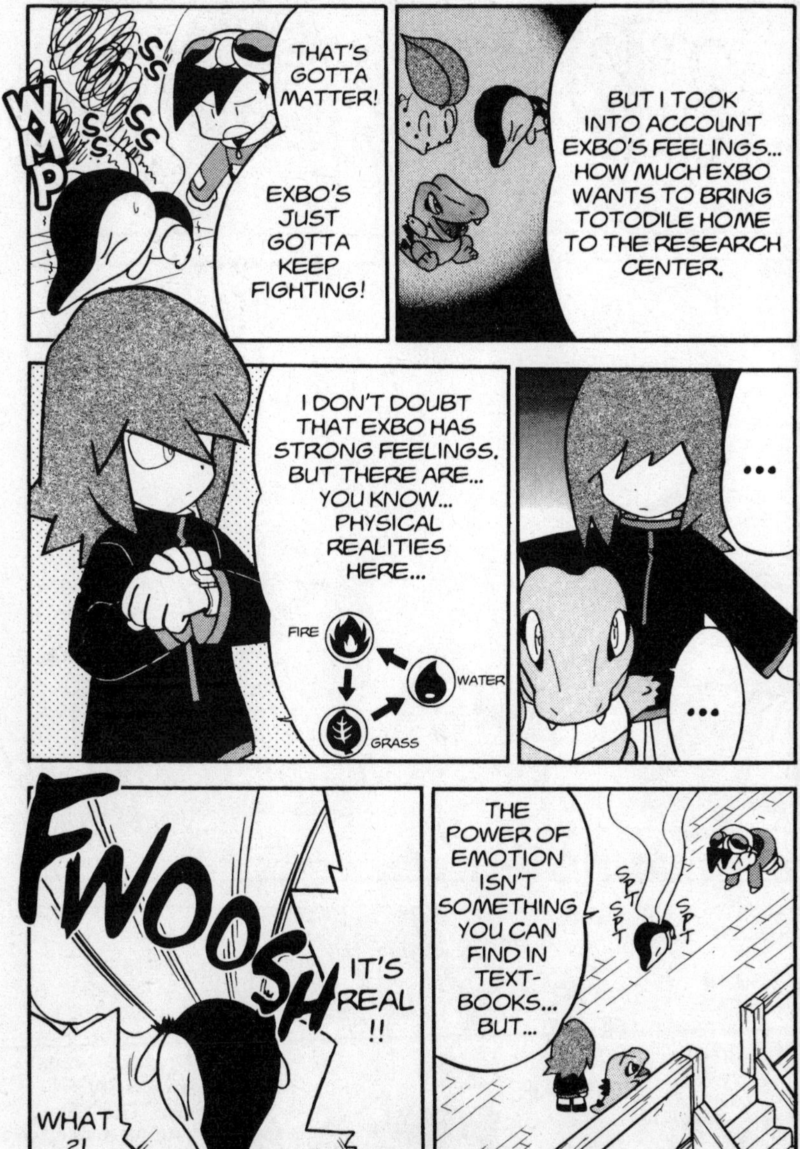
BUT I TOOK INTO ACCOUNT EXBO'S FEELINGS... HOW MUCH EXBO WANTS TO BRING TOTODILE HOME TO THE RESEARCH CENTER.
THAT'S GOTTA MATTER!
WMP
SS
SS
SS
EXBO'S JUST GOTTA KEEP FIGHTING!
...
...
I DON'T DOUBT THAT EXBO HAS STRONG FEELINGS. BUT THERE ARE... YOU KNOW... PHYSICAL REALITIES HERE...
FIRE
WATER
GRASS
THE POWER OF EMOTION ISN'T SOMETHING YOU CAN FIND IN TEXT-BOOKS... BUT...
SPT
SPT
SPT
FWOOSH
IT'S REAL!!
WHAT?!

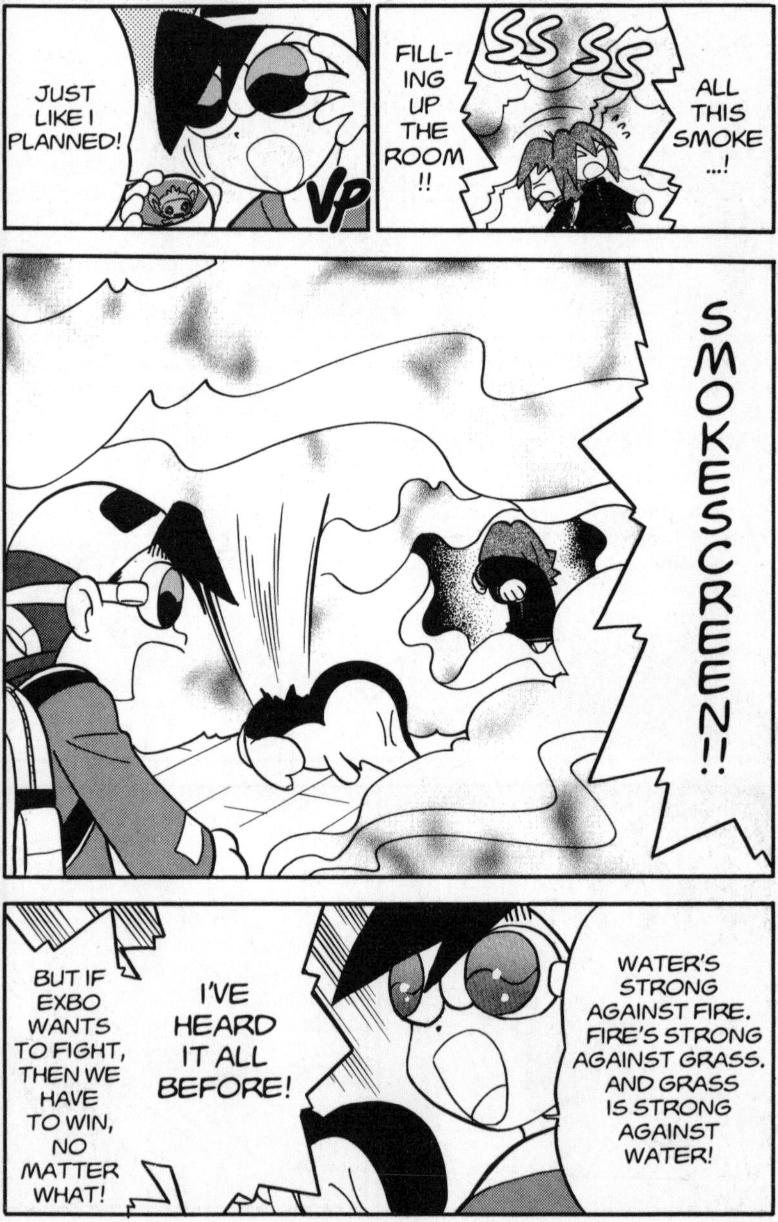
SSSSS
ALL THIS SMOKE ...!
FILL-ING UP THE ROOM !!
JUST LIKE I PLANNED!
VP
SMOKESCREEN!!
WATER'S STRONG AGAINST FIRE. FIRE'S STRONG AGAINST GRASS. AND GRASS IS STRONG AGAINST WATER!
I'VE HEARD IT ALL BEFORE!
BUT IF EXBO WANTS TO FIGHT, THEN WE HAVE TO WIN, NO MATTER WHAT!

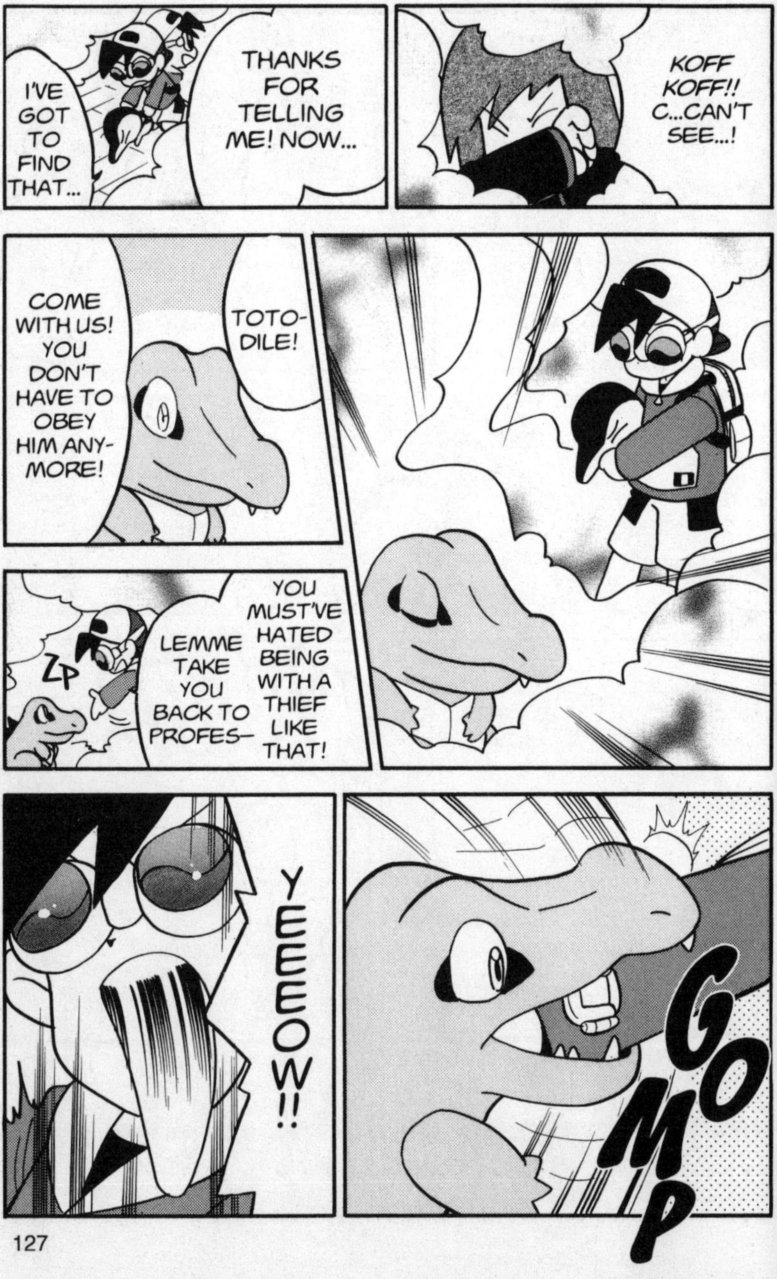
KOFF KOFF!! C...CAN'T SEE...!
THANKS FOR TELLING ME! NOW...
I'VE GOT TO FIND THAT...
TOTO-DILE!
COME WITH US! YOU DON'T HAVE TO OBEY HIM ANYMORE!
YOU MUST'VE HATED BEING WITH A THIEF LIKE THAT!
LEMME TAKE YOU BACK TO PROFES—
ZP
GOMP
YEEEOW!!

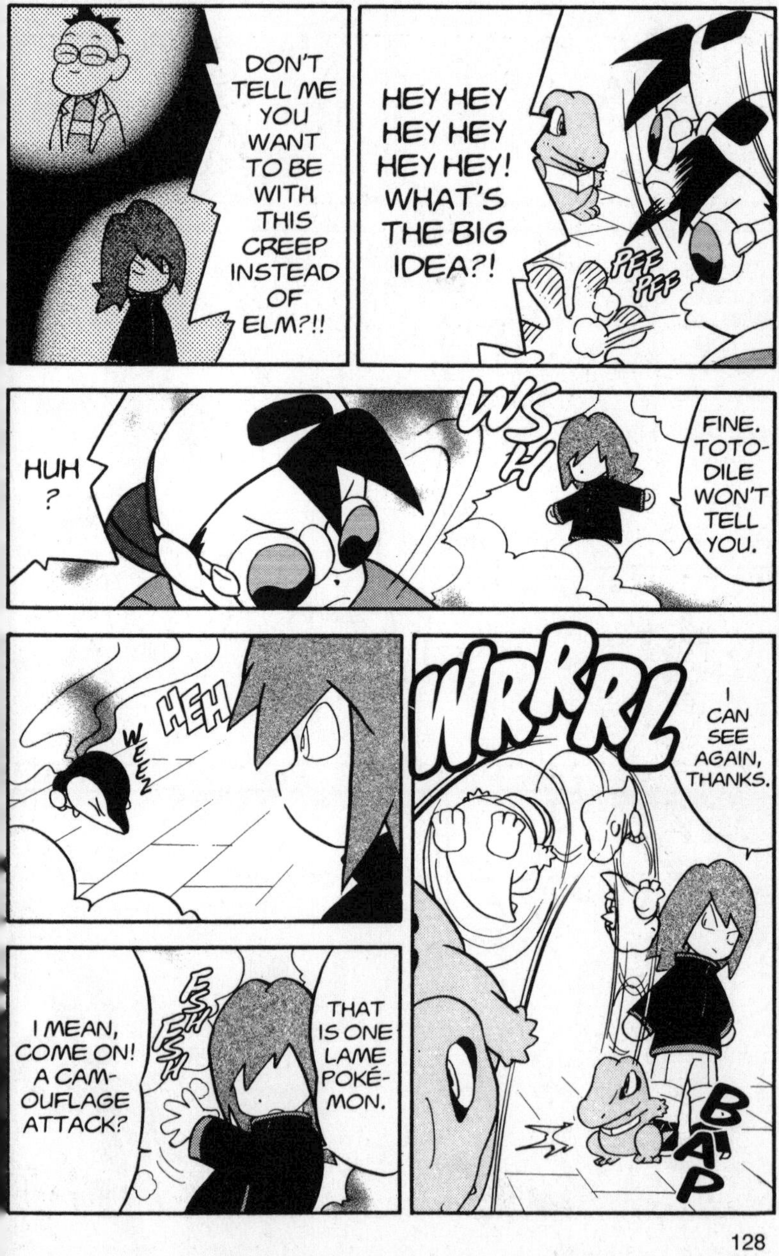
HEY HEY HEY HEY HEY HEY! WHAT'S THE BIG IDEA?!
PFF PFF
DON'T TELL ME YOU WANT TO BE WITH THIS CREEP INSTEAD OF ELM?!!
FINE. TOTO-DILE WON'T TELL YOU.
WSH
HUH?
WRRRL
I CAN SEE AGAIN, THANKS.
BAP
HEH
WEEZ
THAT IS ONE LAME POKÉ-MON.
FSH FSH
I MEAN, COME ON! A CAM-OUFLAGE ATTACK?

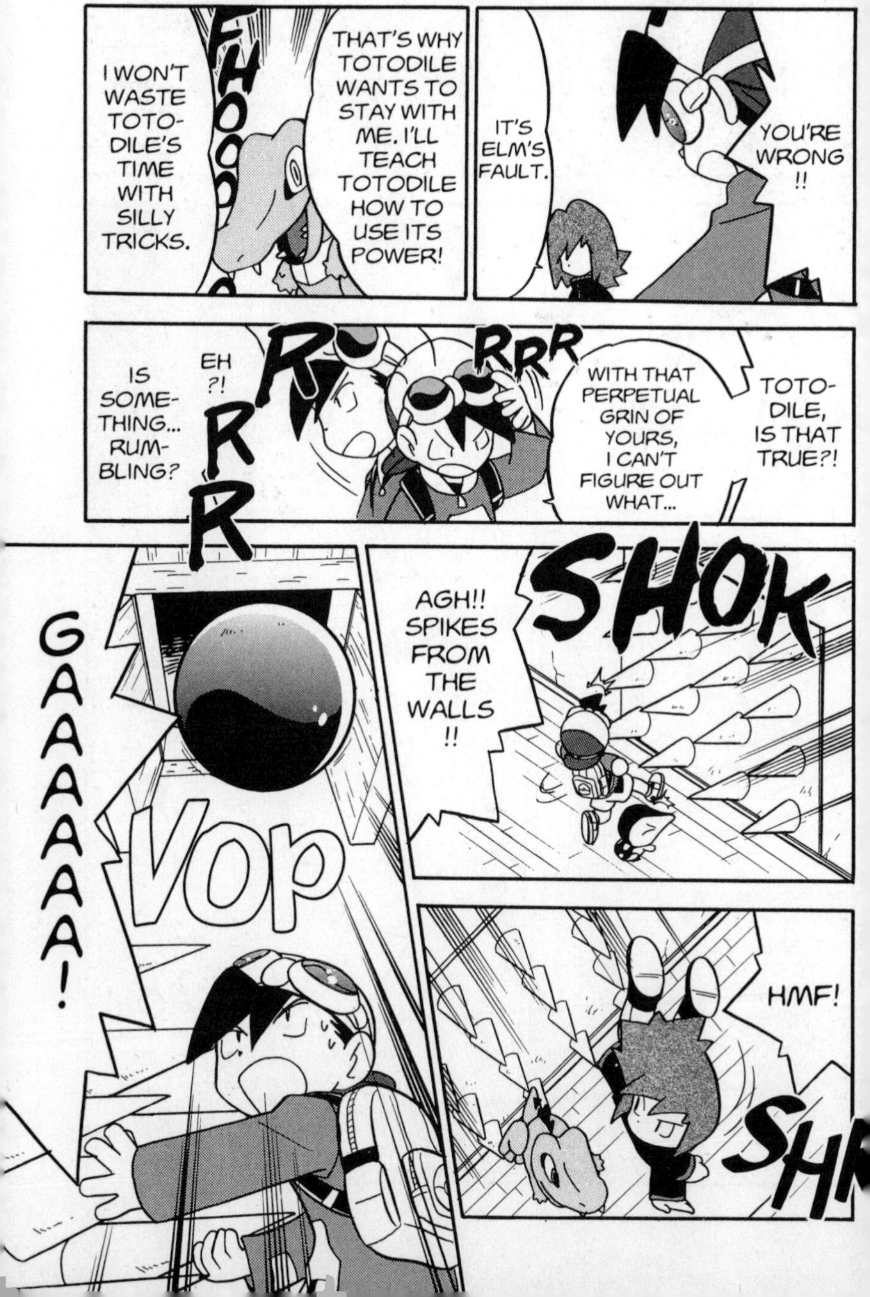

YOU'RE WRONG!!
IT'S ELM'S FAULT.
THAT'S WHY TOTODILE WANTS TO STAY WITH ME. I'LL TEACH TOTODILE HOW TO USE ITS POWER!
FHOOOO
I WON'T WASTE TOTO-DILE'S TIME WITH SILLY TRICKS.
TOTO-DILE, IS THAT TRUE?!
WITH THAT PERPETUAL GRIN OF YOURS, I CAN'T FIGURE OUT WHAT...
RRR
R
EH ?!
IS SOME-THING... RUM-BLING?
RRR
SHOK
AGH!! SPIKES FROM THE WALLS !!
HMF!
SHR
VOP
GAAAAAA!

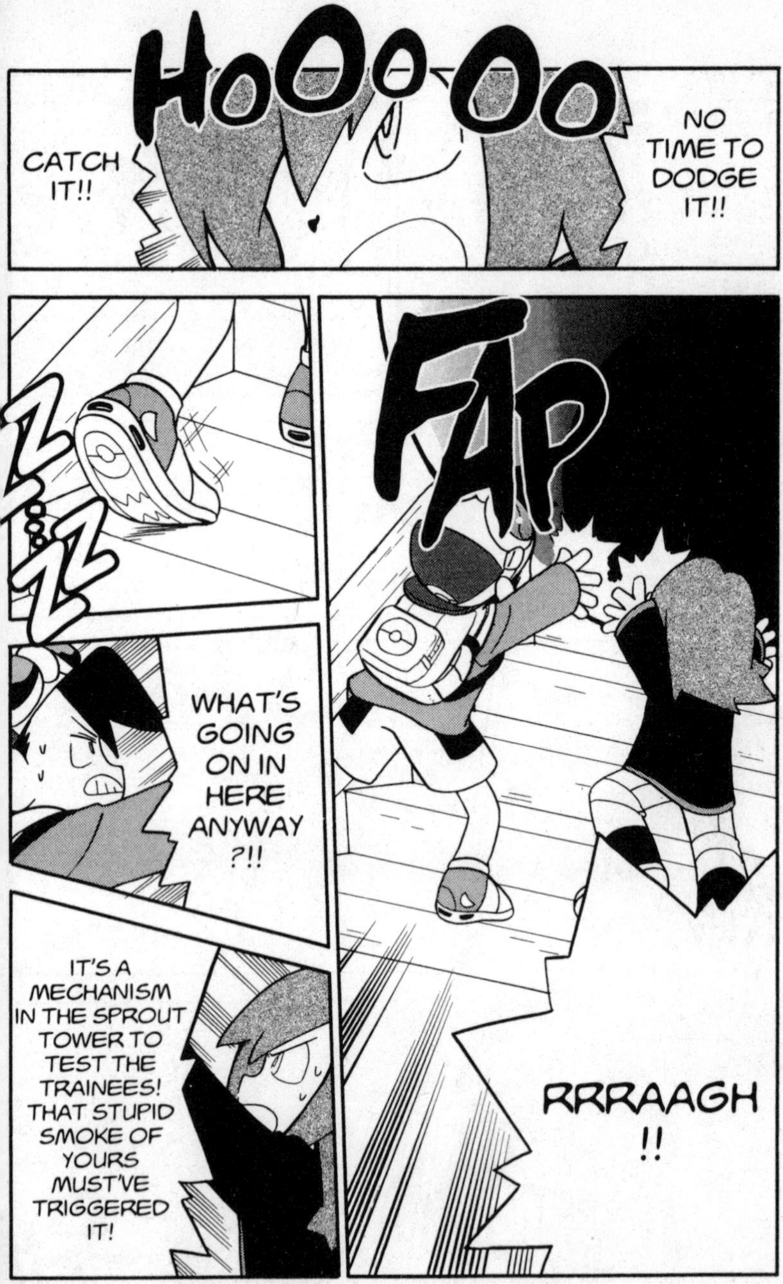
HOOOOO
NO TIME TO DODGE IT!!
CATCH IT!!
FAP
RRRAAGH!!
WHAT'S GOING ON IN HERE ANYWAY?!!
IT'S A MECHANISM IN THE SPROUT TOWER TO TEST THE TRAINEES! THAT STUPID SMOKE OF YOURS MUST'VE TRIGGERED IT!

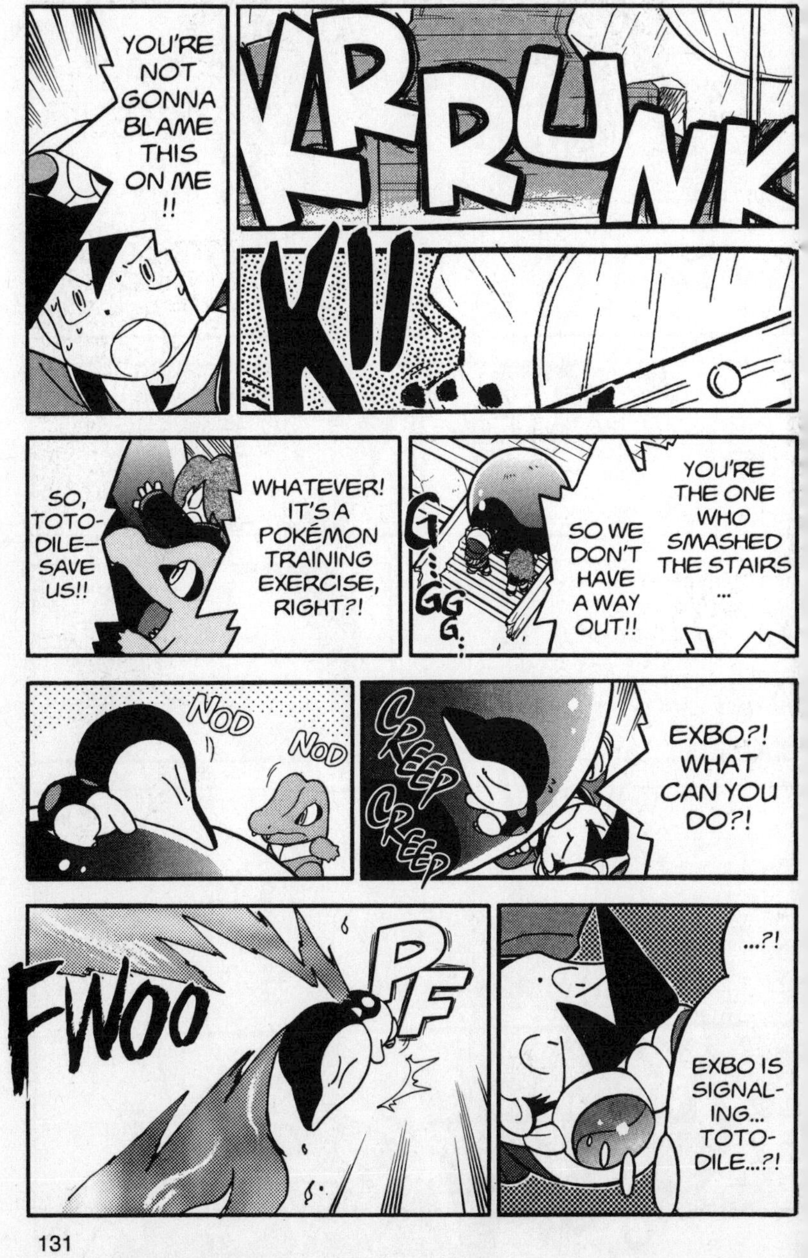
KRRUNK
KU
YOU'RE NOT GONNA BLAME THIS ON ME !!
YOU'RE THE ONE WHO SMASHED THE STAIRS ...
SO WE DON'T HAVE A WAY OUT!!
GGGG...
WHATEVER! IT'S A POKÉMON TRAINING EXERCISE, RIGHT?!
SO, TOTO-DILE— SAVE US!!
EXBO?! WHAT CAN YOU DO?!
CREEP CREEP
NOD
NOD
...?!
EXBO IS SIGNAL-ING... TOTO-DILE...?!
PF
FWOO

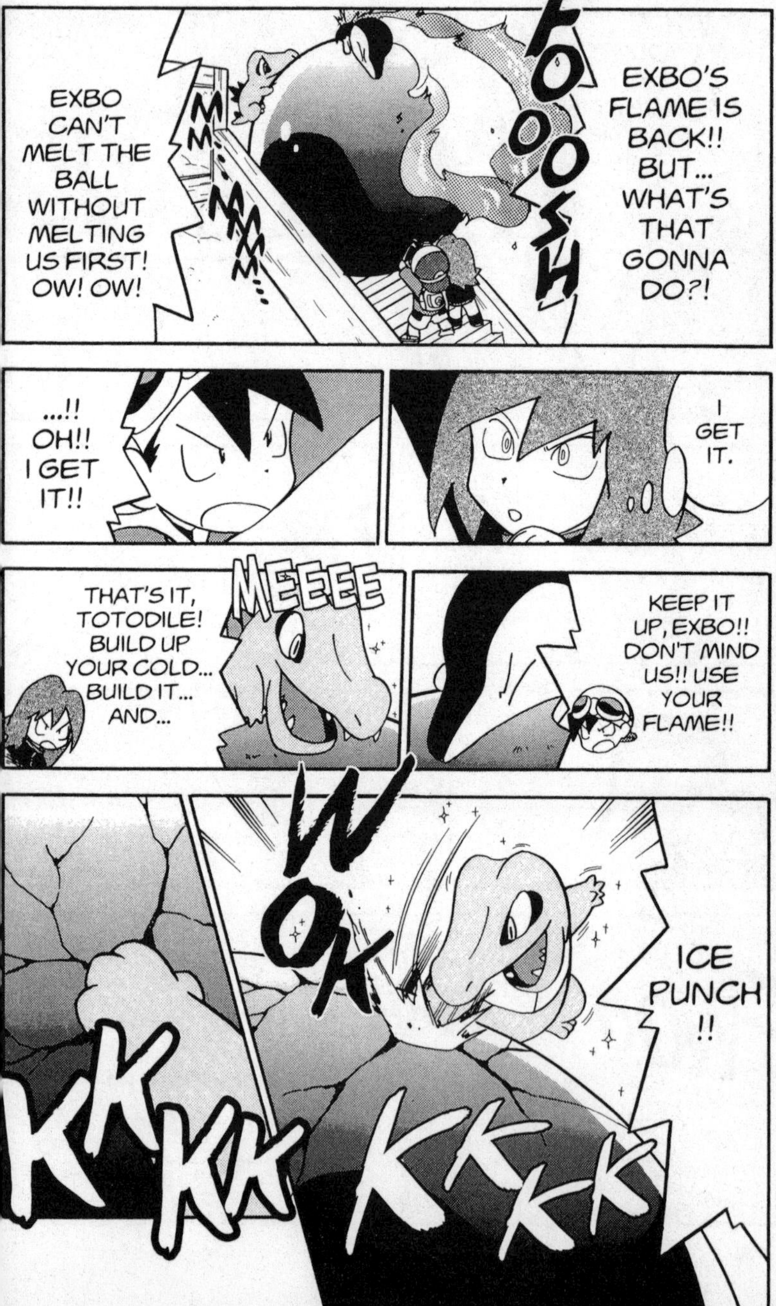
EXBO'S FLAME IS BACK!! BUT... WHAT'S THAT GONNA DO?!
FOOOSH
EXBO CAN'T MELT THE BALL WITHOUT MELTING US FIRST! OW! OW!
I GET IT.
...!! OH!! I GET IT!!
KEEP IT UP, EXBO!! DON'T MIND US!! USE YOUR FLAME!!
MEEEE
THAT'S IT, TOTODILE! BUILD UP YOUR COLD... BUILD IT... AND...
WOK
ICE PUNCH !!

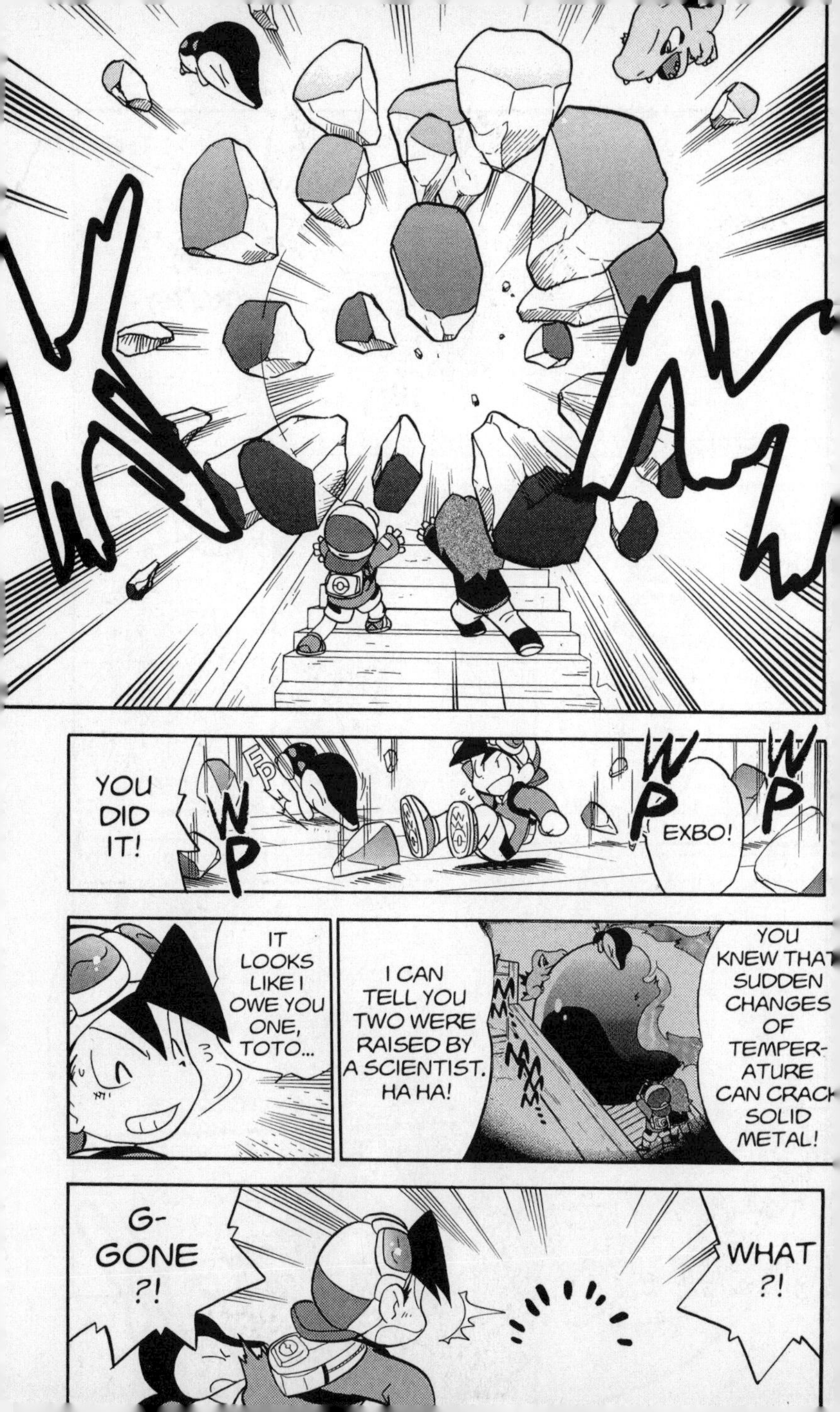
WP
WP
EXBO!
FP
WP
YOU DID IT!
YOU KNEW THAT SUDDEN CHANGES OF TEMPER-ATURE CAN CRACK SOLID METAL!
I CAN TELL YOU TWO WERE RAISED BY A SCIENTIST. HA HA!
IT LOOKS LIKE I OWE YOU ONE, TOTO...
WHAT ?!
G-GONE ?!

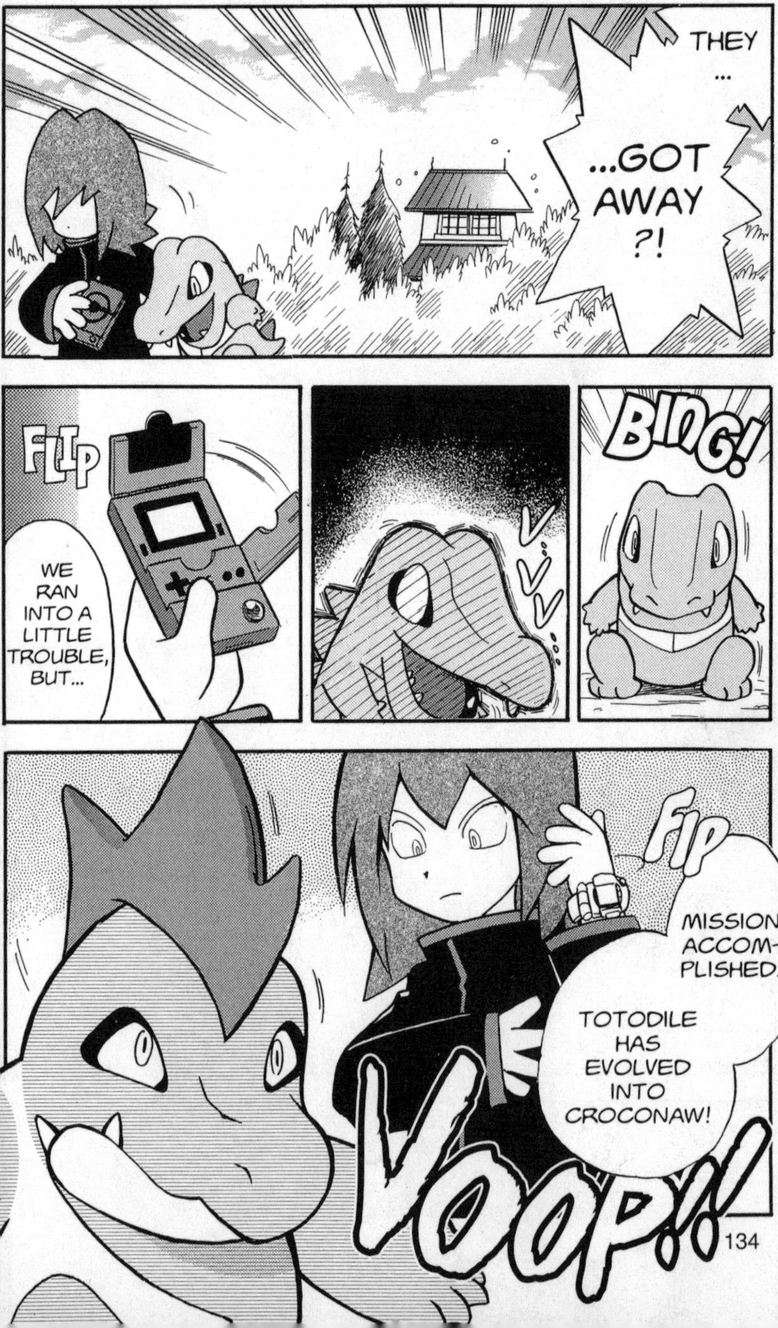

THEY ...
...GOT AWAY ?!
BING!
FLIP
WE RAN INTO A LITTLE TROUBLE, BUT...
FLIP
MISSION ACCOM-PLISHED.
TOTODILE HAS EVOLVED INTO CROCONAW!
VOOP!!

99 Sunkern Treasure

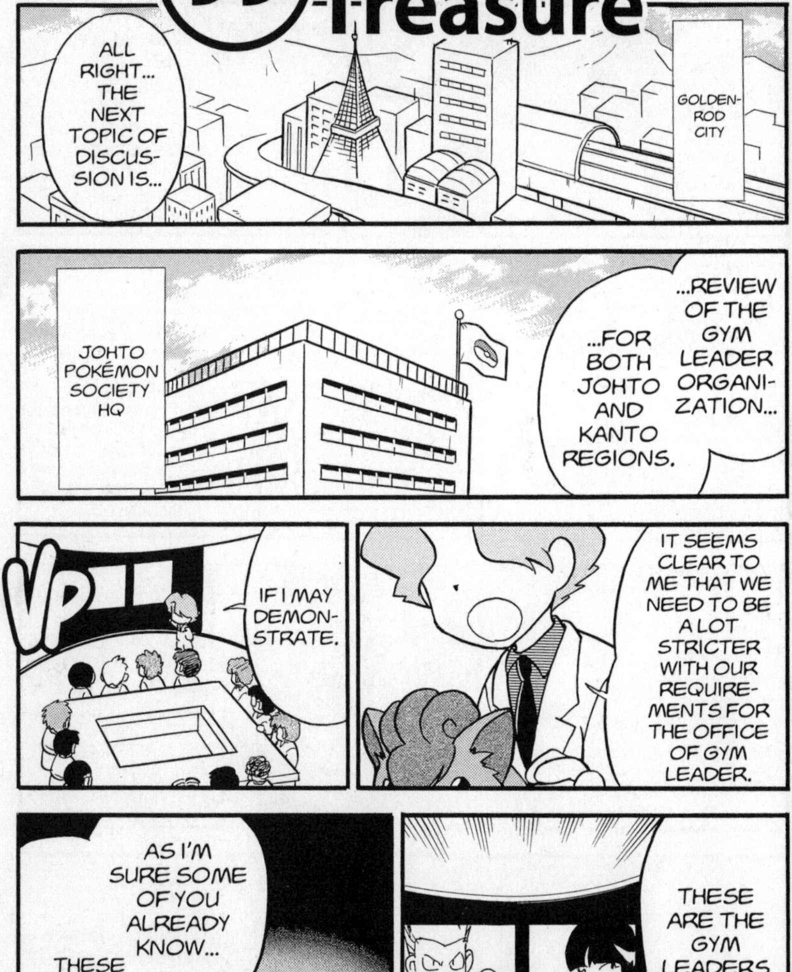
GOLDEN-ROD CITY
ALL RIGHT... THE NEXT TOPIC OF DISCUS-SION IS...
...REVIEW OF THE GYM LEADER ORGANI-ZATION...
...FOR BOTH JOHTO AND KANTO REGIONS.
JOHTO POKÉMON SOCIETY HQ
IT SEEMS CLEAR TO ME THAT WE NEED TO BE A LOT STRICTER WITH OUR REQUIRE-MENTS FOR THE OFFICE OF GYM LEADER.
IF I MAY DEMON-STRATE.
VP
THESE ARE THE GYM LEADERS FOR VER-MILION CITY AND SAFFRON CITY.
AS I'M SURE SOME OF YOU ALREADY KNOW...
THESE TWO WERE SUSPECTED OF HAVING CONSPIRED WITH TEAM ROCKET THREE YEARS AGO.

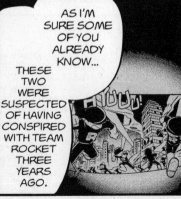

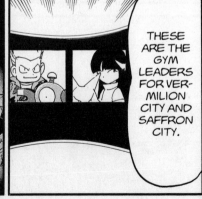

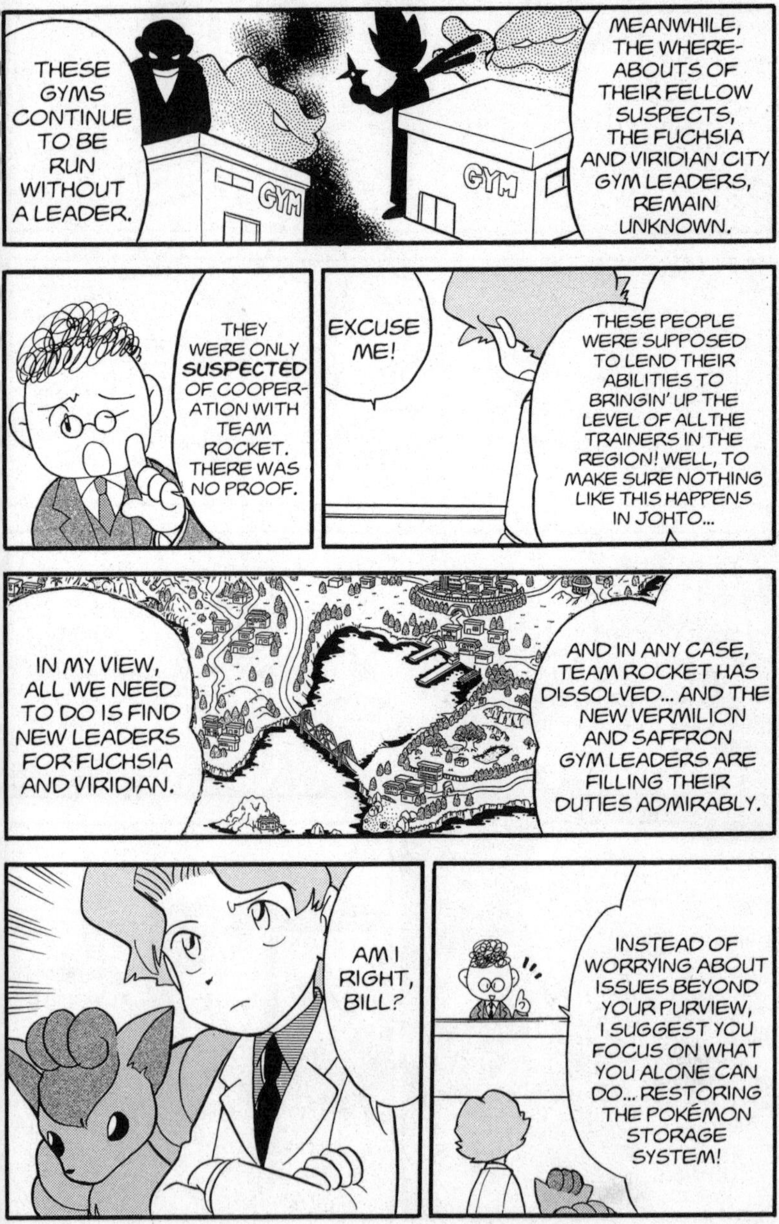
MEANWHILE, THE WHERE-ABOUTS OF THEIR FELLOW SUSPECTS, THE FUCHSIA AND VIRIDIAN CITY GYM LEADERS, REMAIN UNKNOWN.
GYM
GYM
THESE GYMS CONTINUE TO BE RUN WITHOUT A LEADER.
THESE PEOPLE WERE SUPPOSED TO LEND THEIR ABILITIES TO BRINGIN' UP THE LEVEL OF ALL THE TRAINERS IN THE REGION! WELL, TO MAKE SURE NOTHING LIKE THIS HAPPENS IN JOHTO...
EXCUSE ME!
THEY WERE ONLY **SUSPECTED** OF COOPERATION WITH TEAM ROCKET. THERE WAS NO PROOF.
AND IN ANY CASE, TEAM ROCKET HAS DISSOLVED... AND THE NEW VERMILION AND SAFFRON GYM LEADERS ARE FILLING THEIR DUTIES ADMIRABLY.
IN MY VIEW, ALL WE NEED TO DO IS FIND NEW LEADERS FOR FUCHSIA AND VIRIDIAN.
INSTEAD OF WORRYING ABOUT ISSUES BEYOND YOUR PURVIEW, I SUGGEST YOU FOCUS ON WHAT YOU ALONE CAN DO... RESTORING THE POKÉMON STORAGE SYSTEM!
AM I RIGHT, BILL?

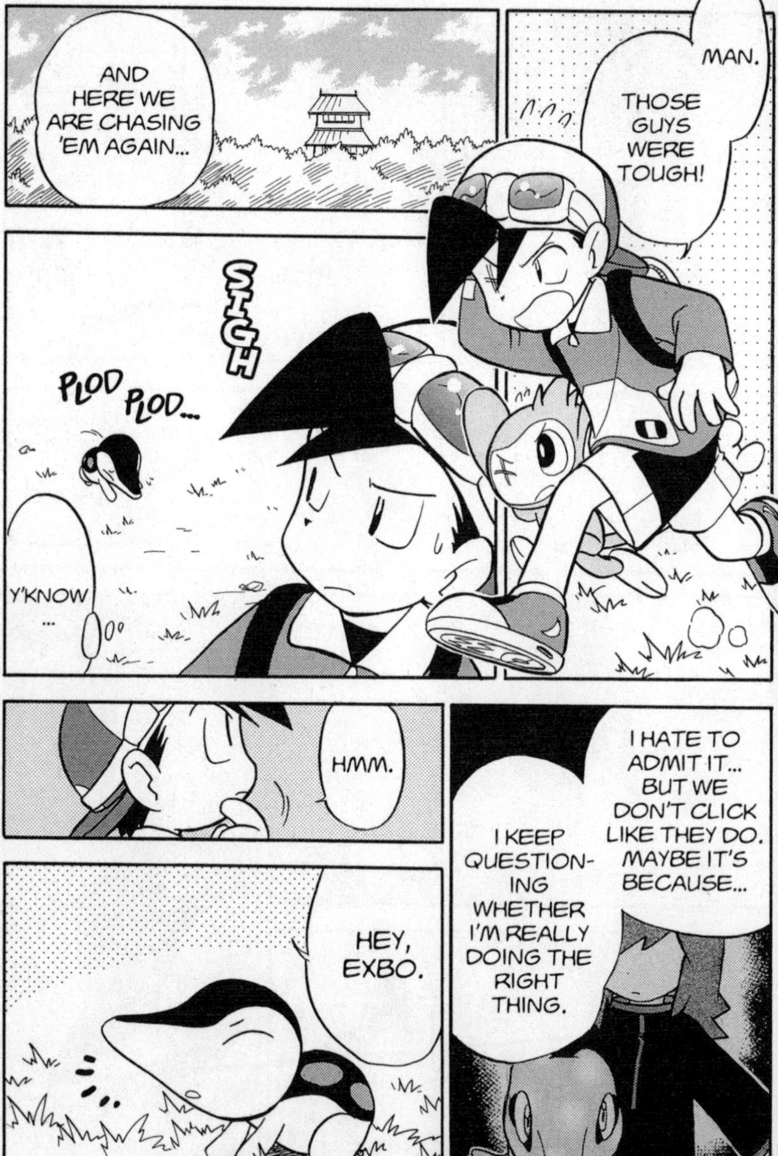
MAN.
THOSE GUYS WERE TOUGH!
AND HERE WE ARE CHASING 'EM AGAIN...
SIGH
PLOD PLOD...
Y'KNOW ...
I HATE TO ADMIT IT... BUT WE DON'T CLICK LIKE THEY DO. MAYBE IT'S BECAUSE...
I KEEP QUESTIONING WHETHER I'M REALLY DOING THE RIGHT THING.
HMM.
HEY, EXBO.

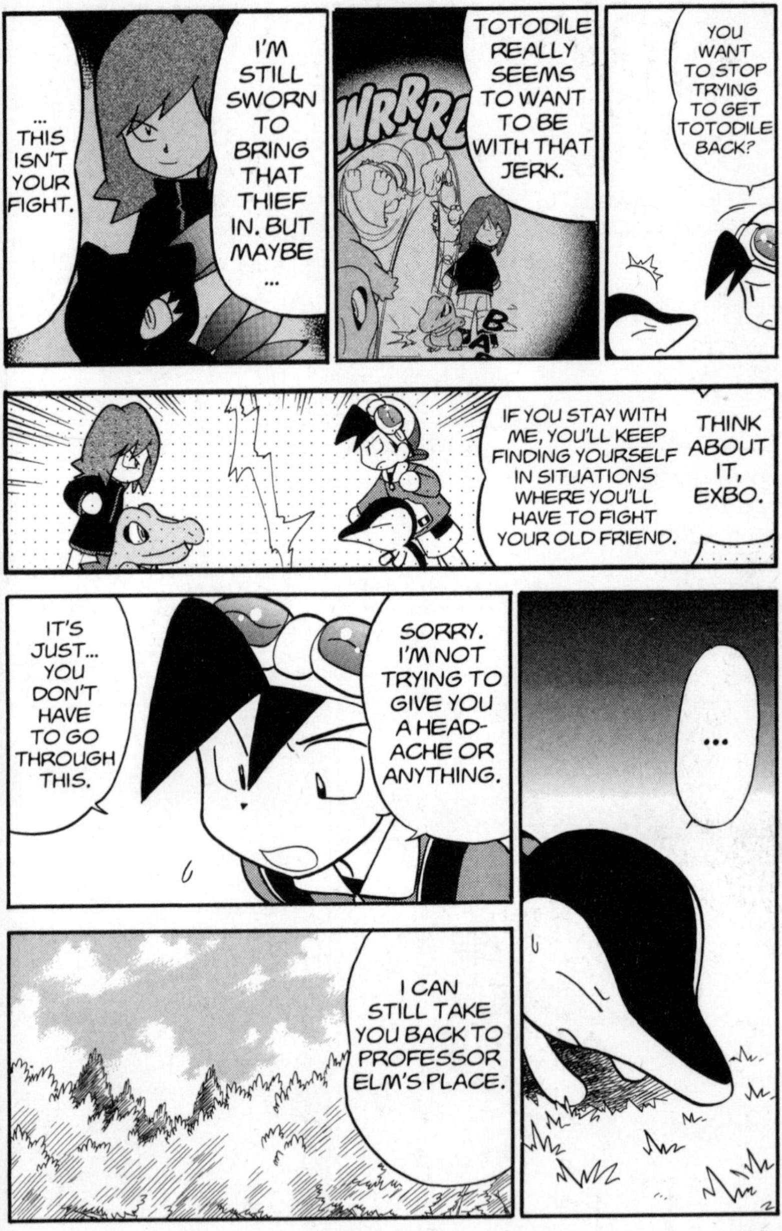
YOU WANT TO STOP TRYING TO GET TOTODILE BACK?
TOTODILE REALLY SEEMS TO WANT TO BE WITH THAT JERK.
WRRRL
I'M STILL SWORN TO BRING THAT THIEF IN. BUT MAYBE ...
... THIS ISN'T YOUR FIGHT.
THINK ABOUT IT, EXBO.
IF YOU STAY WITH ME, YOU'LL KEEP FINDING YOURSELF IN SITUATIONS WHERE YOU'LL HAVE TO FIGHT YOUR OLD FRIEND.
...
SORRY. I'M NOT TRYING TO GIVE YOU A HEADACHE OR ANYTHING.
IT'S JUST... YOU DON'T HAVE TO GO THROUGH THIS.
I CAN STILL TAKE YOU BACK TO PROFESSOR ELM'S PLACE.

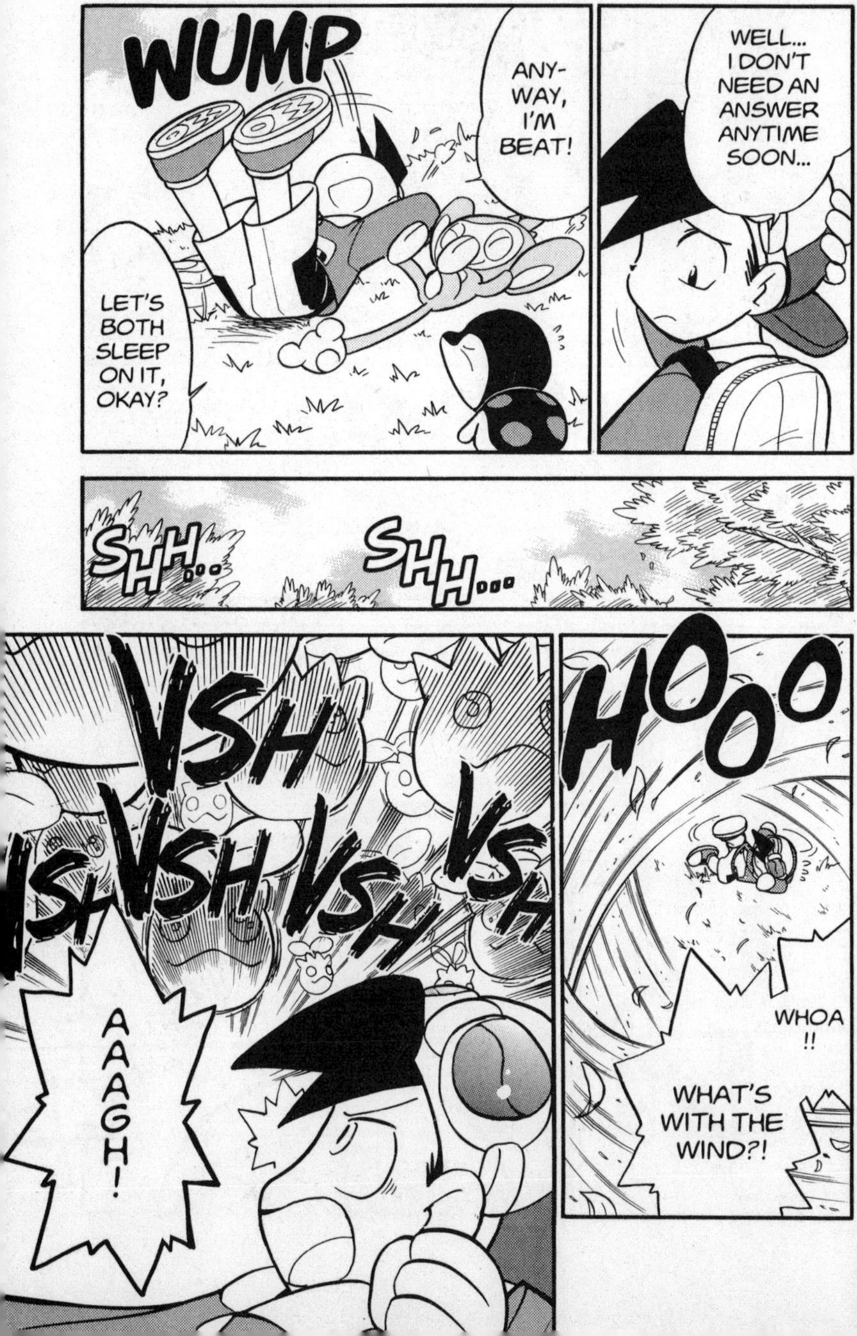
WELL... I DON'T NEED AN ANSWER ANYTIME SOON...
WUMP
ANY-WAY, I'M BEAT!
LET'S BOTH SLEEP ON IT, OKAY?
SHH...
SHH...
HOOO
WHOA !!
WHAT'S WITH THE WIND?!
VSH
VSH
VSH
VSH
VSH
VSH
AAAGH!

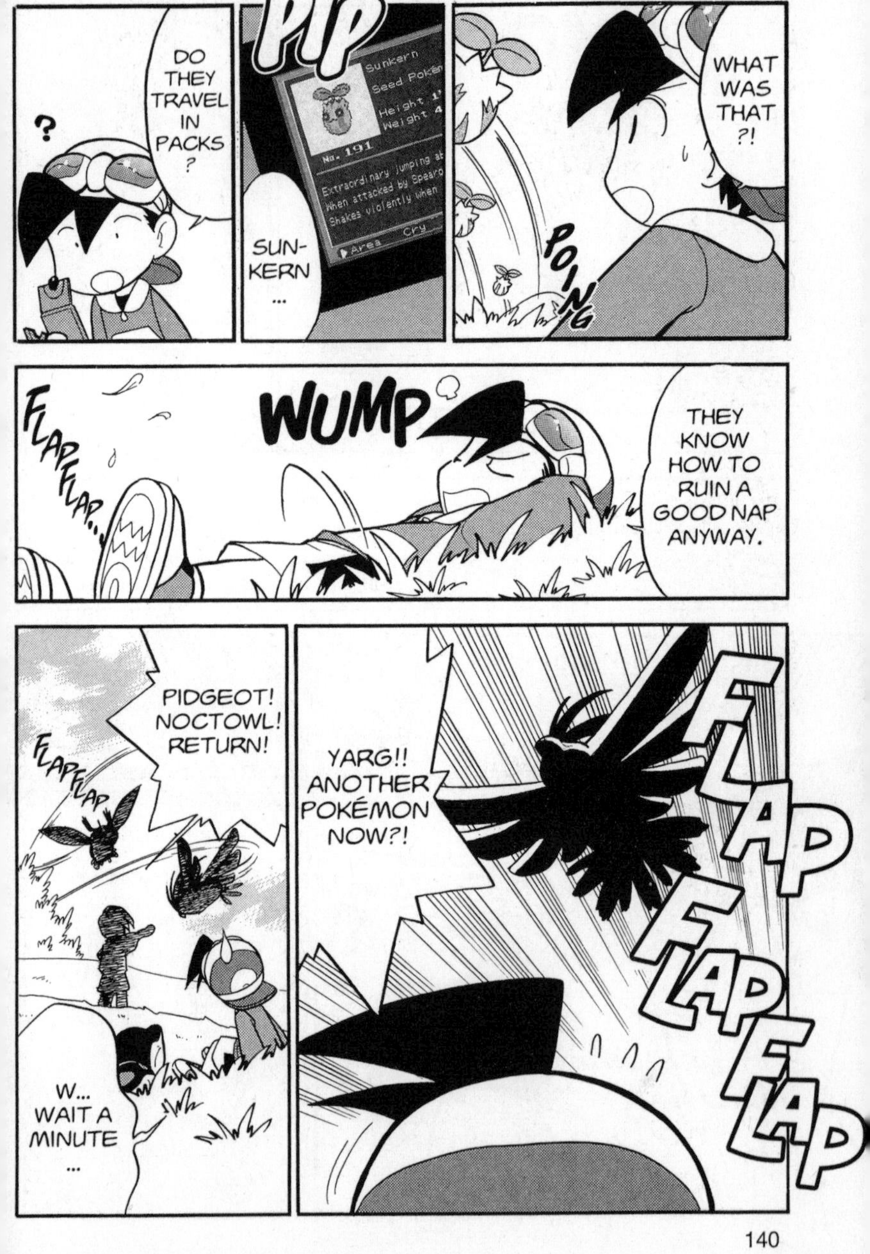
WHAT WAS THAT ?!
POING
PIP
Sunkern
Seed Pokém
Height 1'
Weight 4
No. 191
Extraordinary jumping ab
When attacked by Spearo
Shakes violently when
Area
Cry
SUN-KERN ...
?
DO THEY TRAVEL IN PACKS ?
THEY KNOW HOW TO RUIN A GOOD NAP ANYWAY.
WUMP
FLAPFLAP...
FLAP FLAP FLAP
YARG!! ANOTHER POKÉMON NOW?!
PIDGEOT! NOCTOWL! RETURN!
FLAPFLAP
W... WAIT A MINUTE ...

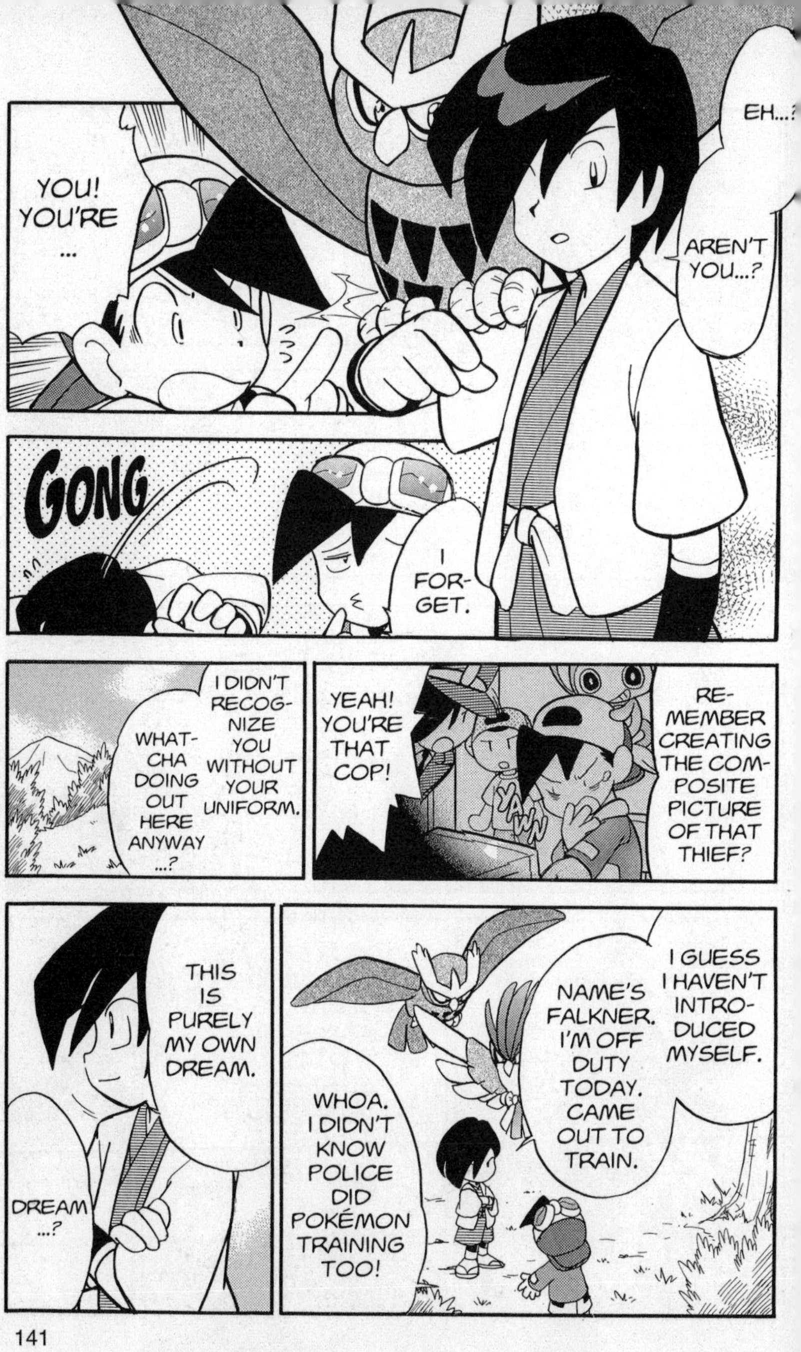
EH...?
AREN'T YOU...?
YOU! YOU'RE ...
I FORGET.
GONG
REMEMBER CREATING THE COMPOSITE PICTURE OF THAT THIEF?
YAWN
YEAH! YOU'RE THAT COP!
I DIDN'T RECOGNIZE YOU WITHOUT YOUR UNIFORM.
WHATCHA DOING OUT HERE ANYWAY ...?
I GUESS I HAVEN'T INTRODUCED MYSELF.
NAME'S FALKNER. I'M OFF DUTY TODAY. CAME OUT TO TRAIN.
WHOA. I DIDN'T KNOW POLICE DID POKÉMON TRAINING TOO!
THIS IS PURELY MY OWN DREAM.
DREAM ...?

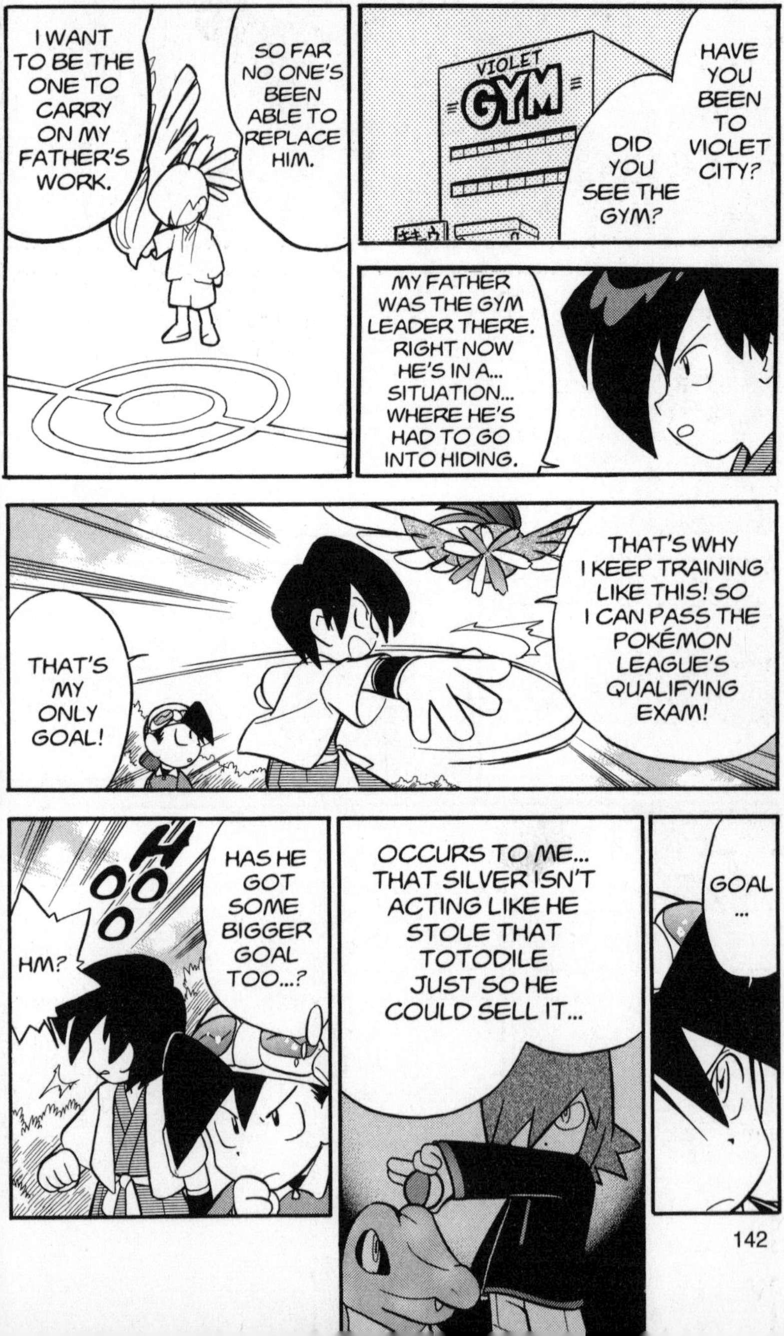
VIOLET
GYM
HAVE YOU BEEN TO VIOLET CITY?
DID YOU SEE THE GYM?
MY FATHER WAS THE GYM LEADER THERE. RIGHT NOW HE'S IN A... SITUATION... WHERE HE'S HAD TO GO INTO HIDING.
SO FAR NO ONE'S BEEN ABLE TO REPLACE HIM.
I WANT TO BE THE ONE TO CARRY ON MY FATHER'S WORK.
THAT'S WHY I KEEP TRAINING LIKE THIS! SO I CAN PASS THE POKÉMON LEAGUE'S QUALIFYING EXAM!
THAT'S MY ONLY GOAL!
GOAL...
OCCURS TO ME... THAT SILVER ISN'T ACTING LIKE HE STOLE THAT TOTODILE JUST SO HE COULD SELL IT...
HAS HE GOT SOME BIGGER GOAL TOO...?
HOOO
HM?

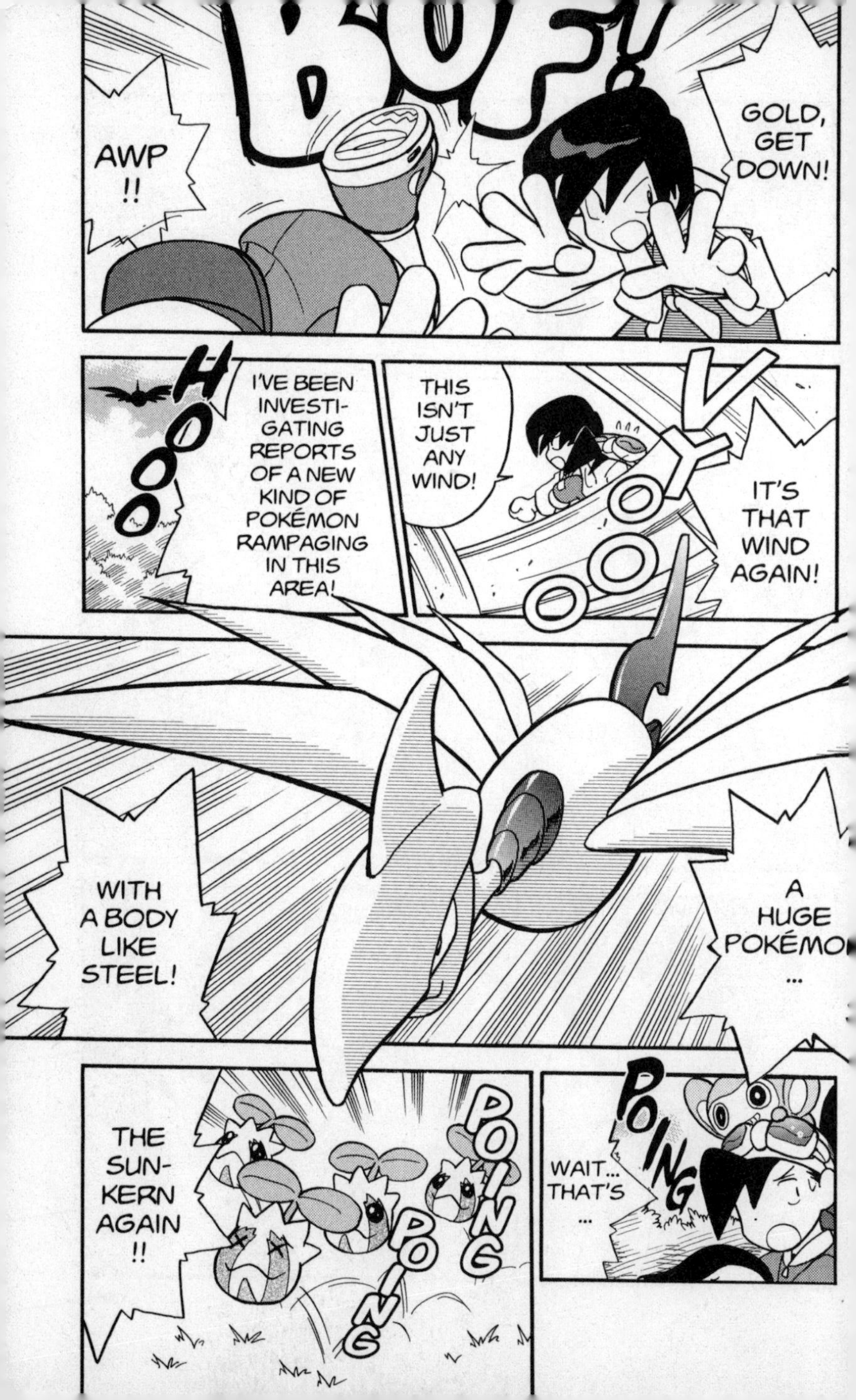
GOLD, GET DOWN!
AWP !!
IT'S THAT WIND AGAIN!
THIS ISN'T JUST ANY WIND!
I'VE BEEN INVESTI-GATING REPORTS OF A NEW KIND OF POKÉMON RAMPAGING IN THIS AREA!
HOOOO
A HUGE POKÉMO ...
WITH A BODY LIKE STEEL!
POING
WAIT... THAT'S ...
POING
POING
THE SUN-KERN AGAIN !!

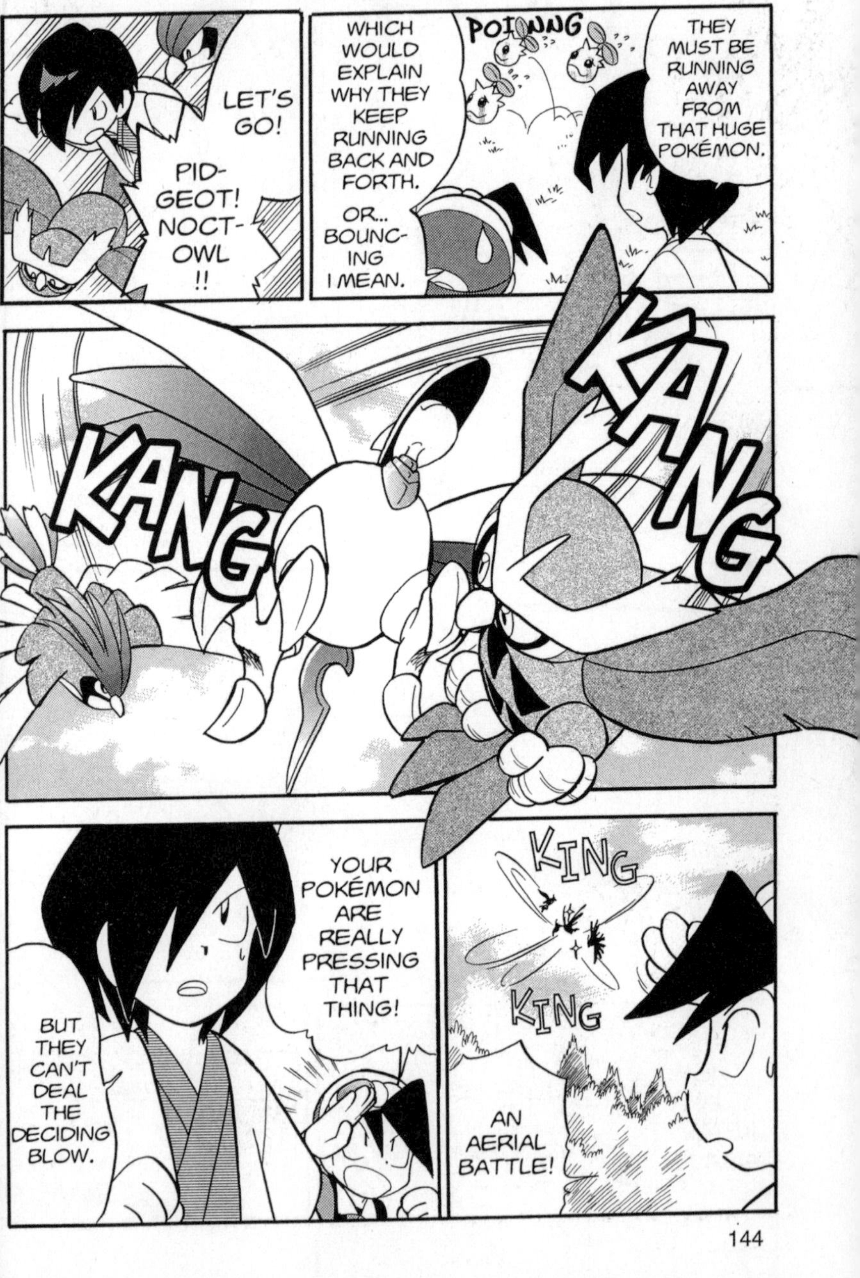
THEY MUST BE RUNNING AWAY FROM THAT HUGE POKÉMON.
POINNG
WHICH WOULD EXPLAIN WHY THEY KEEP RUNNING BACK AND FORTH.
OR... BOUNCING I MEAN.
LET'S GO!
PID-GEOT! NOCT-OWL!!
KANG
KANG
KING
KING
AN AERIAL BATTLE!
YOUR POKÉMON ARE REALLY PRESSING THAT THING!
BUT THEY CAN'T DEAL THE DECIDING BLOW.

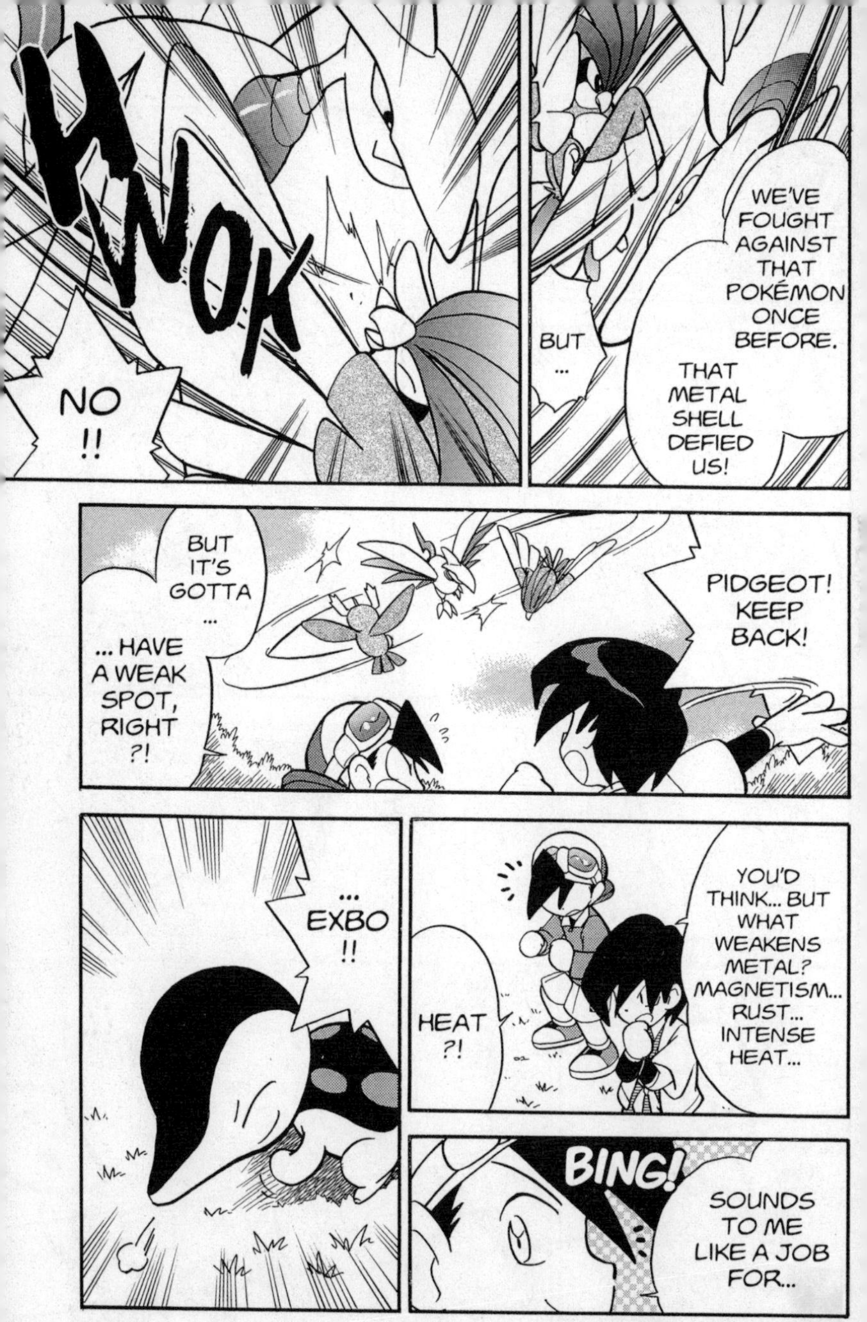
WE'VE FOUGHT AGAINST THAT POKÉMON ONCE BEFORE.
THAT METAL SHELL DEFIED US!
BUT ...
WHOK
NO !!
PIDGEOT! KEEP BACK!
BUT IT'S GOTTA ...
... HAVE A WEAK SPOT, RIGHT ?!
YOU'D THINK... BUT WHAT WEAKENS METAL? MAGNETISM... RUST... INTENSE HEAT...
HEAT ?!
BING!
SOUNDS TO ME LIKE A JOB FOR...
... EXBO !!

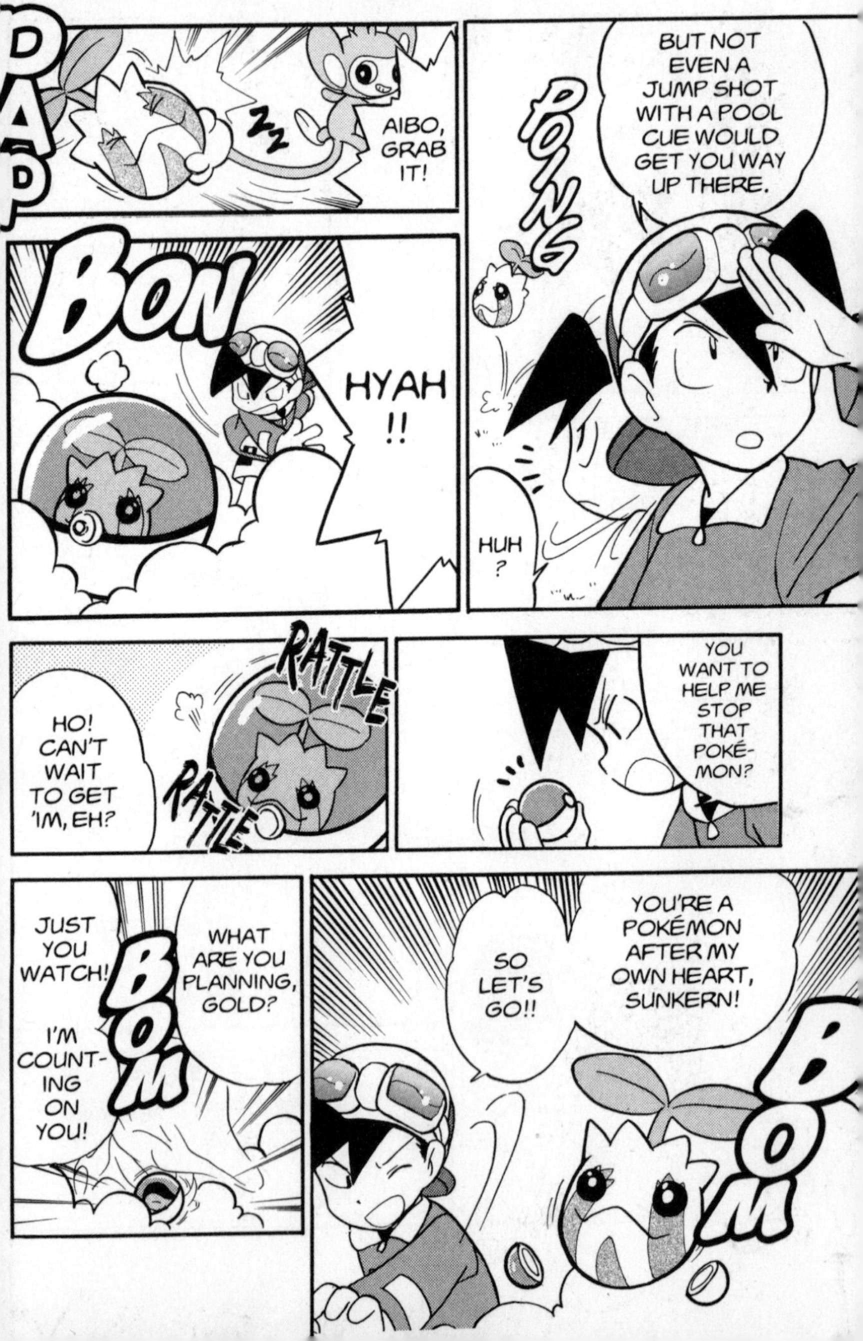
BUT NOT EVEN A JUMP SHOT WITH A POOL CUE WOULD GET YOU WAY UP THERE.
POING
HUH?
DAP
AIBO, GRAB IT!
BON
HYAH!!
YOU WANT TO HELP ME STOP THAT POKÉMON?
RATTLE
RATTLE
HO! CAN'T WAIT TO GET 'IM, EH?
YOU'RE A POKÉMON AFTER MY OWN HEART, SUNKERN!
SO LET'S GO!!
BOM
WHAT ARE YOU PLANNING, GOLD?
JUST YOU WATCH!
I'M COUNTING ON YOU!
BOM

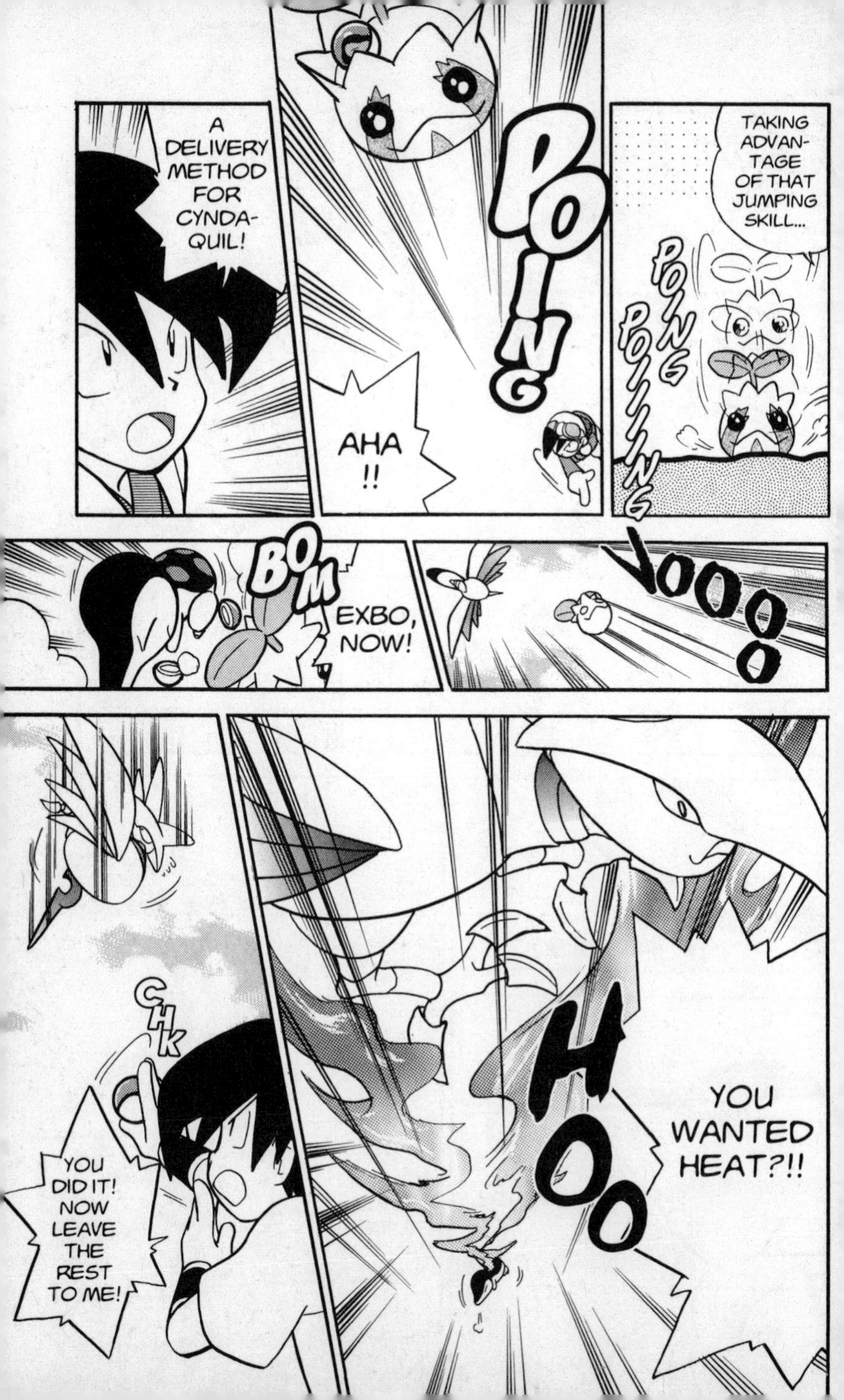
TAKING ADVANTAGE OF THAT JUMPING SKILL...
POING
POING
POIIIING
POING
AHA!!
A DELIVERY METHOD FOR CYNDAQUIL!
VOOOOO
BOM
EXBO, NOW!
YOU WANTED HEAT?!!
HOOO
CHK
YOU DID IT! NOW LEAVE THE REST TO ME!

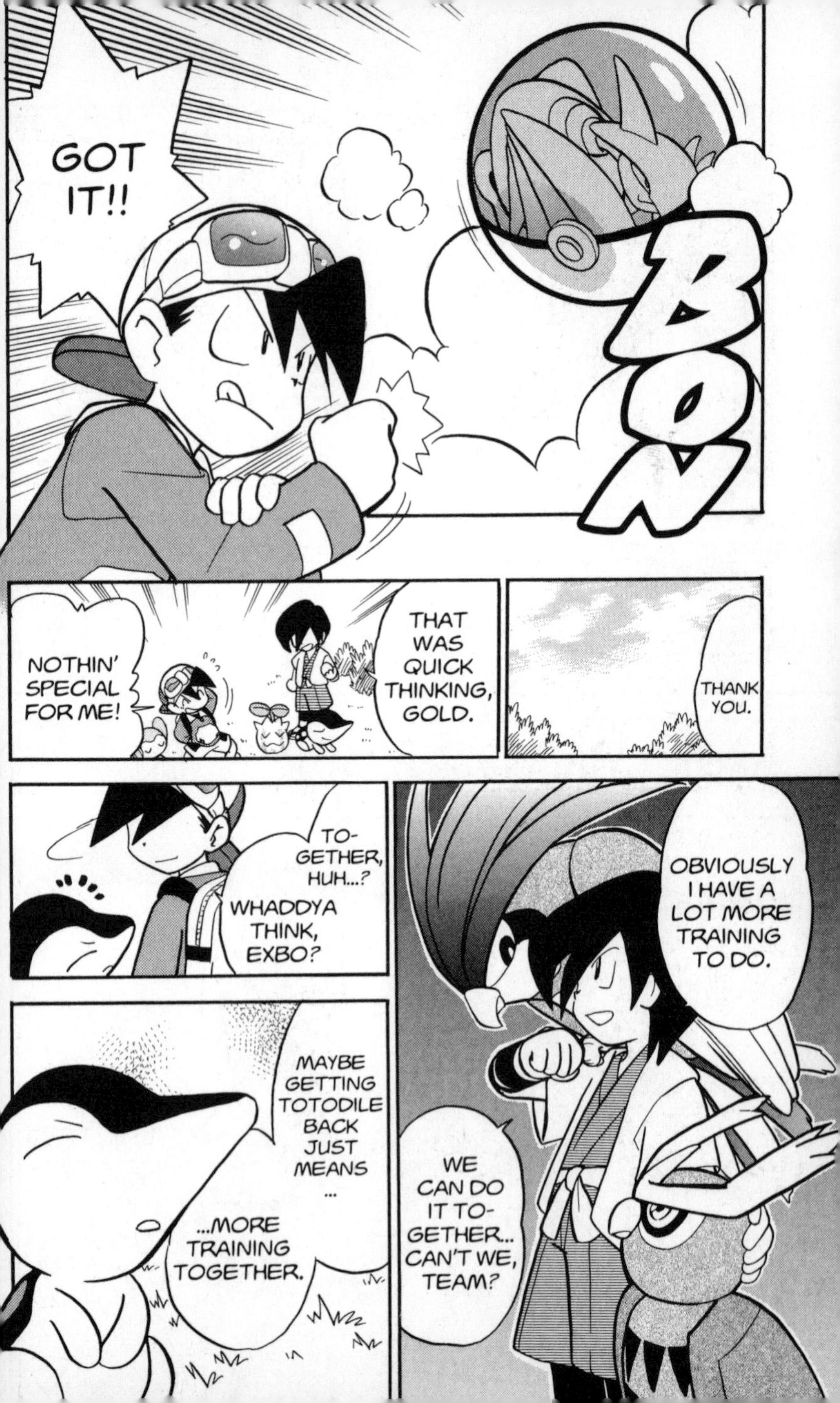
GOT IT!!
BON
THANK YOU.
THAT WAS QUICK THINKING, GOLD.
NOTHIN' SPECIAL FOR ME!
OBVIOUSLY I HAVE A LOT MORE TRAINING TO DO.
WE CAN DO IT TO-GETHER... CAN'T WE, TEAM?
TO-GETHER, HUH...?
WHADDYA THINK, EXBO?
MAYBE GETTING TOTODILE BACK JUST MEANS ...
...MORE TRAINING TOGETHER.

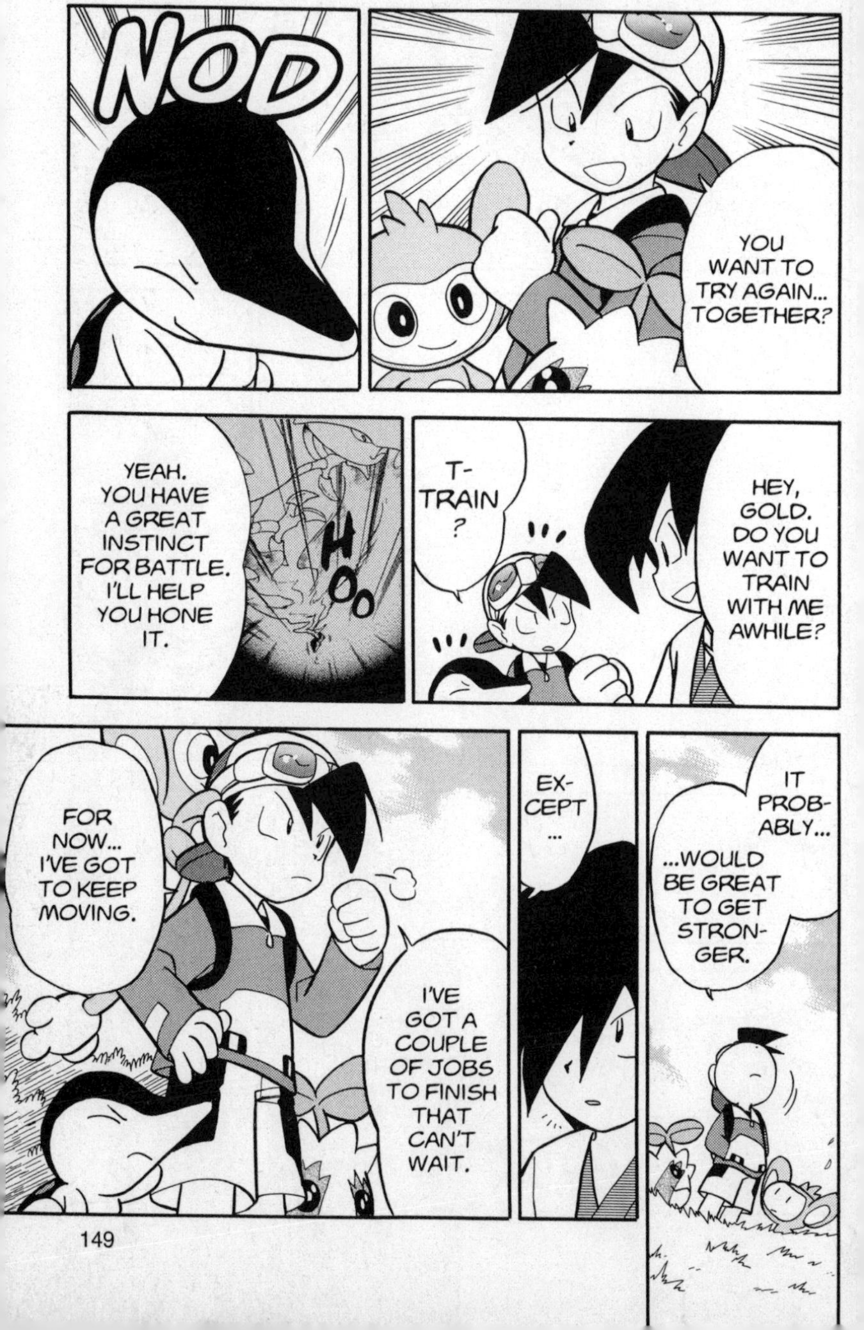
YOU WANT TO TRY AGAIN... TOGETHER?
NOD
HEY, GOLD. DO YOU WANT TO TRAIN WITH ME AWHILE?
T-TRAIN?
YEAH. YOU HAVE A GREAT INSTINCT FOR BATTLE. I'LL HELP YOU HONE IT.
HOO
IT PROBABLY...
...WOULD BE GREAT TO GET STRONGER.
EXCEPT...
FOR NOW... I'VE GOT TO KEEP MOVING.
I'VE GOT A COUPLE OF JOBS TO FINISH THAT CAN'T WAIT.

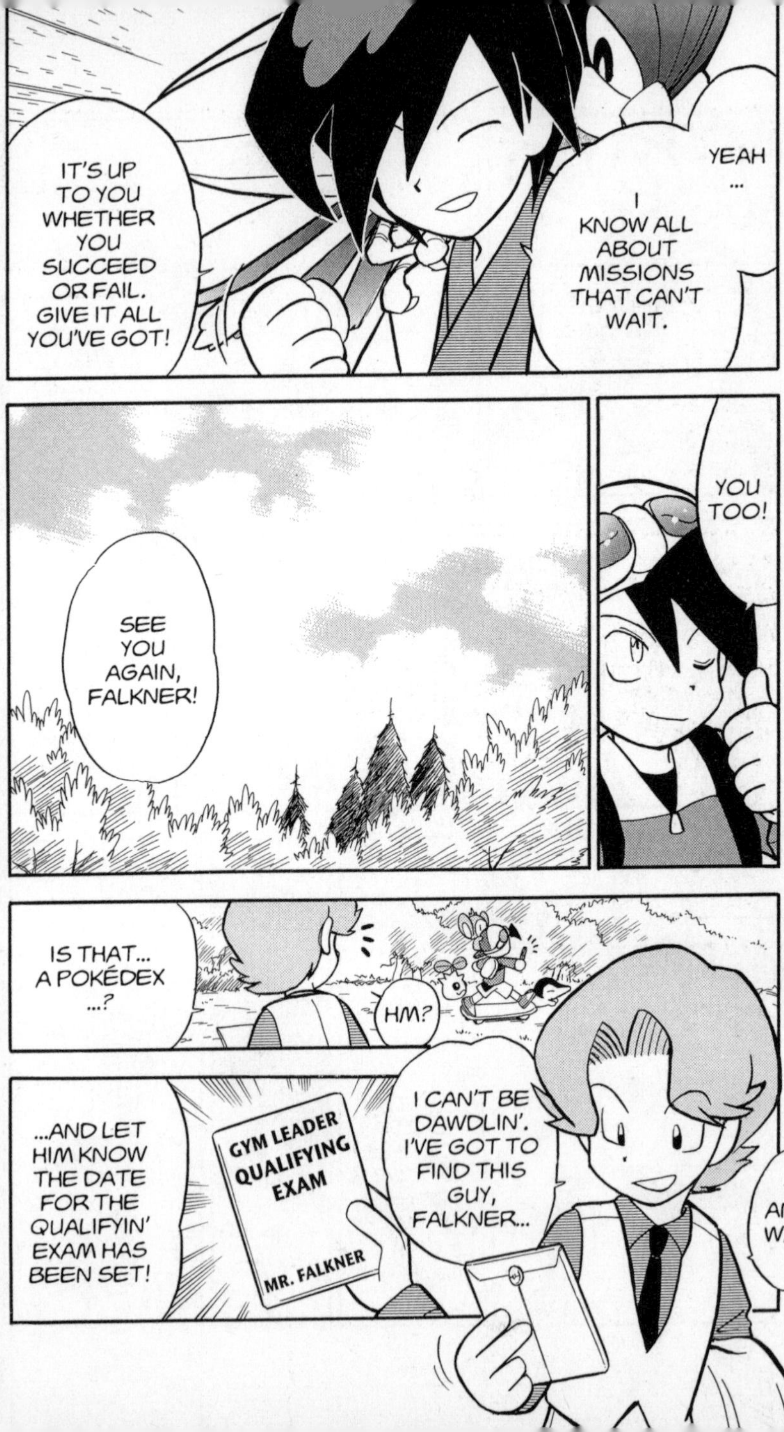

YEAH ... I KNOW ALL ABOUT MISSIONS THAT CAN'T WAIT.
IT'S UP TO YOU WHETHER YOU SUCCEED OR FAIL. GIVE IT ALL YOU'VE GOT!
YOU TOO!
SEE YOU AGAIN, FALKNER!
HM?
IS THAT... A POKÉDEX ...?
ANY-WAY.
I CAN'T BE DAWDLIN'. I'VE GOT TO FIND THIS GUY, FALKNER...
GYM LEADER QUALIFYING EXAM
MR. FALKNER
...AND LET HIM KNOW THE DATE FOR THE QUALIFYIN' EXAM HAS BEEN SET!

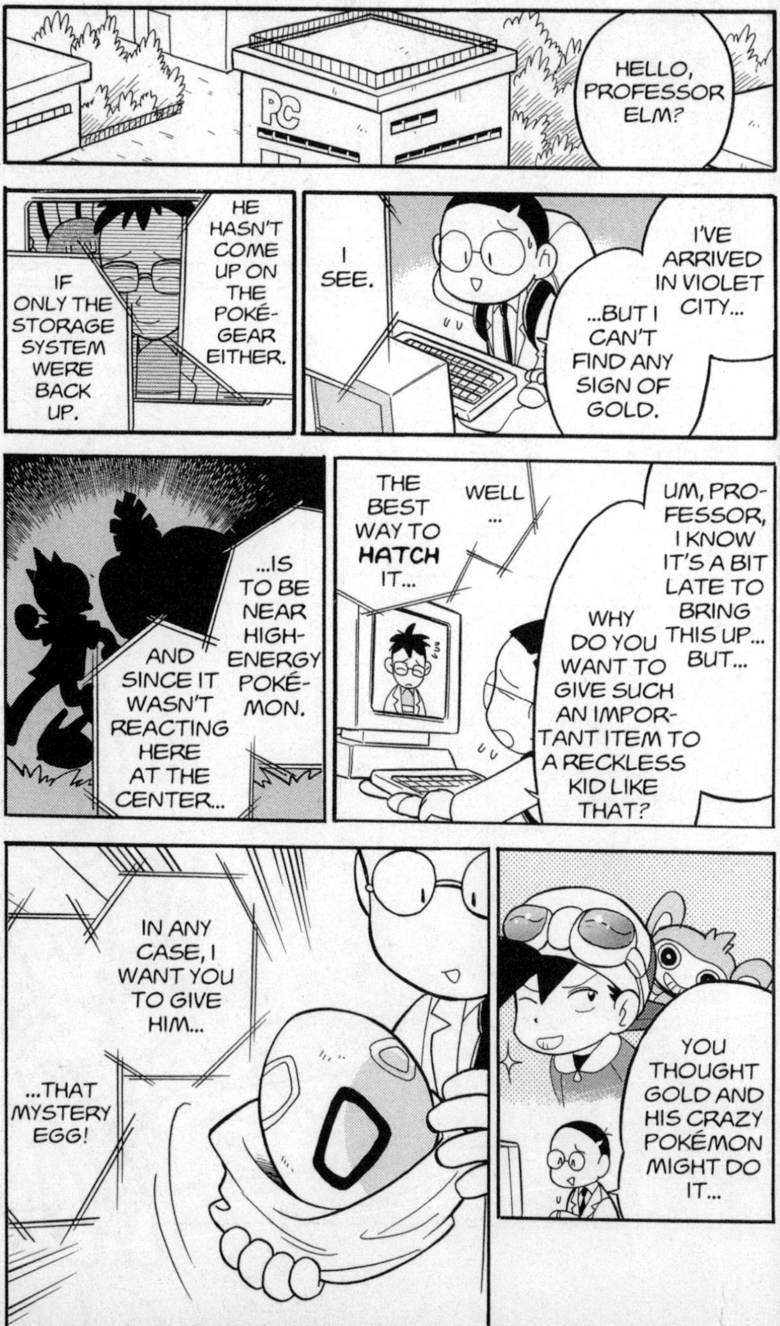
HELLO, PROFESSOR ELM?
I'VE ARRIVED IN VIOLET CITY...
...BUT I CAN'T FIND ANY SIGN OF GOLD.
I SEE.
HE HASN'T COME UP ON THE POKÉ-GEAR EITHER.
IF ONLY THE STORAGE SYSTEM WERE BACK UP.
UM, PRO-FESSOR, I KNOW IT'S A BIT LATE TO BRING THIS UP... BUT...
WHY DO YOU WANT TO GIVE SUCH AN IMPOR-TANT ITEM TO A RECKLESS KID LIKE THAT?
WELL ...
THE BEST WAY TO HATCH IT...
...IS TO BE NEAR HIGH-ENERGY POKÉ-MON.
AND SINCE IT WASN'T REACTING HERE AT THE CENTER...
YOU THOUGHT GOLD AND HIS CRAZY POKÉMON MIGHT DO IT...
IN ANY CASE, I WANT YOU TO GIVE HIM...
...THAT MYSTERY EGG!

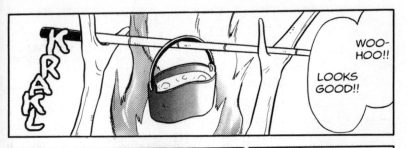

WOO-HOO!!

LOOKS GOOD!!

HMM. NOT THERE QUITE YET. EXBO, COULD YOU TURN UP THE HEAT A LITTLE?

SLURP

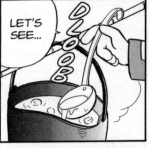

LET'S SEE...

DROOB

SSSSZZZ

...

WAGH!!

FOOSH

152

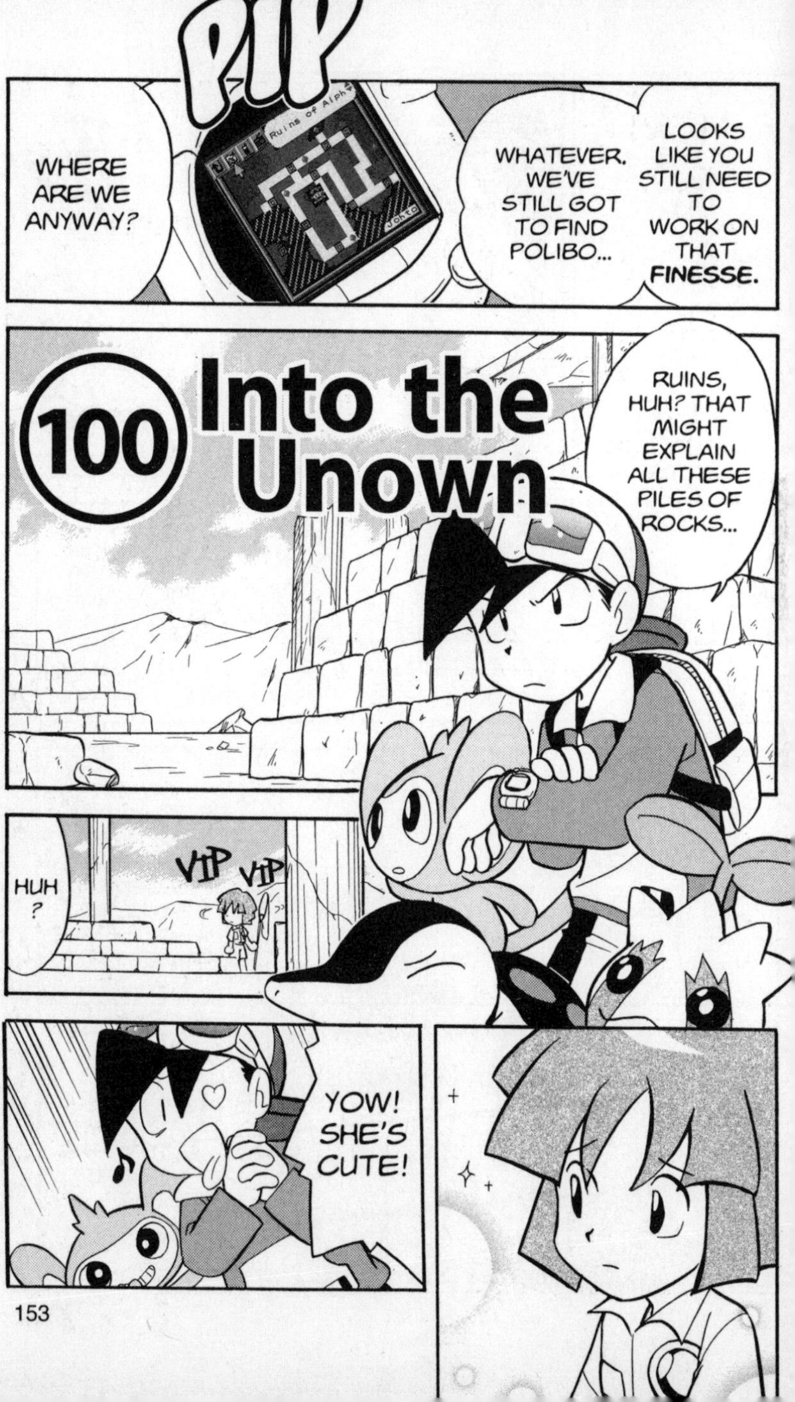

PIP
Ruins of Alph
Johto
LOOKS LIKE YOU STILL NEED TO WORK ON THAT FINESSE.
WHATEVER. WE'VE STILL GOT TO FIND POLIBO...
WHERE ARE WE ANYWAY?
100 Into the Unown
RUINS, HUH? THAT MIGHT EXPLAIN ALL THESE PILES OF ROCKS...
VIP VIP
HUH ?
YOW! SHE'S CUTE!

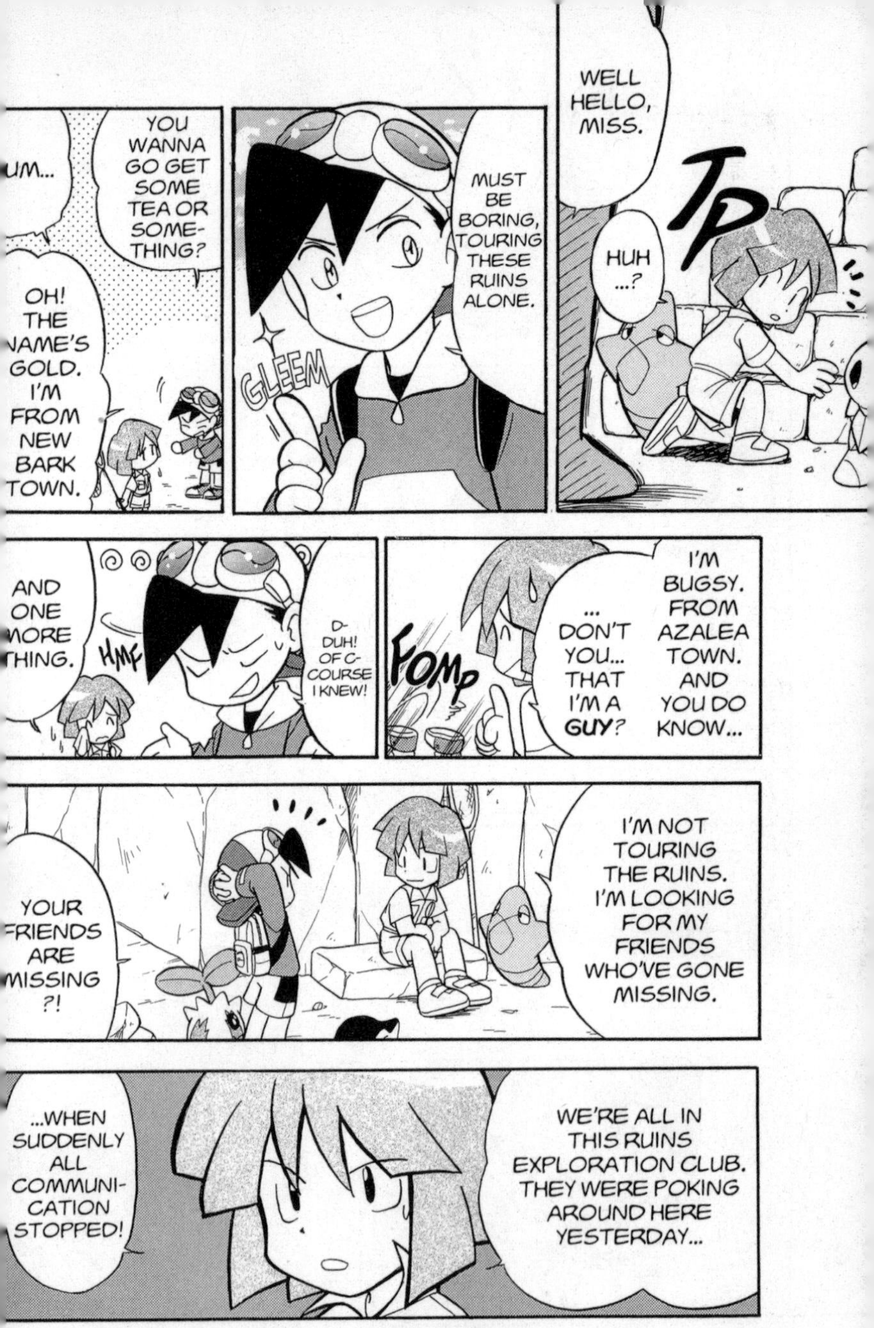
WELL HELLO, MISS.
TP
HUH ...?
MUST BE BORING, TOURING THESE RUINS ALONE.
GLEEM
YOU WANNA GO GET SOME TEA OR SOME-THING?
UM...
OH! THE NAME'S GOLD. I'M FROM NEW BARK TOWN.
I'M BUGSY. FROM AZALEA TOWN. AND YOU DO KNOW...
... DON'T YOU... THAT I'M A **GUY**?
FOMP
D-DUH! OF C-COURSE I KNEW!
HMF
AND ONE MORE THING.
I'M NOT TOURING THE RUINS. I'M LOOKING FOR MY FRIENDS WHO'VE GONE MISSING.
YOUR FRIENDS ARE MISSING ?!
WE'RE ALL IN THIS RUINS EXPLORATION CLUB. THEY WERE POKING AROUND HERE YESTERDAY...
...WHEN SUDDENLY ALL COMMUNI-CATION STOPPED!

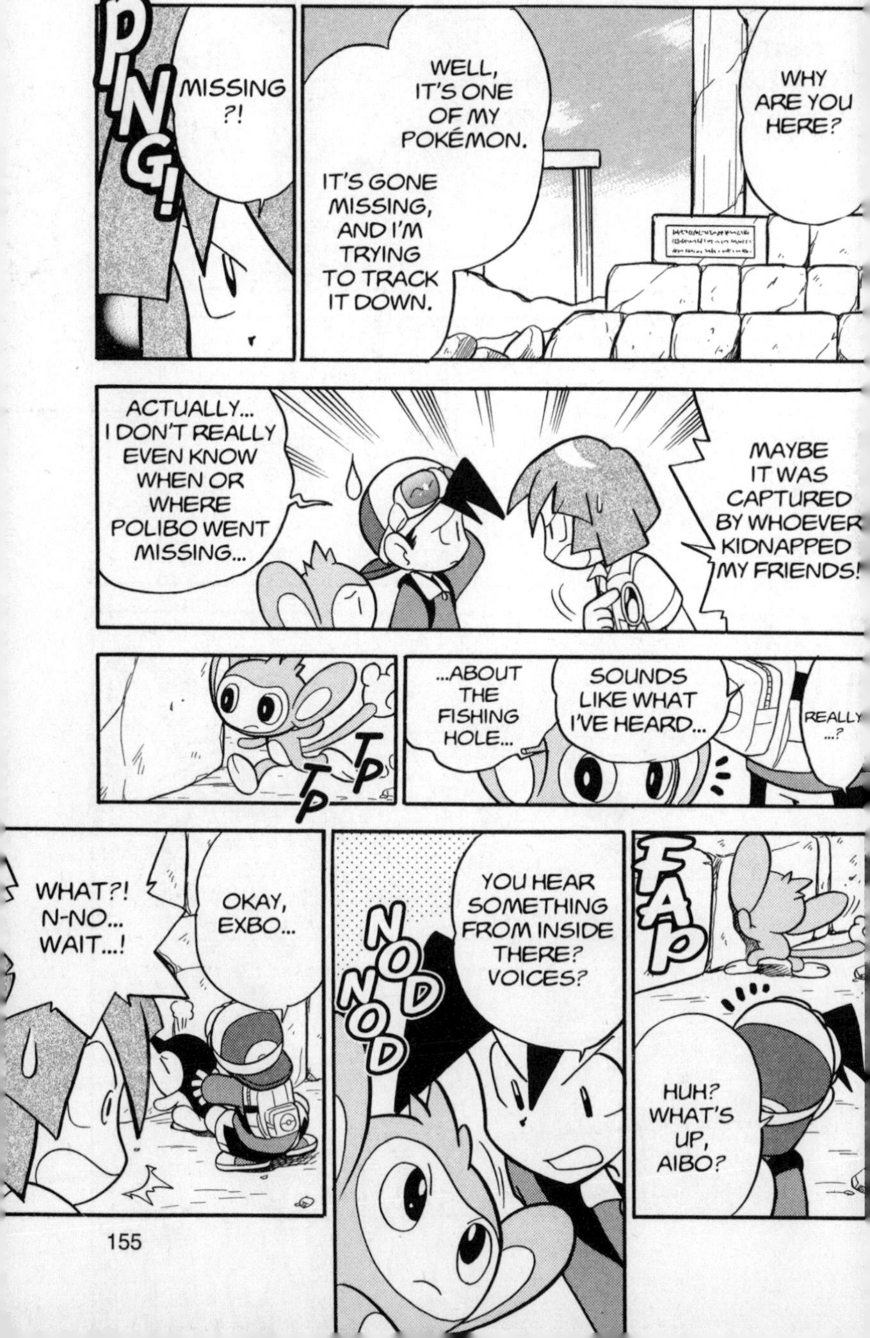
WHY ARE YOU HERE?
WELL, IT'S ONE OF MY POKÉMON.
IT'S GONE MISSING, AND I'M TRYING TO TRACK IT DOWN.
PING!
MISSING ?!
MAYBE IT WAS CAPTURED BY WHOEVER KIDNAPPED MY FRIENDS!
ACTUALLY... I DON'T REALLY EVEN KNOW WHEN OR WHERE POLIBO WENT MISSING...
REALLY ...?
SOUNDS LIKE WHAT I'VE HEARD...
...ABOUT THE FISHING HOLE...
TP TP
FAP
HUH? WHAT'S UP, AIBO?
YOU HEAR SOMETHING FROM INSIDE THERE? VOICES?
NOD NOD
OKAY, EXBO...
WHAT?! N-NO... WAIT...!

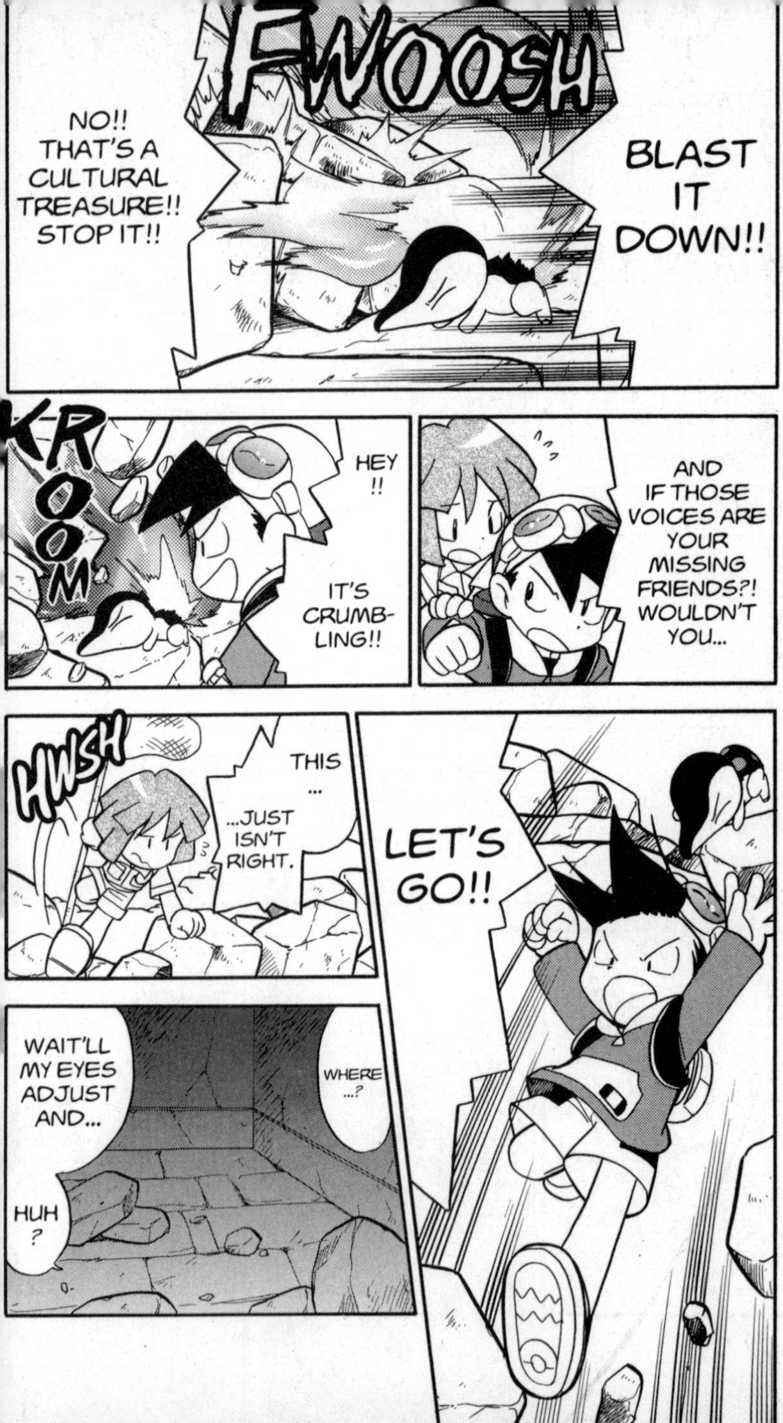
FWOOSH
BLAST IT DOWN!!
NO!! THAT'S A CULTURAL TREASURE!! STOP IT!!
AND IF THOSE VOICES ARE YOUR MISSING FRIENDS?! WOULDN'T YOU...
KROOOM
HEY!!
IT'S CRUMBLING!!
LET'S GO!!
HWSH
THIS...
...JUST ISN'T RIGHT.
WHERE...?
WAIT'LL MY EYES ADJUST AND...
HUH?

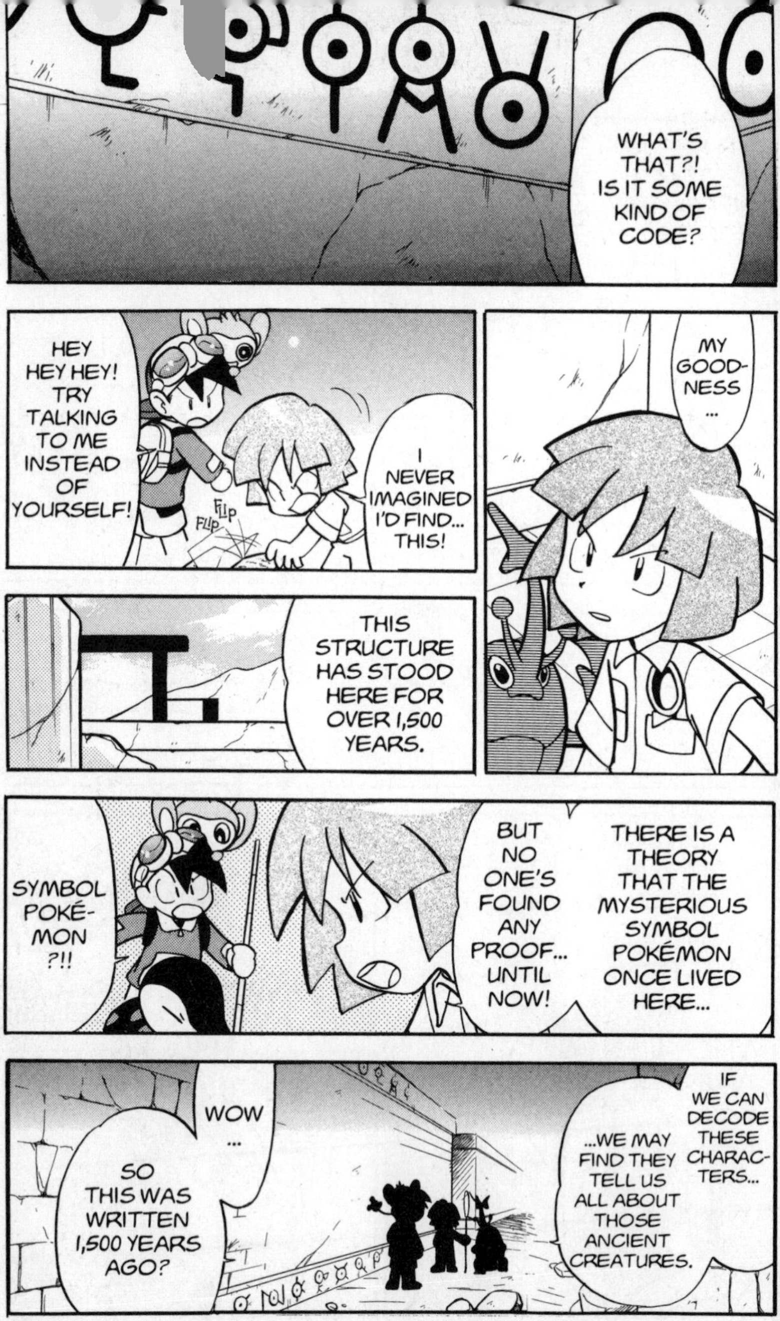
WHAT'S THAT?! IS IT SOME KIND OF CODE?
MY GOODNESS ...
I NEVER IMAGINED I'D FIND... THIS!
HEY HEY HEY! TRY TALKING TO ME INSTEAD OF YOURSELF!
FLIP FLIP
THIS STRUCTURE HAS STOOD HERE FOR OVER 1,500 YEARS.
THERE IS A THEORY THAT THE MYSTERIOUS SYMBOL POKÉMON ONCE LIVED HERE...
BUT NO ONE'S FOUND ANY PROOF... UNTIL NOW!
SYMBOL POKÉ-MON ?!!
IF WE CAN DECODE THESE CHARAC-TERS...
...WE MAY FIND THEY TELL US ALL ABOUT THOSE ANCIENT CREATURES.
WOW ...
SO THIS WAS WRITTEN 1,500 YEARS AGO?

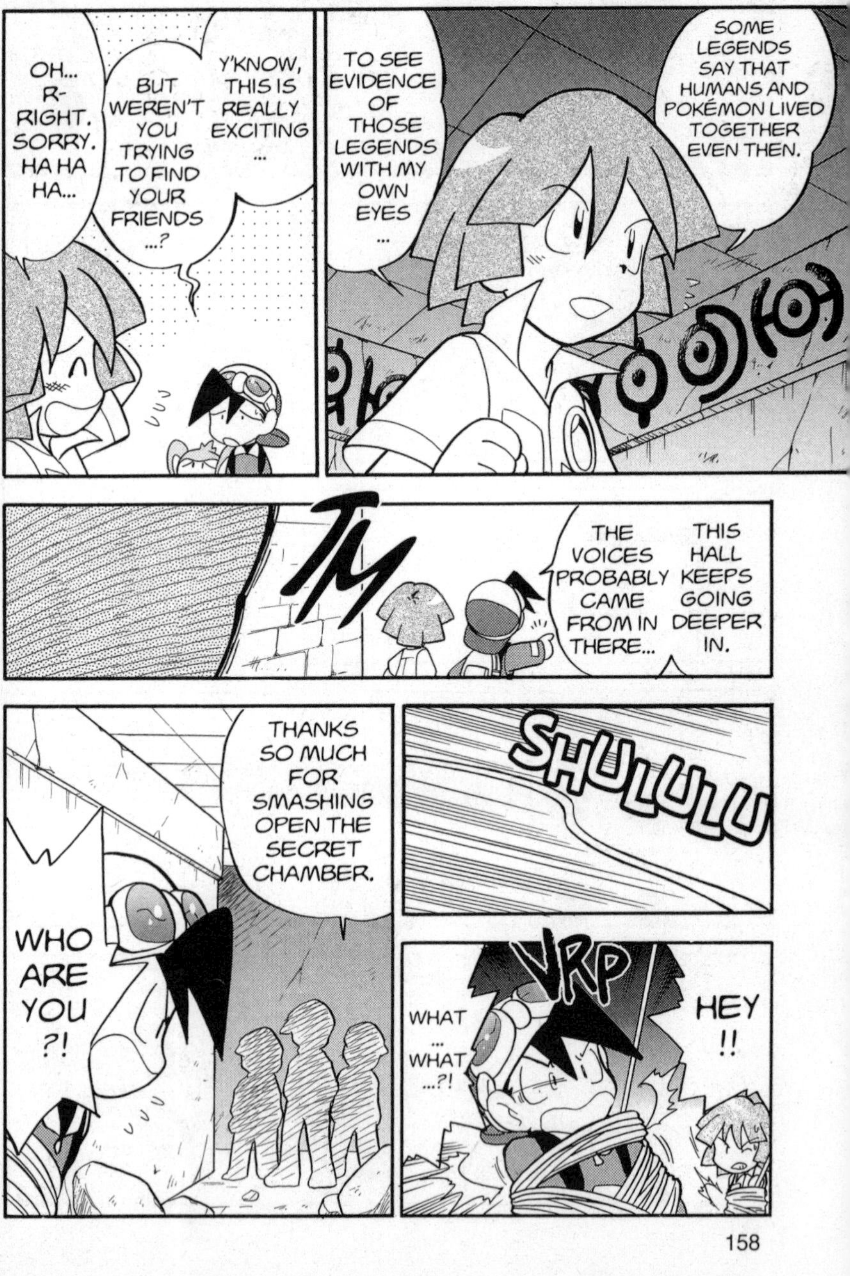
SOME LEGENDS SAY THAT HUMANS AND POKÉMON LIVED TOGETHER EVEN THEN.
TO SEE EVIDENCE OF THOSE LEGENDS WITH MY OWN EYES ...
Y'KNOW, THIS IS REALLY EXCITING ...
BUT WEREN'T YOU TRYING TO FIND YOUR FRIENDS ...?
OH... R-RIGHT. SORRY. HA HA HA...
THIS HALL KEEPS GOING DEEPER IN.
THE VOICES PROBABLY CAME FROM IN THERE...
TM
SHULULU
VRP
HEY !!
WHAT ... WHAT ...?!
THANKS SO MUCH FOR SMASHING OPEN THE SECRET CHAMBER.
WHO ARE YOU ?!

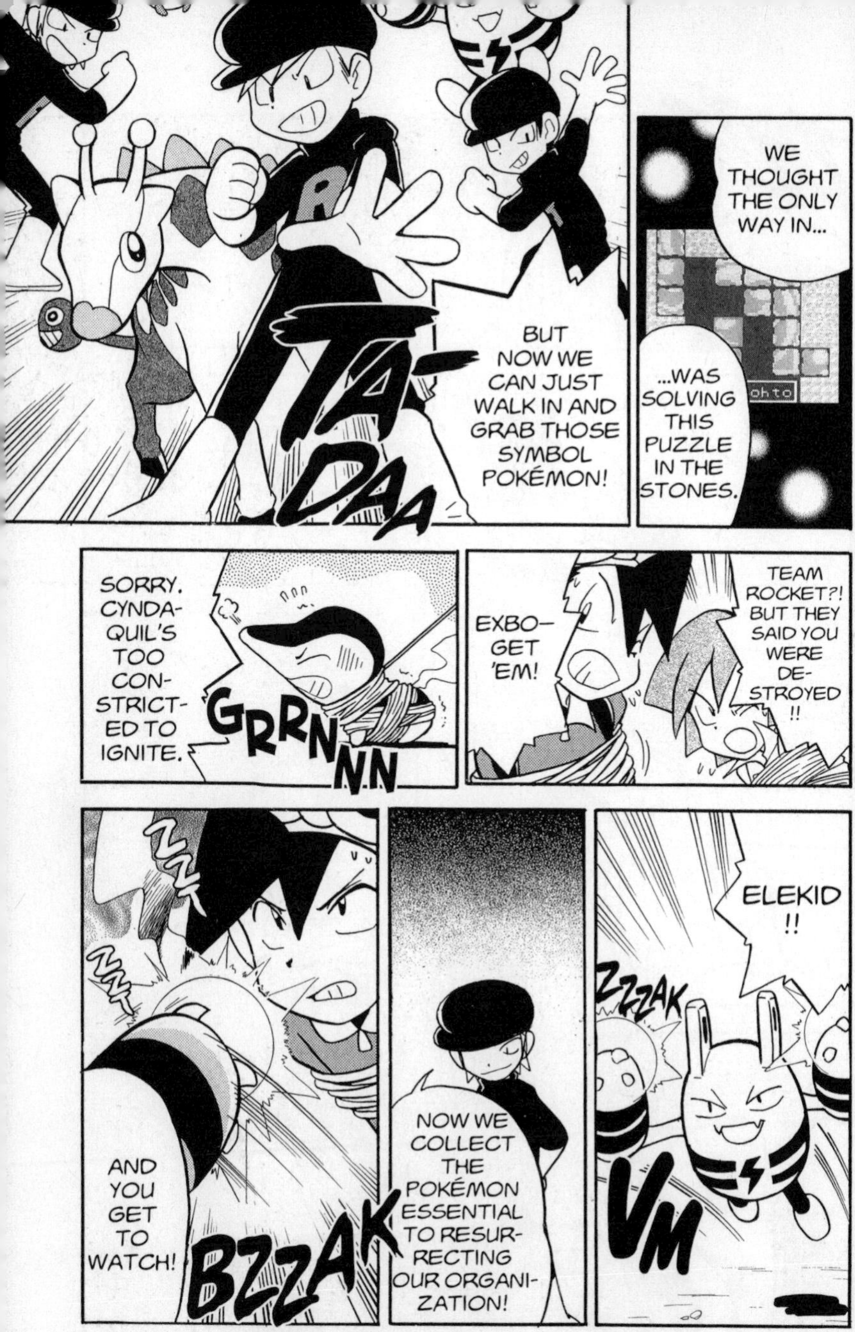

WE THOUGHT THE ONLY WAY IN...
...WAS SOLVING THIS PUZZLE IN THE STONES.
BUT NOW WE CAN JUST WALK IN AND GRAB THOSE SYMBOL POKÉMON!
TA-DAA
TEAM ROCKET?! BUT THEY SAID YOU WERE DE-STROYED!!
EXBO—GET 'EM!
SORRY. CYNDA-QUIL'S TOO CON-STRICT-ED TO IGNITE.
GRRNNNN
ELEKID!!
ZZZAK
VM
NOW WE COLLECT THE POKÉMON ESSENTIAL TO RESUR-RECTING OUR ORGANI-ZATION!
NNK
NNK
AND YOU GET TO WATCH!
BZZAK

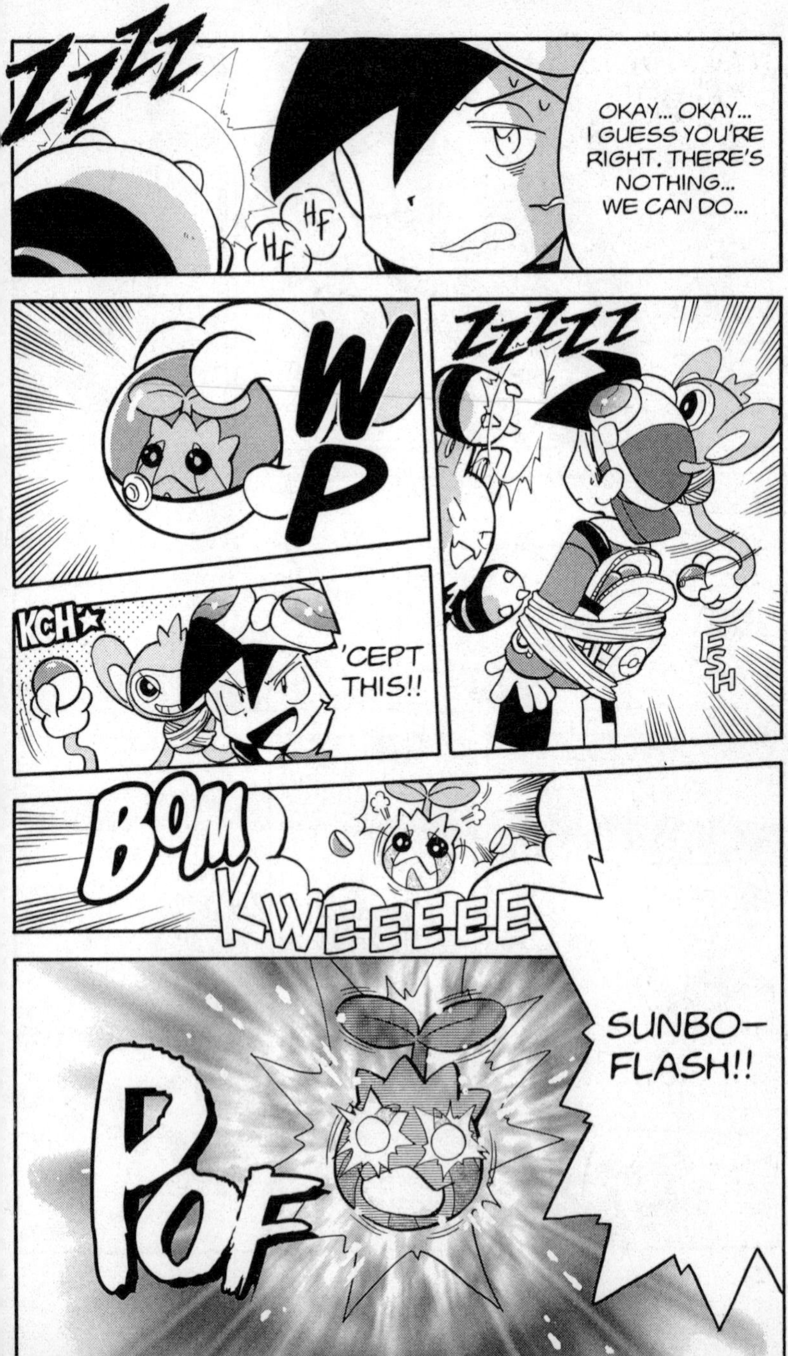
ZZZZ
HF HF
OKAY... OKAY... I GUESS YOU'RE RIGHT. THERE'S NOTHING... WE CAN DO...
ZZZZZZ
FSH
WP
KCH
'CEPT THIS!!
BOOM
KWEEEEEE
POOF
SUNBO—FLASH!!

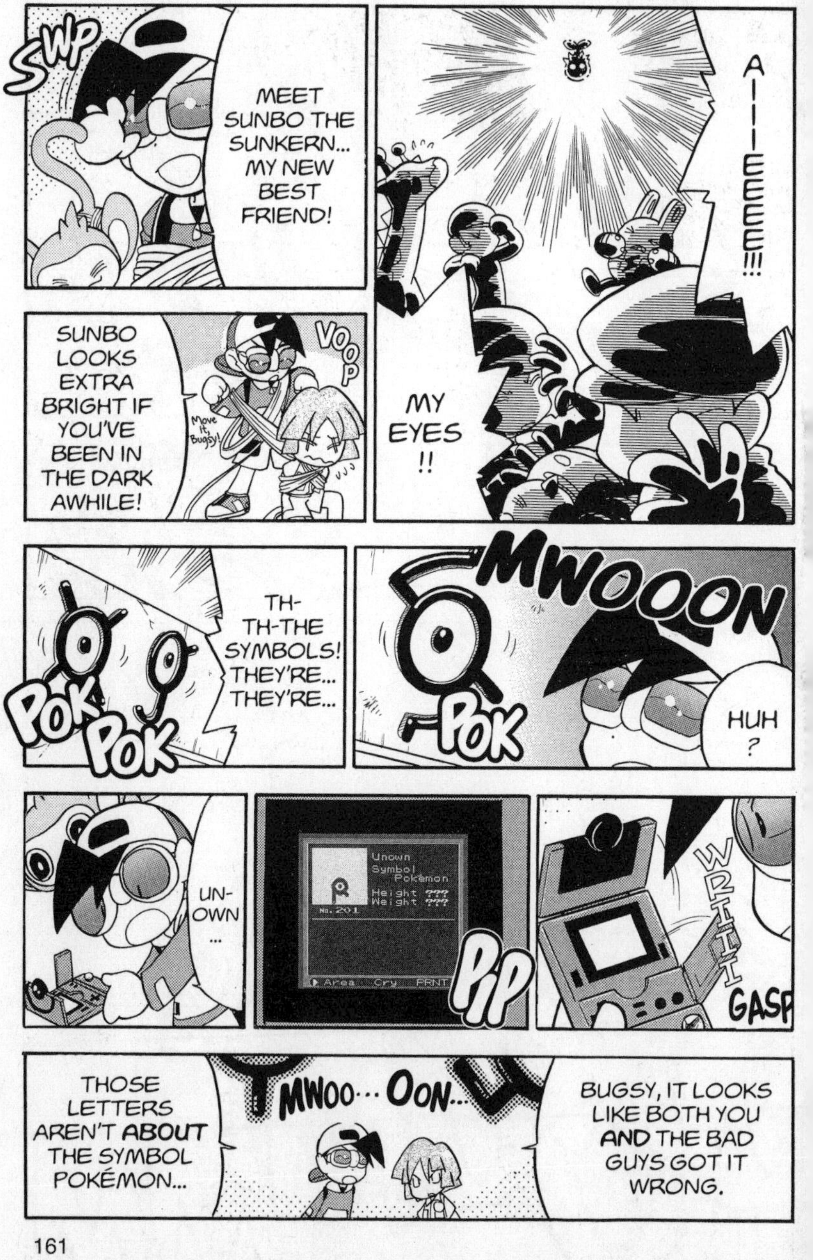
AIIIEEEE!!!
MY EYES!!
SWP
MEET SUNBO THE SUNKERN... MY NEW BEST FRIEND!
VOOP
SUNBO LOOKS EXTRA BRIGHT IF YOU'VE BEEN IN THE DARK AWHILE!
Move it, Bugsy!
MWOOON
POK
HUH?
TH-TH-THE SYMBOLS! THEY'RE... THEY'RE...
POK POK
WRIIII
GASP
Unown
Symbol Pokemon
Height ???
Weight ???
No. 201
Area Cry PRNT
PIP
UN-OWN...
BUGSY, IT LOOKS LIKE BOTH YOU **AND** THE BAD GUYS GOT IT WRONG.
MWOO...OON...
THOSE LETTERS AREN'T **ABOUT** THE SYMBOL POKÉMON...

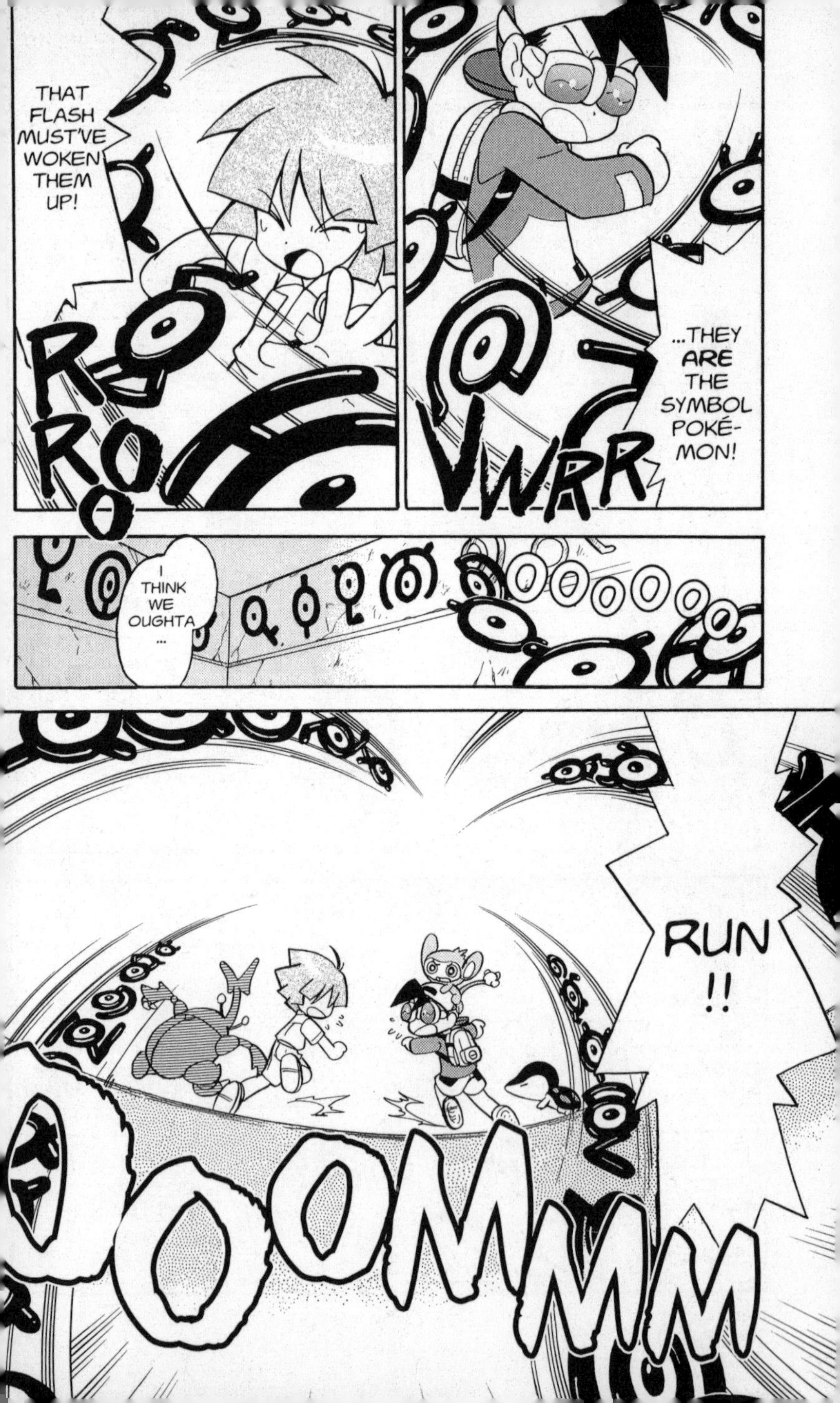
...THEY ARE THE SYMBOL POKÉMON!
VWRR
THAT FLASH MUST'VE WOKEN THEM UP!
RORO
I THINK WE OUGHTA ...
RUN !!
OOMMMM

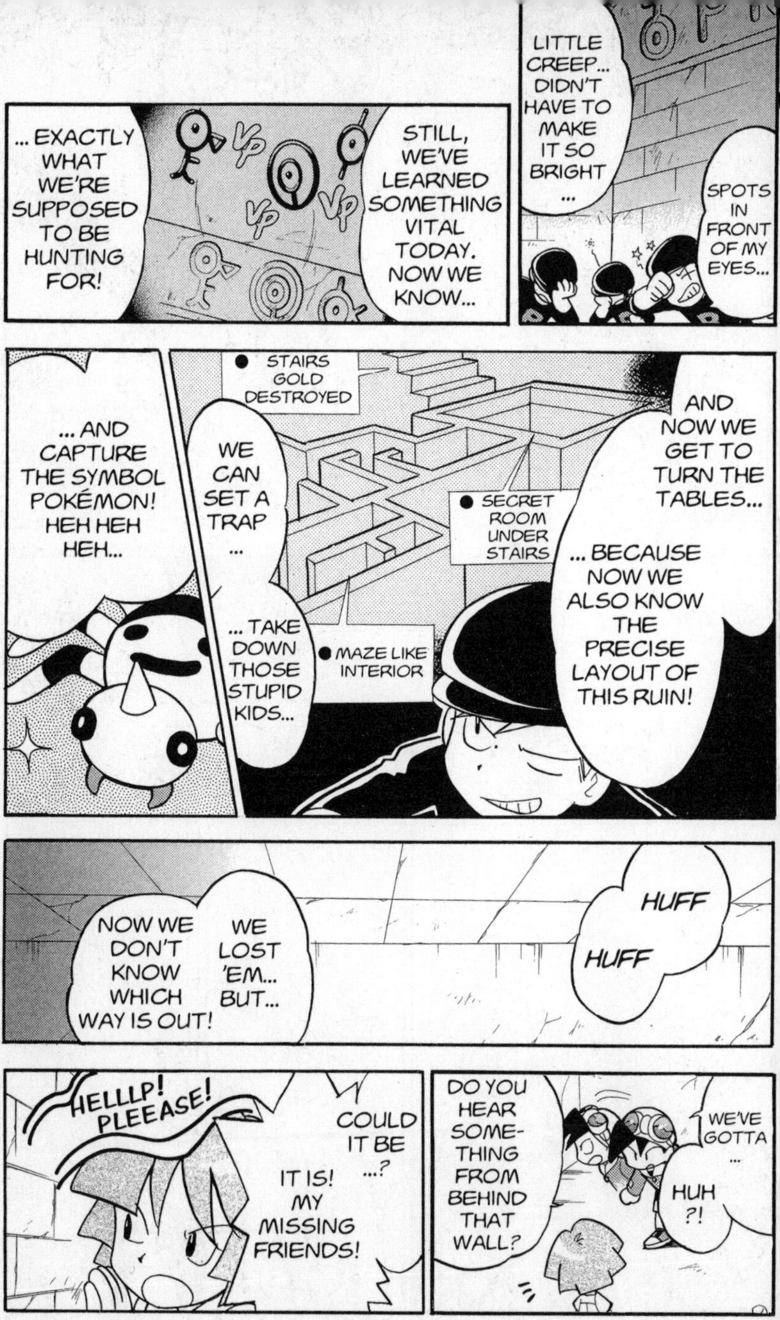
LITTLE CREEP... DIDN'T HAVE TO MAKE IT SO BRIGHT ...
SPOTS IN FRONT OF MY EYES...
STILL, WE'VE LEARNED SOMETHING VITAL TODAY. NOW WE KNOW...
... EXACTLY WHAT WE'RE SUPPOSED TO BE HUNTING FOR!
AND NOW WE GET TO TURN THE TABLES...
... BECAUSE NOW WE ALSO KNOW THE PRECISE LAYOUT OF THIS RUIN!
● STAIRS GOLD DESTROYED
● SECRET ROOM UNDER STAIRS
● MAZE LIKE INTERIOR
WE CAN SET A TRAP ...
... TAKE DOWN THOSE STUPID KIDS...
... AND CAPTURE THE SYMBOL POKÉMON! HEH HEH HEH...
HUFF
HUFF
WE LOST 'EM... BUT...
NOW WE DON'T KNOW WHICH WAY IS OUT!
WE'VE GOTTA ...
HUH ?!
DO YOU HEAR SOME-THING FROM BEHIND THAT WALL?
HELLLP! PLEEASE!
COULD IT BE ...?
IT IS! MY MISSING FRIENDS!

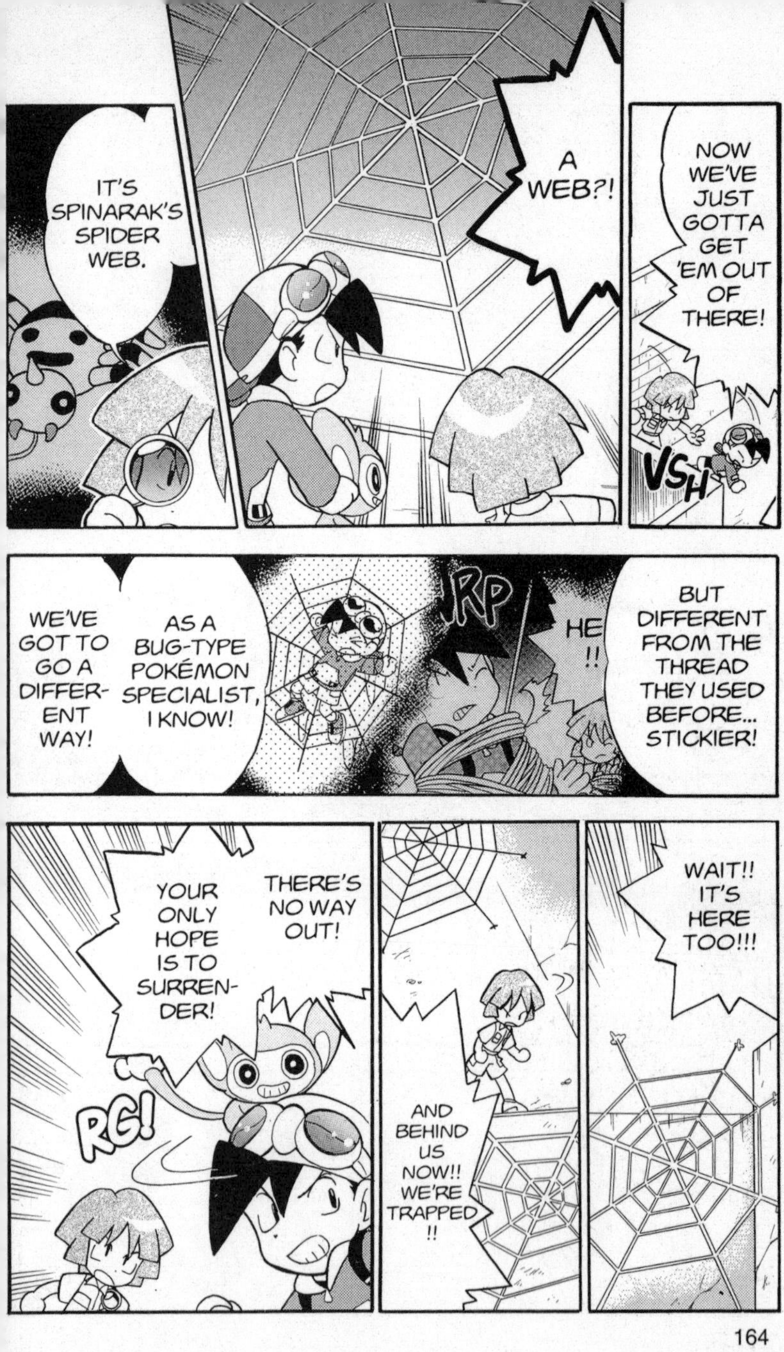
NOW WE'VE JUST GOTTA GET 'EM OUT OF THERE!
VSH
A WEB?!
IT'S SPINARAK'S SPIDER WEB.
BUT DIFFERENT FROM THE THREAD THEY USED BEFORE... STICKIER!
HE !!
JRP
AS A BUG-TYPE POKÉMON SPECIALIST, I KNOW!
WE'VE GOT TO GO A DIFFERENT WAY!
WAIT!! IT'S HERE TOO!!!
AND BEHIND US NOW!! WE'RE TRAPPED !!
THERE'S NO WAY OUT!
YOUR ONLY HOPE IS TO SURRENDER!
RG!

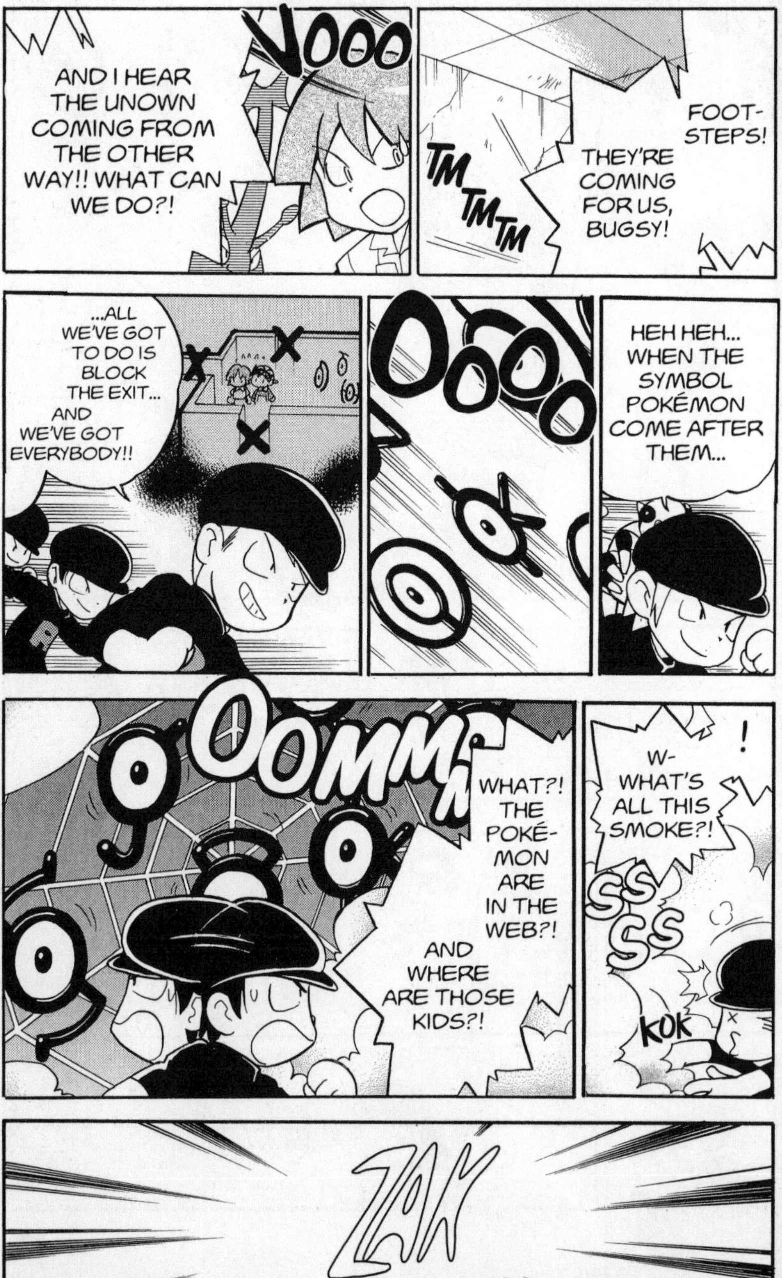
FOOT-STEPS!
THEY'RE COMING FOR US, BUGSY!
TM TM TM TM
VOOO
AND I HEAR THE UNOWN COMING FROM THE OTHER WAY!! WHAT CAN WE DO?!
HEH HEH... WHEN THE SYMBOL POKÉMON COME AFTER THEM...
OOOOO
...ALL WE'VE GOT TO DO IS BLOCK THE EXIT...
AND WE'VE GOT EVERYBODY!!
!
W-WHAT'S ALL THIS SMOKE?!
SSSS
KOK
OOMMM
WHAT?! THE POKÉMON ARE IN THE WEB?!
AND WHERE ARE THOSE KIDS?!
ZAK

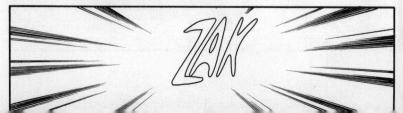

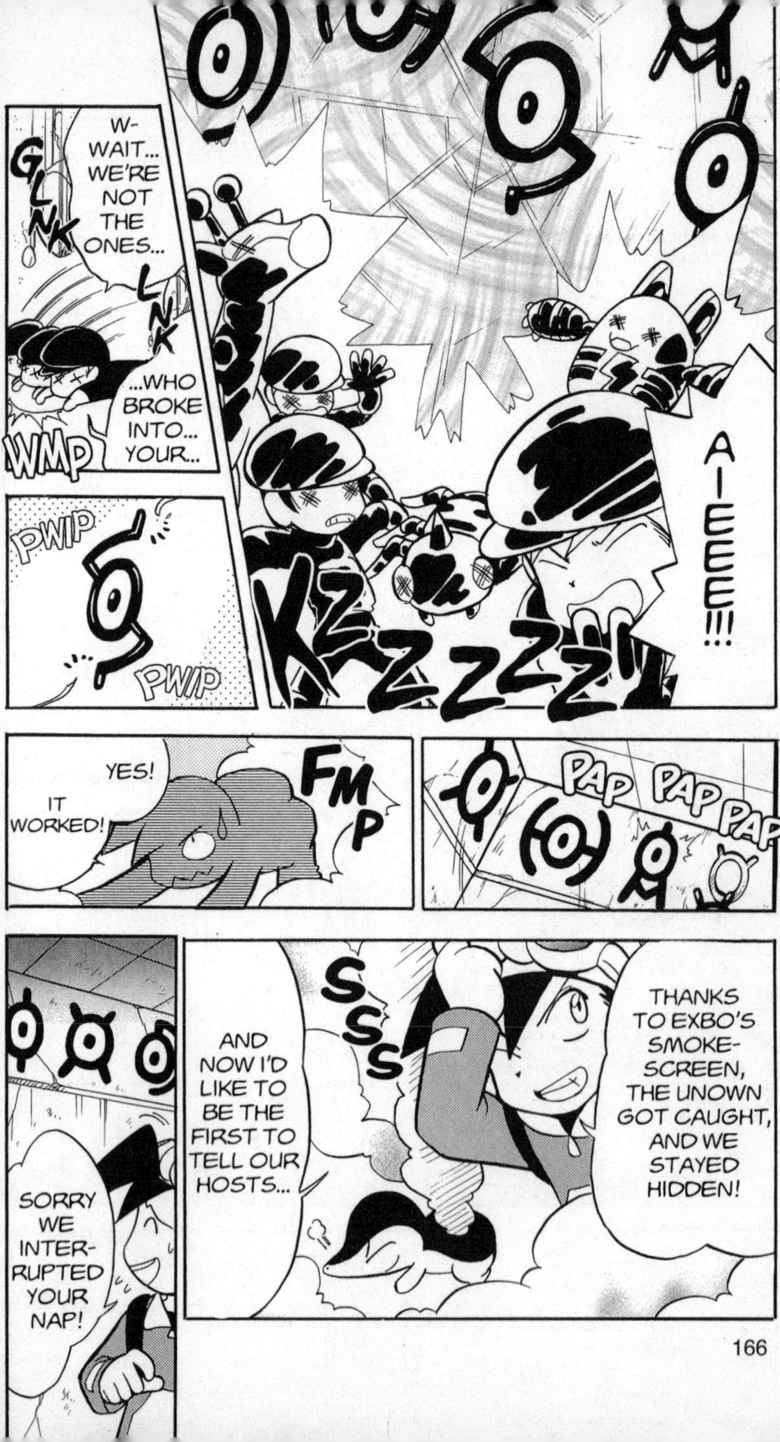
A-IEEE!!!
KZZZZZ
GLNK
W-WAIT... WE'RE NOT THE ONES...
LNK
...WHO BROKE INTO... YOUR...
WMP
PWIP
PWIP
PAP PAP PAP PAP
FMP
YES! IT WORKED!
THANKS TO EXBO'S SMOKE-SCREEN, THE UNOWN GOT CAUGHT, AND WE STAYED HIDDEN!
SSS
AND NOW I'D LIKE TO BE THE FIRST TO TELL OUR HOSTS...
SORRY WE INTERRUPTED YOUR NAP!

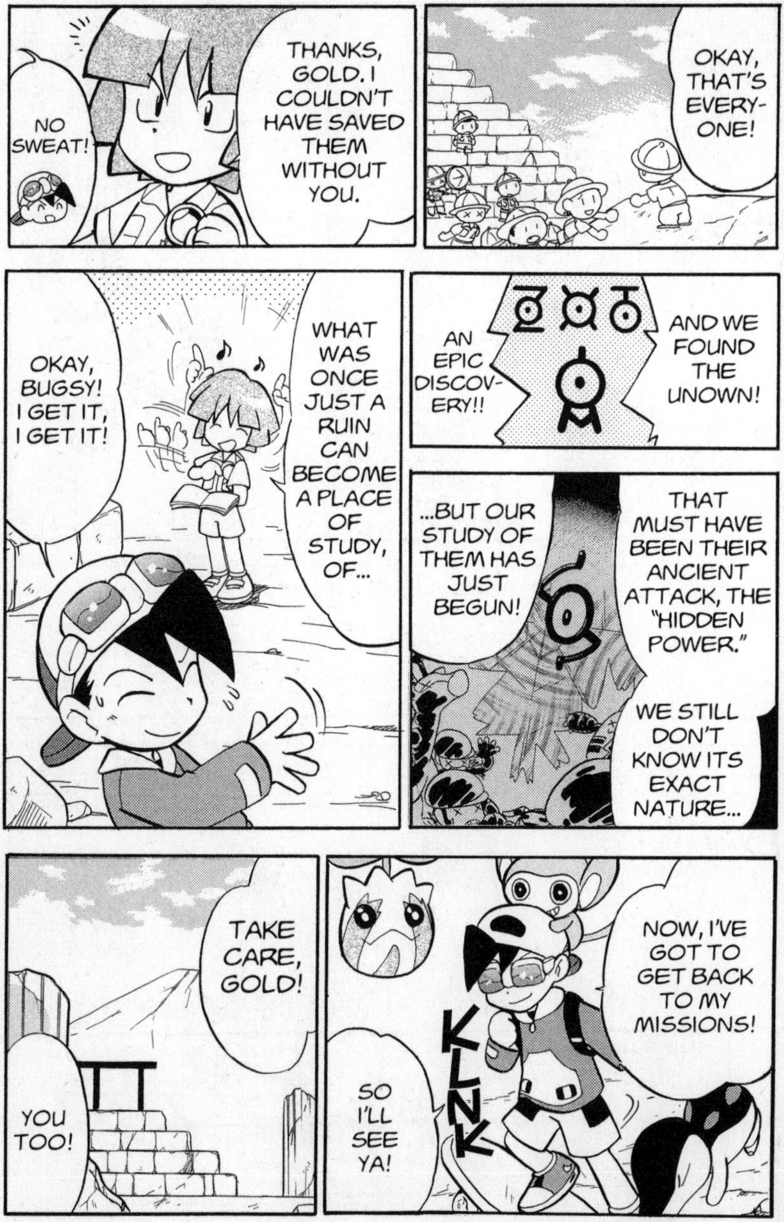
OKAY, THAT'S EVERY-ONE!
THANKS, GOLD. I COULDN'T HAVE SAVED THEM WITHOUT YOU.
NO SWEAT!
AND WE FOUND THE UNOWN!
AN EPIC DISCOV-ERY!!
THAT MUST HAVE BEEN THEIR ANCIENT ATTACK, THE "HIDDEN POWER."
WE STILL DON'T KNOW ITS EXACT NATURE...
...BUT OUR STUDY OF THEM HAS JUST BEGUN!
WHAT WAS ONCE JUST A RUIN CAN BECOME A PLACE OF STUDY, OF...
OKAY, BUGSY! I GET IT, I GET IT!
NOW, I'VE GOT TO GET BACK TO MY MISSIONS!
KLNK
SO I'LL SEE YA!
TAKE CARE, GOLD!
YOU TOO!

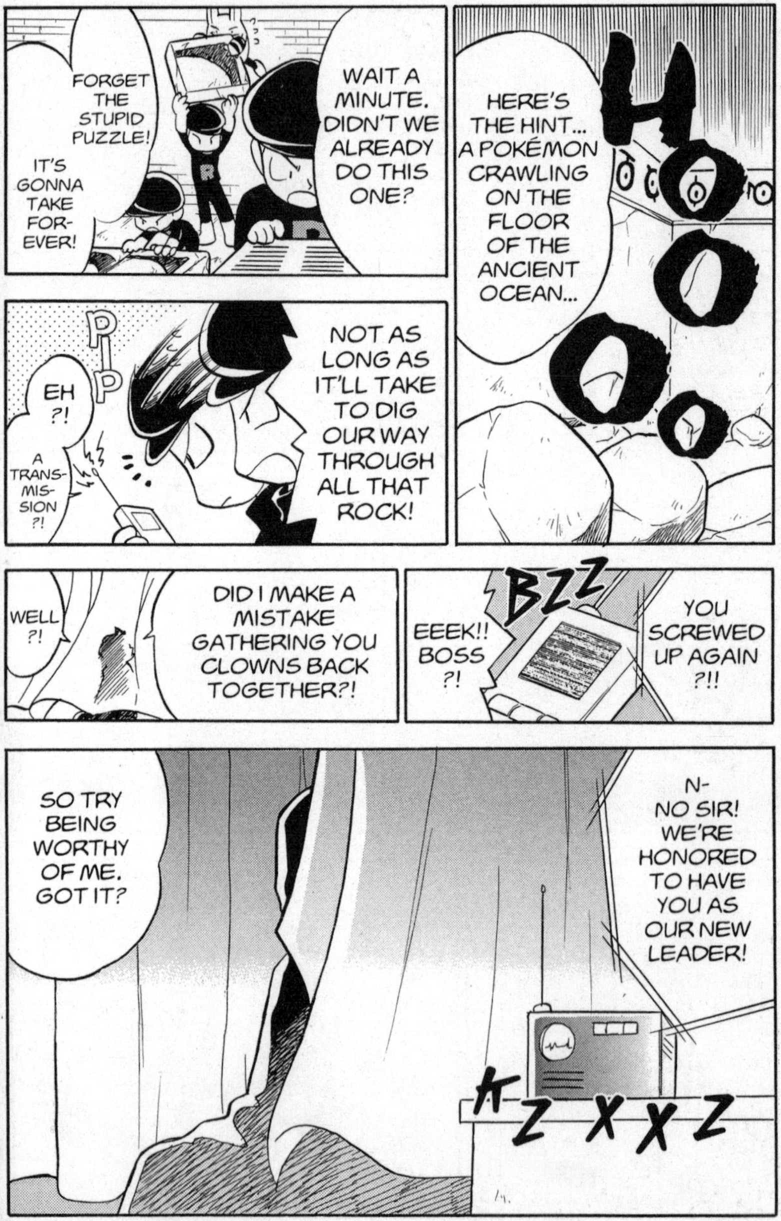
HERE'S THE HINT... A POKÉMON CRAWLING ON THE FLOOR OF THE ANCIENT OCEAN...
HOOOO
WAIT A MINUTE. DIDN'T WE ALREADY DO THIS ONE?
FORGET THE STUPID PUZZLE!
IT'S GONNA TAKE FOR-EVER!
NOT AS LONG AS IT'LL TAKE TO DIG OUR WAY THROUGH ALL THAT ROCK!
PIP
EH ?!
A TRANS-MIS-SION ?!
BZZ
YOU SCREWED UP AGAIN ?!!
EEEK!! BOSS ?!
DID I MAKE A MISTAKE GATHERING YOU CLOWNS BACK TOGETHER?!
WELL ?!
N- NO SIR! WE'RE HONORED TO HAVE YOU AS OUR NEW LEADER!
SO TRY BEING WORTHY OF ME. GOT IT?
KZXXZ

101 Teddiursa's Picnic

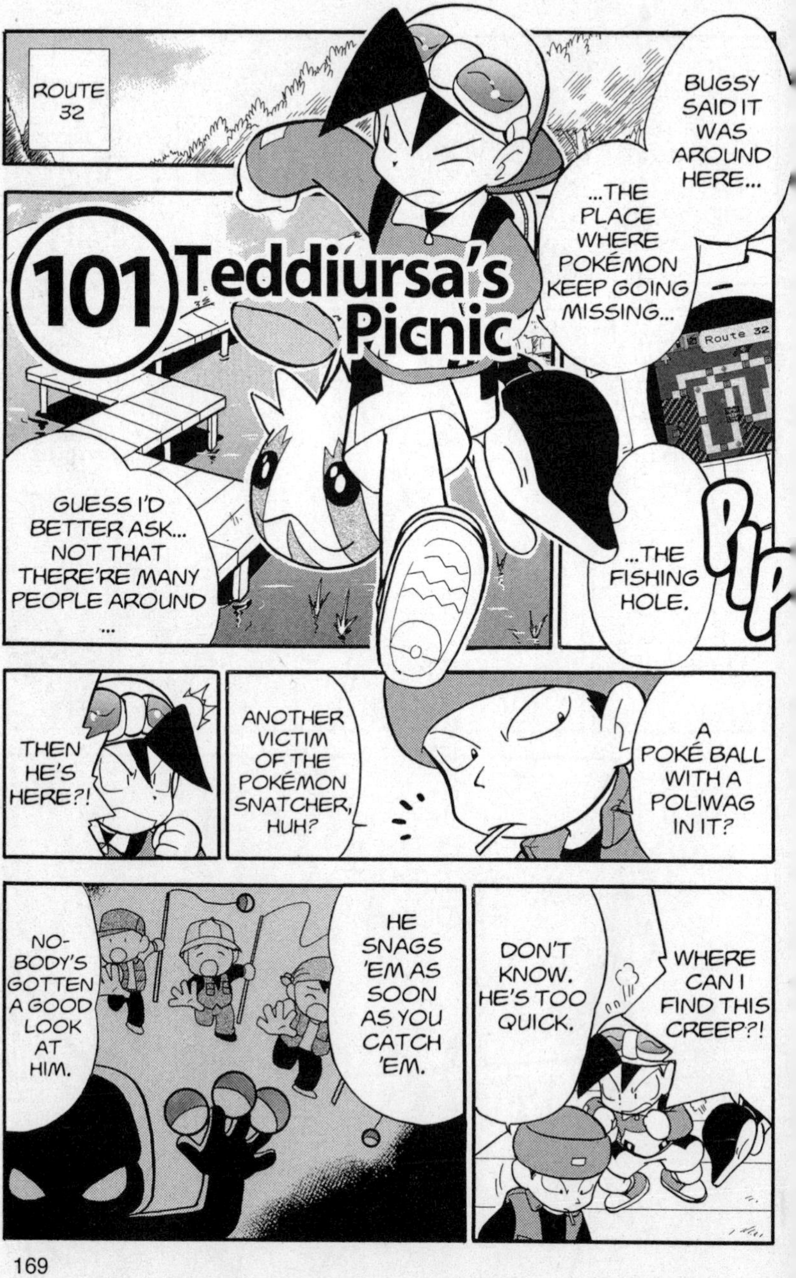
ROUTE 32
BUGSY SAID IT WAS AROUND HERE...
...THE PLACE WHERE POKÉMON KEEP GOING MISSING...
Route 32
PIP
...THE FISHING HOLE.
GUESS I'D BETTER ASK... NOT THAT THERE'RE MANY PEOPLE AROUND ...
A POKÉ BALL WITH A POLIWAG IN IT?
ANOTHER VICTIM OF THE POKÉMON SNATCHER, HUH?
THEN HE'S HERE?!
WHERE CAN I FIND THIS CREEP?!
DON'T KNOW. HE'S TOO QUICK.
HE SNAGS 'EM AS SOON AS YOU CATCH 'EM.
NO-BODY'S GOTTEN A GOOD LOOK AT HIM.

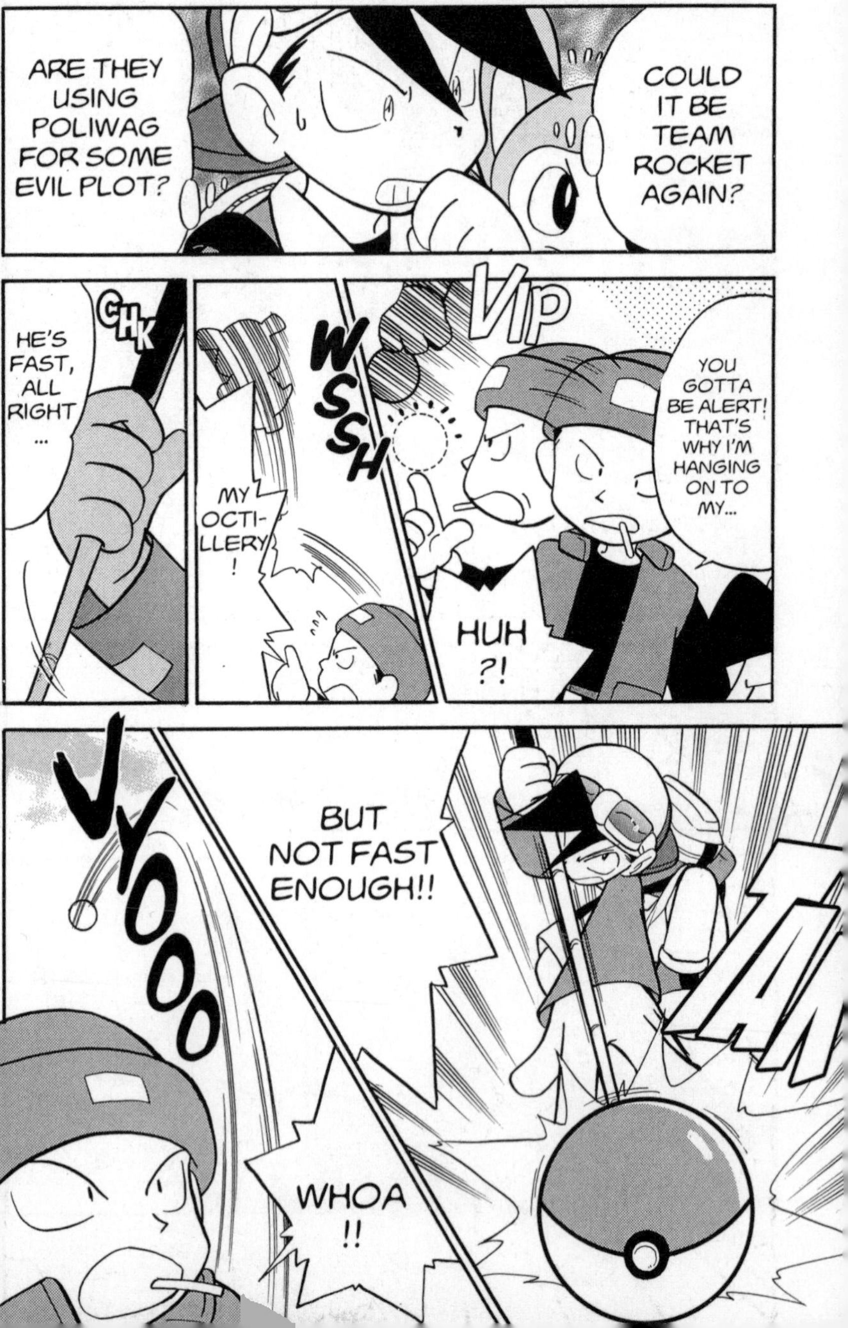

COULD IT BE TEAM ROCKET AGAIN?
ARE THEY USING POLIWAG FOR SOME EVIL PLOT?
VIP
YOU GOTTA BE ALERT! THAT'S WHY I'M HANGING ON TO MY...
WSSH
MY OCTILLERY!
HUH?!
CHK
HE'S FAST, ALL RIGHT...
BUT NOT FAST ENOUGH!!
VYOOO
WHOA!!

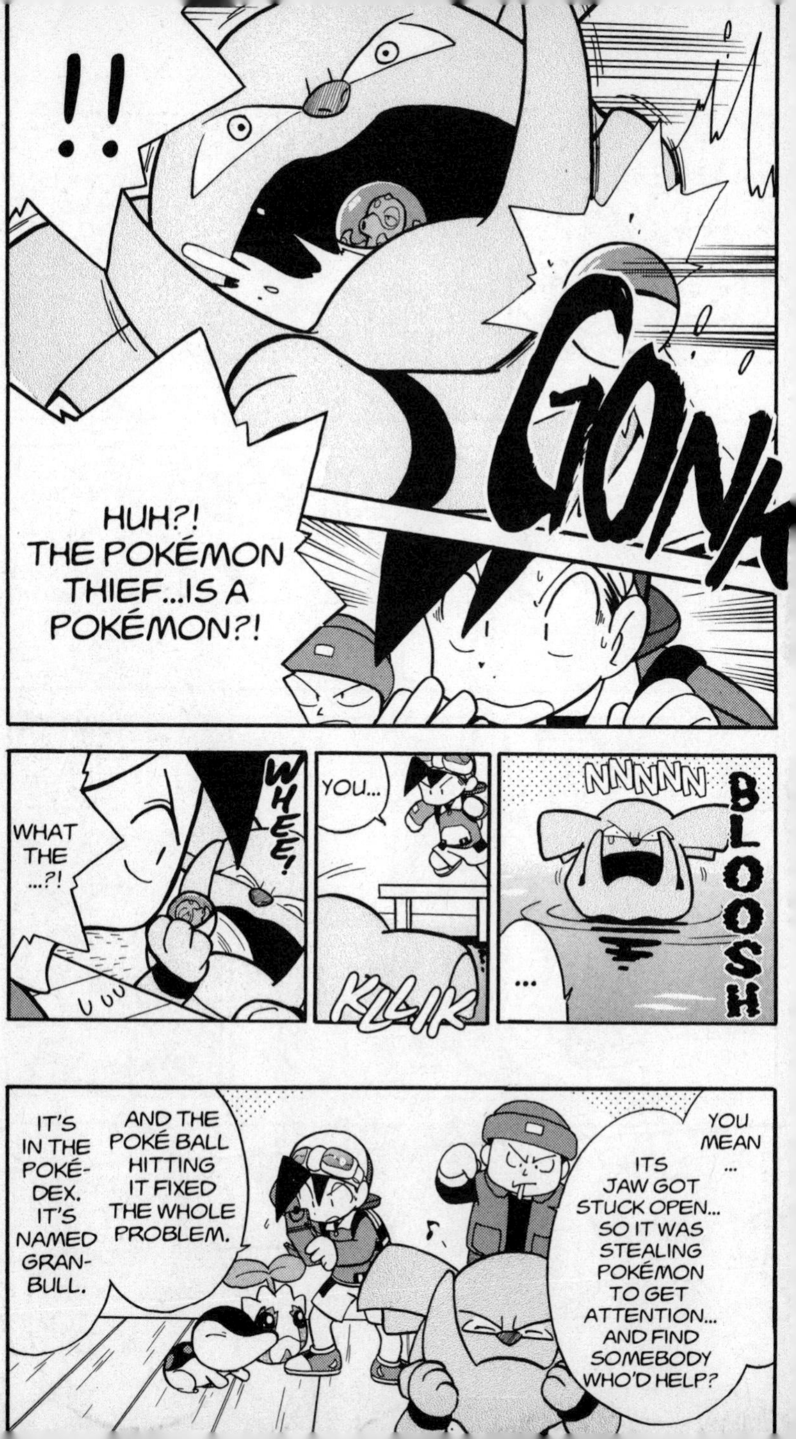
GONK
!!
HUH?! THE POKÉMON THIEF...IS A POKÉMON?!
NNNNN
BLOOSH
...
YOU...
KLLIK
WHEE!
WHAT THE ...?!
YOU MEAN ...
ITS JAW GOT STUCK OPEN... SO IT WAS STEALING POKÉMON TO GET ATTENTION... AND FIND SOMEBODY WHO'D HELP?
IT'S IN THE POKÉ-DEX. IT'S NAMED GRAN-BULL.
AND THE POKÉ BALL HITTING IT FIXED THE WHOLE PROBLEM.

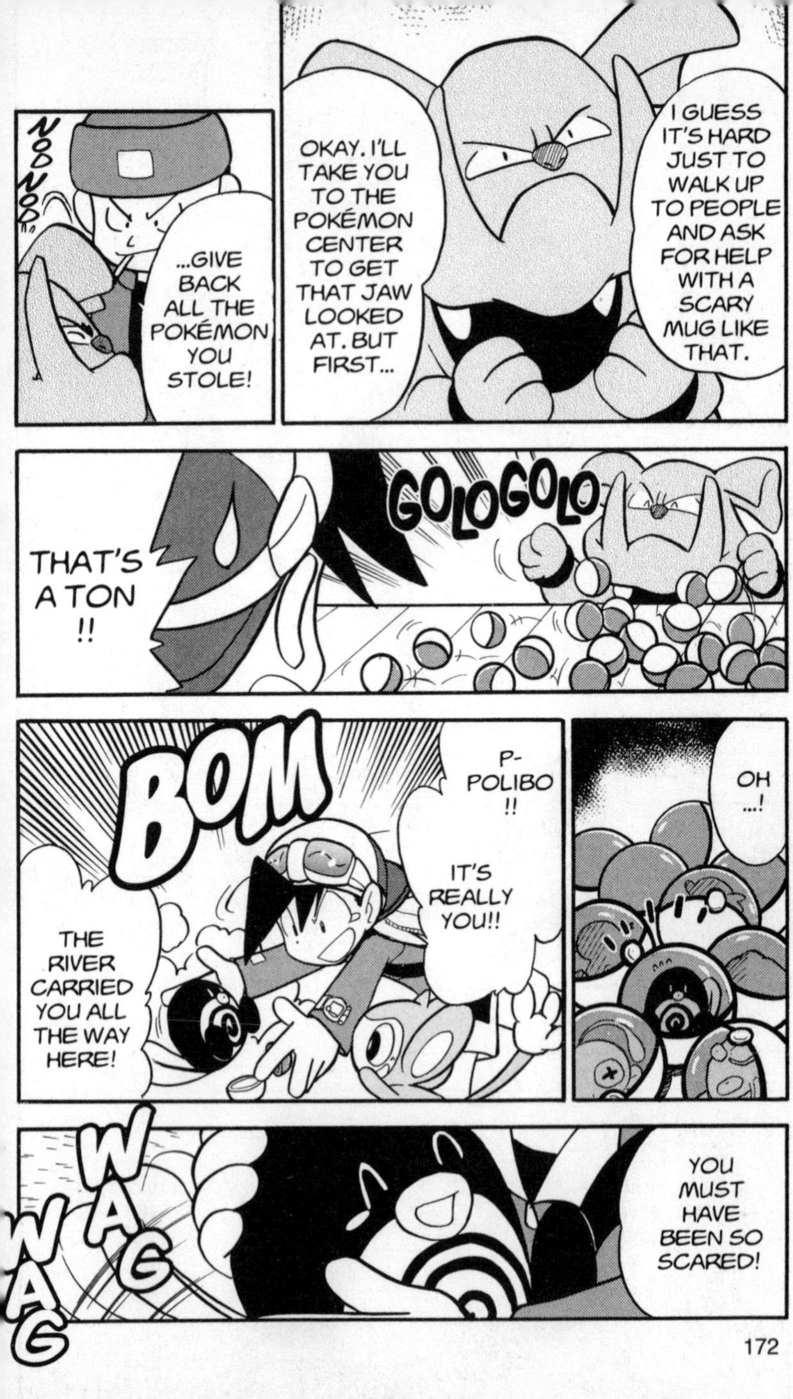
I GUESS IT'S HARD JUST TO WALK UP TO PEOPLE AND ASK FOR HELP WITH A SCARY MUG LIKE THAT.
OKAY. I'LL TAKE YOU TO THE POKÉMON CENTER TO GET THAT JAW LOOKED AT. BUT FIRST...
...GIVE BACK ALL THE POKÉMON YOU STOLE!
NOONOO
GOLOGOLO
THAT'S A TON !!
OH ...!
P-POLIBO !!
IT'S REALLY YOU!!
BOM
THE RIVER CARRIED YOU ALL THE WAY HERE!
YOU MUST HAVE BEEN SO SCARED!
WAG
WAG

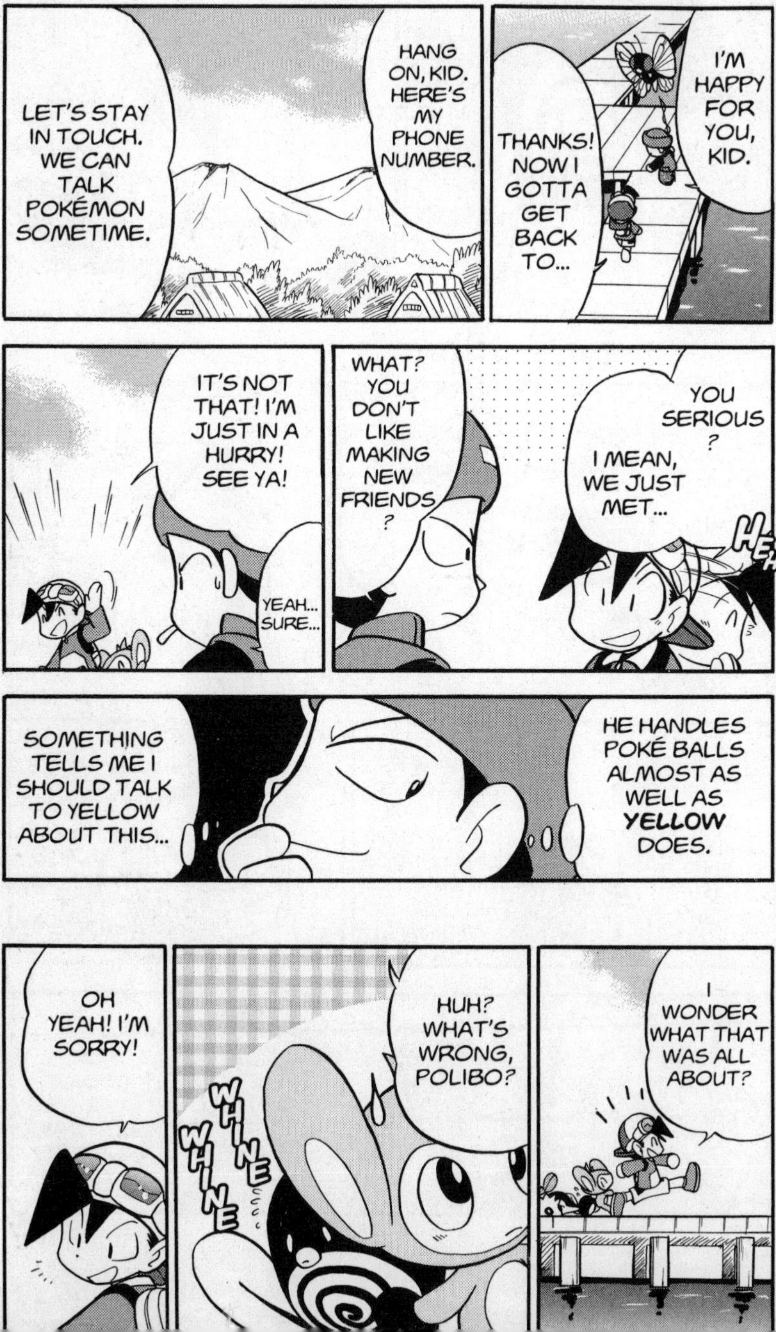
I'M HAPPY FOR YOU, KID.
THANKS! NOW I GOTTA GET BACK TO...
HANG ON, KID. HERE'S MY PHONE NUMBER.
LET'S STAY IN TOUCH. WE CAN TALK POKÉMON SOMETIME.
YOU SERIOUS?
I MEAN, WE JUST MET...
HEH
WHAT? YOU DON'T LIKE MAKING NEW FRIENDS?
IT'S NOT THAT! I'M JUST IN A HURRY! SEE YA!
YEAH... SURE...
HE HANDLES POKÉ BALLS ALMOST AS WELL AS **YELLOW** DOES.
SOMETHING TELLS ME I SHOULD TALK TO YELLOW ABOUT THIS...
I WONDER WHAT THAT WAS ALL ABOUT?
HUH? WHAT'S WRONG, POLIBO?
WHINE
WHINE
OH YEAH! I'M SORRY!

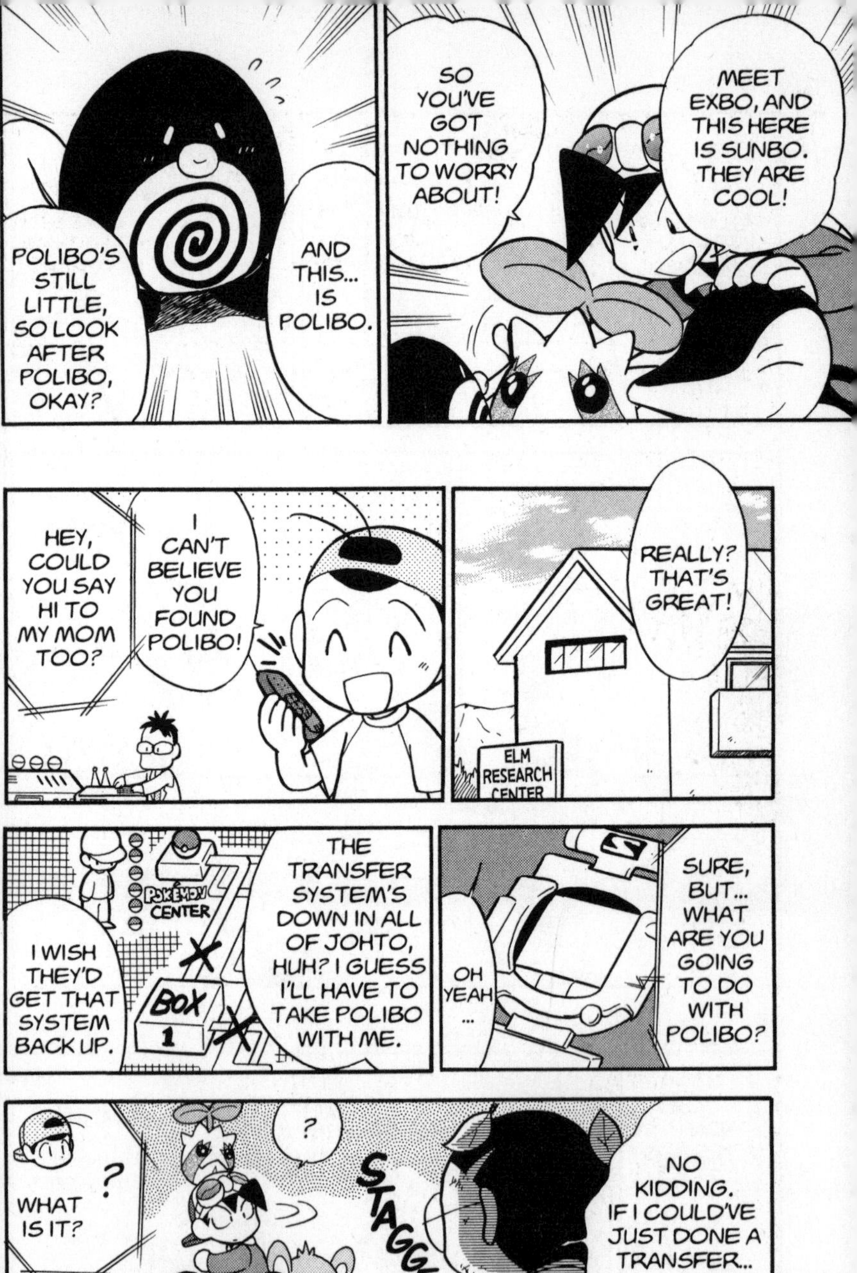
MEET EXBO, AND THIS HERE IS SUNBO. THEY ARE COOL!
SO YOU'VE GOT NOTHING TO WORRY ABOUT!
AND THIS... IS POLIBO.
POLIBO'S STILL LITTLE, SO LOOK AFTER POLIBO, OKAY?
REALLY? THAT'S GREAT!
ELM RESEARCH CENTER
I CAN'T BELIEVE YOU FOUND POLIBO!
HEY, COULD YOU SAY HI TO MY MOM TOO?
SURE, BUT... WHAT ARE YOU GOING TO DO WITH POLIBO?
OH YEAH ...
THE TRANSFER SYSTEM'S DOWN IN ALL OF JOHTO, HUH? I GUESS I'LL HAVE TO TAKE POLIBO WITH ME.
POKéMON CENTER
BOX 1
I WISH THEY'D GET THAT SYSTEM BACK UP.
NO KIDDING. IF I COULD'VE JUST DONE A TRANSFER...
STAGGER
?
?
WHAT IS IT?

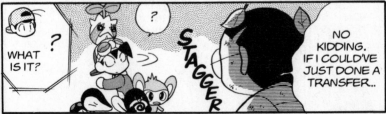

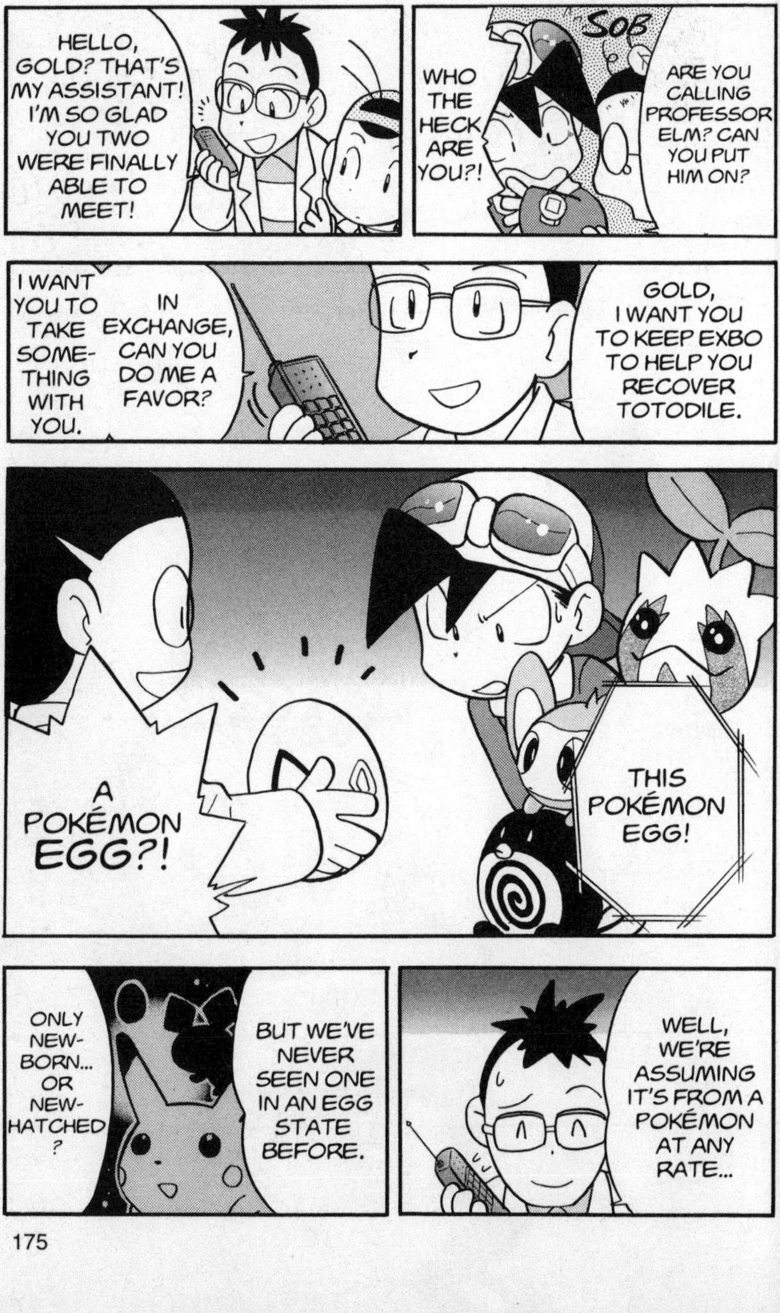
SOB
ARE YOU CALLING PROFESSOR ELM? CAN YOU PUT HIM ON?
WHO THE HECK ARE YOU?!
HELLO, GOLD? THAT'S MY ASSISTANT! I'M SO GLAD YOU TWO WERE FINALLY ABLE TO MEET!
GOLD, I WANT YOU TO KEEP EXBO TO HELP YOU RECOVER TOTODILE.
IN EXCHANGE, CAN YOU DO ME A FAVOR?
I WANT YOU TO TAKE SOME-THING WITH YOU.
THIS POKÉMON EGG!
A POKÉMON EGG?!
WELL, WE'RE ASSUMING IT'S FROM A POKÉMON AT ANY RATE...
BUT WE'VE NEVER SEEN ONE IN AN EGG STATE BEFORE.
ONLY NEW-BORN... OR NEW-HATCHED?

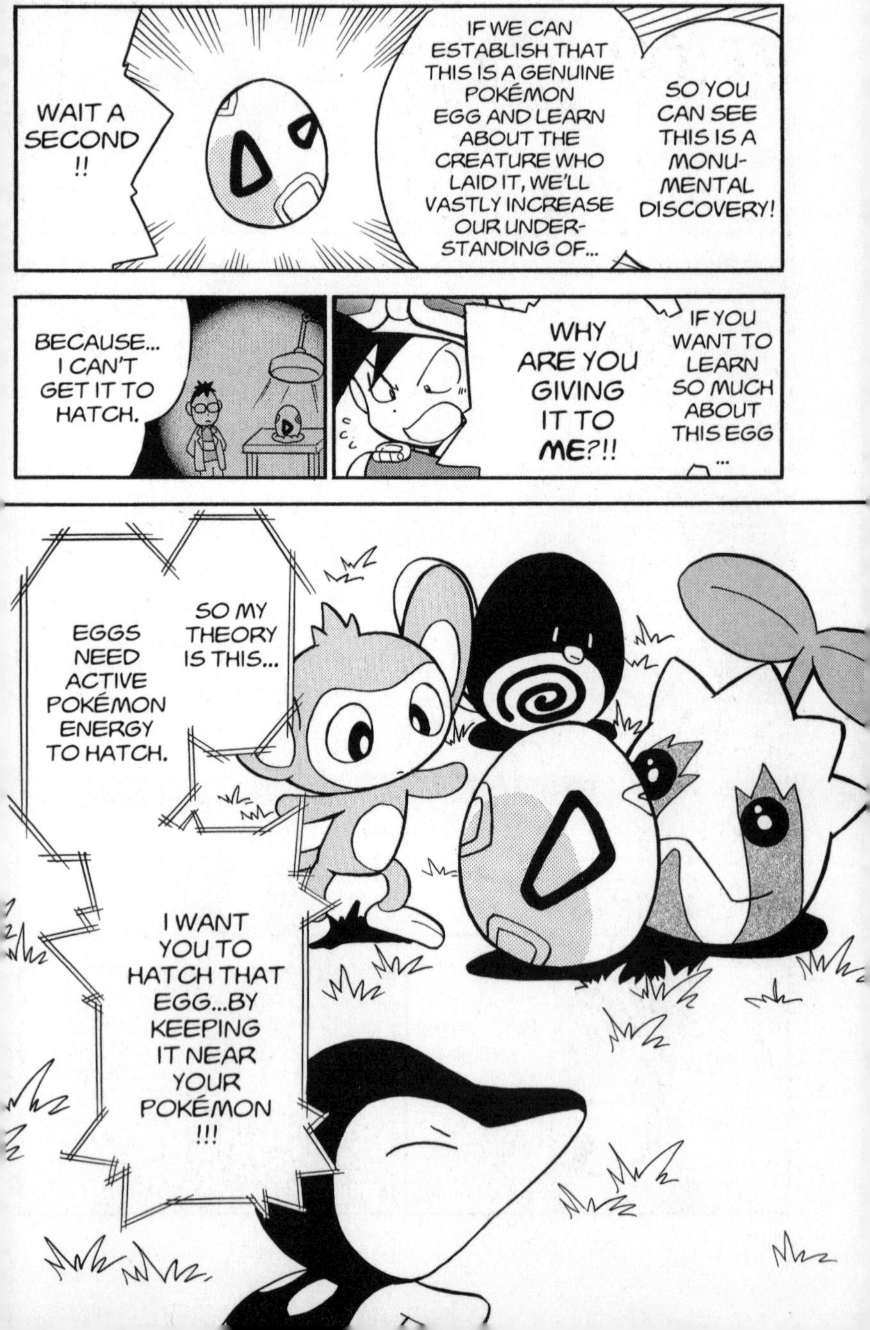
SO YOU CAN SEE THIS IS A MONU-MENTAL DISCOVERY!
IF WE CAN ESTABLISH THAT THIS IS A GENUINE POKÉMON EGG AND LEARN ABOUT THE CREATURE WHO LAID IT, WE'LL VASTLY INCREASE OUR UNDER-STANDING OF...
WAIT A SECOND !!
IF YOU WANT TO LEARN SO MUCH ABOUT THIS EGG ...
WHY ARE YOU GIVING IT TO ME?!!
BECAUSE... I CAN'T GET IT TO HATCH.
SO MY THEORY IS THIS...
EGGS NEED ACTIVE POKÉMON ENERGY TO HATCH.
I WANT YOU TO HATCH THAT EGG...BY KEEPING IT NEAR YOUR POKÉMON !!!

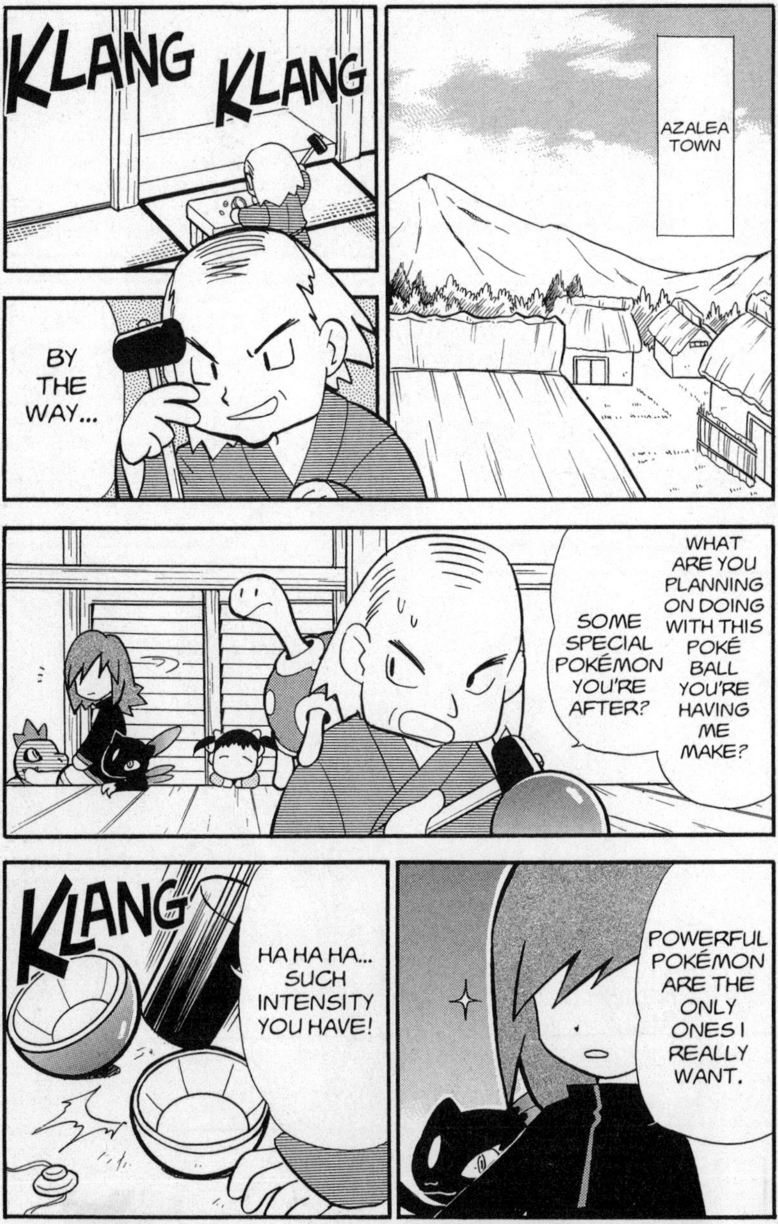
AZALEA TOWN
KLANG KLANG
BY THE WAY...
WHAT ARE YOU PLANNING ON DOING WITH THIS POKÉ BALL YOU'RE HAVING ME MAKE?
SOME SPECIAL POKÉMON YOU'RE AFTER?
POWERFUL POKÉMON ARE THE ONLY ONES I REALLY WANT.
KLANG
HA HA HA... SUCH INTENSITY YOU HAVE!

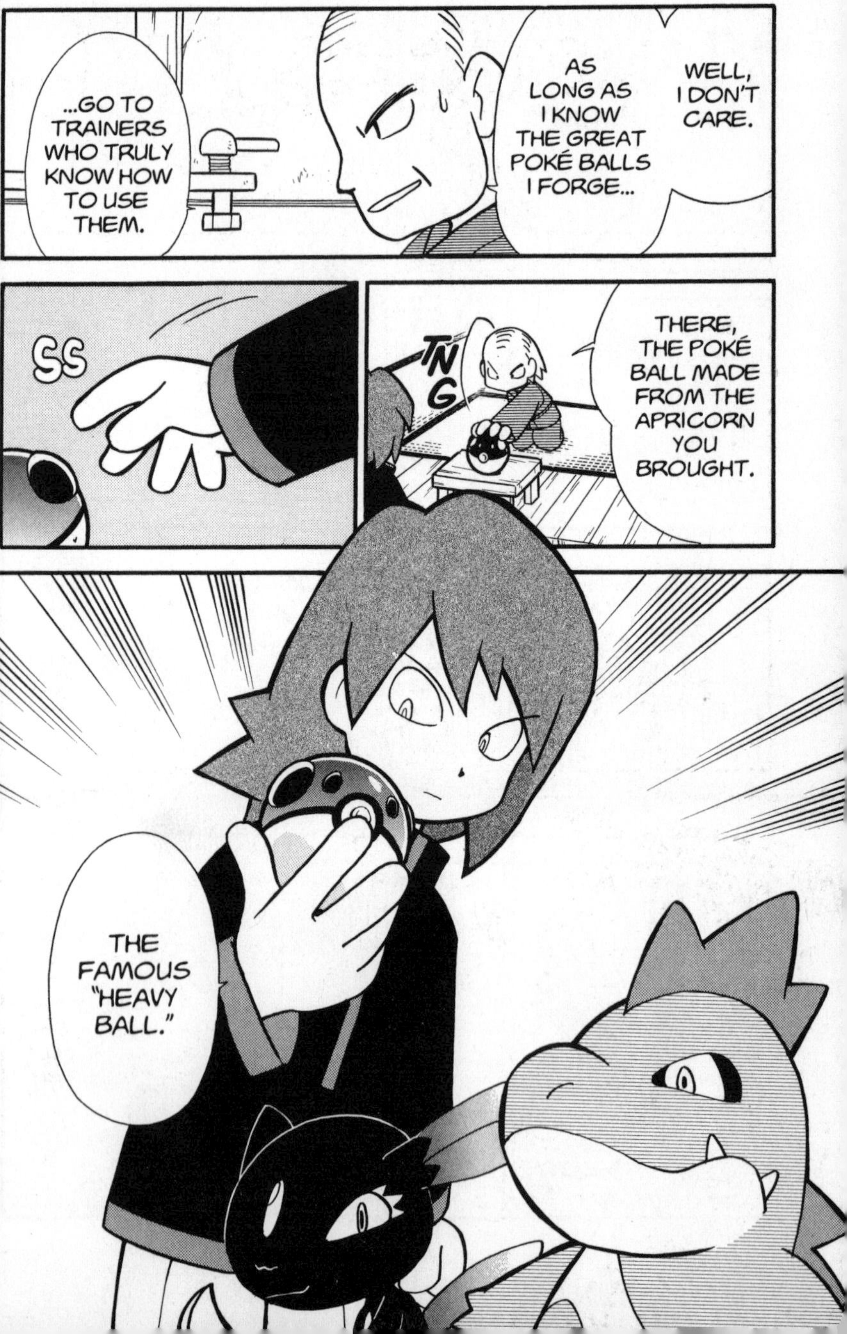
WELL, I DON'T CARE.
AS LONG AS I KNOW THE GREAT POKÉ BALLS I FORGE...
...GO TO TRAINERS WHO TRULY KNOW HOW TO USE THEM.
THERE, THE POKÉ BALL MADE FROM THE APRICORN YOU BROUGHT.
TNG
SS
THE FAMOUS "HEAVY BALL."

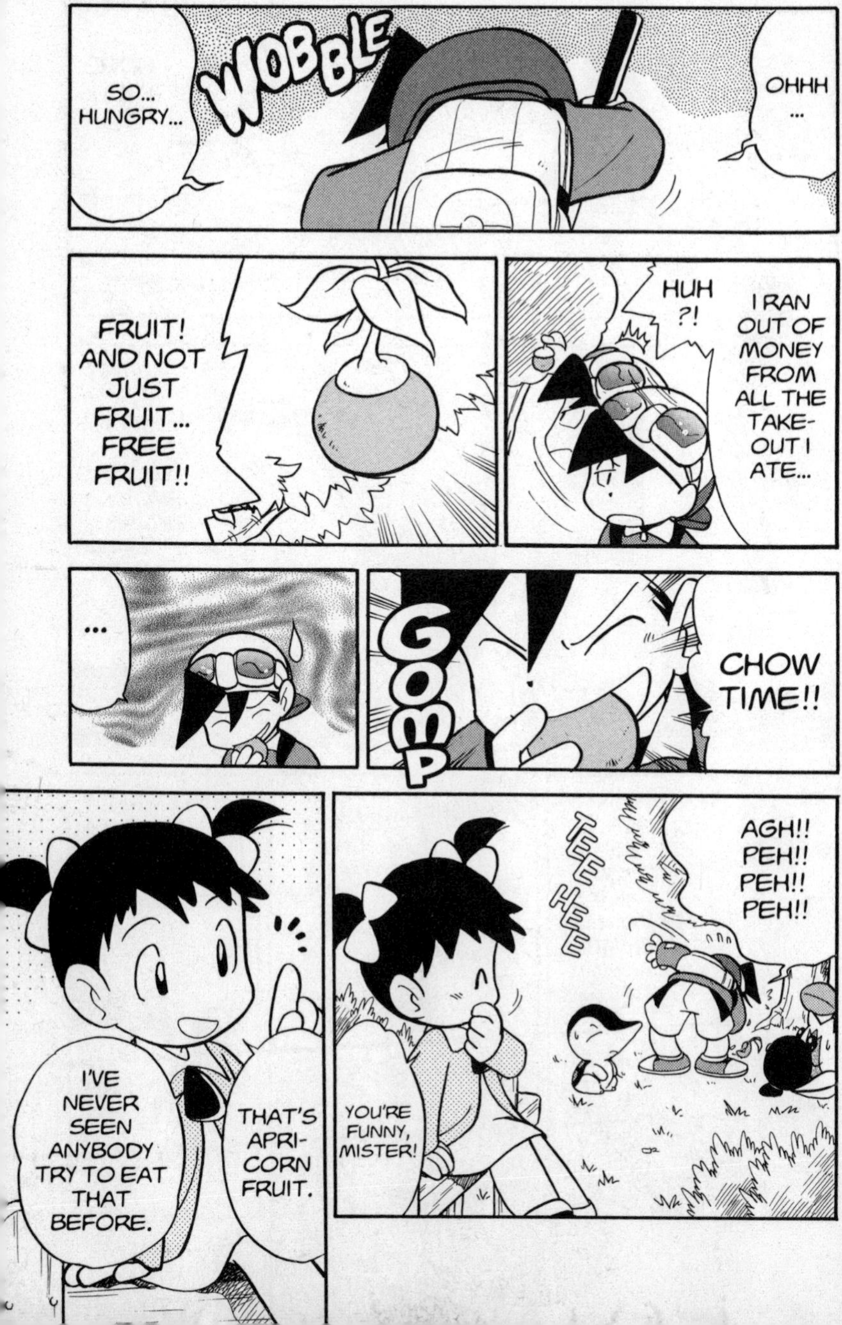
OHHH ...
WOBBLE
SO... HUNGRY...
I RAN OUT OF MONEY FROM ALL THE TAKE-OUT I ATE...
HUH ?!
FRUIT! AND NOT JUST FRUIT... FREE FRUIT!!
CHOW TIME!!
GOMP
...
AGH!! PEH!! PEH!! PEH!!
TEE HEE
YOU'RE FUNNY, MISTER!
THAT'S APRI-CORN FRUIT.
I'VE NEVER SEEN ANYBODY TRY TO EAT THAT BEFORE.

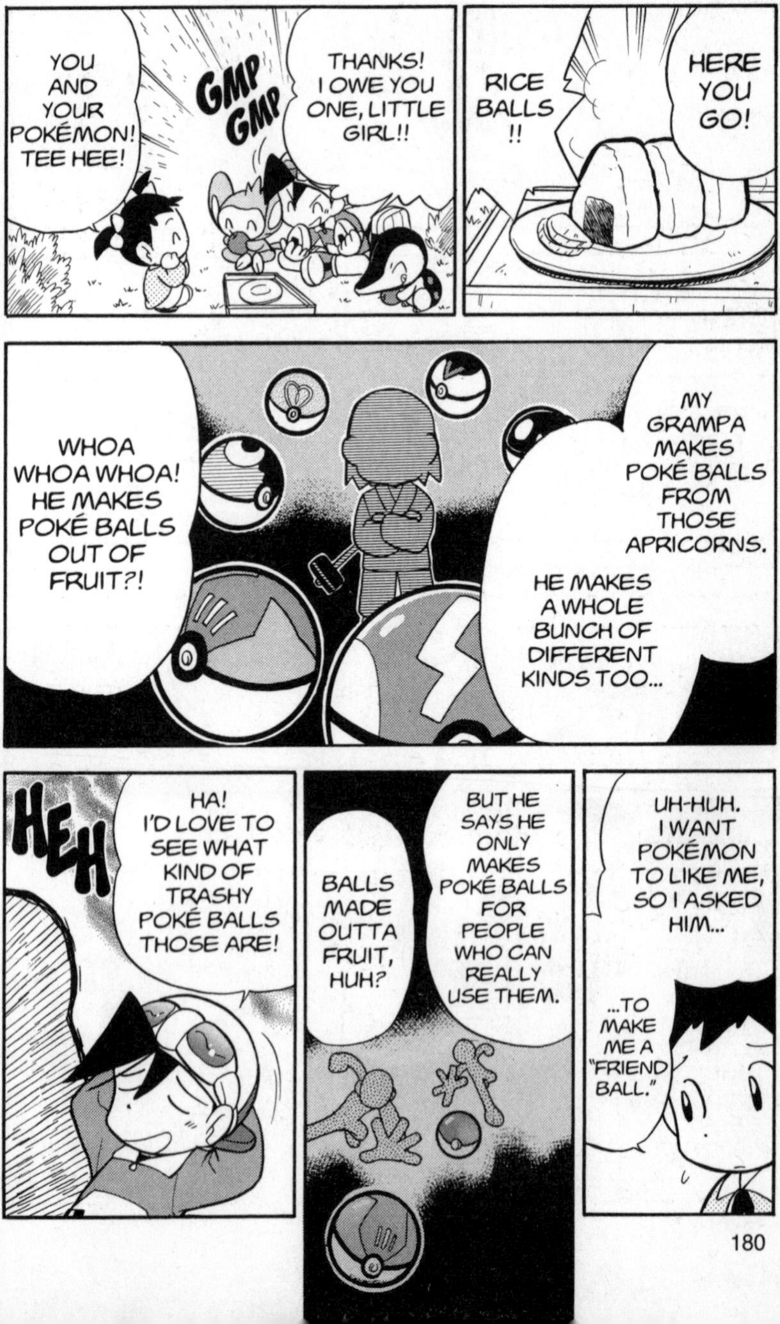
HERE YOU GO!
RICE BALLS !!
THANKS! I OWE YOU ONE, LITTLE GIRL!!
GMP GMP
YOU AND YOUR POKÉMON! TEE HEE!
MY GRAMPA MAKES POKÉ BALLS FROM THOSE APRICORNS.
HE MAKES A WHOLE BUNCH OF DIFFERENT KINDS TOO...
WHOA WHOA WHOA! HE MAKES POKÉ BALLS OUT OF FRUIT?!
UH-HUH. I WANT POKÉMON TO LIKE ME, SO I ASKED HIM...
...TO MAKE ME A "FRIEND BALL."
BUT HE SAYS HE ONLY MAKES POKÉ BALLS FOR PEOPLE WHO CAN REALLY USE THEM.
BALLS MADE OUTTA FRUIT, HUH?
HA! I'D LOVE TO SEE WHAT KIND OF TRASHY POKÉ BALLS THOSE ARE!
HEH

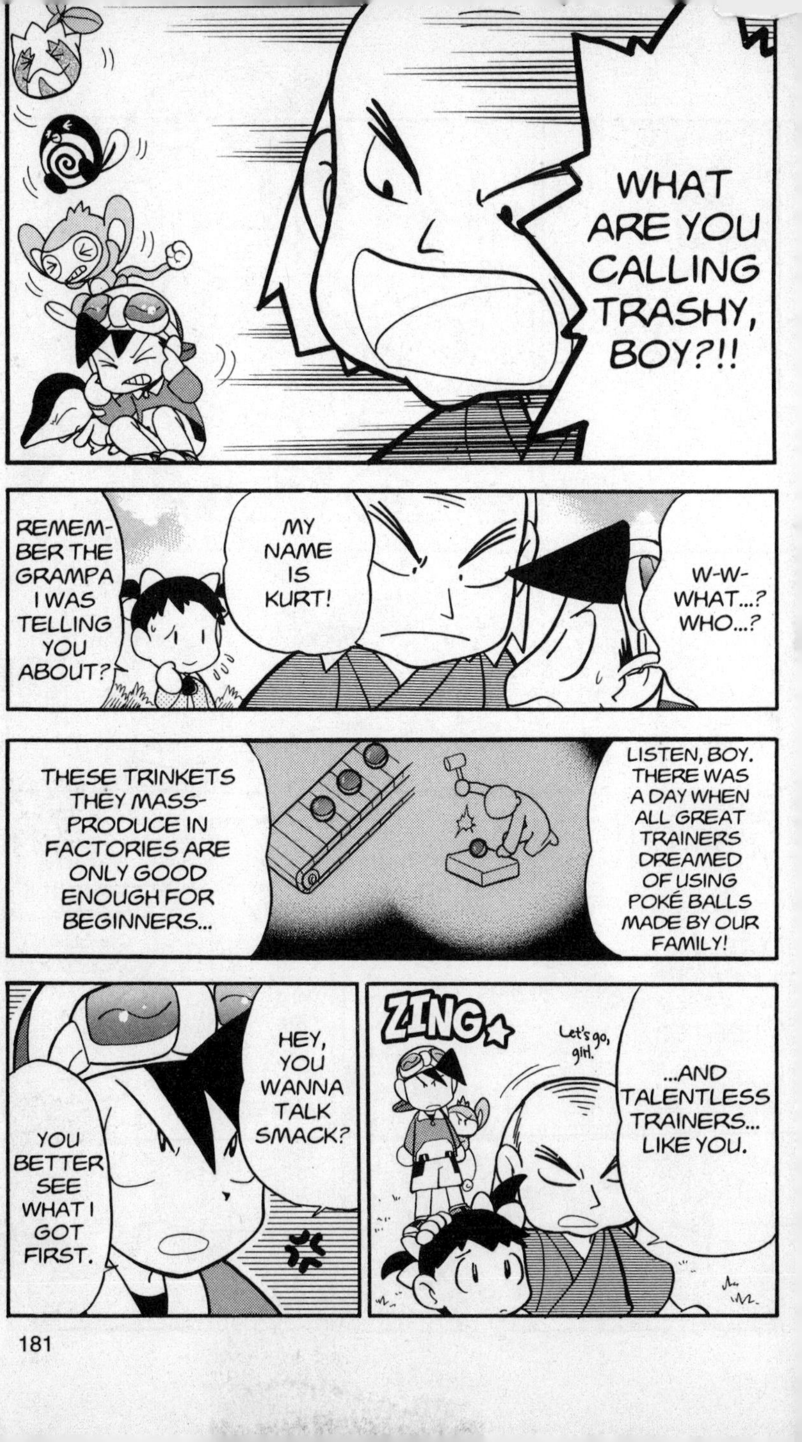
WHAT ARE YOU CALLING TRASHY, BOY?!!
W-W-WHAT...? WHO...?
MY NAME IS KURT!
REMEMBER THE GRAMPA I WAS TELLING YOU ABOUT?
LISTEN, BOY. THERE WAS A DAY WHEN ALL GREAT TRAINERS DREAMED OF USING POKÉ BALLS MADE BY OUR FAMILY!
THESE TRINKETS THEY MASS-PRODUCE IN FACTORIES ARE ONLY GOOD ENOUGH FOR BEGINNERS...
...AND TALENTLESS TRAINERS... LIKE YOU.
Let's go, girl.
ZING
HEY, YOU WANNA TALK SMACK?
YOU BETTER SEE WHAT I GOT FIRST.

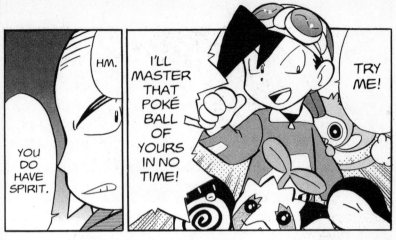

TRY ME!
I'LL MASTER THAT POKÉ BALL OF YOURS IN NO TIME!
HM.
YOU DO HAVE SPIRIT.
AND IF YOU CAN'T MASTER IT?
THEN I'LL WORK AS YOUR ASSISTANT FOR THE REST OF MY LIFE.
THOSE ARE BIG WORDS!
ALL RIGHT THEN. I'LL MAKE ONE JUST FOR YOU.
CHOOSE THE TYPE OF POKÉ BALL YOU WANT... AND BRING ME AN APRI-CORN.
TUG
WHAT?! I HAVE TO SUPPLY THE MATERIALS?!
BETTER GET IT BEFORE THE SUN SETS!
BRRR
BRRR

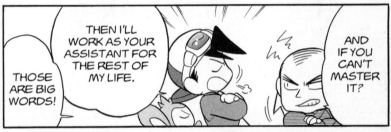

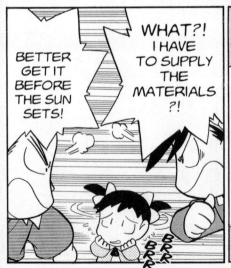

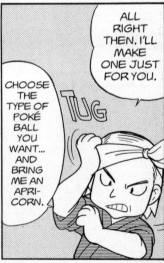

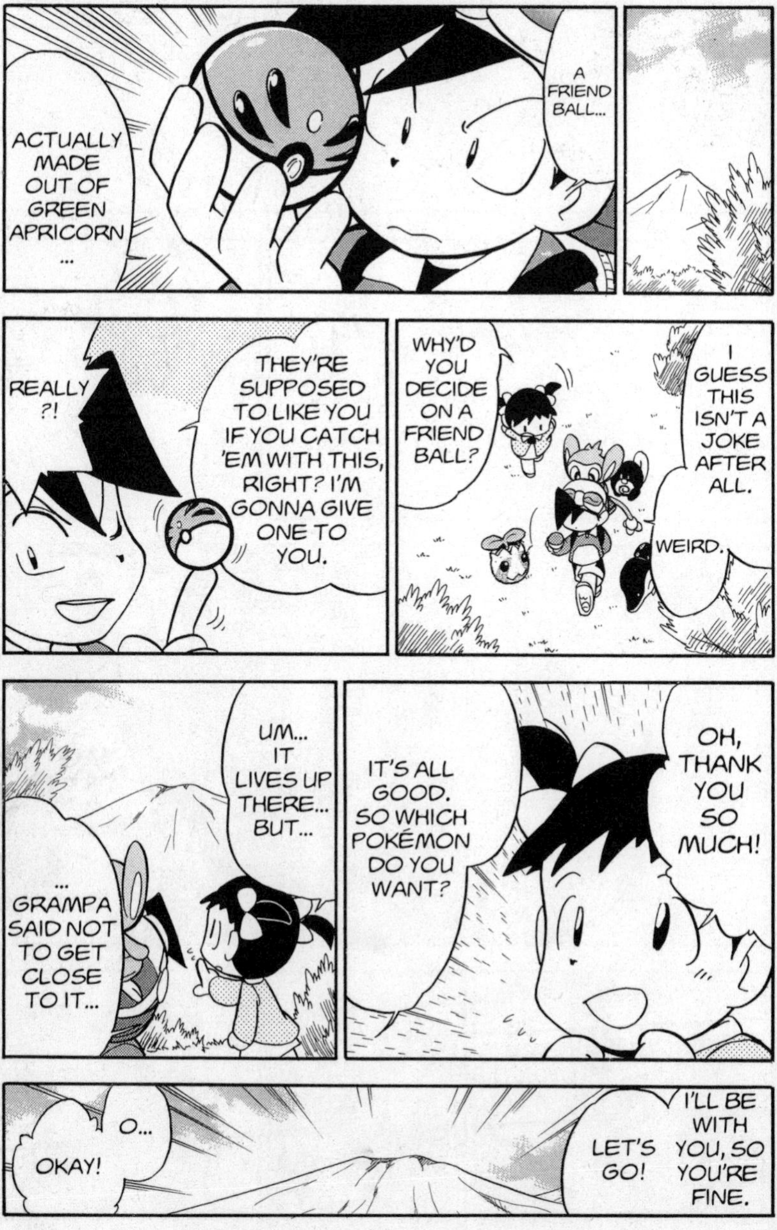
A FRIEND BALL...
ACTUALLY MADE OUT OF GREEN APRICORN...
I GUESS THIS ISN'T A JOKE AFTER ALL.
WEIRD.
WHY'D YOU DECIDE ON A FRIEND BALL?
THEY'RE SUPPOSED TO LIKE YOU IF YOU CATCH 'EM WITH THIS, RIGHT? I'M GONNA GIVE ONE TO YOU.
REALLY ?!
OH, THANK YOU SO MUCH!
IT'S ALL GOOD. SO WHICH POKÉMON DO YOU WANT?
UM... IT LIVES UP THERE... BUT...
...GRAMPA SAID NOT TO GET CLOSE TO IT...
I'LL BE WITH YOU, SO YOU'RE FINE.
LET'S GO!
O... OKAY!

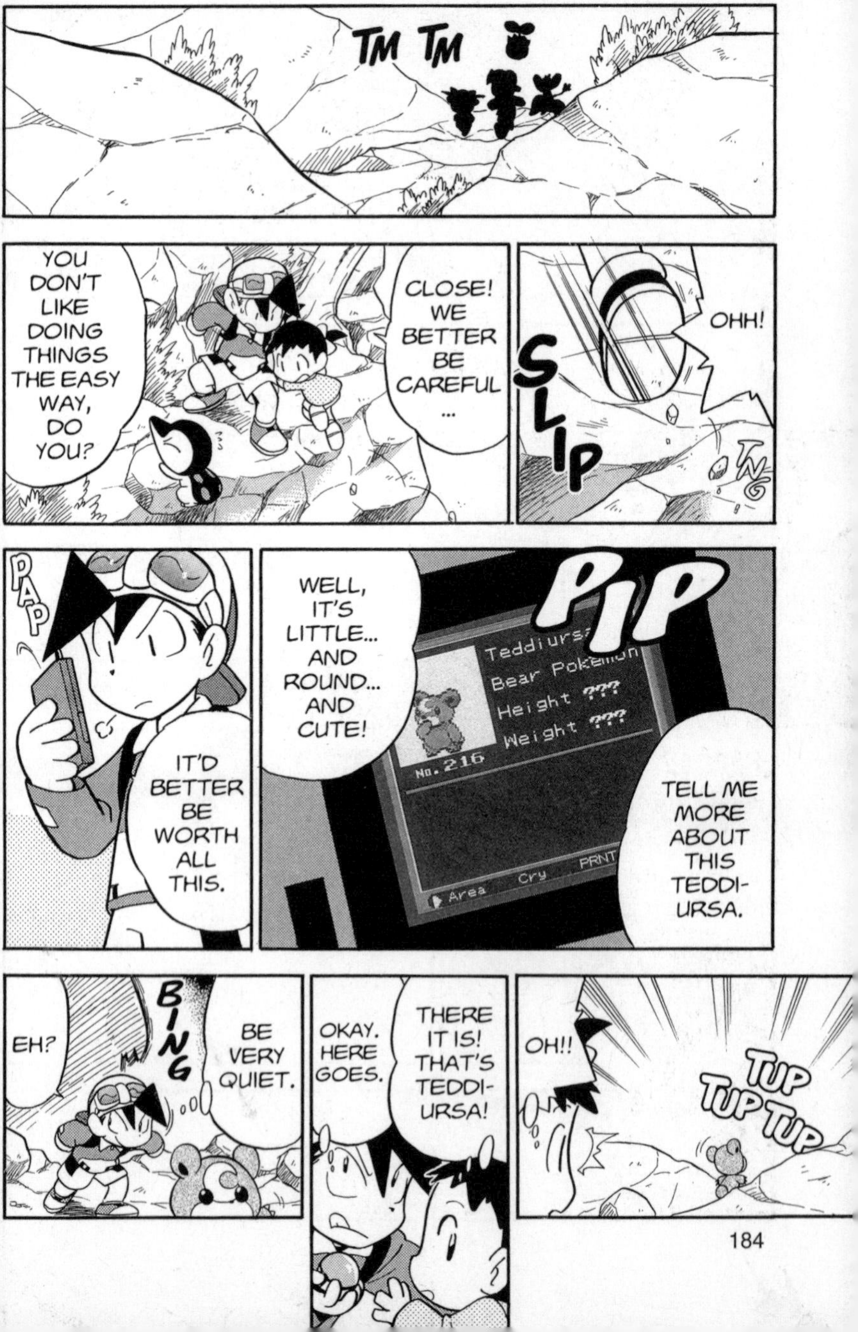
TM TM
SLIP
OHH!
TNG
CLOSE! WE BETTER BE CAREFUL...
YOU DON'T LIKE DOING THINGS THE EASY WAY, DO YOU?
PIP
WELL, IT'S LITTLE... AND ROUND... AND CUTE!
Teddiursa
Bear Pokemon
Height ???
Weight ???
No.216
Area Cry PRNT
TELL ME MORE ABOUT THIS TEDDI-URSA.
PAP
IT'D BETTER BE WORTH ALL THIS.
OH!!
TUP TUP TUP
THERE IT IS! THAT'S TEDDI-URSA!
OKAY. HERE GOES.
BE VERY QUIET.
BING
EH?

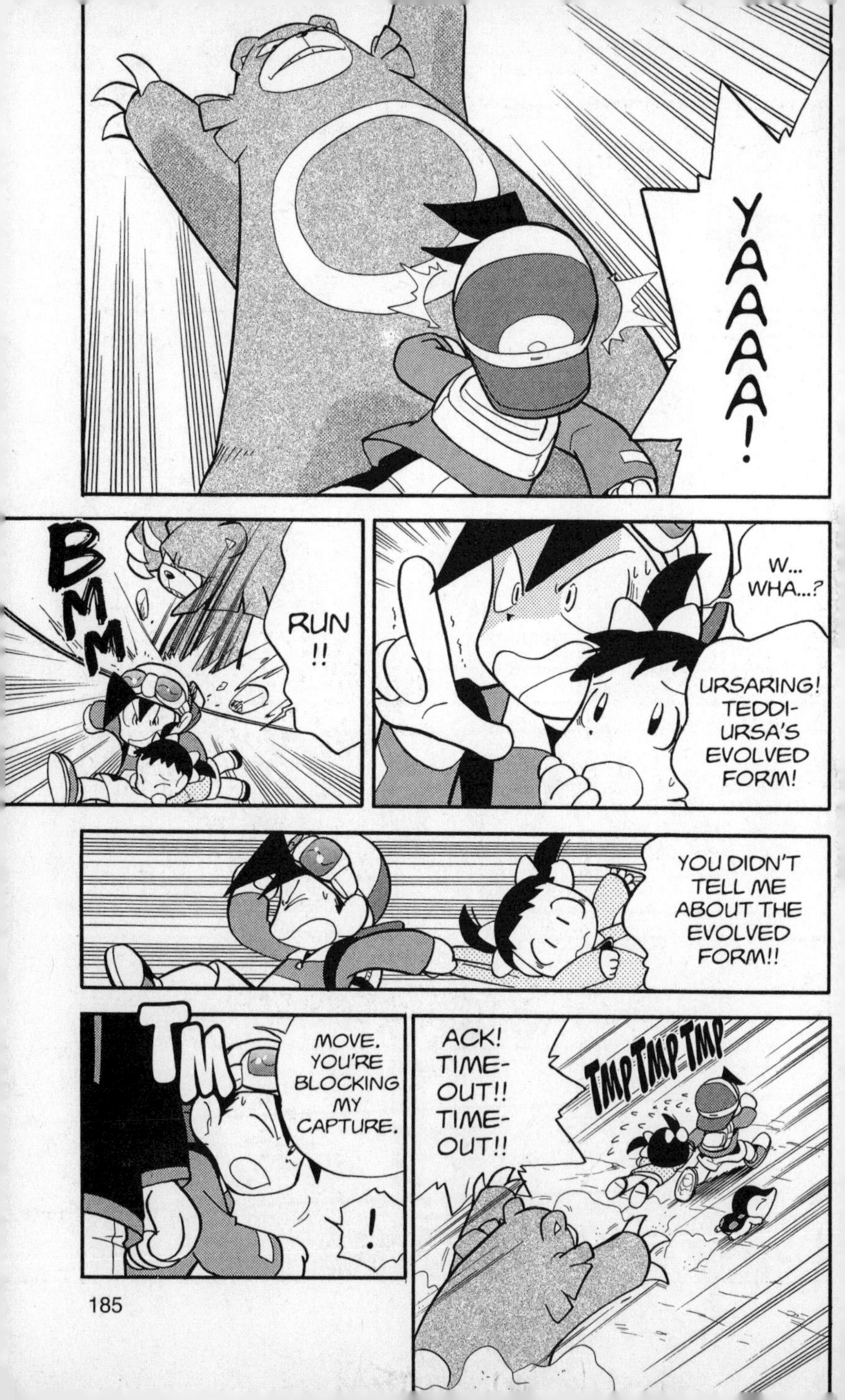
YAAAA!
W... WHA...?
URSARING! TEDDI-URSA'S EVOLVED FORM!
RUN!!
BMMM
YOU DIDN'T TELL ME ABOUT THE EVOLVED FORM!!
ACK! TIME-OUT!! TIME-OUT!!
TMP TMP TMP
TM
MOVE. YOU'RE BLOCKING MY CAPTURE.
!

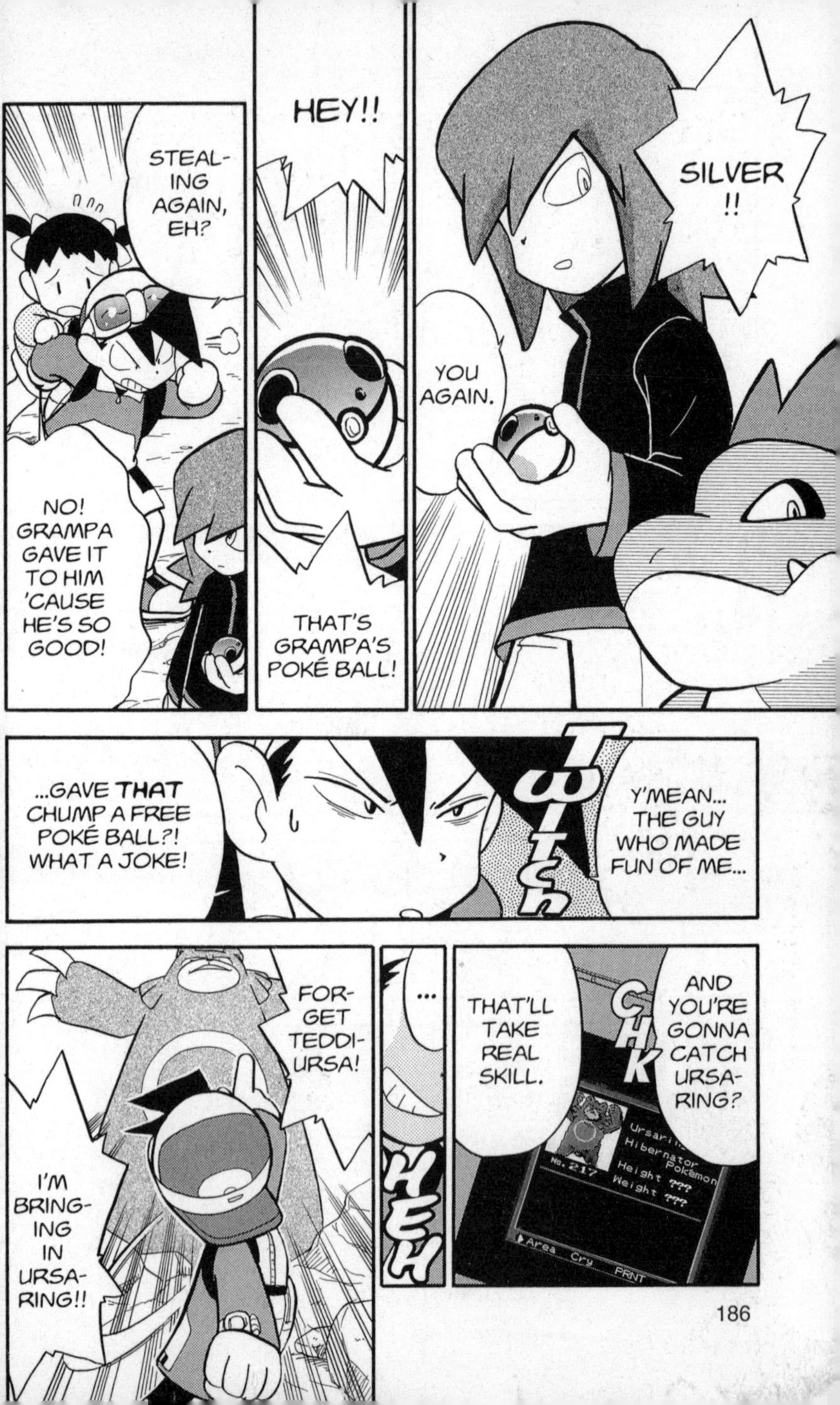
SILVER!!
YOU AGAIN.
HEY!!
THAT'S GRAMPA'S POKÉ BALL!
STEAL-ING AGAIN, EH?
NO! GRAMPA GAVE IT TO HIM 'CAUSE HE'S SO GOOD!
Y'MEAN... THE GUY WHO MADE FUN OF ME...
TWITCH
...GAVE **THAT** CHUMP A FREE POKÉ BALL?! WHAT A JOKE!
AND YOU'RE GONNA CATCH URSA-RING?
CHK
THAT'LL TAKE REAL SKILL.
Ursari
Hibernator Pokémon
No. 217
Height ???
Weight ???
Area Cry PRNT
...
HEH HEH
FOR-GET TEDDI-URSA!
I'M BRING-ING IN URSA-RING!!

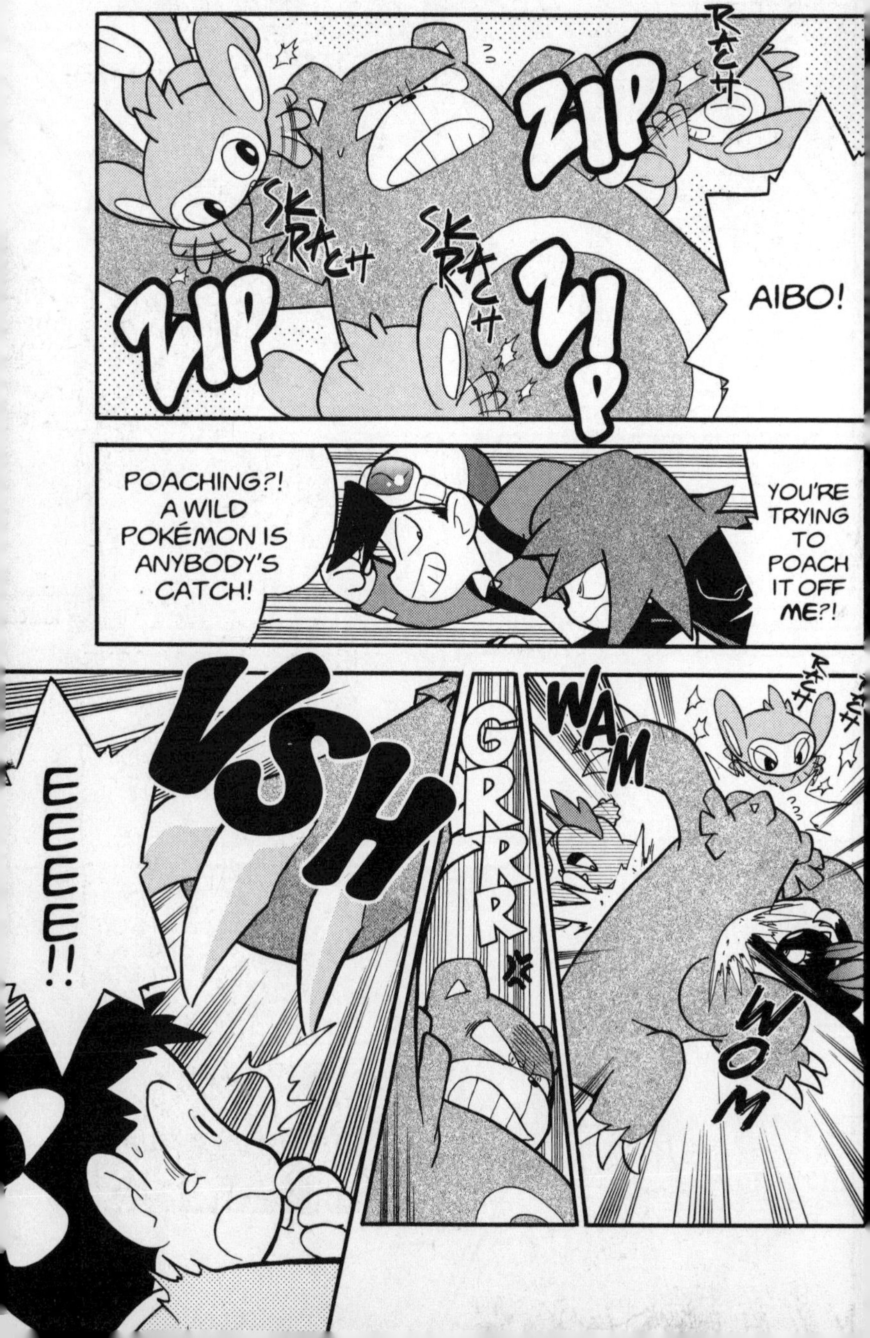
RACH
ZIP
AIBO!
SKRACH
ZIP
SKRACH
ZIP
YOU'RE TRYING TO POACH IT OFF ME?!
POACHING?! A WILD POKÉMON IS ANYBODY'S CATCH!
RACH
WAM
WOM
GRRR
VSH
EEEEE!!

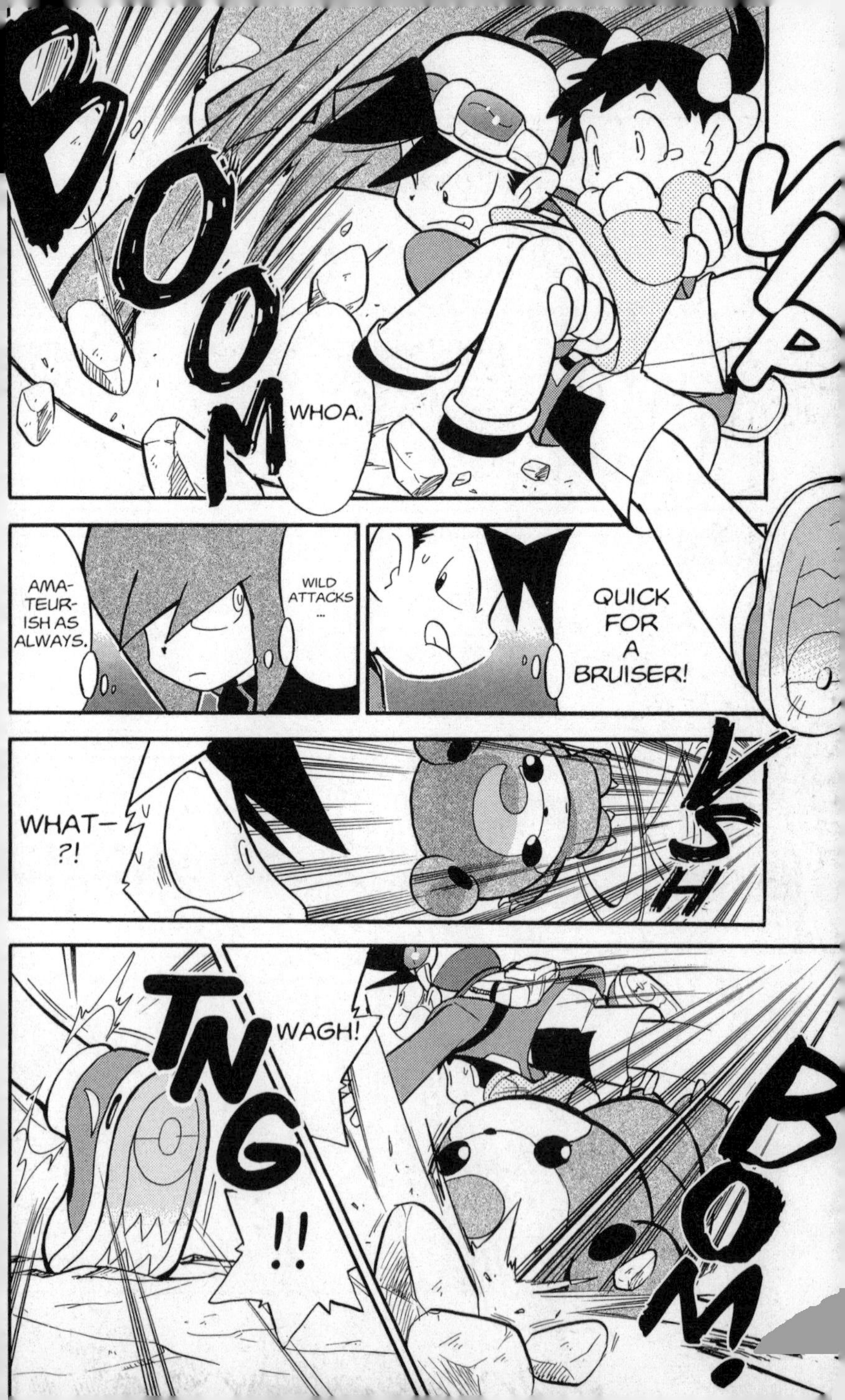
VIP
BOOM
WHOA.
QUICK FOR A BRUISER!
WILD ATTACKS...
AMATEURISH AS ALWAYS.
VSH
WHAT—?!
BOOM!
TNG!!
WAGH!

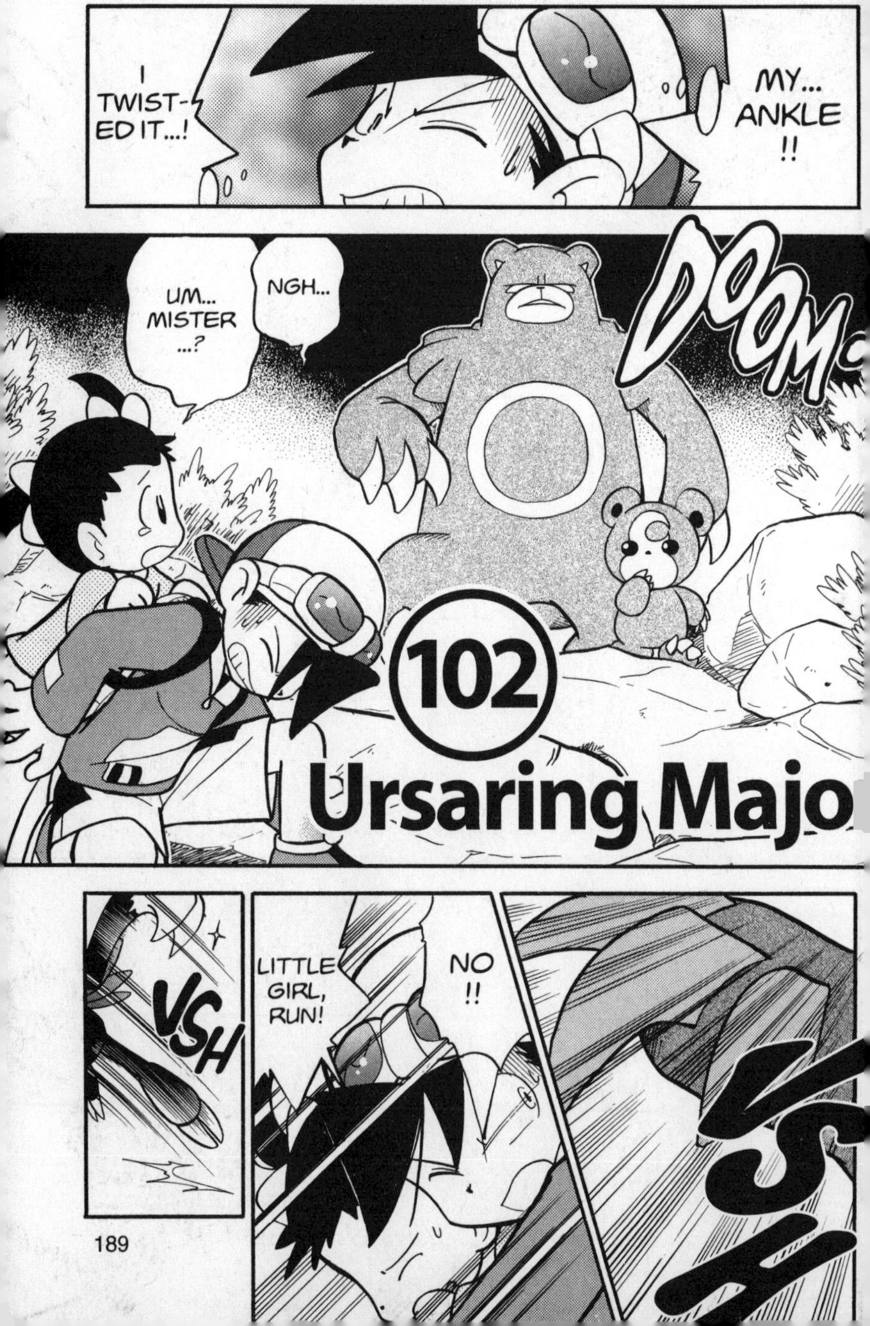

MY... ANKLE !!
I TWIST-ED IT...!
DOOM
NGH...
UM... MISTER ...?
102
Ursaring Majo
VSH
NO !!
LITTLE GIRL, RUN!
VSH

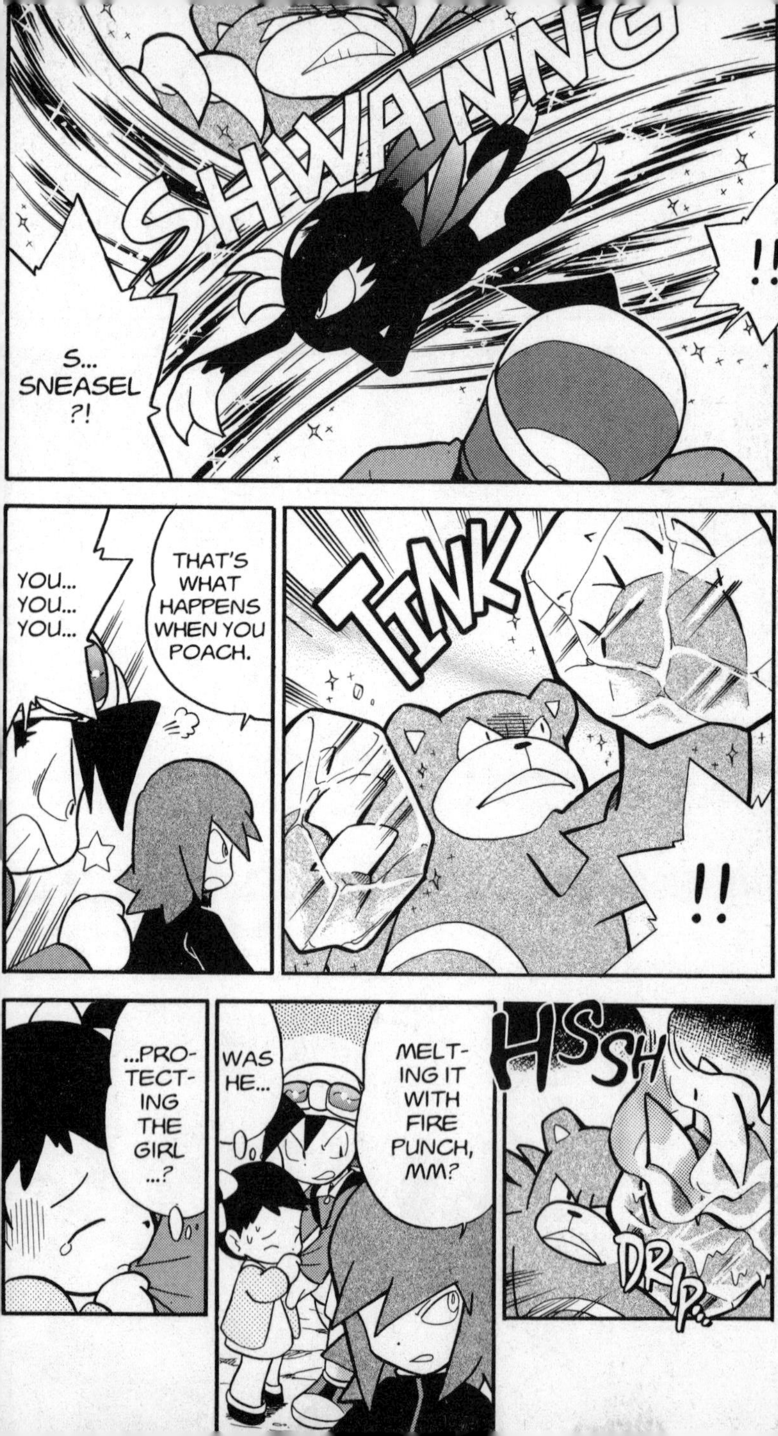
SHWANNG
!!
S... SNEASEL ?!
TINK
!!
THAT'S WHAT HAPPENS WHEN YOU POACH.
YOU... YOU... YOU...
HSSSH
DRIP...
MELT-ING IT WITH FIRE PUNCH, MM?
WAS HE...
...PRO-TECT-ING THE GIRL ...?

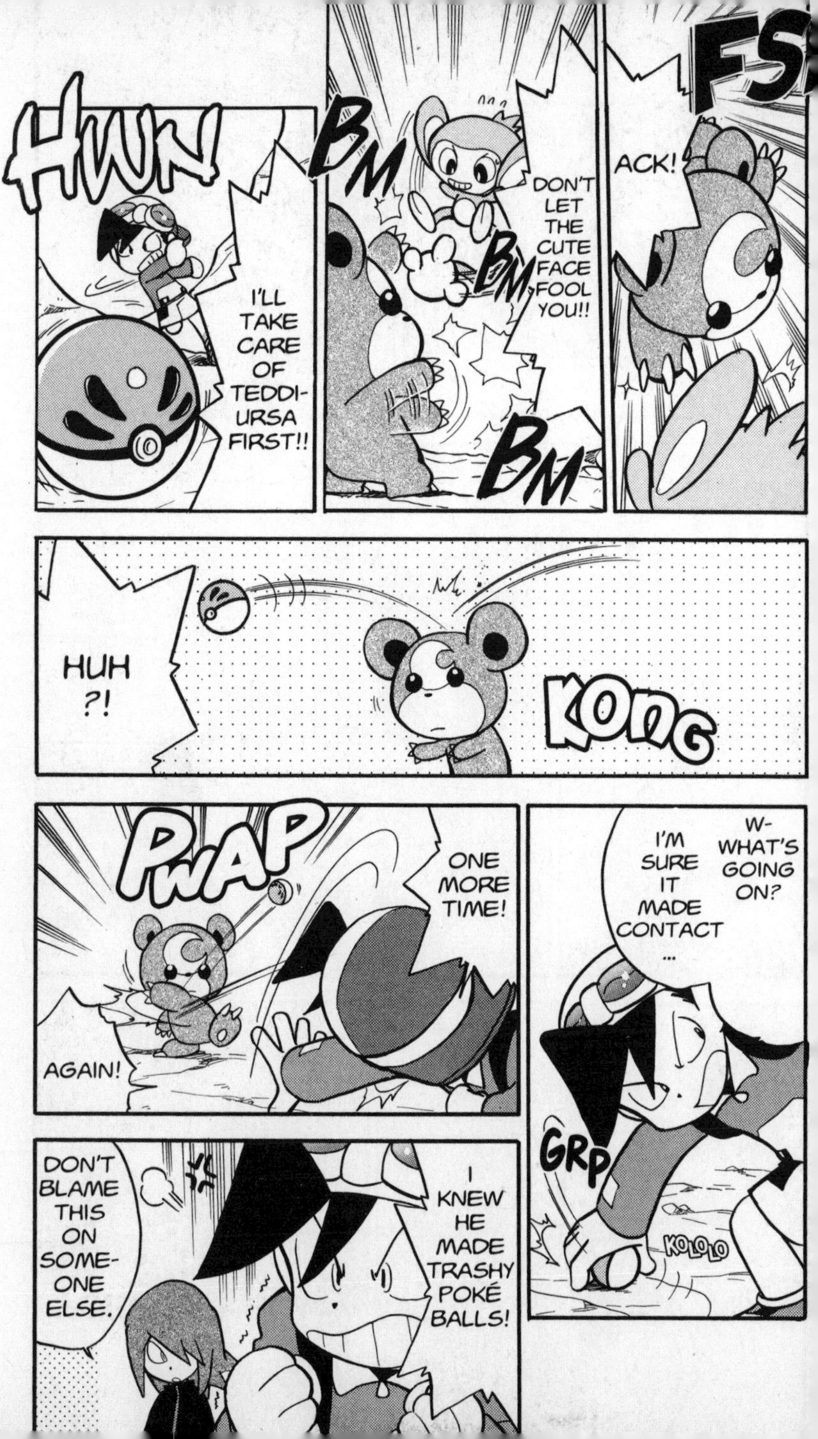
FS
ACK!
BM
DON'T LET THE CUTE FACE FOOL YOU!!
BM
BM
HWN
I'LL TAKE CARE OF TEDDI-URSA FIRST!!
KONG
HUH ?!
W-WHAT'S GOING ON?
I'M SURE IT MADE CONTACT ...
GRP
KOLOLO
ONE MORE TIME!
PWAP
AGAIN!
I KNEW HE MADE TRASHY POKÉ BALLS!
DON'T BLAME THIS ON SOME-ONE ELSE.

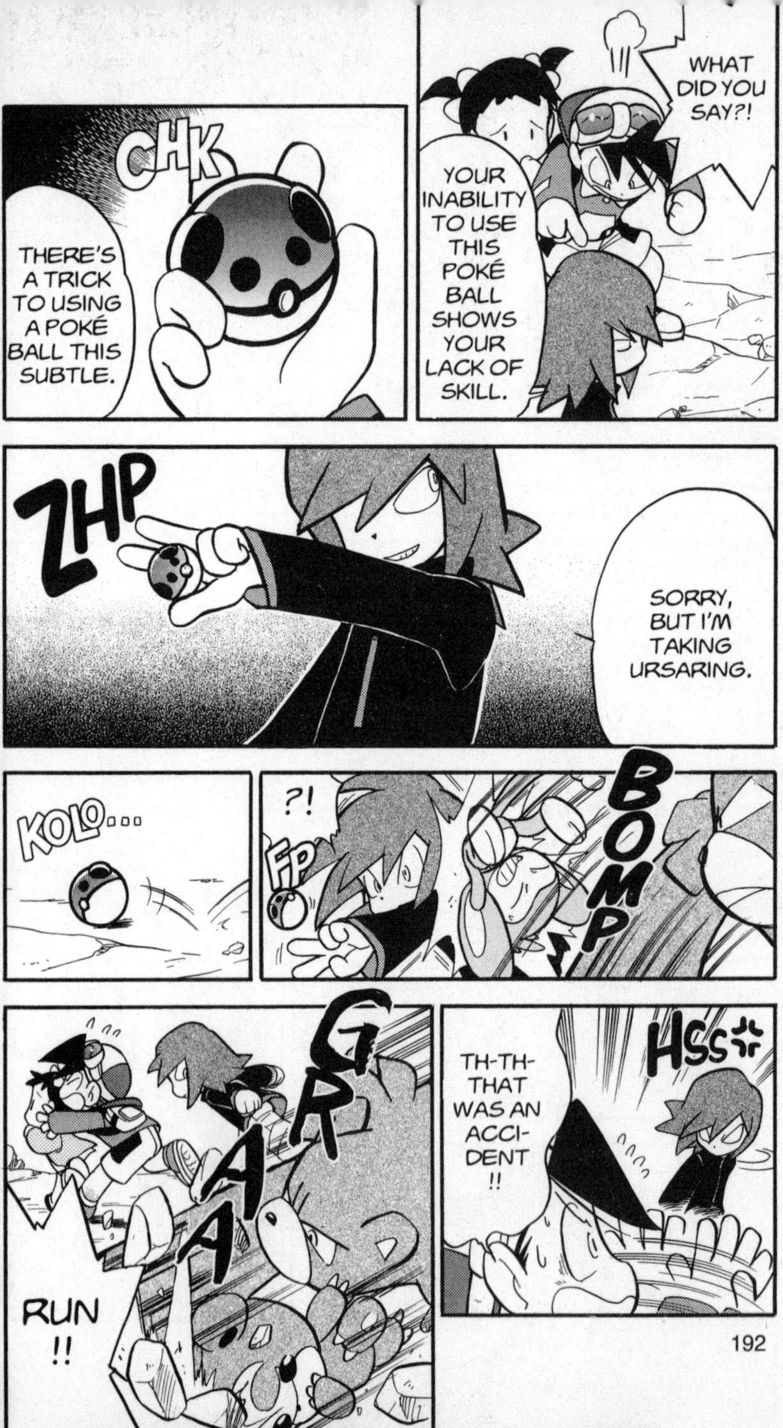
WHAT DID YOU SAY?!
YOUR INABILITY TO USE THIS POKÉ BALL SHOWS YOUR LACK OF SKILL.
CHK
THERE'S A TRICK TO USING A POKÉ BALL THIS SUBTLE.
SORRY, BUT I'M TAKING URSARING.
ZHP
BOMP
?!
FP
KOLO...
HSS
TH-TH-THAT WAS AN ACCI-DENT !!
GRAA
RUN !!

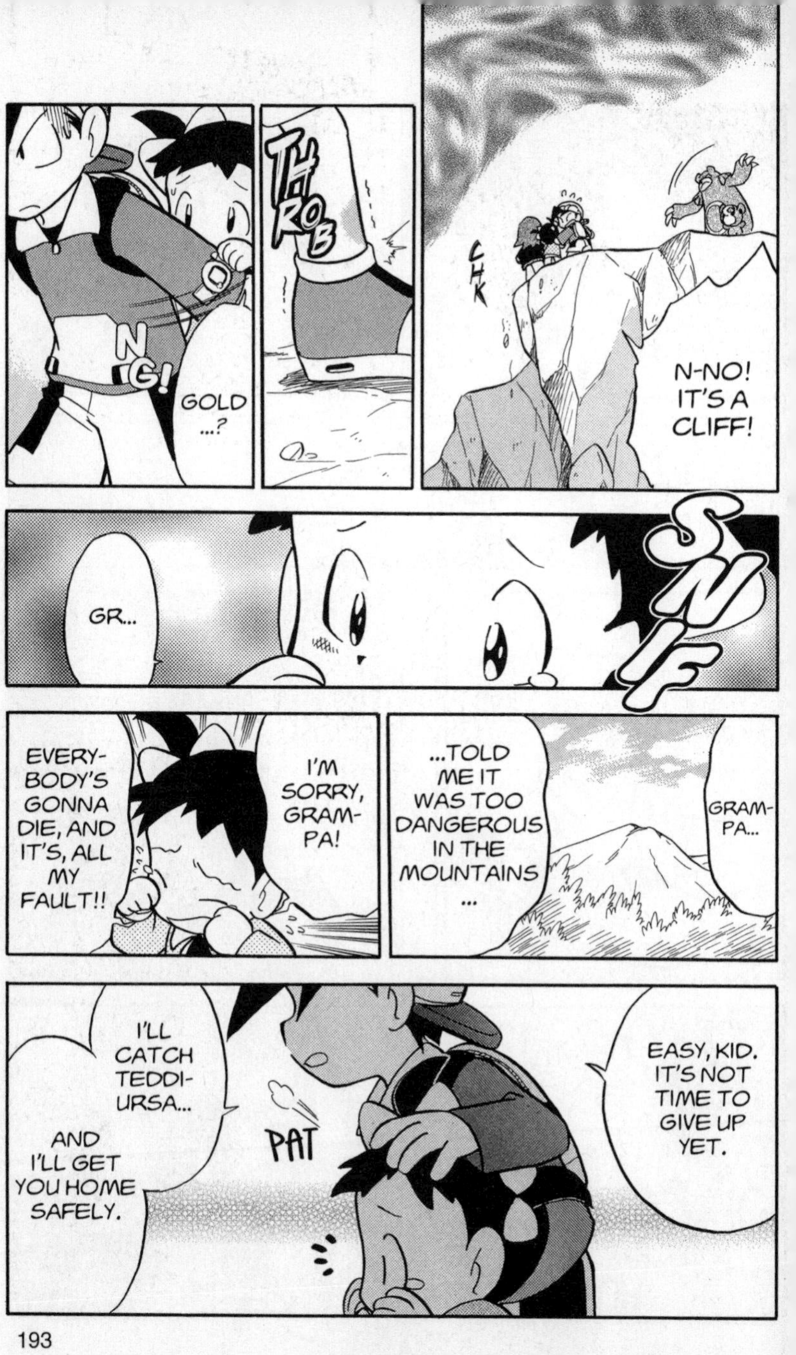
CHK
N-NO! IT'S A CLIFF!
THROB
NG!
GOLD ...?
SNIFF
GR...
GRAM-PA...
...TOLD ME IT WAS TOO DANGEROUS IN THE MOUNTAINS ...
I'M SORRY, GRAM-PA!
EVERY-BODY'S GONNA DIE, AND IT'S, ALL MY FAULT!!
EASY, KID. IT'S NOT TIME TO GIVE UP YET.
PAT
I'LL CATCH TEDDI-URSA...
AND I'LL GET YOU HOME SAFELY.

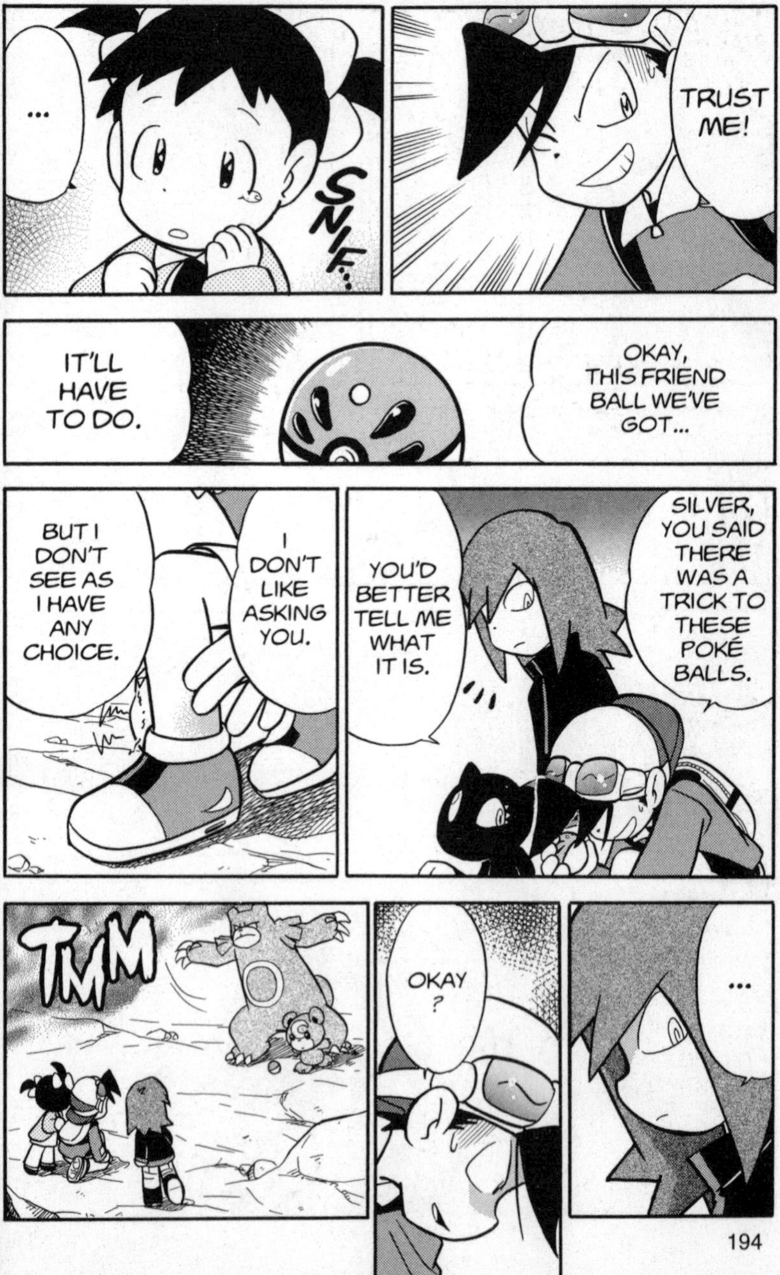
TRUST ME!
...
SNIF...
OKAY, THIS FRIEND BALL WE'VE GOT...
IT'LL HAVE TO DO.
SILVER, YOU SAID THERE WAS A TRICK TO THESE POKÉ BALLS.
YOU'D BETTER TELL ME WHAT IT IS.
I DON'T LIKE ASKING YOU.
BUT I DON'T SEE AS I HAVE ANY CHOICE.
...
OKAY?
TMM

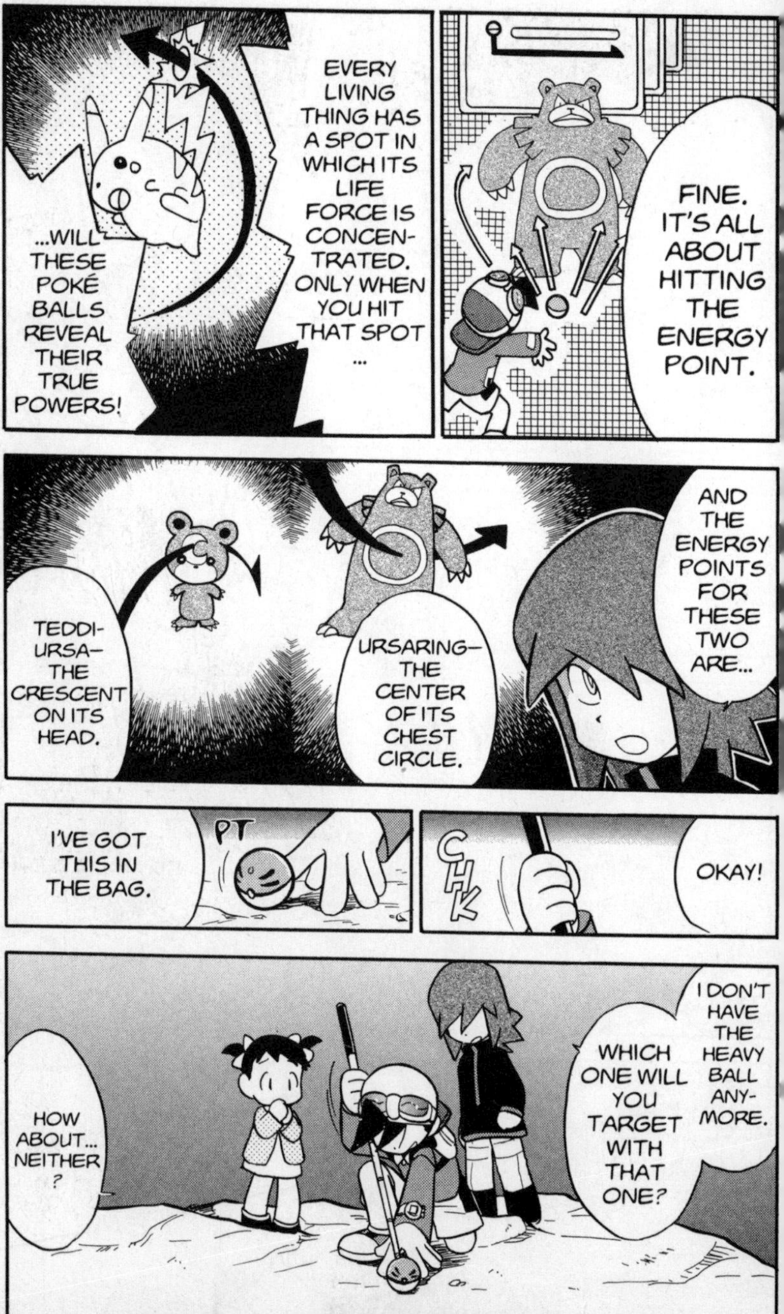
FINE. IT'S ALL ABOUT HITTING THE ENERGY POINT.
EVERY LIVING THING HAS A SPOT IN WHICH ITS LIFE FORCE IS CONCENTRATED. ONLY WHEN YOU HIT THAT SPOT ...
...WILL THESE POKÉ BALLS REVEAL THEIR TRUE POWERS!
AND THE ENERGY POINTS FOR THESE TWO ARE...
URSARING—THE CENTER OF ITS CHEST CIRCLE.
TEDDIURSA—THE CRESCENT ON ITS HEAD.
CHK
OKAY!
PT
I'VE GOT THIS IN THE BAG.
I DON'T HAVE THE HEAVY BALL ANYMORE.
WHICH ONE WILL YOU TARGET WITH THAT ONE?
HOW ABOUT... NEITHER?

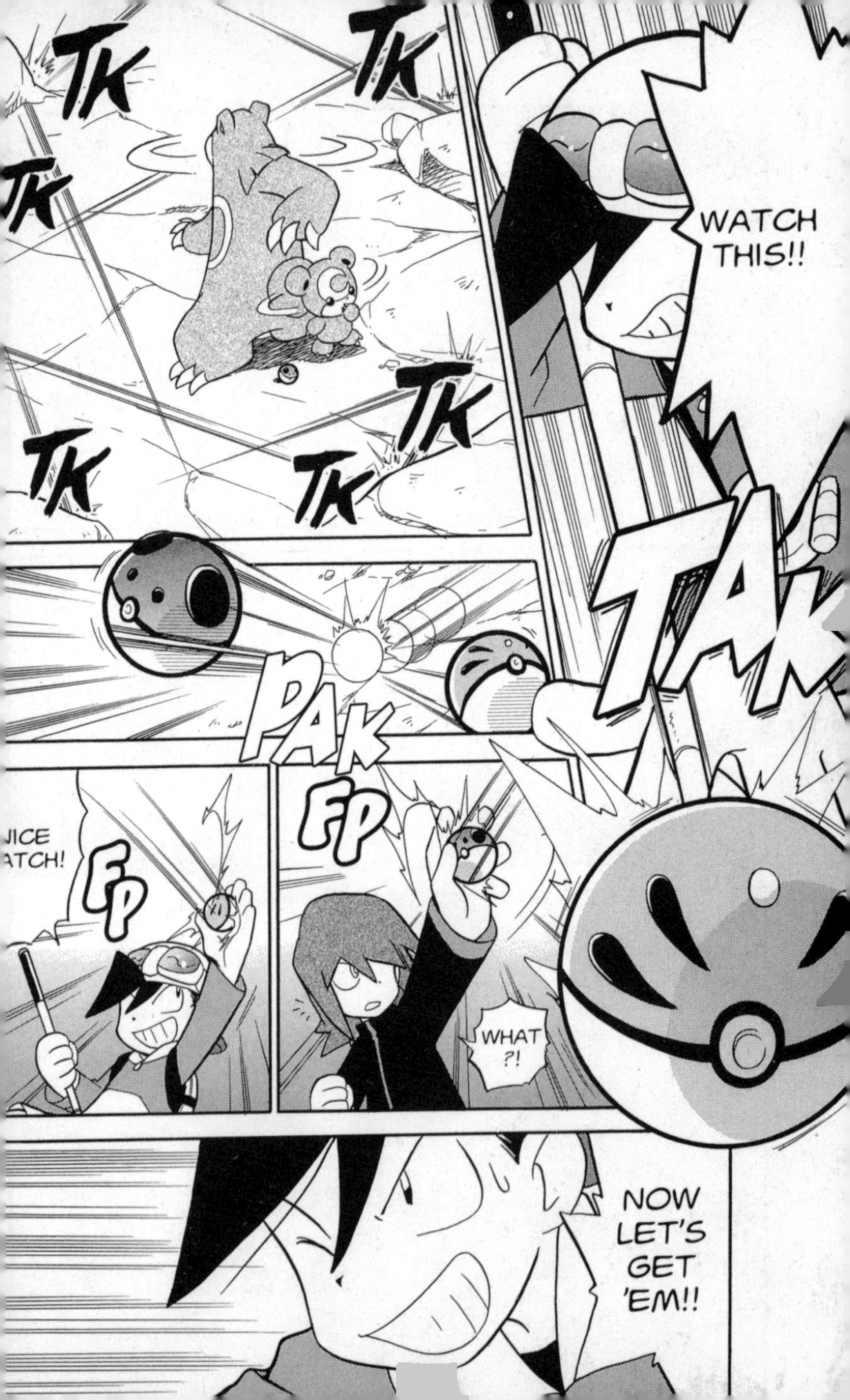
WATCH THIS!!
TAK
TK
TK
TK
TK
TK
TK
PAK
FP
WHAT ?!
NICE
ATCH!
FP
NOW LET'S GET 'EM!!

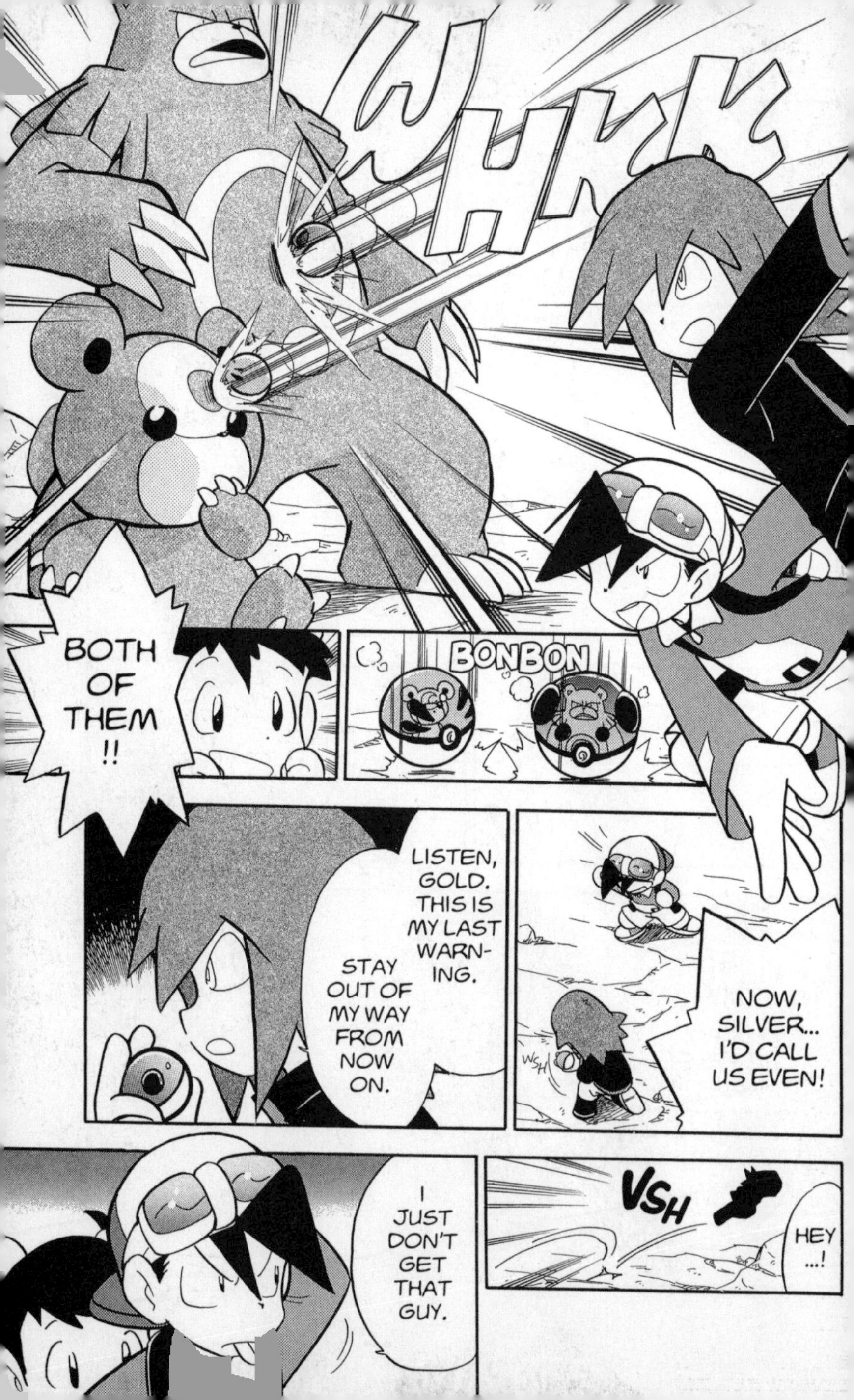
WHKK
BOTH OF THEM !!
BONBON
NOW, SILVER... I'D CALL US EVEN!
WSH
LISTEN, GOLD. THIS IS MY LAST WARNING.
STAY OUT OF MY WAY FROM NOW ON.
VSH
HEY ...!
I JUST DON'T GET THAT GUY.

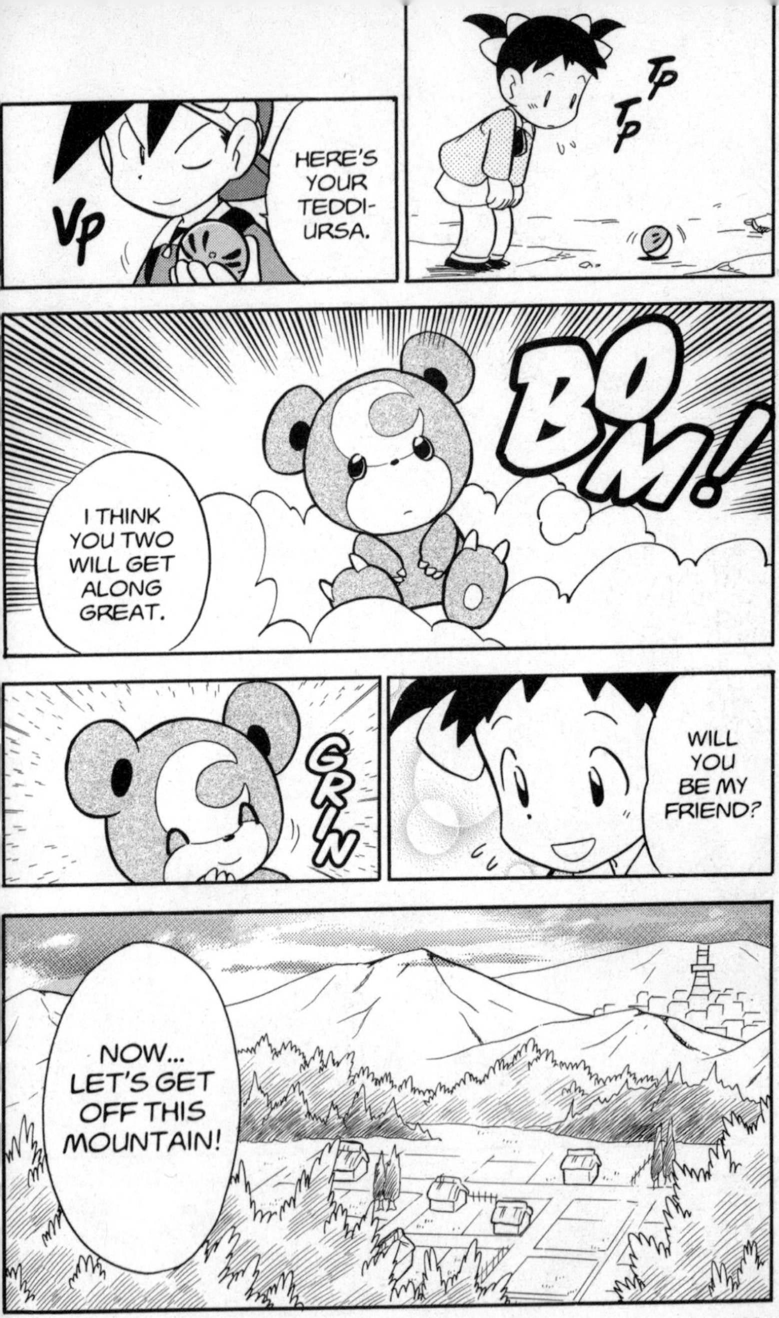
Tp Tp
Vp
HERE'S YOUR TEDDIURSA.
BOOM!
I THINK YOU TWO WILL GET ALONG GREAT.
WILL YOU BE MY FRIEND?
GRIN
NOW... LET'S GET OFF THIS MOUNTAIN!

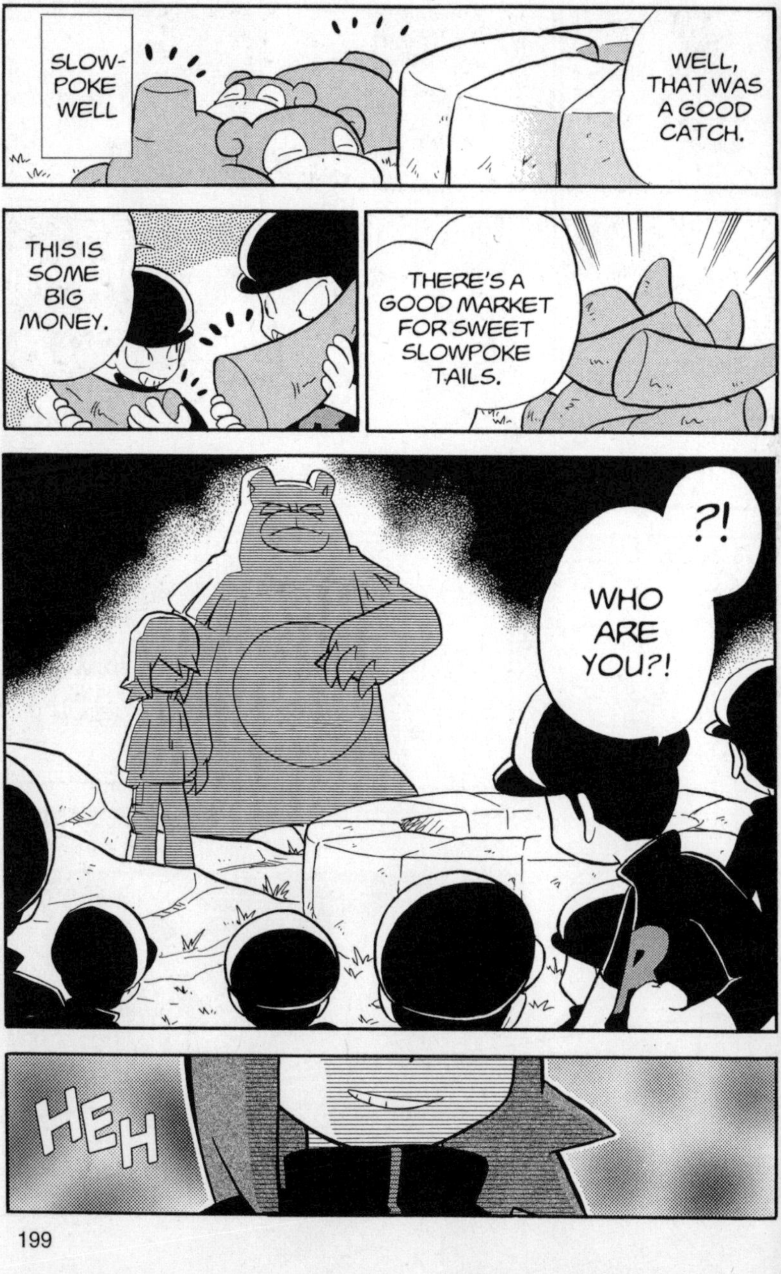
WELL, THAT WAS A GOOD CATCH.
SLOW-POKE WELL
THERE'S A GOOD MARKET FOR SWEET SLOWPOKE TAILS.
THIS IS SOME BIG MONEY.
?!
WHO ARE YOU?!
HEH

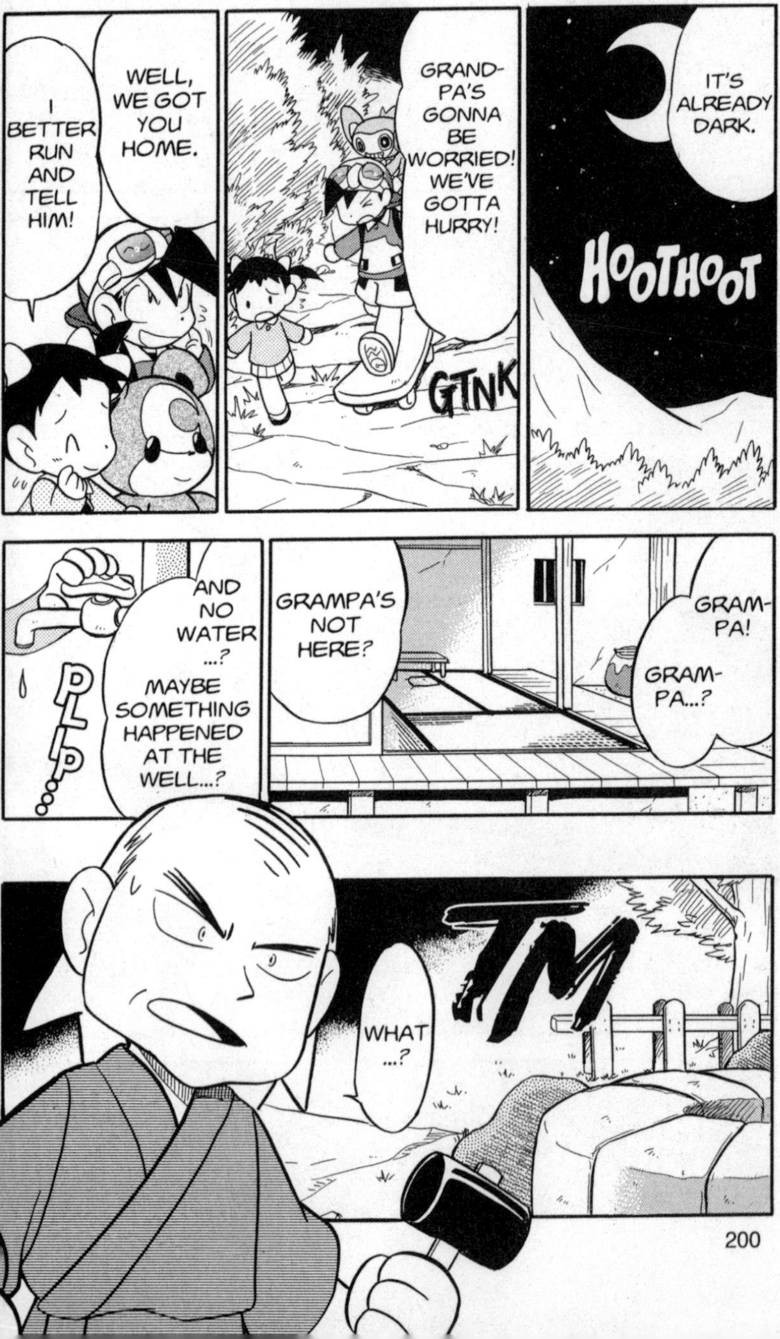
IT'S ALREADY DARK.
HOOTHOOT
GRAND-PA'S GONNA BE WORRIED! WE'VE GOTTA HURRY!
GTNK
WELL, WE GOT YOU HOME.
I BETTER RUN AND TELL HIM!
GRAM-PA!
GRAM-PA...?
GRAMPA'S NOT HERE?
AND NO WATER ...? MAYBE SOMETHING HAPPENED AT THE WELL...?
PLIP
TM
WHAT ...?

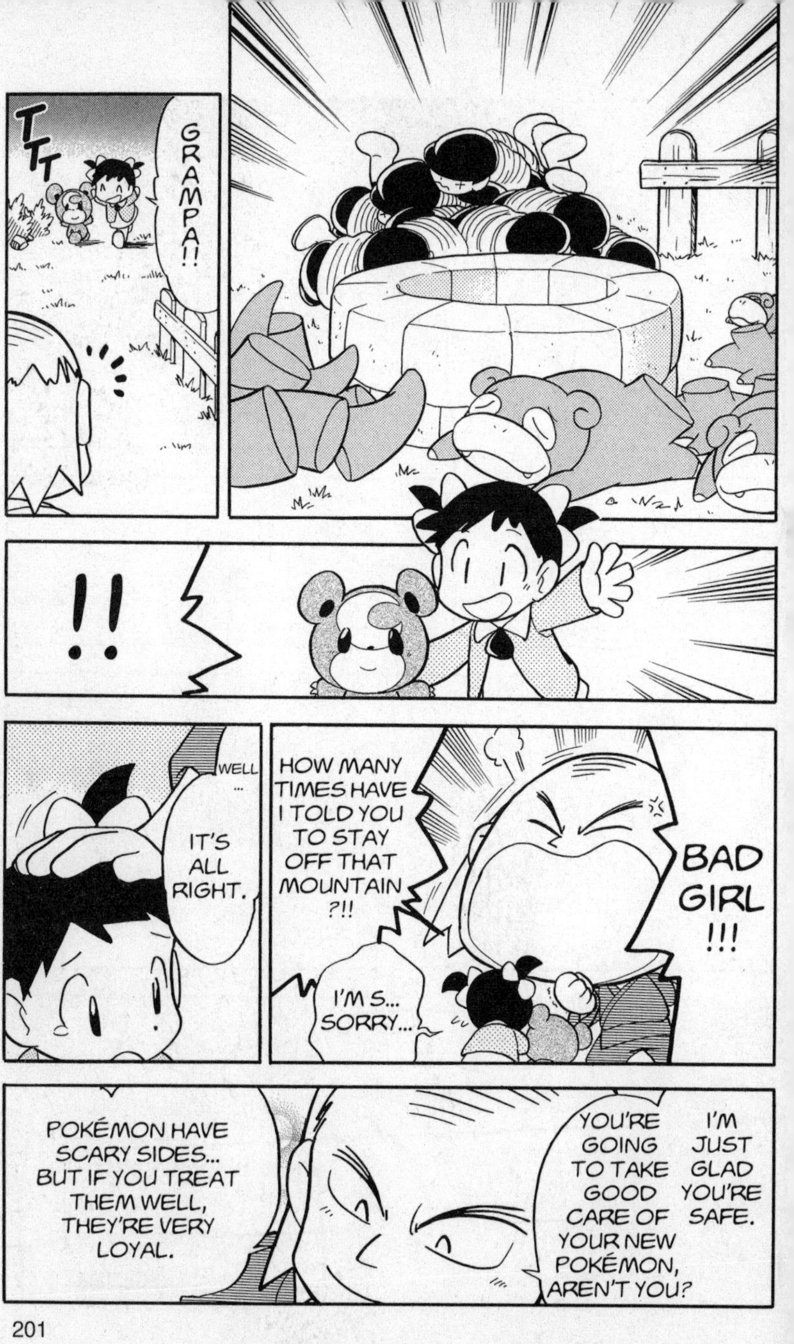
GRAMPA!!
TTT
!!
BAD GIRL !!!
HOW MANY TIMES HAVE I TOLD YOU TO STAY OFF THAT MOUNTAIN ?!!
I'M S... SORRY...
WELL ...
IT'S ALL RIGHT.
I'M JUST GLAD YOU'RE SAFE.
YOU'RE GOING TO TAKE GOOD CARE OF YOUR NEW POKÉMON, AREN'T YOU?
POKÉMON HAVE SCARY SIDES... BUT IF YOU TREAT THEM WELL, THEY'RE VERY LOYAL.

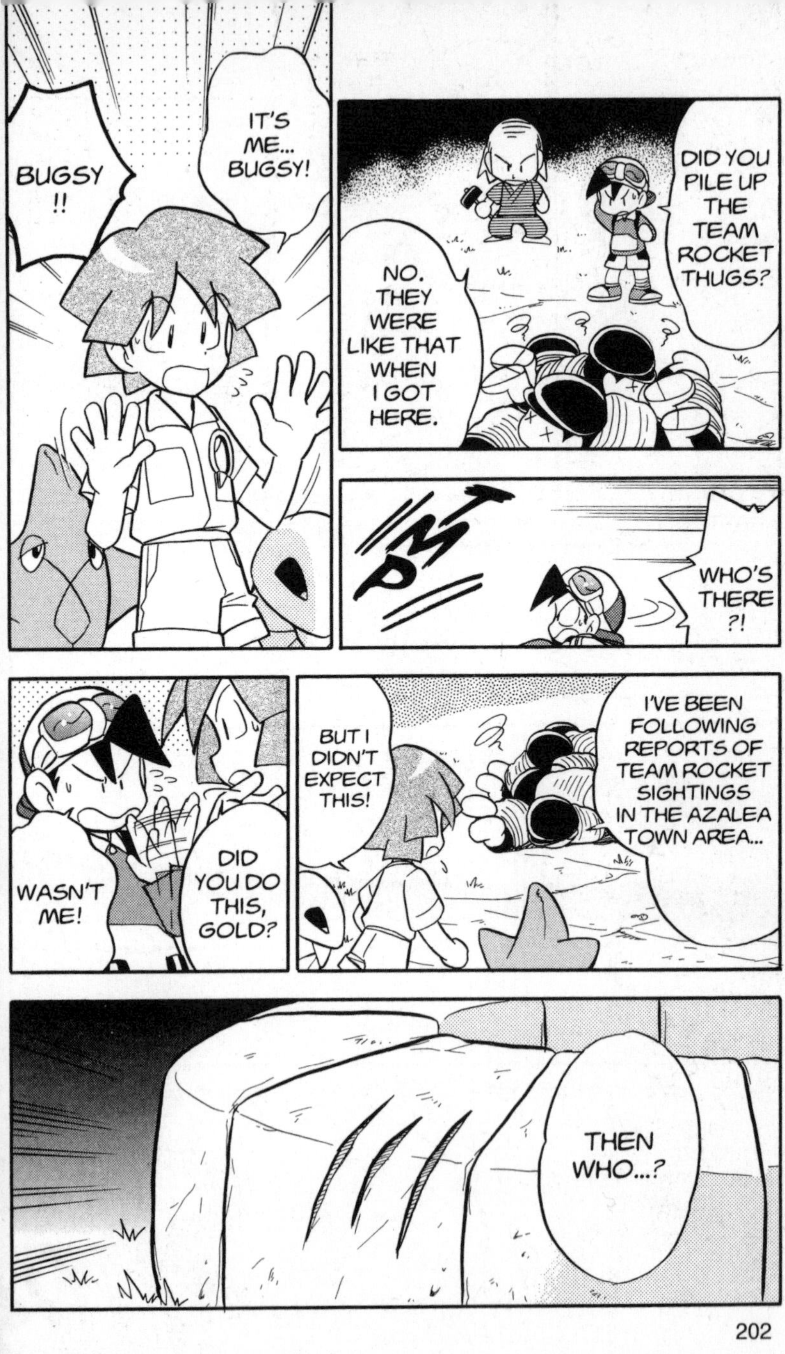
DID YOU PILE UP THE TEAM ROCKET THUGS?
NO. THEY WERE LIKE THAT WHEN I GOT HERE.
WHO'S THERE ?!
TMP
IT'S ME... BUGSY!
BUGSY !!
I'VE BEEN FOLLOWING REPORTS OF TEAM ROCKET SIGHTINGS IN THE AZALEA TOWN AREA...
BUT I DIDN'T EXPECT THIS!
DID YOU DO THIS, GOLD?
WASN'T ME!
THEN WHO...?

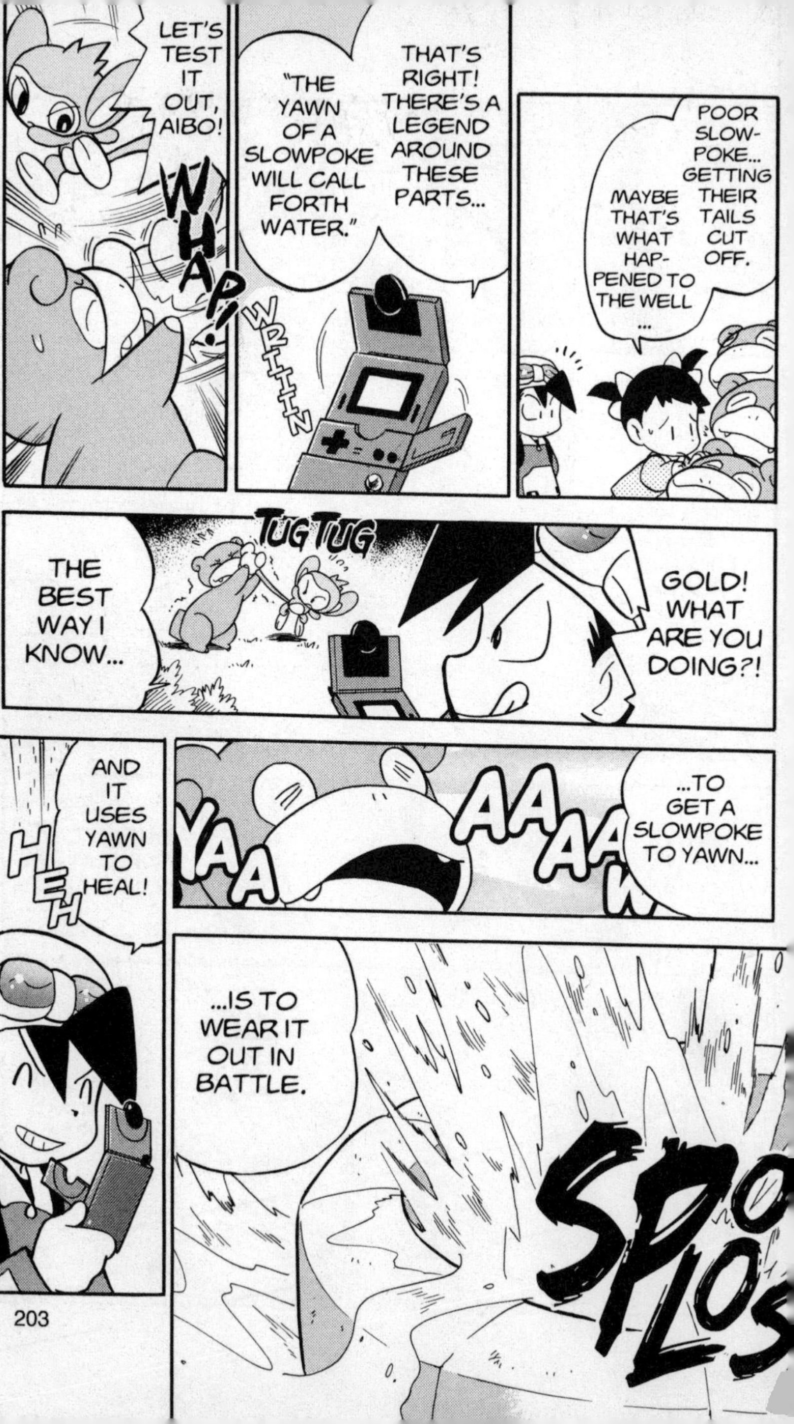
POOR SLOWPOKE... GETTING THEIR TAILS CUT OFF.
MAYBE THAT'S WHAT HAPPENED TO THE WELL...
THAT'S RIGHT! THERE'S A LEGEND AROUND THESE PARTS...
"THE YAWN OF A SLOWPOKE WILL CALL FORTH WATER."
WRIIIN
LET'S TEST IT OUT, AIBO!
WHAP!
GOLD! WHAT ARE YOU DOING?!
TUG TUG
THE BEST WAY I KNOW...
...TO GET A SLOWPOKE TO YAWN...
YAAAAAAW
...IS TO WEAR IT OUT IN BATTLE.
SPLOOS
AND IT USES YAWN TO HEAL!
HEH

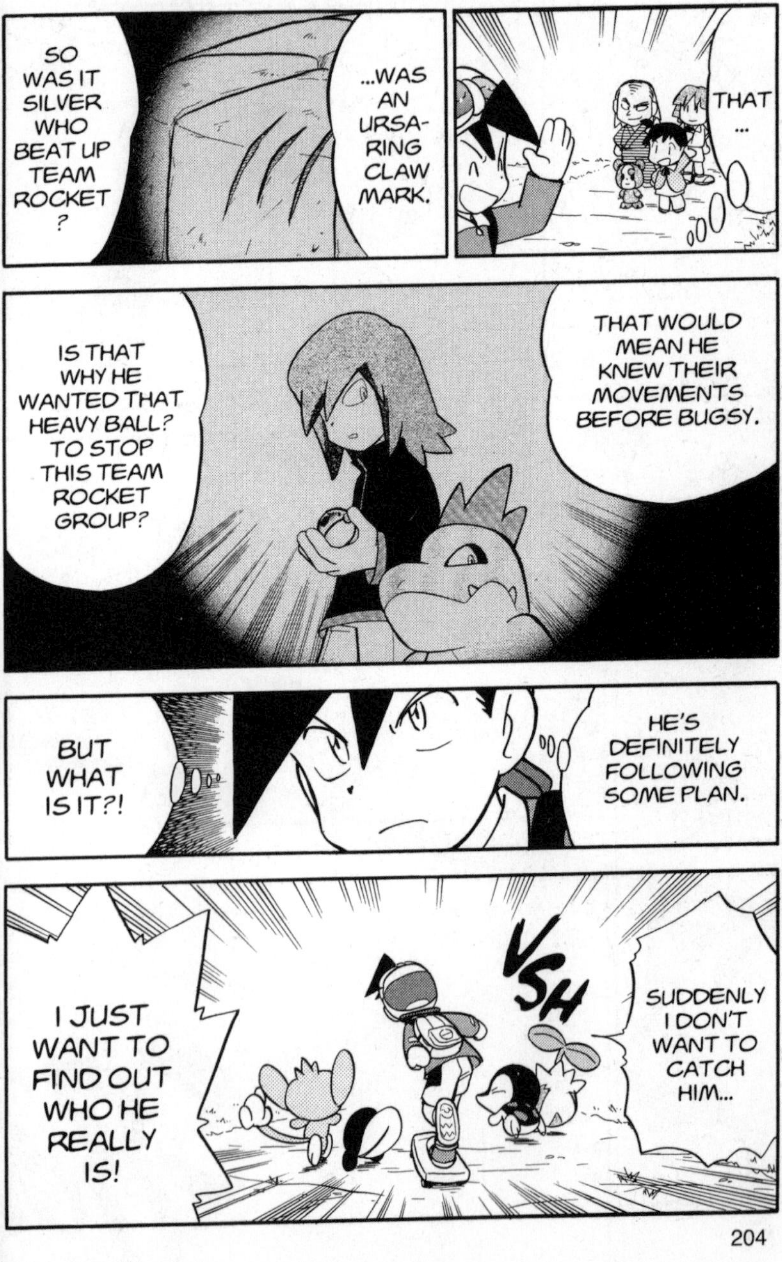
THAT...
...WAS AN URSARING CLAW MARK.
SO WAS IT SILVER WHO BEAT UP TEAM ROCKET?
THAT WOULD MEAN HE KNEW THEIR MOVEMENTS BEFORE BUGSY.
IS THAT WHY HE WANTED THAT HEAVY BALL? TO STOP THIS TEAM ROCKET GROUP?
HE'S DEFINITELY FOLLOWING SOME PLAN.
BUT WHAT IS IT?!
SUDDENLY I DON'T WANT TO CATCH HIM...
VSH
I JUST WANT TO FIND OUT WHO HE REALLY IS!

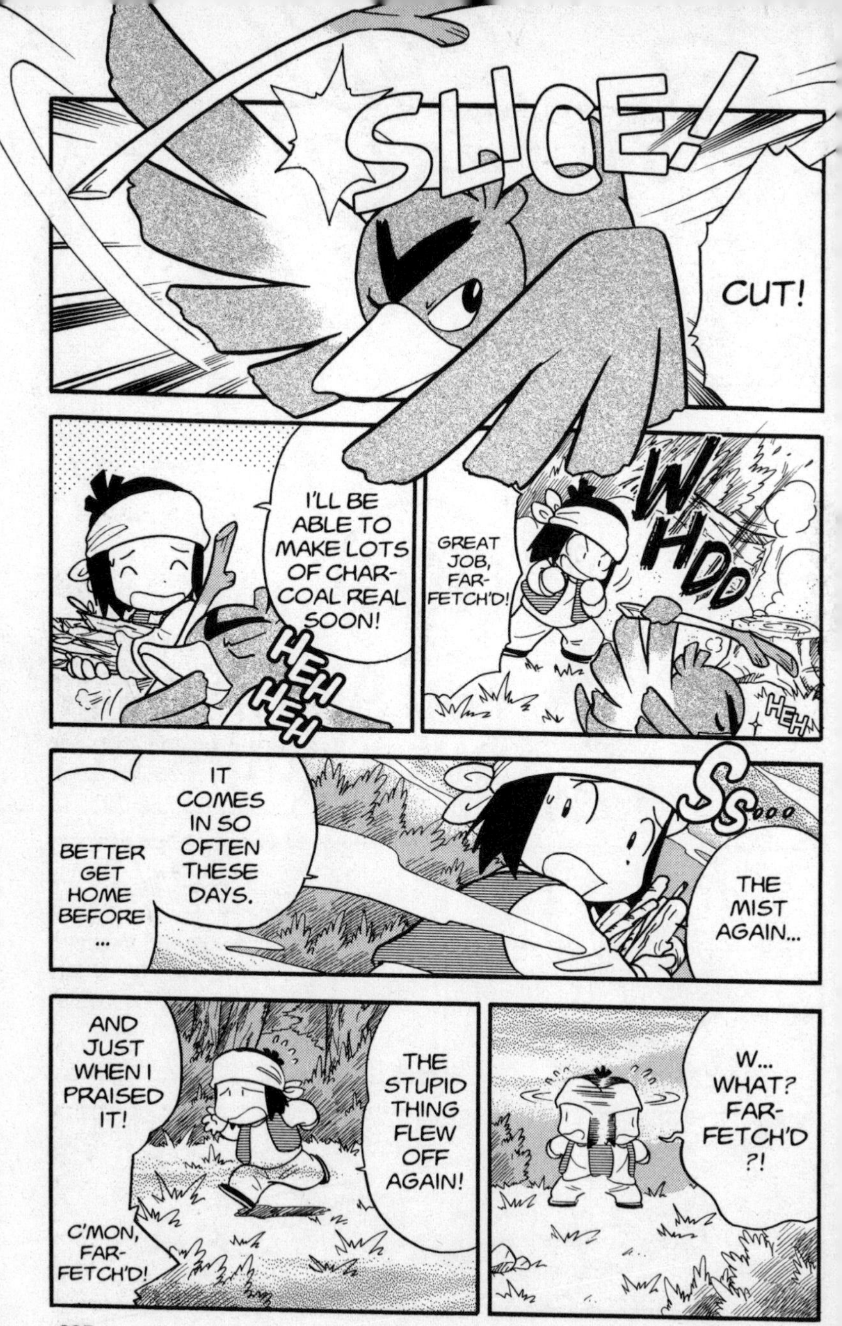
SLICE!
CUT!
WHDD
GREAT JOB, FAR-FETCH'D!
HEH
I'LL BE ABLE TO MAKE LOTS OF CHAR-COAL REAL SOON!
HEH HEH
Ssooo
THE MIST AGAIN...
IT COMES IN SO OFTEN THESE DAYS.
BETTER GET HOME BEFORE ...
W... WHAT? FAR-FETCH'D?!
THE STUPID THING FLEW OFF AGAIN!
AND JUST WHEN I PRAISED IT!
C'MON, FAR-FETCH'D!

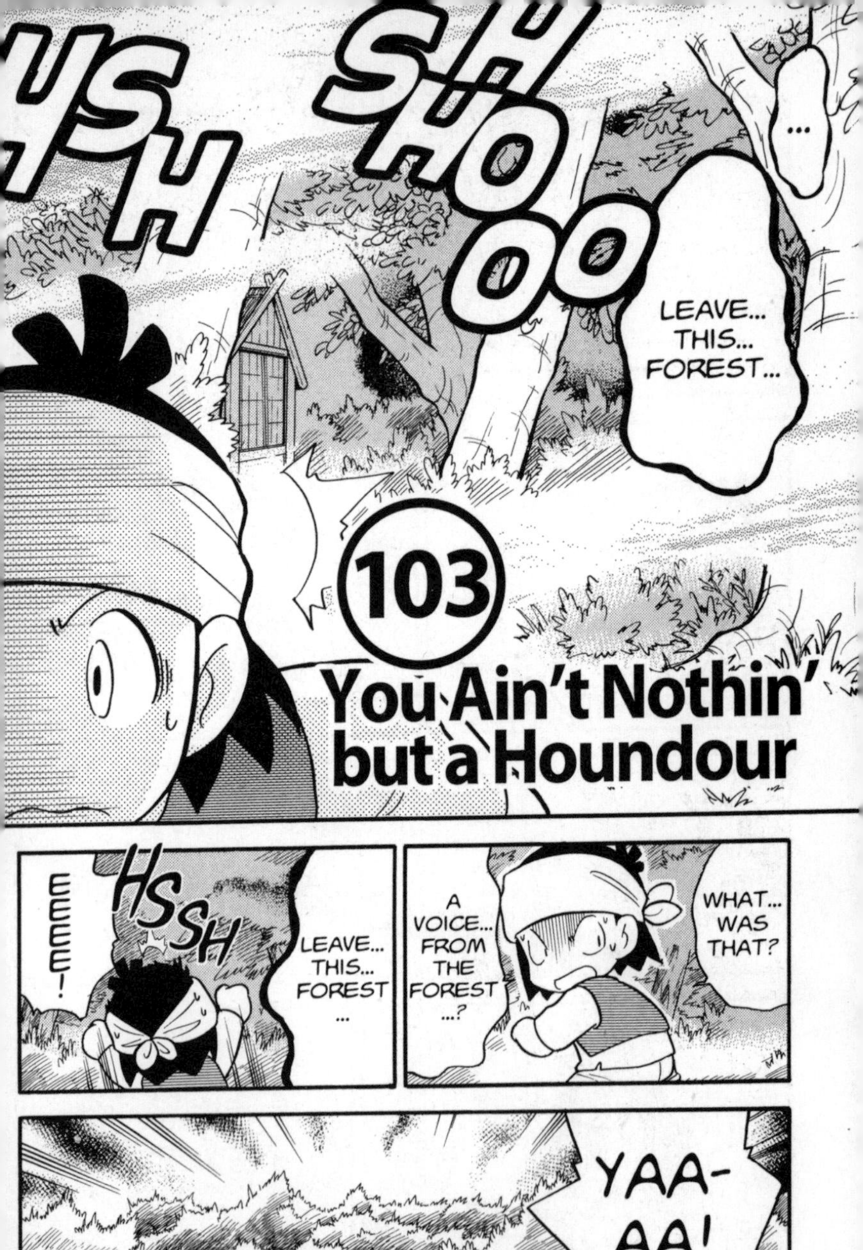
...
LEAVE... THIS... FOREST...
103
You Ain't Nothin' but a Houndour
WHAT... WAS THAT?
A VOICE... FROM THE FOREST ...?
LEAVE... THIS... FOREST ...
HSSH
EEEE!
YAA-AA!

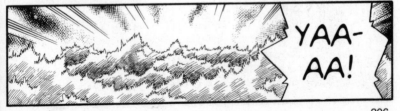

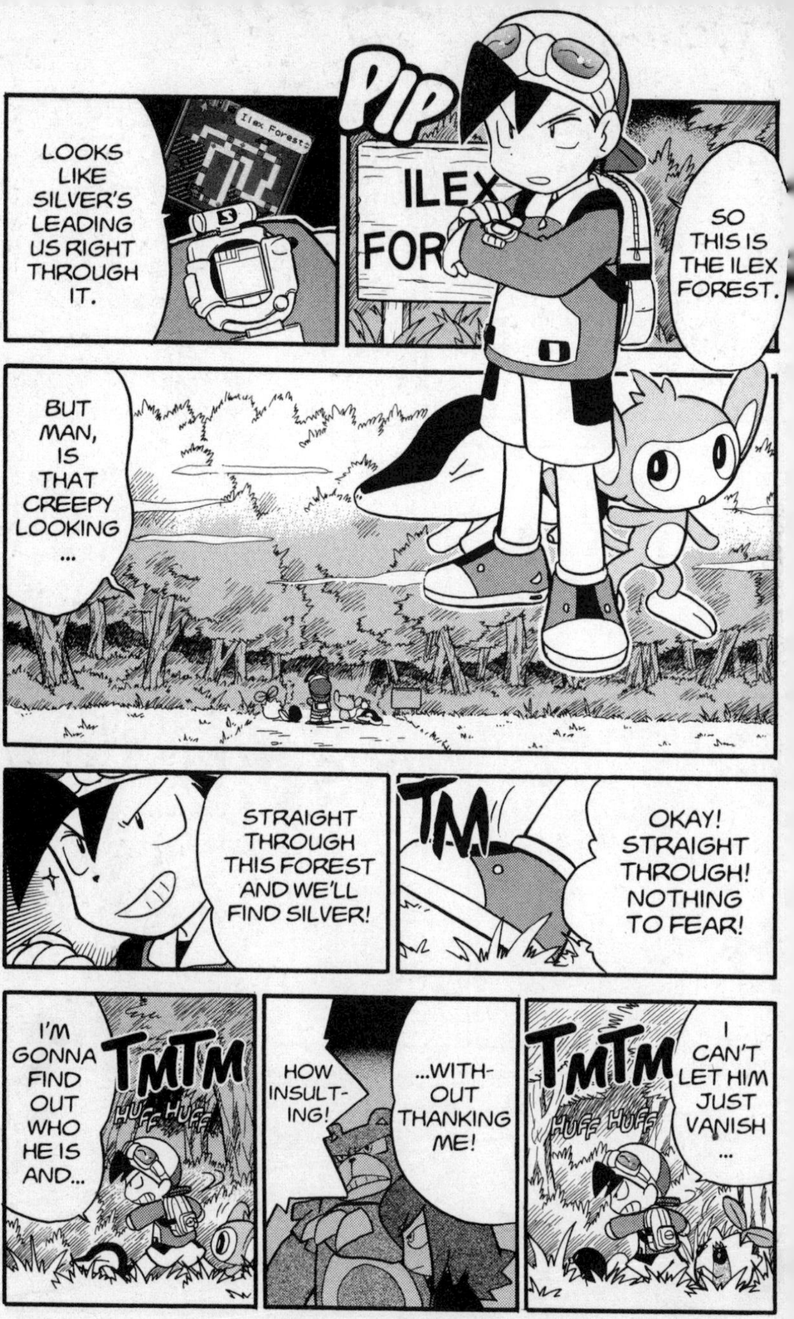
PIP
ILEX FOR
SO THIS IS THE ILEX FOREST.
Ilex Forest
LOOKS LIKE SILVER'S LEADING US RIGHT THROUGH IT.
BUT MAN, IS THAT CREEPY LOOKING ...
TM
OKAY! STRAIGHT THROUGH! NOTHING TO FEAR!
STRAIGHT THROUGH THIS FOREST AND WE'LL FIND SILVER!
TMTM
HUFF HUFF
I CAN'T LET HIM JUST VANISH ...
...WITH-OUT THANKING ME!
HOW INSULT-ING!
TMTM
HUFF HUFF
I'M GONNA FIND OUT WHO HE IS AND...

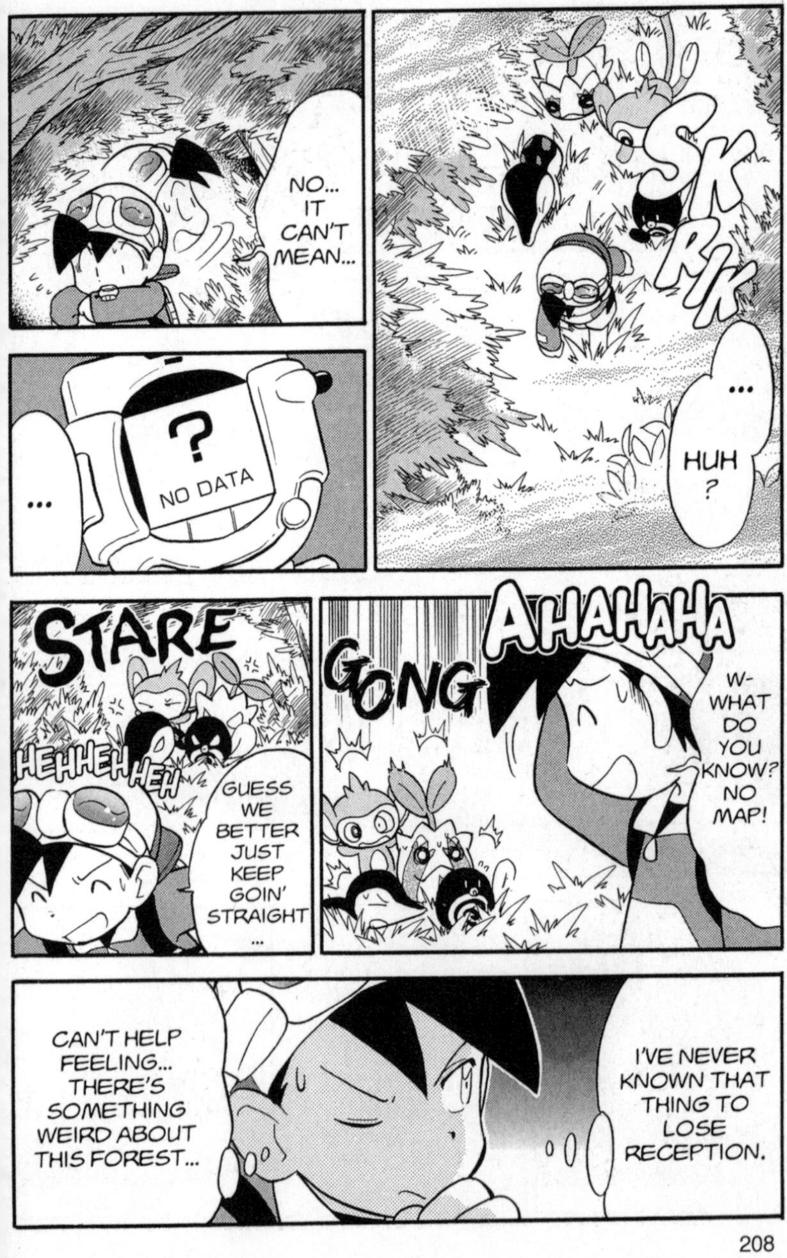
SKRIK
...
HUH?
NO... IT CAN'T MEAN...
?
NO DATA
...
AHAHAHA
W-WHAT DO YOU KNOW? NO MAP!
GONG
STARE
HEHHEHHEH
GUESS WE BETTER JUST KEEP GOIN' STRAIGHT ...
I'VE NEVER KNOWN THAT THING TO LOSE RECEPTION.
CAN'T HELP FEELING... THERE'S SOMETHING WEIRD ABOUT THIS FOREST...

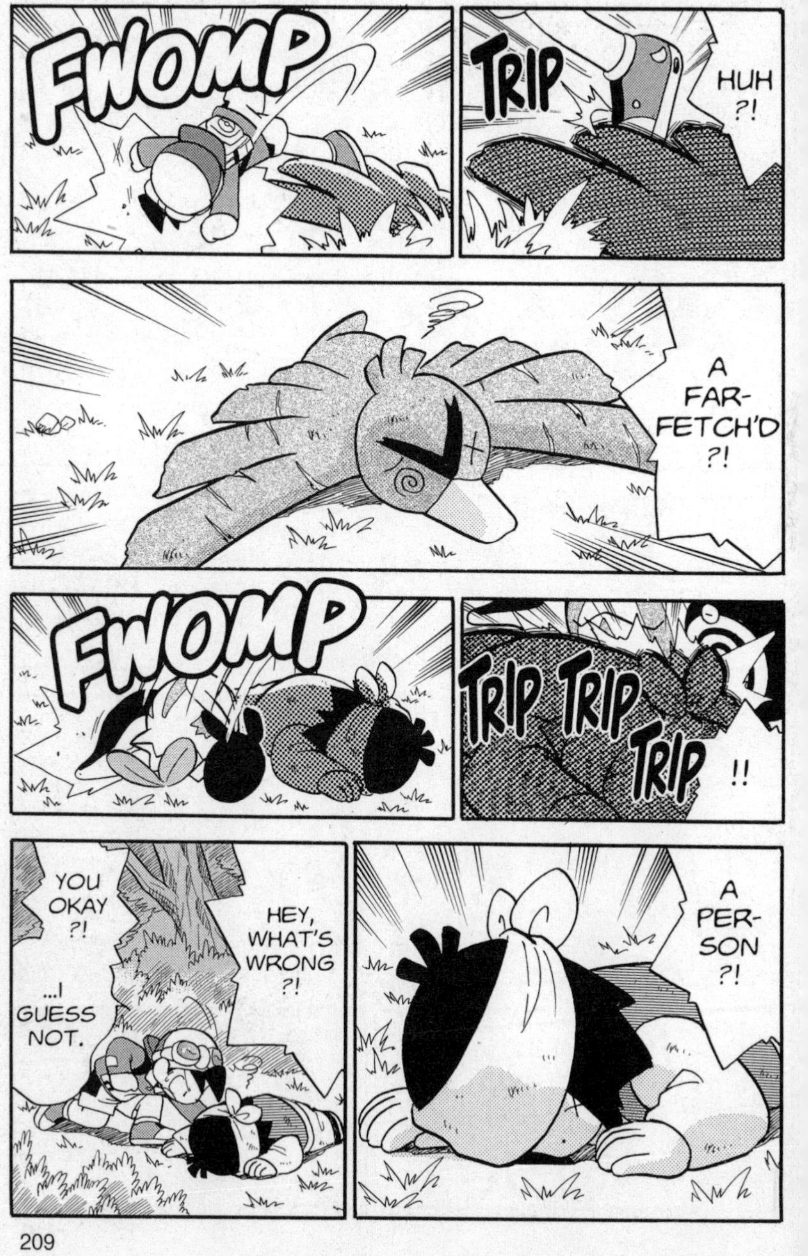
TRIP
HUH ?!
FWOMP
A FAR-FETCH'D ?!
TRIP TRIP TRIP
!!
FWOMP
A PER-SON ?!
HEY, WHAT'S WRONG ?!
YOU OKAY ?!
...I GUESS NOT.

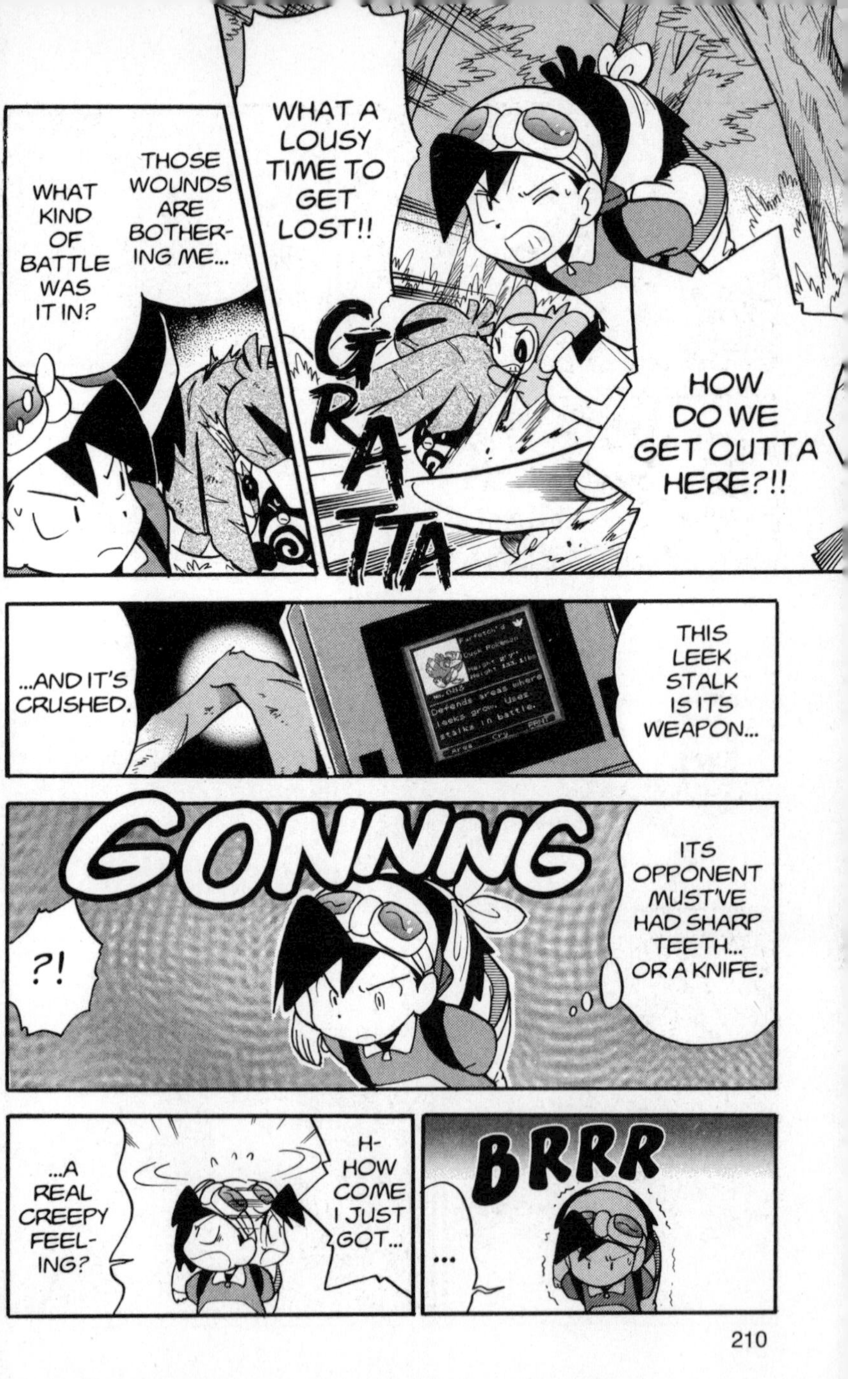
WHAT A LOUSY TIME TO GET LOST!!
HOW DO WE GET OUTTA HERE?!!
GRATTA
THOSE WOUNDS ARE BOTHERING ME...
WHAT KIND OF BATTLE WAS IT IN?
THIS LEEK STALK IS ITS WEAPON...
Farfetch'd
Defends areas where leeks grow. Uses stalks in battle.
Area Cry
...AND IT'S CRUSHED.
ITS OPPONENT MUST'VE HAD SHARP TEETH... OR A KNIFE.
GONNNG
?!
BRRR
...
H-HOW COME I JUST GOT...
...A REAL CREEPY FEELING?

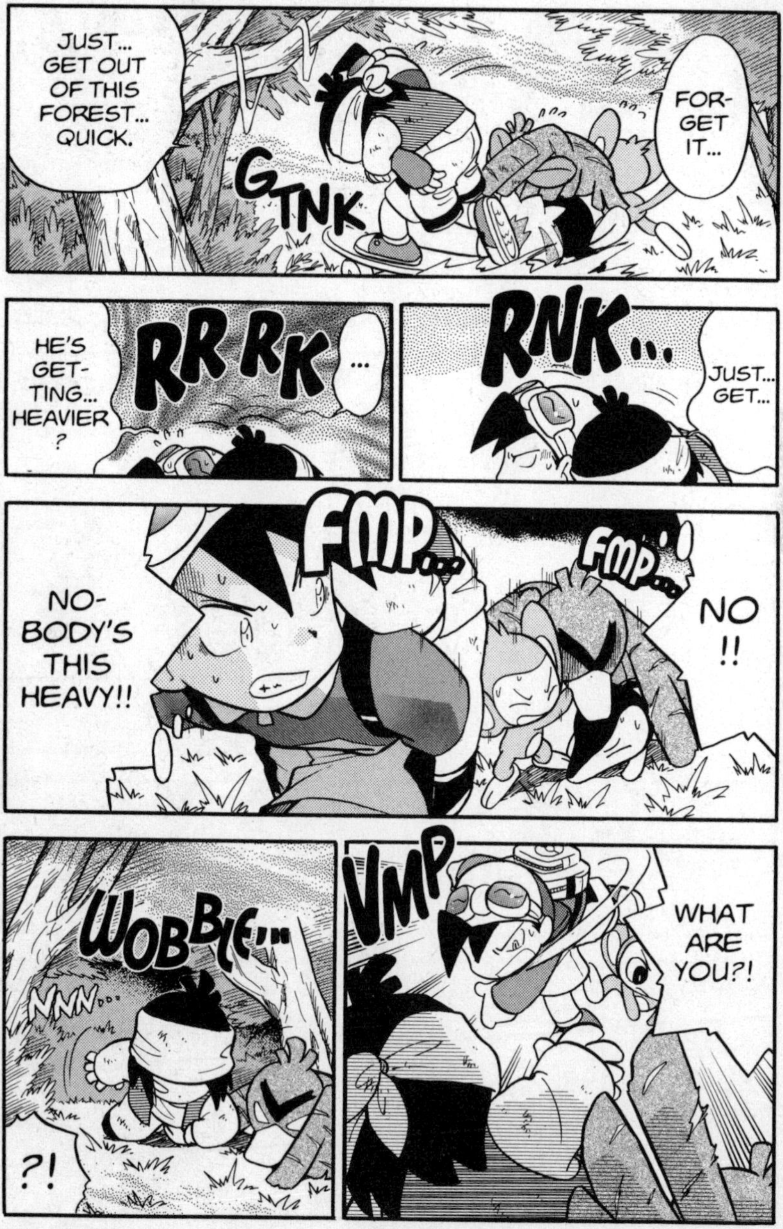
FOR-GET IT...
JUST... GET OUT OF THIS FOREST... QUICK.
GTNK
RNK...
JUST... GET...
...
RR RK
HE'S GET-TING... HEAVIER?
FMP...
FMP...
NO!!
NO-BODY'S THIS HEAVY!!
VMP
WHAT ARE YOU?!
WOBBLE..
NNN...
?!

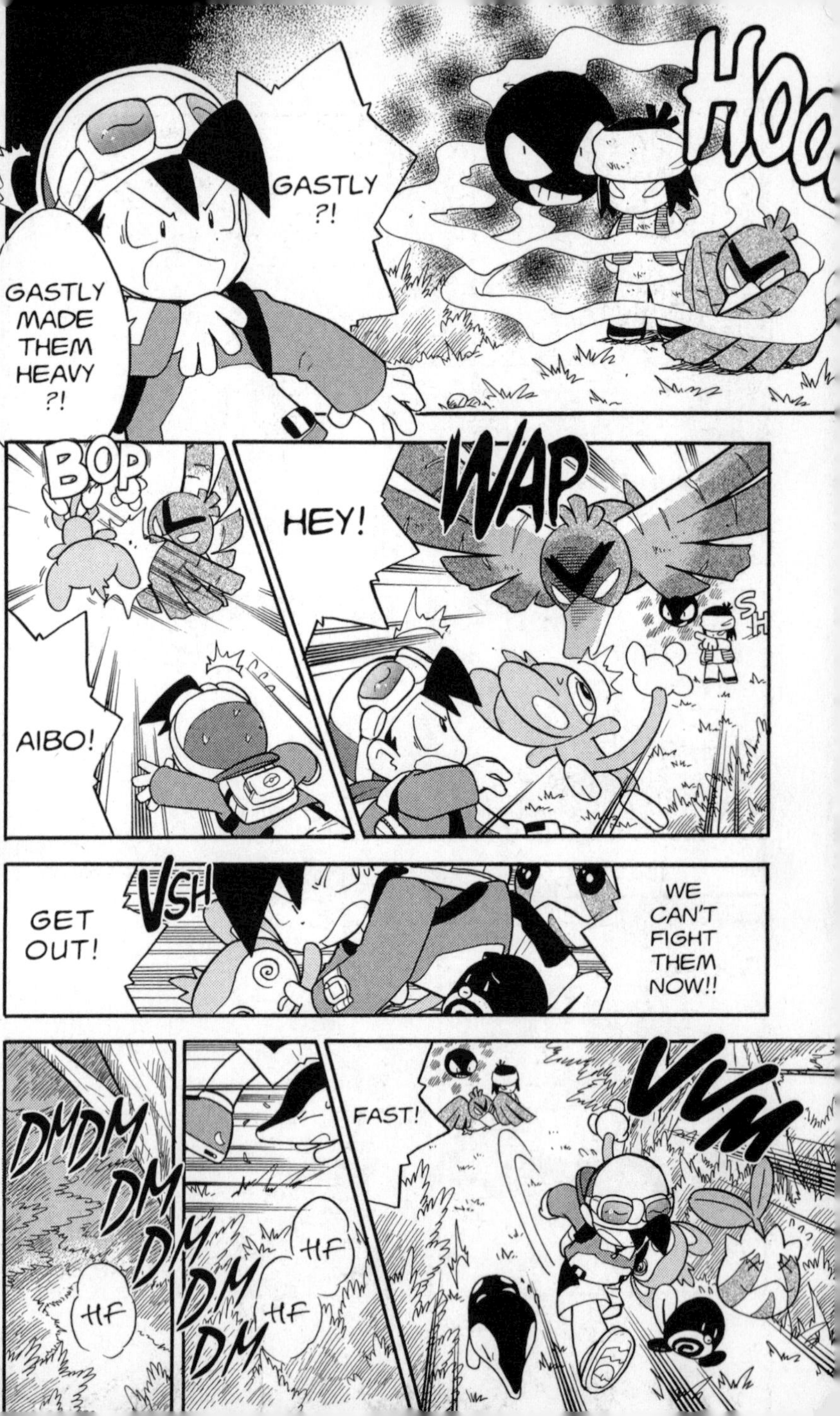
HOO
GASTLY ?!
GASTLY MADE THEM HEAVY ?!
WAP
HEY!
SH
BOP
AIBO!
WE CAN'T FIGHT THEM NOW!!
VSH
GET OUT!
VVM
FAST!
HF
HF
DMDM DM DM DM DM
HF

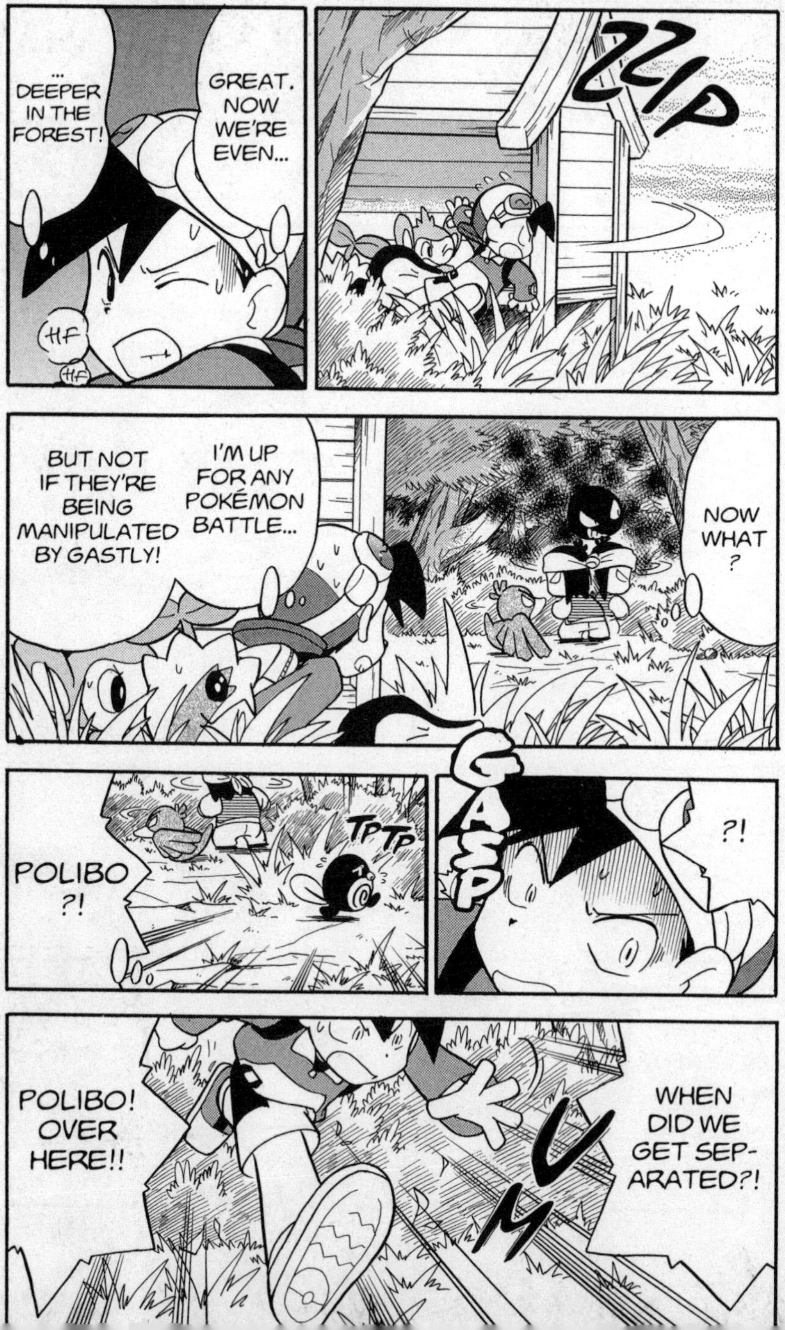
ZZIP
GREAT. NOW WE'RE EVEN...
... DEEPER IN THE FOREST!
HF HF
NOW WHAT?
I'M UP FOR ANY POKÉMON BATTLE...
BUT NOT IF THEY'RE BEING MANIPULATED BY GASTLY!
GASP
?!
TPTP
POLIBO?!
WHEN DID WE GET SEP-ARATED?!
VUM
POLIBO! OVER HERE!!

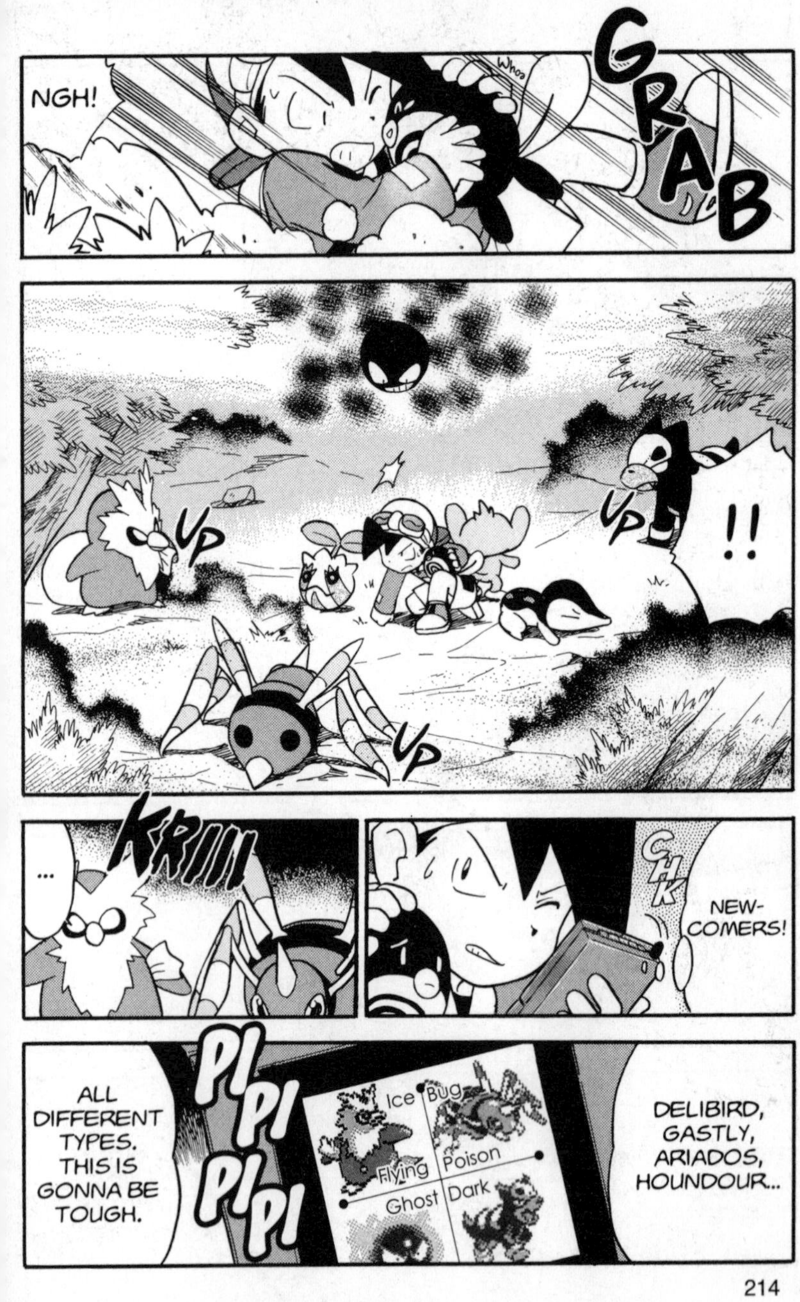
GRAB
Whoa
NGH!
UP
!!
UP
UP
CHK
NEW-COMERS!
KRIIII
...
DELIBIRD, GASTLY, ARIADOS, HOUNDOUR...
PIPI PIPI
Ice
Bug
Flying
Poison
Ghost
Dark
ALL DIFFERENT TYPES. THIS IS GONNA BE TOUGH.

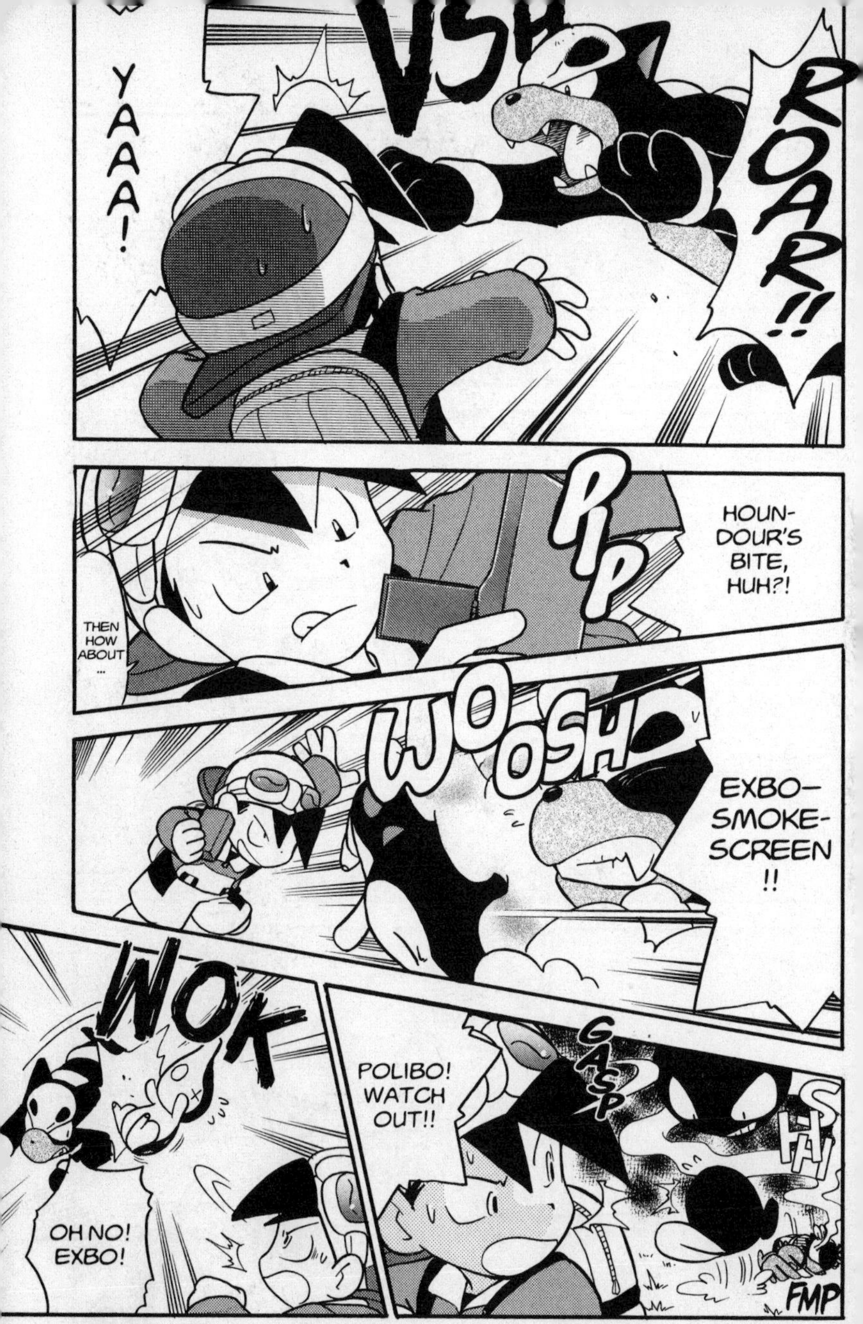
VSH
ROAR!!
YAAAA!
HOUN-
DOUR'S
BITE,
HUH?!
PIP
THEN
HOW
ABOUT
...
EXBO-
SMOKE-
SCREEN
!!
WOOSH
SHH
GASP
POLIBO!
WATCH
OUT!!
FMP
WOK
OH NO!
EXBO!

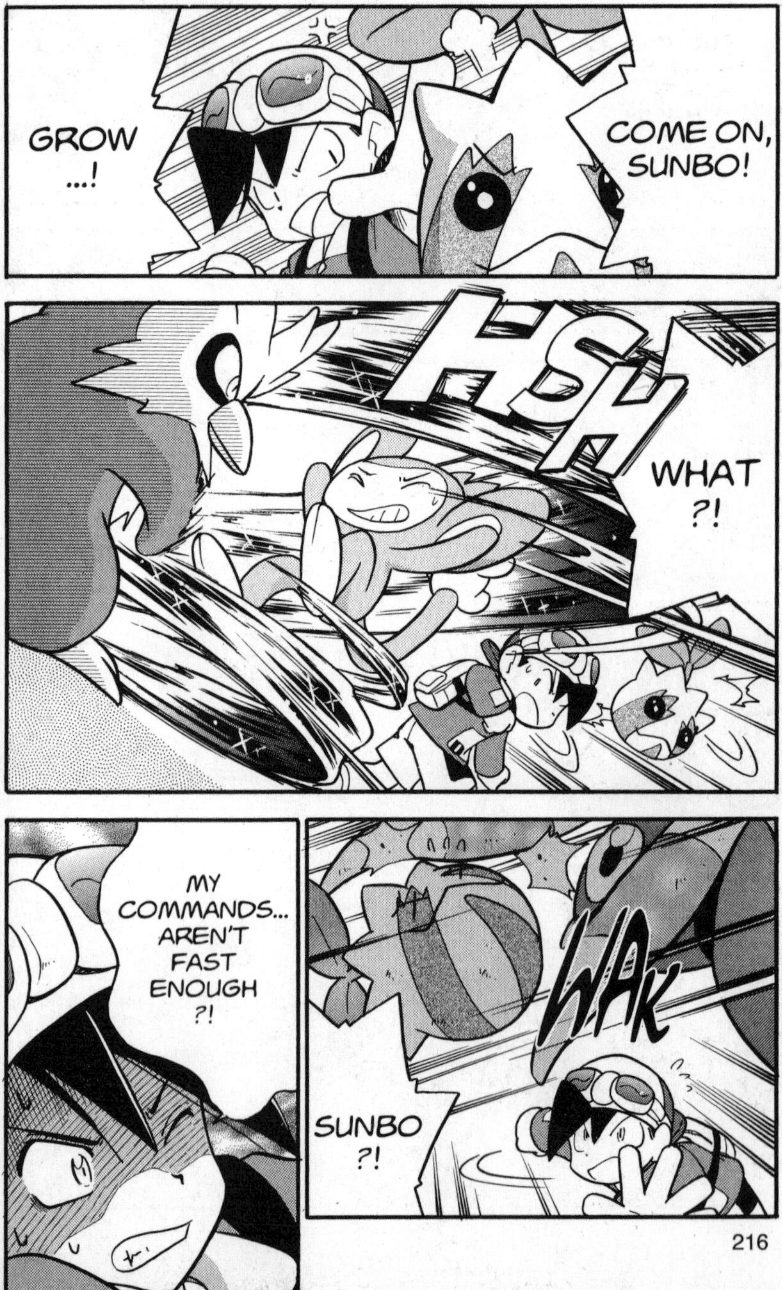
COME ON, SUNBO!
GROW ...!
HSH
WHAT ?!
WAK
SUNBO ?!
MY COMMANDS... AREN'T FAST ENOUGH ?!

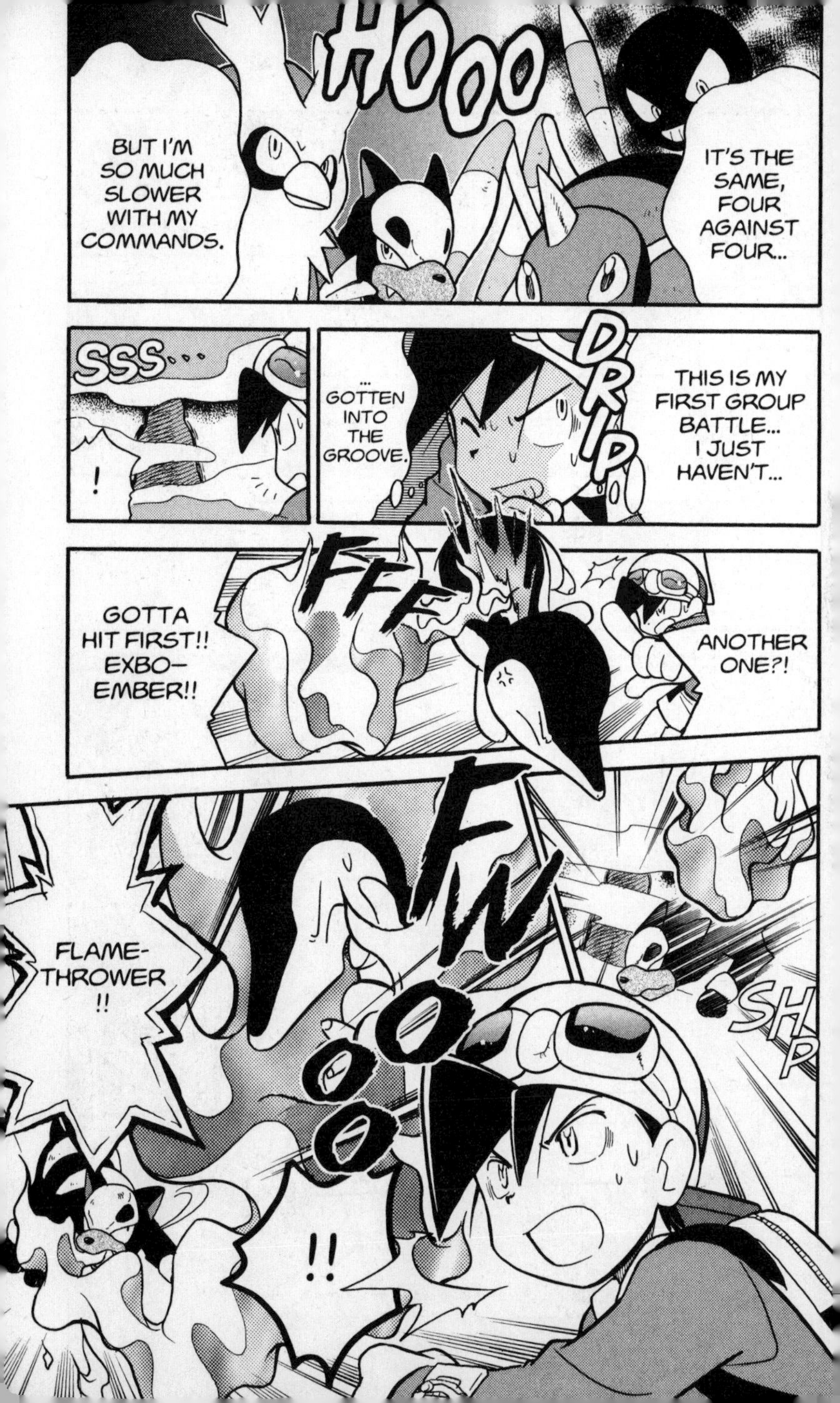

HOOO
IT'S THE SAME, FOUR AGAINST FOUR...
BUT I'M SO MUCH SLOWER WITH MY COMMANDS.
DRIP
THIS IS MY FIRST GROUP BATTLE... I JUST HAVEN'T...
... GOTTEN INTO THE GROOVE.
SSS...
!
ANOTHER ONE?!
FFF
GOTTA HIT FIRST!! EXBO- EMBER!!
FWOOOO
SHP
FLAME-THROWER !!
!!

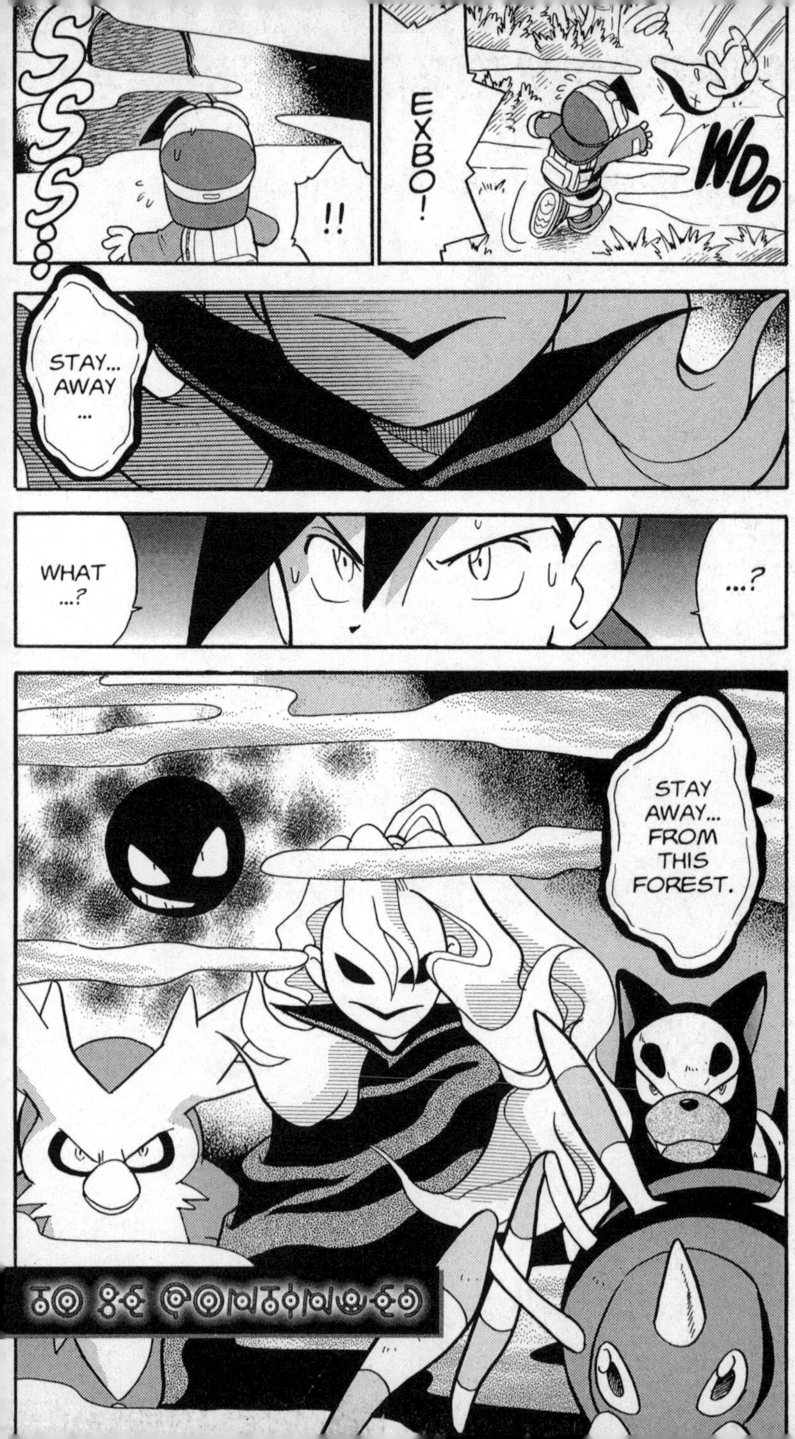
EXBO!
WDD
SSSS
!!
STAY... AWAY ...
...?
WHAT ...?
STAY AWAY... FROM THIS FOREST.
TO BE CONTINUED

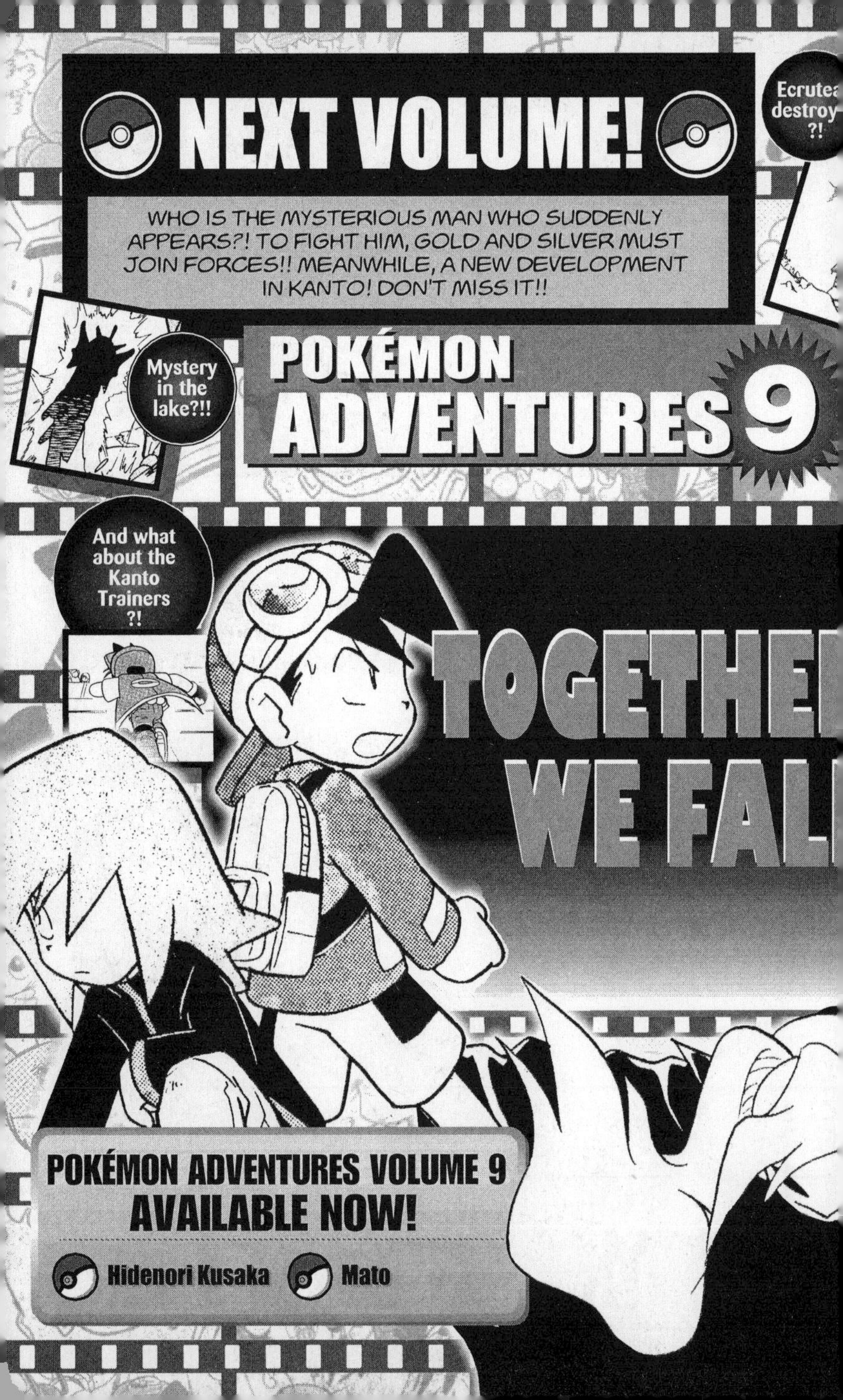
NEXT VOLUME!
Ecrutea destroy ?!
WHO IS THE MYSTERIOUS MAN WHO SUDDENLY APPEARS?! TO FIGHT HIM, GOLD AND SILVER MUST JOIN FORCES!! MEANWHILE, A NEW DEVELOPMENT IN KANTO! DON'T MISS IT!!
Mystery in the lake?!!
POKÉMON ADVENTURES 9
And what about the Kanto Trainers ?!
TOGETHE
WE FAL
POKÉMON ADVENTURES VOLUME 9
AVAILABLE NOW!
Hidenori Kusaka
Mato

Johto region—the arena in which Gold's battle with Silver plays out!

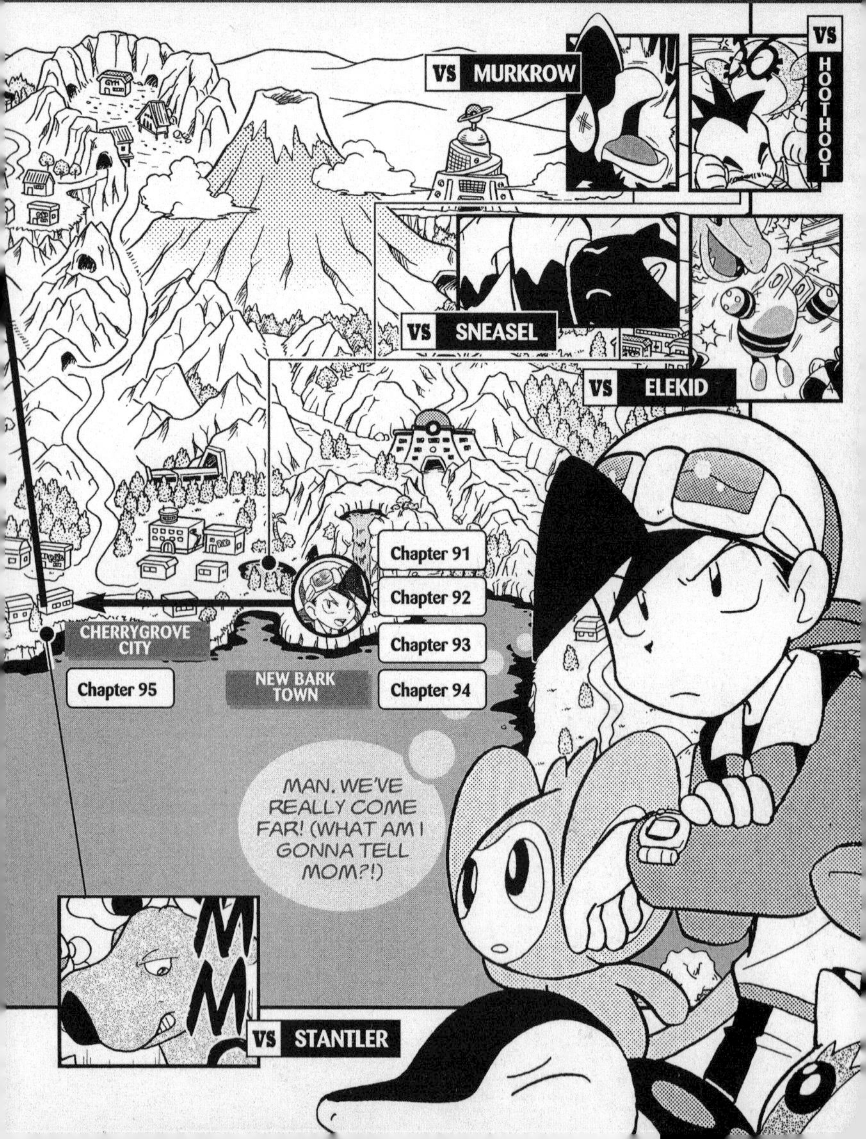
VS HOOTHOOT
VS MURKROW
VS SNEASEL
VS ELEKID
Chapter 91
Chapter 92
Chapter 93
Chapter 94
NEW BARK TOWN
CHERRYGROVE CITY
Chapter 95
MAN. WE'VE REALLY COME FAR! (WHAT AM I GONNA TELL MOM?!)
VS STANTLER

“GOTTA CATCH ’EM ALL” ADVENTURE ROUTE MAP 8

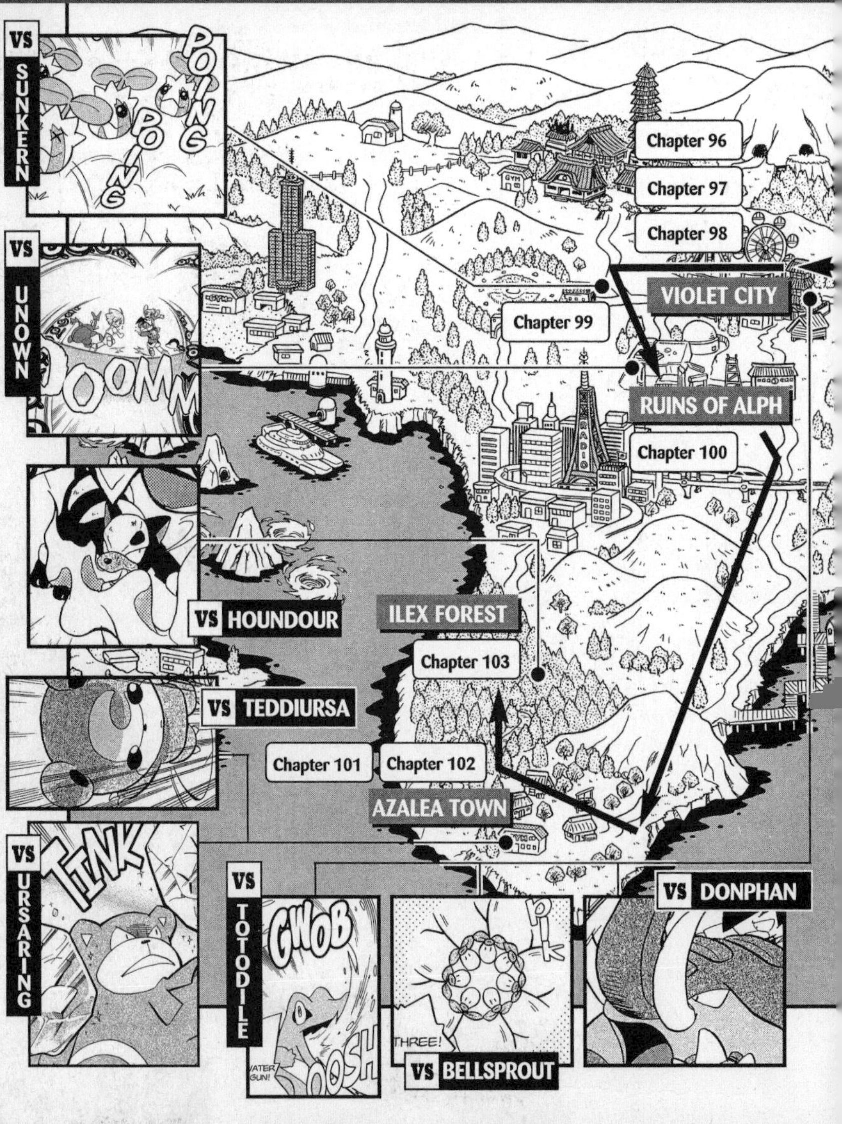

Chapter 96
Chapter 97
Chapter 98
VIOLET CITY
Chapter 99
RUINS OF ALPH
Chapter 100
ILEX FOREST
Chapter 103
Chapter 102
Chapter 101
AZALEA TOWN
VS SUNKERN
POING
POING
VS UNOWN
OOMM
VS HOUNDOUR
VS TEDDIURSA
VS URSARING
TINK
VS TOTODILE
GWOB
WATER GUN!
OOSH
VS BELLSPROUT
THREE!
VS DONPHAN

GOLD TEAM

POKÉDEX SECRETS

POKÉDEX	
▶155 ⊖	CYNDAQUIL
156	-------------
157	-------------
158	TOTODILE
159	CROCONAW
160	-------------
016	PIDGEY
017	PIDGEOTTO
018	PIDGEOT

MAIN CHARACTER: GOLD
BADGES: 0
POKÉDEX: 6 POKÉMON

NUMBER SEEN
35
NUMBER CAUGHT
6

Uses Pokédex mainly during battle. Catch number has not increased.

Gold's Team

Although all his Pokémon are at low levels, they've kept going on brains and determination.

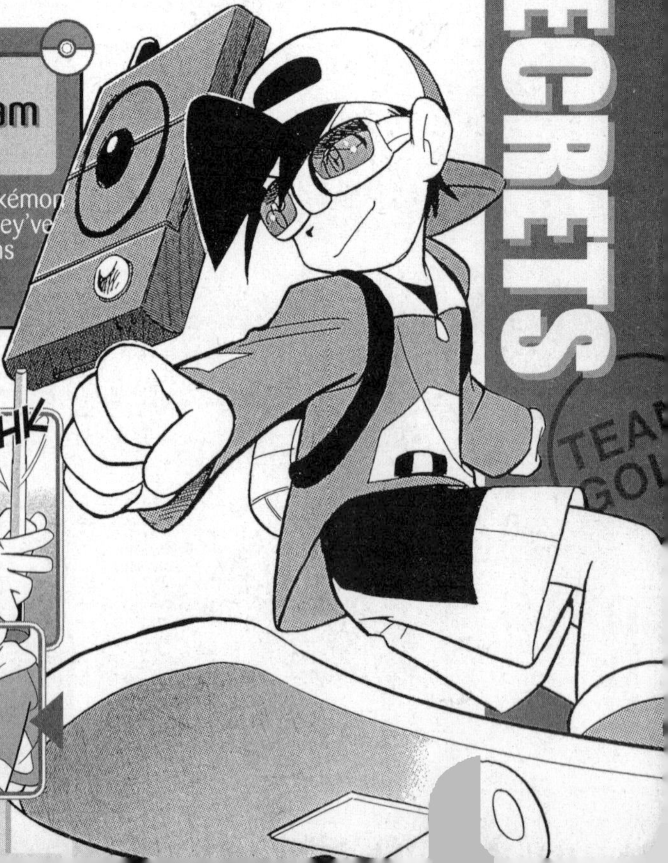
TEAM
GOL

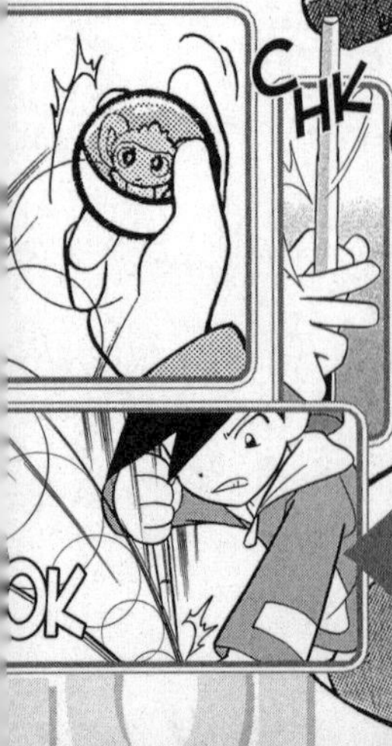
CHK

POKÉMON

AIPOM

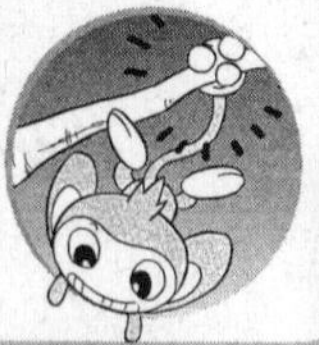

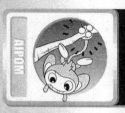

AIBO
TYPE 1 / NORMAL
TRAINER / GOLD

LIKE FAMILY TO GOLD. AIBO HELPED OUT MANY TIMES WITH THAT TAIL THAT'S MORE DEXTROUS THAN HANDS!

NO.190

CYNDAQUIL

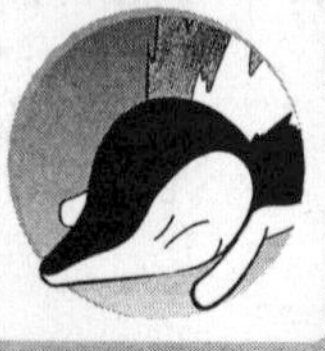

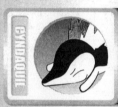

EXBO
TYPE 1 / FIRE
TRAINER / GOLD

ON "LOAN" FROM PROFESSOR ELM. USES THE FLAME ON ITS BACK AS A WEAPON!

NO.155

SUNKERN

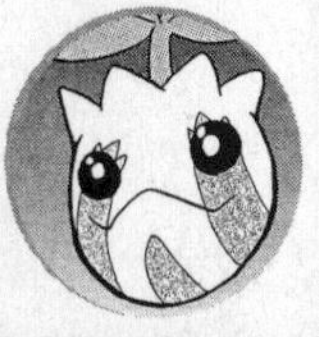

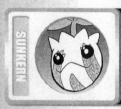

SUNBO
TYPE 1 / GRASS
TRAINER / GOLD

EARNEST AND HONEST, A POKÉMON WHO'LL ALWAYS STAND UP FOR THOSE IN NEED!!

NO.191

POLIWAG

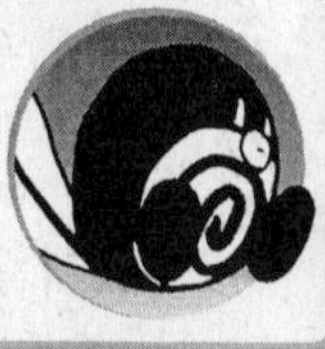

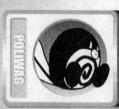

POLIBO
TYPE 1 / WATER
TRAINER / GOLD

THRILLED TO BE BACK WITH GOLD AFTER BEING SWEPT AWAY BY THE RIVER. POLIBO'S FUTURE SHOULD BE EXCITING!!

NO.060

EGG

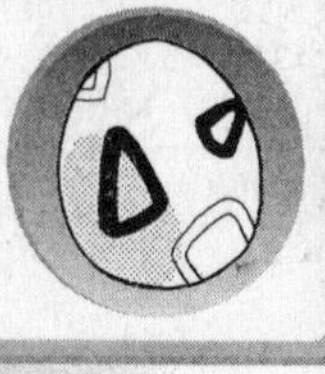

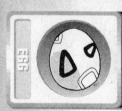

EGG: ???

A MYSTERIOUS EGG FOUND AT A POKÉMON BREEDER'S HOME. BUT WHAT WILL HATCH OUT OF IT...?!

NO.???

POKÉMON

Message from
Hidenori Kusaka

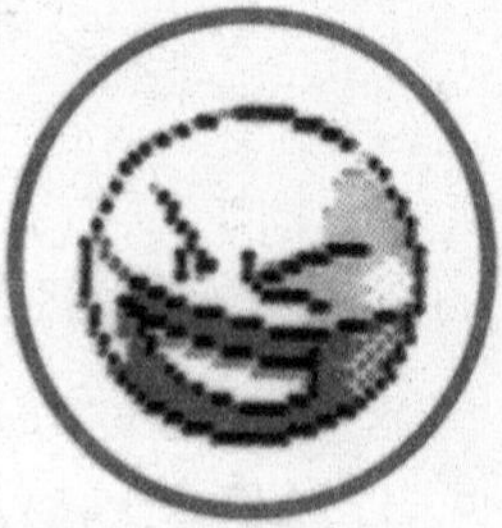

A year has passed since the battle against the Elite Four—and the adventures of Gold, Silver and Crystal are here at last!! Whenever I start a new storyline, I feel sharp and focused all over again—wait'll you see chapter 3, where I went back to my original concept for the series!

Message from
MATO

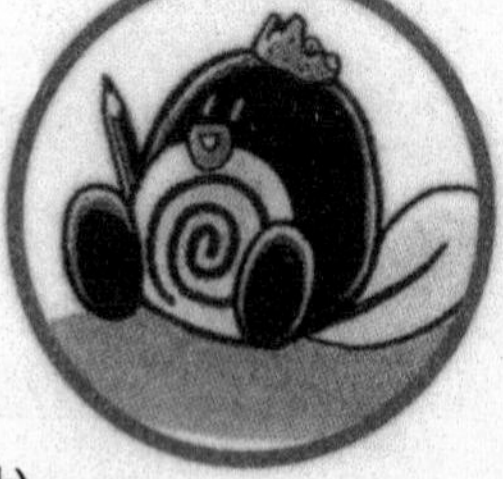

It's been too long, but I'm glad to be back! We'll have to say goodbye to Red, Green, Blue and Yellow for a while, but I'm looking forward to getting to know Gold (who's a bit of a clown) and Silver (who's kind of a punk) and all the other new characters!

More Adventures Coming Soon...

The adventure, starring Gold and his rival Silver, continues! Gold is still trying to track down Silver when he uncovers a far bigger threat. Can these two Trainers put aside their differences to fight a common enemy?

Keep an eye on Team Rocket, Gold and Silver... Will they be the toughest opponents yet?

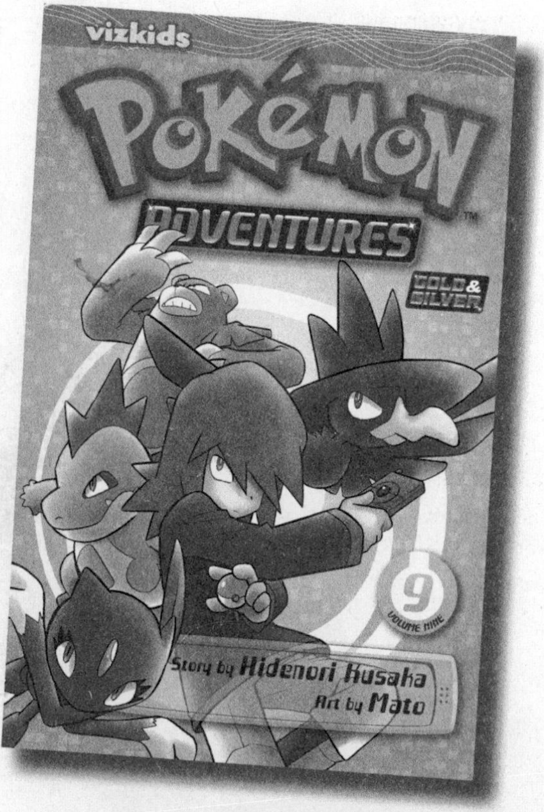

vizkids
POKÉMON
ADVENTURES
GOLD & SILVER
9
VOLUME NINE
Story by Hidenori Kusaka
Art by Mato

AVAILABLE NOW!

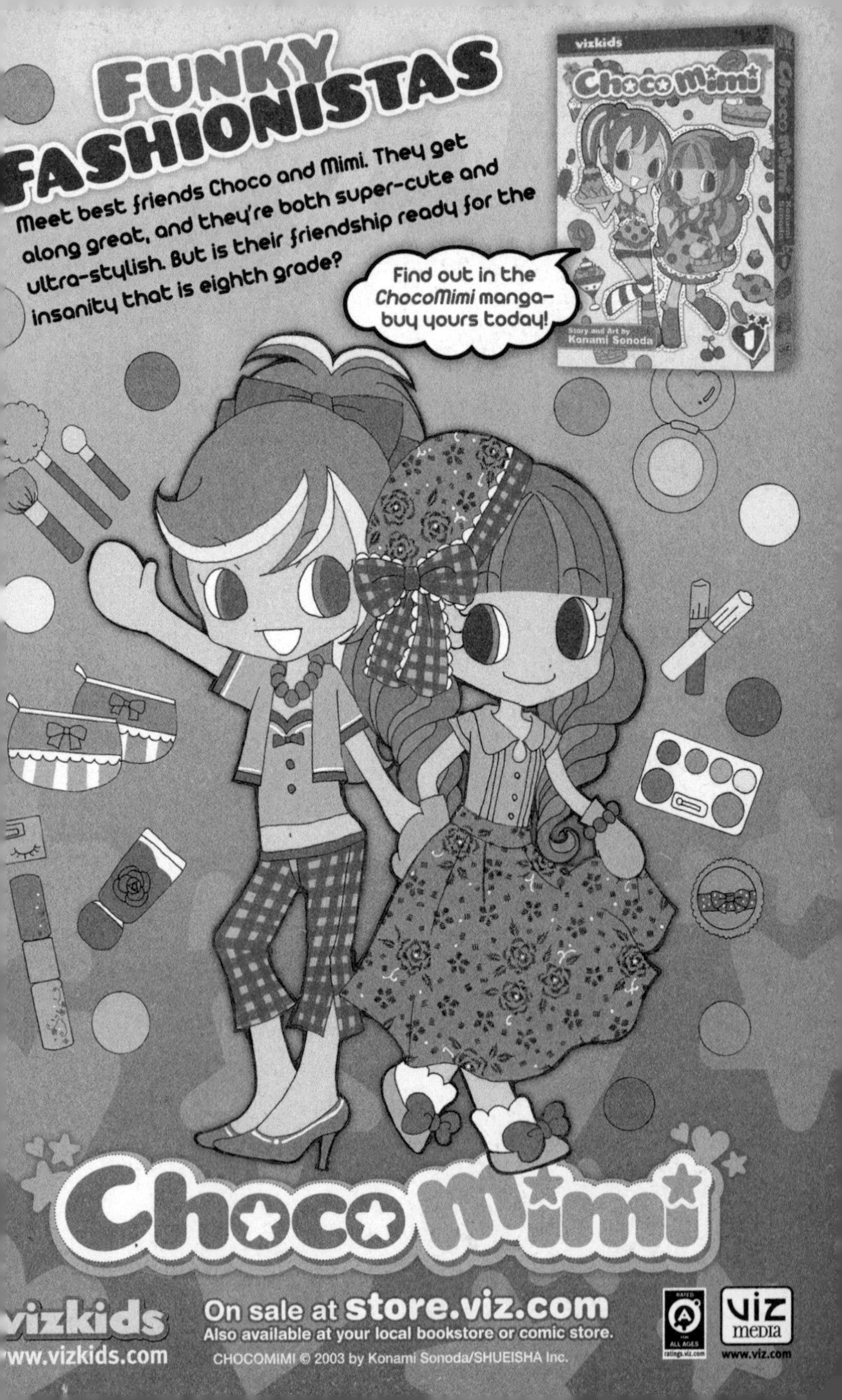
FUNKY FASHIONISTAS
Meet best friends Choco and Mimi. They get along great, and they're both super-cute and ultra-stylish. But is their friendship ready for the insanity that is eighth grade?
Find out in the ChocoMimi manga–buy yours today!
vizkids
Choco Mimi
Story and Art by Konami Sonoda
1
Choco Mimi
vizkids
www.vizkids.com
On sale at store.viz.com
Also available at your local bookstore or comic store.
CHOCOMIMI © 2003 by Konami Sonoda/SHUEISHA Inc.
RATED A ALL AGES ratings.viz.com
VIZ media
www.viz.com

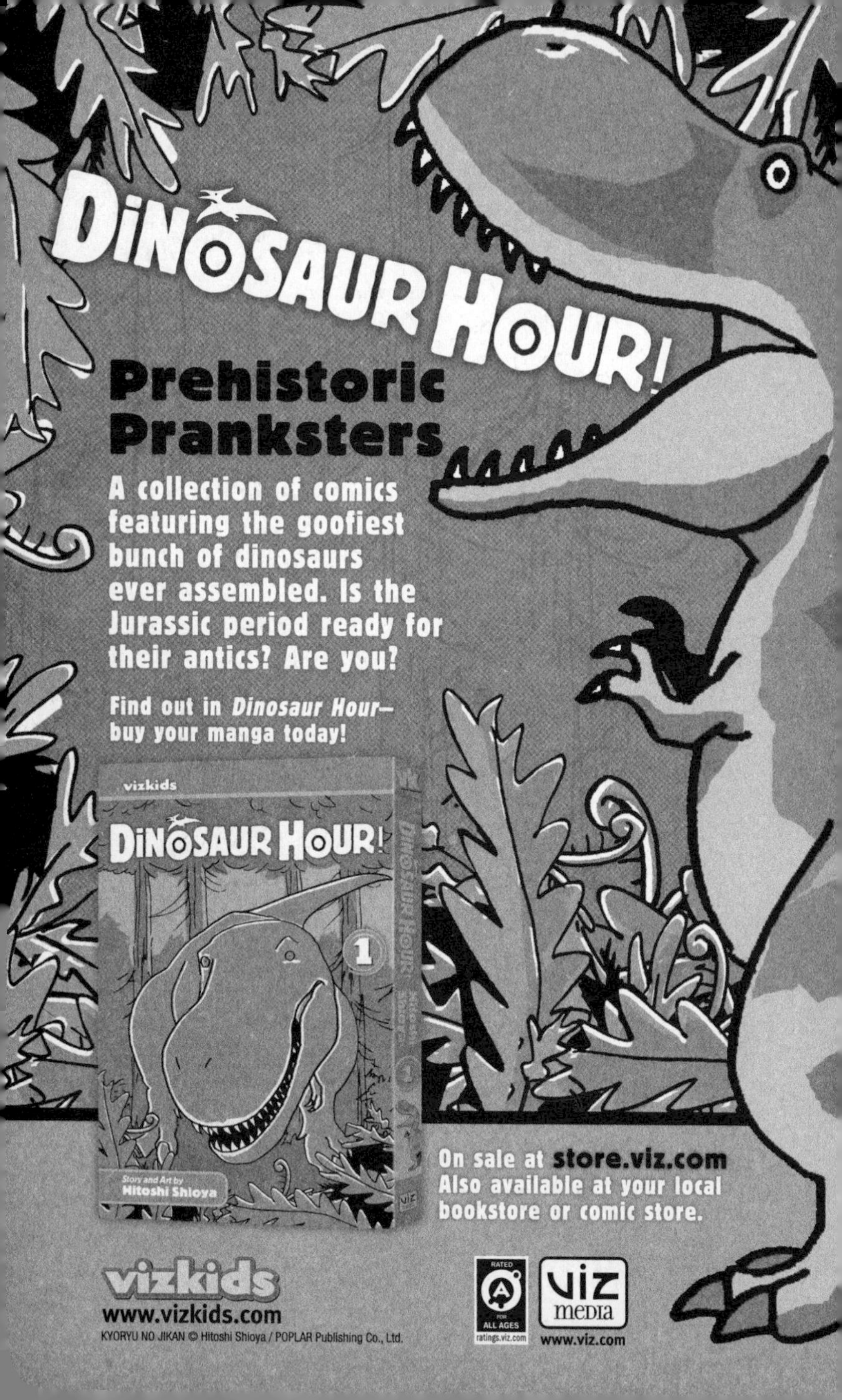
DINOSAUR HOUR!
Prehistoric Pranksters
A collection of comics featuring the goofiest bunch of dinosaurs ever assembled. Is the Jurassic period ready for their antics? Are you?
Find out in Dinosaur Hour—buy your manga today!
vizkids
DINOSAUR HOUR!
1
Story and Art by Hitoshi Shioya
On sale at store.viz.com
Also available at your local bookstore or comic store.
vizkids
www.vizkids.com
KYORYU NO JIKAN © Hitoshi Shioya / POPLAR Publishing Co., Ltd.
RATED A FOR ALL AGES
ratings.viz.com
VIZ MEDIA
www.viz.com

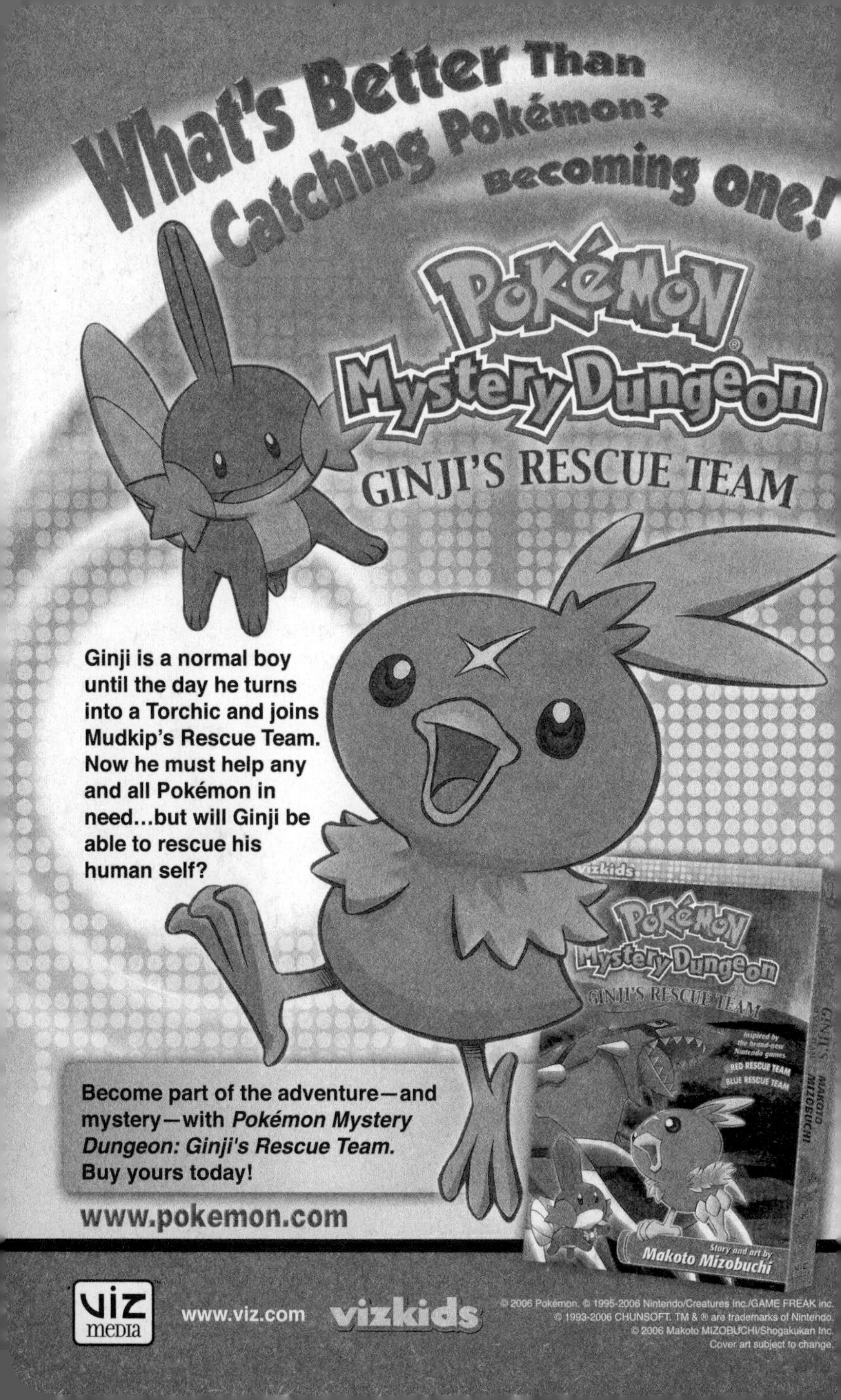

What's Better Than
Catching Pokémon?
Becoming one!
Pokémon®
Mystery Dungeon
GINJI'S RESCUE TEAM
Ginji is a normal boy until the day he turns into a Torchic and joins Mudkip's Rescue Team. Now he must help any and all Pokémon in need...but will Ginji be able to rescue his human self?
vizkids
Pokémon
Mystery Dungeon
GINJI'S RESCUE TEAM
Story and art by
Makoto Mizobuchi
Become part of the adventure—and mystery—with *Pokémon Mystery Dungeon: Ginji's Rescue Team.* Buy yours today!
www.pokemon.com
viz media
www.viz.com
vizkids
© 2006 Pokémon. © 1995-2006 Nintendo/Creatures Inc./GAME FREAK inc.
© 1993-2006 CHUNSOFT. TM & ® are trademarks of Nintendo.
© 2006 Makoto MIZOBUCHI/Shogakukan Inc.
Cover art subject to change.

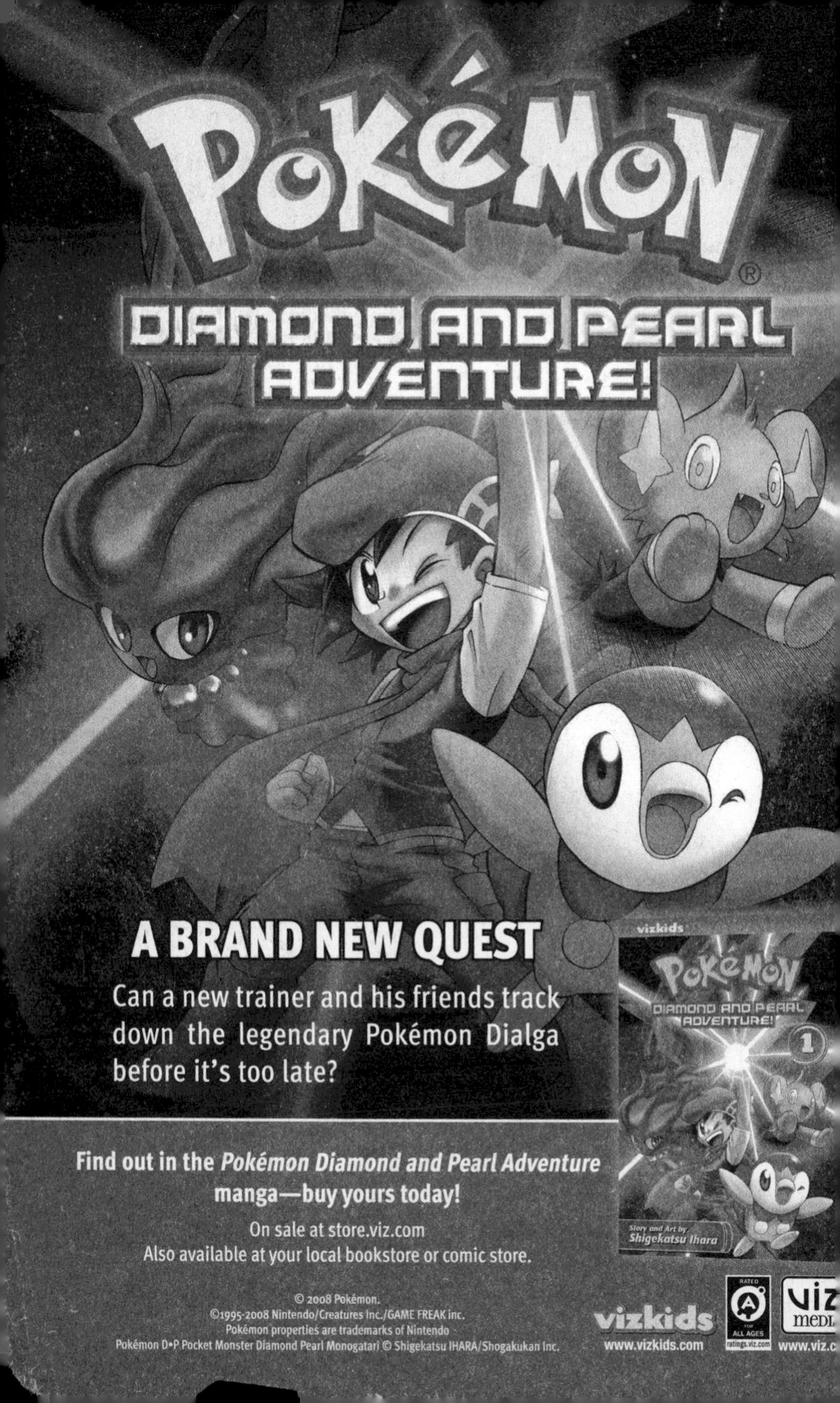
POKéMON®
DIAMOND AND PEARL ADVENTURE!
A BRAND NEW QUEST
Can a new trainer and his friends track down the legendary Pokémon Dialga before it's too late?
vizkids
POKéMON
DIAMOND AND PEARL ADVENTURE!
1
Story and Art by Shigekatsu Ihara
Find out in the *Pokémon Diamond and Pearl Adventure* manga—buy yours today!
On sale at store.viz.com
Also available at your local bookstore or comic store.
© 2008 Pokémon.
©1995-2008 Nintendo/Creatures Inc./GAME FREAK inc.
Pokémon properties are trademarks of Nintendo
Pokémon D•P Pocket Monster Diamond Pearl Monogatari © Shigekatsu IHARA/Shogakukan Inc.
vizkids
www.vizkids.com
RATED A FOR ALL AGES
ratings.viz.com
www.viz.c

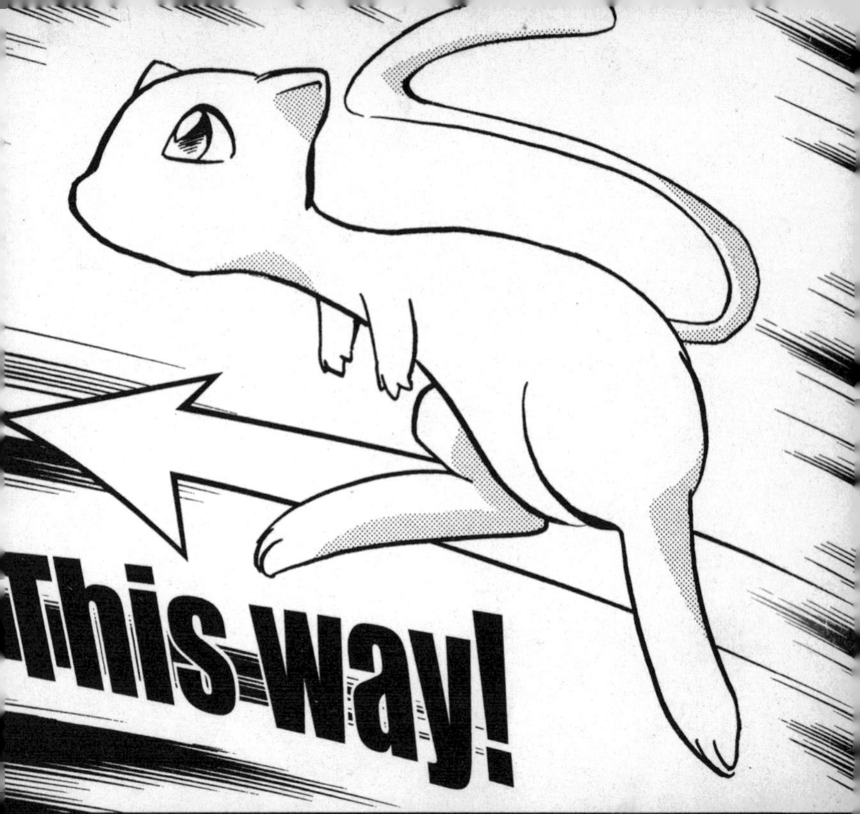
This way!

THIS IS THE END OF THIS GRAPHIC NOVEL!

To properly enjoy this VIZ Media graphic novel, please turn it around and begin reading from right to left.

This book has been printed in the original Japanese format in order to preserve the orientation of the original artwork. Have fun with it!

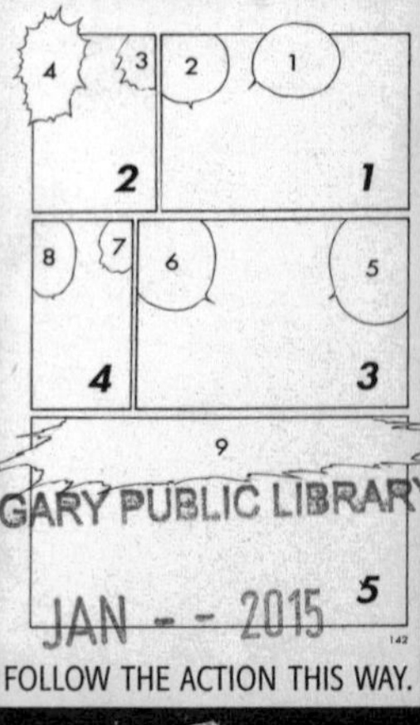

FOLLOW THE ACTION THIS WAY.